BACKLASH

BY

IAN COATES

Backlash

First published in 2024
by Wallace Publishing, United Kingdom
www.wallacepublishing.co.uk

Typesetting courtesy of Wallace Author Services, United Kingdom
www.wallaceauthorservices.weebly.com

Cover design courtesy of KGHH Publishing, United Kingdom

CHAPTER ONE

It was Trish McGowan's addiction to a daily half-packet of Lambert & Butlers that saved her life. She had been leaning against the back wall in the small delivery yard and had her mouth open when it happened. They said afterwards that had helped too – something about protecting inner organs from the pressure wave that threw her across the concrete.

As she had unlocked the shop's door on that April morning there had been no sign that the premises of Sylver & McGowan Interiors weren't as she'd left them, no sign that someone had circumvented the security system. Trish used her reflection in the picture window to adjust her fringe of green and pink hair. She winked at herself before casting an eye over the display the other side of the glass. It still wasn't quite right, and she made a mental note to try moving the cushions closer to the curls of wallpaper. She let herself in and disabled the alarm. With nostrils full of the aroma of fabrics and of vanilla from the neatly arranged candles, she headed for the back office. She passed the watercolour she'd painted for her aunt of Rectory Cottage with the slogan *We listen to customers and design to exceed expectations*. It still took pride-of-place on the wall behind the counter. She now reckoned it sounded cheesy, but had left it there in Flo's memory.

Trish lit the gas heater, booted her PC, and went to fill the kettle in the tiny alcove she considered the kitchen. Just time for a ciggie while the water boiled. Humming gently to herself, she unlocked the back and strolled into the rear delivery yard. There was nothing suspicious, nothing anywhere to suggest someone had broken in.

She pulled a packet of cigarettes from her jeans' pocket. 'Never smoke in the shop,' Aunt Flo had instilled in her. 'The smell puts punters off.' When breast cancer had ripped her spinster aunt from her and left her with no-one, it had become Trish's shop, but she still held Flo Sylver's edicts as law.

Trish leant back against the wall and drew in a mouthful of smoke, holding it inside her mouth for a few seconds before attempting to puff a smoke ring into the still air and failing as always.

The world suddenly turned white. A blow to her back hurled her across the yard, slammed her down onto concrete. There was no sound. Something sharp dug into the back of her head and arms. She tried to yell for help, but no scream came out. *God, what's happening?*

Needles pierced her jeans and jumper, stabbed into her skin. She tried to push herself up but her arms collapsed. She fell forward, cracking her jaw on the ground. Warm liquid seeped across her thighs, sending more panic surging through her. Was she bleeding? Desperately, she tried to twist, to feel between her legs, but a spasm of pain immobilised her. She screamed, heard nothing.

Out of the corner of her eye she saw something long and dark crash into the ground and break apart in a cloud of dust.

She couldn't breathe. Her chest heaved in vain as she tried to suck air into her lungs. *Why can't I breathe?*

Suddenly a raging heat scorched her legs and the back of her neck. She tried to crawl – to escape it – but her arms were useless. Her lungs burned as she gasped for oxygen before slumping into unconscious.

***

The wind that swept across Hampstead Heath plucked at Matt Casey's hoodie when he emerged from the trees. He adjusted the hood to keep his face hidden. He was walking slowly towards the car park that had been chosen, waiting for the second text message. He slowed further, his tatty trainers making little sound on the footpath. Can't afford to get there too early. He unconsciously scratched at his sparse goatee and licked his lips. The next couple of hours would be the worst bit – the point where it could all go wrong.

A crisp packet scudded across the grass before disappearing into the stream of cars on the nearby road. Between the tree trunks to his right, he caught glimpses of the pond. He'd been here a few times as a boy, had memories of flying kites followed by an ice cream at the cafe.

Casey, keeping his face down, passed a couple of

chattering dog walkers going the other way, while their dogs sniffed at last winter's leaves.

His phone suddenly vibrated, and his entire body jumped, even though he'd been expecting the text. He stopped walking, opened the message with his heart racing. Short and to the point as always, but it contained what he needed: vehicle type and registration. Casey memorised them, deleted the message and hurried to the parked cars he could see ahead.

He scanned the dusty area for a white VW Golf, spotted it right in the middle and glanced around. A woman with bare legs and a short red skirt that quivered in the wind stood at a Range Rover. She leant over a toddler that screamed loudly as it fought to get out of its buggy. Good – anyone who looked in this direction would remember them, not him. She had a great figure, but this wasn't the time to stare. An old man in a flat cap peered over his glasses at the ticket machine. They were both oblivious to what he was doing.

Casey pulled on leather gloves and walked casually to the car, the stone chippings crunching loudly underfoot. He pulled a key from the rear wheel arch and, with pulse quickening, dropped into the driver's seat. There was no need to check the boot; he knew what would be inside.

The cabin stank of pine air freshener, reminding him with disgust of his old school assembly hall. Keeping his hood up, he fired the engine, keen to be away. There was no doubt the car was stolen. The plates would have been changed, but he couldn't know how much time that might give him.

The journey would be over an hour, out to the M25, then south towards Guildford. He drove cautiously. At one point on the motorway, a police car overtook him, and Casey stared straight forward, keeping well below seventy. He imagined them radioing in to check the car. *Don't be paranoid*, he scolded himself.

The crawl past Heathrow made him late, and it was approaching lunch by the time he swapped the main roads for ones that curved through stretches of woodland and along the edges of freshly sown fields. Casey slowed, searching for landmarks he might recognize from last time. Half a mile on, he spotted the familiar lay-by, pulled in, and cut the engine.

Trees stretched to the kerbside in eerie silence. Patches of purple rhododendron bloom were the only things breaking its brown-green monotony. There were no houses in sight, no pavement, no streetlamps, no bustle. Alien territory.

Casey took the large empty envelope that had been left for him in the glove box and hurried with it to the boot. After a nervous glance around, he grabbed the parcel that lay there and slit it open with a penknife. Hunched over, worried the wind might snatch its contents, Casey pulled out wads of twenty-pound notes and transferred them to the envelope, his gloved hands fumbling slightly.

Some notes were new, others crumpled and dog-eared. He hurriedly rammed them into the envelope, slammed the boot, and pushed the original Jiffy bag deep into the roadside bin. If anyone had secreted a tracker in its padding, it wouldn't help them now.

He climbed back into the Volkswagen and waited. A single car swept past in the other direction before the road again fell silent. *Come on. I can't sit in a stolen car all day.*

He tapped his fingers against the wheel, then pulled his phone from his pocket, checked it had signal, and dropped it on the passenger seat. He continued to drum gloved fingers. His hands sweated inside the leather.

He'd feigned a stomach upset to get the day off work to do this. How many more times could he get away with that, he wondered? Do it too often and the dragon in HR would demand a chat.

The text message arrived three minutes later. He snatched up the phone and read the single word. "Now".

***

The room had bright white walls and ceiling. Trish McGowan tried to focus her blurred vision, but pain stabbed through her skull. She quickly screwed her eyes shut again.

Hospital. She recalled disjointed threads of memory, people leaning over her, talking to her, movement. They'd told her she was in hospital, but she couldn't remember why. She wiggled her toes, felt the brush of rough sheets. She did the same with her fingers. Everything was there, everything worked. She slipped back into blackness, away from the pain.

Trish drifted in and out of sleep while various doctors and nurses came and went. 'You were very lucky,' they kept repeating.

'Just as well you were outside ...'

'No permanent damage ...'

'Do your ears still ring? That'll fade in time ...'

There were other women in the ward – all sorts of ages, varying levels of noisiness. She noticed little of it.

The nightmare realisation of what had happened started to dawn during the afternoon with the arrival of the first policeman and his questions. He looked a few years younger than she, mid-twenties maybe. He sat awkwardly on the hard plastic chair at her bedside. 'What happened in the shop this morning?' he asked.

Can't remember.

When she didn't reply, he prompted gently, 'Any gas appliances? Anything that could have exploded?'

She tried to nod but pain spiked through her head. Instead, she mumbled, 'A Calor Gas heater. I use it if I'm cold.'

'Could it have been leaking?'

'It's fine.'

Why was he asking such stupid questions? She stared at him intently, noting for the first time that he was slightly boss-eyed and that his cheeks still bore the scars of childhood acne. Trish pushed a lock of green hair back out of her eyes. Her right shoulder throbbed like hell. 'Why are you here?'

'They're just routine questions,' he said defensively. 'We need to be sure of what happened.'

What the hell's he talking about? She tried to sit up, gave up. No strength. 'What d'you mean?'

'Well, the fire brigade has largely finished ...'

Fire brigade? 'I don't know what you're talking about.' Panic rose in her chest.

'Didn't they tell you? You were caught in an explosion.'

She couldn't remember. 'Where?'

'At your shop.' That snapped her into full awareness for the first time. She stared at him, and the panic became an unstoppable tsunami. It pumped adrenaline through her bloodstream, fighting the drugs the hospital had fed her.

He continued, 'There's no need to worry. The brigade has made everything secure.'

Trish closed her eyes again and leant back, breathing heavily. *Stay calm.* She felt as if she might faint. She ignored him, kept her eyes tightly closed. *An accident? He's presuming it was an accident, but how can he be so sure?*

Kurt Wendell. It had to be him. She remembered the emails and the letter. This couldn't be an accident. *The bastard just tried to kill me.*

Calm down. It won't help to panic.

All those months ago, she should have stood up for herself, should have refused to comply. It had just been one stupid mistake, but now she was involved right up to her idiotic neck. No escape.

She heard the scrape of the chair as the policeman stood. 'I'll come back later once you've had a chance to rest,' he said softly, and his footsteps receded across the ward.

Wendell tried to kill me, she thought with rising panic, trying to calm herself with the thought that she was safe here.

Eventually, she slipped into a light doze, waking later to

the clatter of trolleys outside the ward, the presage of a meal. A nurse helped her out of bed and allowed her to limp to the toilet rather than insisting on the indignity of the bedpan. Trish stared at herself in the tiny mirror above the sink, leaning closer to examine the swelling on her left eyebrow. She touched it gingerly and flinched. The surrounding skin, normally pale and smooth, was grazed and starting to darken with a bruise. Her little snub nose, too, looked scratched. She ran a slender finger across it, but it seemed undamaged. Her hair that was normally so full of bounce – blonde except for the colourful fringe – now hung limply across her shoulders. She pushed it off her ears, the room's downlighter causing the diamond ear studs to sparkle. The movement sent a spasm of pain up her arm that made her wince as she studied the side of her face. A school boyfriend had described her ears as "small and cute", but the plaster now enveloping part of the left one made it look enormous. Trish straightened the top of the pyjamas the hospital had provided, hiding the swallow tattoos on her shoulder, before carefully making her way back across the ward.

He tried to murder me she repeated, but it suddenly struck her as she climbed into bed that Wendell had no reason to think he'd failed. He would think her dead after the explosion. And if Wendell thought he'd succeeded, she would be safe. She relaxed and lay back on the pillow, breathing deeply and listening to the sound of food being plated.

***

That evening, her two employees at the interior design

business visited her in hospital – Cliff and Beth. Cliff's lanky body hesitated at the open door to the ward. Beth, her round face full of concern, pushed past and hurried over.

Trish propped herself up on the pillows. 'How's the shop?' she asked hoarsely, even before they'd dragged chairs round to face the bed.

'Stuff the shop,' Cliff said. 'How are *you*?' He ran slender hands through his waves of hair. 'They wouldn't let us visit this morning. They said you were resting. What happened?'

Beth added, 'We were told there had been some sort of explosion and that you were in hospital.'

'Really, I'm fine,' she insisted. 'Everyone keeps telling me I've been very lucky. It's just some bruises and cuts. Now, tell me about the shop, please.' She sounded almost pleading.

Cliff and Beth looked at each other for a moment, and Cliff winced. 'It's a bit of a mess to be honest.'

Beth said quickly, 'But we'll soon have it tidied. Don't worry. All the glass blew out at the front and back, but that's been boarded up already and we can easily get it re-glazed as soon as the insurance company's been round.'

'There's quite a lot of fire and water damage on the stock, though,' Cliff said.

Trish felt tears prick at her eyes. *Sorry Aunt Flo – this is all my fault.* Beth noticed the look on Trish's face and continued quickly, 'I think we can salvage much of it, though. Cliff and I can deal with everything. Just you relax.'

'What about diary appointments? I was meant to be visiting that big house over in Amersham tomorrow and I haven't finished the mood board yet.'

Beth laid a hand on hers. 'Don't worry,' she said firmly. 'I'll finish it. I know what you were aiming to achieve. I'll have a stab this evening and bring it over in the morning for you to see, and we can make changes before I take it round. I'll present it to the client for you. Okay?'

Beth's soft brown eyes locked with hers, re-assuring. She was a good designer. It was just that her natural style leaned more towards Art Deco, whereas the client wanted Riviera. *Oh, just let her do it*, Trish told herself. *She'll be fine. Beth can adapt.*

By the time they left, Trish was feeling calmer. It helped, too, to remember that Wendell would think he had succeeded. Her optimism was shattered two days later.

By Thursday she was recovering well, but it was what Beth brought with her in the afternoon that thrust Trish back into the nightmare and threatened to change her life forever.

Beth dropped that week's Bucks Herald on the sheets. 'We thought you might like to see this. You're a celebrity. Look at the front page.'

Trish stared in horror at the article. *Smoking Saves Shop Owner's Life*. There was even a picture of the shattered front of Sylver & McGowan Interiors with a fire engine outside and hoses that snaked through the front door.

Her guts tightened. She'd been telling herself that Wendell would think she was dead. Not now, though. One look at the local paper and he would know he had failed, which meant he would come back. And the next time, she mightn't be so lucky.

CHAPTER TWO

Early Saturday morning, Matt Casey pulled on latex gloves and slid a small envelope out from its cellophane packet. He didn't know whether the police could lift fingerprints from paper but he certainly wasn't going to take the risk. Moments later, the printer on his windowsill whirred as it printed the address. Could forensics tell which brand of ink had been used? Perhaps he should bin the cartridge and switch to a different make. *No. That's too expensive.*

Casey erased the file from his laptop before sliding the message into the envelope and sealing it using a wet sponge to moisten the gum. He had no intention of leaving traces of DNA anywhere.

The brakes of a lorry hissed in the street below as it slowed for the lights. Somewhere within the block of flats a front door slammed and footsteps shuffled down the corridor. Old Mrs Kozlowski would be trudging to the corner shop with her string bag. The lift was bust again, so she would have to wheeze up and down the stairs. A pang of guilt at not offering to help rose up inside him, but he couldn't do it today.

His gloved hand was trembling when he picked up the envelope. One long deep breath. *Don't be stupid, Matt, you can do this. You've got to.*

He scooped the keys to his Renault from the frayed sofa. The stair door scraped, and he hesitated. He didn't want to catch up the old woman and be forced into small talk right now. Casey waited. He studied the scale model Avro Lancaster that hung from the hall ceiling. He'd made a good job of her. He tapped it gently and watched it swing. He fancied doing the Dornier Night Fighter next, if his mother sent a little money for his birthday as she usually did.

He waited another minute, shifting his weight from one leg to the other before letting himself out. Clutching the letter, he quietly took the two flights of stairs to the street.

It would take nearly an hour to reach Bromley by car, but this couldn't be done on his own patch. He drove with the stereo wound high to the beat of King Nun to distract him, but his stomach still twisted and churned. It felt as if every other driver was watching him. He left Hackney and joined the rows of vehicles that crawled through Blackwall Tunnel to the south bank of the Thames. At least it wasn't hot this time of year – his car had once had air-conditioning but it had packed up a month after he bought the damn thing.

He passed the wide green of Greenwich Park, then took to side streets to avoid the CCTV around Bromley's shopping centre. Soon, lime trees that were coming into vibrant green leaf lined the roads, along with large detached houses that sheltered behind neat hedges and freshly painted gateposts. It was so different to the litter-strewn pavements he was familiar with and the rows of concrete flats. This was Classy. One day he would live somewhere like this, he decided. Now that he'd cleared his debts, he could start saving. He badly missed his ex-girlfriend, Alicia, but at least his credit cards were now recovering from taking her out. Her tastes had been expensive.

Casey spotted a pillar box, pulled over, and dropped the envelope inside. Once safely back behind the wheel he removed the latex gloves and rubbed the sweat from his hands. He turned in the road and headed back, his mouth dry.

Give it a week, and he knew he would have another task.

CHAPTER THREE

'I'm being blackmailed.'

It was a few days after Casey mailed the letter and Craig Tyler was admiring the view from the CEO's office window. The outskirts of Warminster were laid out before him, with the hills beyond rolling gently upwards towards Imber. When he'd been a young "squaddie" – several lifetimes ago – he had exercised up there. He snapped his focus back to the skinny businessman. 'You're what?'

'I'm being blackmailed, Craig, and I want to ask if you can help me.'

Tyler had got used to the public-school accent during the few months he'd known Art Bradon, but today an uncharacteristically rough edge was breaking through. Bradon: early sixties, face drawn, dark eyes burning intensely below thick eyebrows, owner and CEO of Bradon Defence Electronics. The charcoal suit that hung loosely from his body made him look like a scrawny scarecrow. 'I know this is not what I contracted you for,' Bradon was saying, 'but this is a purely personal thing and nothing to do with my company.'

'Uh-huh.'

'I've come to know you over the past weeks while you've been working for me on our writing project and I reckon I can trust you. Do you think you can help?'

Excitement fluttered in Tyler's chest. It certainly wasn't why he'd found himself in BDE's head office, and he had to admit he sometimes hankered for the adrenaline rush of the old SAS days. But that was a younger man's game. He'd left it years ago to make his name as a thriller writer. He scratched the stubble on his chin. 'What about the company history book you commissioned me to write? It'll impact my work on that. You wanted it done by the end of June, but I'll be hard pushed to meet that if I'm off chasing blackmailers.'

'Can you somehow do both?'

Tyler laughed, but Bradon studied him without emotion. Suddenly Bradon gave a slight nod. 'I'm sorry, Craig. I guess you've got your own creative work to do on top of what I'm asking. Have you got a publisher's deadline coming up?'

Been and gone, thought Tyler. He shrugged. It was because of Sandra. How could he concentrate while she filed for divorce and constantly sent him sniping messages? He'd lost track of how many times recently he'd tried to outline a new thriller and ended up scrunching the page into a ball. That's why he'd taken Bradon's contract. A book about BDE's history, that's what Bradon had wanted – ready for their fiftieth anniversary celebrations. They'd been put in touch by the former major of Tyler's SAS squadron who now held a position high up in the Ministry of Defence. Apparently, Bradon had mentioned his hope to create the book while socialising with the major after a procurement meeting, and the major suggested Tyler. A professional writer who knew the workings of the military had seemed the perfect combination to them, and Tyler had thought the task would be a pleasant distraction.

Bradon broke the silence. 'I'll pay extra for your help of course.'

Tyler hid the smile that threatened his look of indifference by examining the blue-green tattoos of a winged sword and skulls on his forearm. 'Maybe,' he said and crossed his legs. 'Tell me about it first and I'll see. If I can't do it, I can probably recommend someone who could.'

'Oh no,' Bradon said, flapping his hands wildly. 'I wouldn't want to get someone I didn't know involved. It's too …' He hesitated. '… too confidential.'

Tyler waited. What was it? Some sort of sex scandal?

Bradon shifted awkwardly. 'When I was a boy, I made a stupid mistake.' He sighed and shook his head. 'It was an accident, but I never admitted what I'd done. If I'd been brave enough to do so, I'd have prevented all the problems our family suffered afterwards.' Bradon paused for a sip of water. 'The thing is, I kept a diary when I was a boy and was naively honest about what happened. I'd forgotten all about what I'd written until a couple of months ago when I got a letter addressed to me here. Inside was a photocopy of some of the pages of the diary and a typed note asking if I remembered the summer of nineteen-seventy-four.'

'Do you still have the letter?'

Bradon shook his head. 'I burned everything straight away and tried to ignore it. Then a week or so later, I got another one demanding a large sum of money in exchange for his silence, which I paid. It was signed by someone called "Argus".'

'Signed?'

'Well, typed.'

'Does "Argus" mean anything to you?'

Bradon shrugged, and his expensive jacket trembled across his shoulders. 'No.'

'Do you still have that second letter?'

'I'm sorry, no. I didn't think at the time. I burned it.'

'Why did you give in to him so easily?'

Bradon got up and paced in front of the view of the hills for a moment before turning to face Tyler. 'As you might know, I've been getting increasingly involved in local politics. BDE has been my life, but I'm starting to release the reins to others, which gives me more time to do something for the community. I'm standing as the Liberal Democrat candidate for my constituency next year.' He sighed and locked his flinty eyes with Tyler's. 'If the contents of that diary get out, with the fact I've never admitted what I did and how I allowed it to rip our family apart … if that gets out, I'd be finished as a politician.' He slammed a fist into the palm of his other hand. 'I honestly reckon I could make a difference in local government. I don't want something I really regret from a long time ago ruining that.'

It was probably the first time Tyler had ever believed a

politician. Most were lying arseholes, but Bradon actually seemed genuine.

The businessman leant his back against the tall plate-glass window. 'I know it's not what I hired you for, but bearing in mind your background as a commander in the SAS, I thought you might know how to ...' Bradon tailed off with an apologetic shrug. It was clear he wanted an answer.

'How could anyone have gotten hold of your old diary? I mean, wouldn't that imply it's got to be someone close to you?'

'I've thought about that a lot, but I'd even forgotten I used to write one, let alone know where the hell they were. I'd have said they were probably lost in one of my parent's house moves or thrown out as rubbish at some point.'

'Even though the contents were that explosive?'

Bradon was already shaking his head. 'But they weren't at the time. At least, they didn't seem so, not to a schoolboy.' There was silence for a moment. Bradon watched him intently.

'Tell me what happened when you handed over the money.'

Bradon returned to his seat and took another sip of water. 'I withdrew cash and sealed it in a large Jiffy bag. He made me go all the way up to London. Told me to go by train to Waterloo and then over to Hampstead Heath station where I was to wait. What a stinking journey that was, I can tell you. I'd been there a bit when I got a text telling me to go to a particular car park where I would find a white VW Golf.'

'Have you still got that message?'

'No. I deleted it immediately afterwards. I thought it might be considered incriminating. Anyway, I had to put the money in the boot and just walk away. And that's what I did.'

'Have you got the car registration?'

In answer, Bradon opened a desk drawer and pulled out a slip of paper that he handed over. 'So, you'll help?'

Tyler nodded slowly. 'It looks like it, doesn't it.'

'Good, because I received this yesterday.' Bradon lifted a white envelope from the drawer, and his eyes burned with anger as he waved it at Tyler. 'I thought, apparently naively, that if I paid this "Argus" it would all be over, but he's already come back for more. I won't keep paying. It's as simple as that. I saved my money for this political campaign, and if I keep handing it over to this blackmailer, I'll have nothing left. Then I won't be able to stand anyway. If that happens, he might as well have just published that damned diary in the first place. Ironic, isn't it? I lose what I want either way.'

He tossed the envelope on to Tyler's side of the desk. The address had been printed by what looked like an inkjet. Tyler slid out a single sheet, read it quickly, then asked, 'And what would you like me to do?'

'Quietly recover the diary and keep the whole thing hushed up.' Bradon studied him carefully. 'Do you think you can do that?'

'Sure.' He paused. 'Does your wife know about any of this?'

'Of course not.' Bradon looked horrified at the suggestion. 'She's turfed me out into the spare room because I'm tossing and turning all night with worry. Madi just thinks things are difficult at work.'

Tyler looked at the letter again. 'Right. You need to deliver a further twenty thousand in three days' time in the same manner as before. D'you know where the pickup will be yet?'

A shake of the head.

Tyler thought fast. 'Can you get that amount in time?'

Bradon squirmed. 'I think so, just about. But it pretty much cleans me out.'

'Okay. Let me know the second you get told where the car's going to be waiting.'

CHAPTER FOUR

Tyler's powerful BMW swept up the switchback, a road barely wide enough for two cars. This early, nothing was coming the other way. The morning sun was barely glowing through the trees.

The call had come for Bradon just before sunrise – a computer-generated voice. 'Drive into Surrey,' he'd been told. 'Be at Dorking railway station at six-thirty this morning and wait there for instructions.' Bradon barely had time to reach the spot; for Tyler it would be impossible.

While waiting among the bustle of early commuters, Bradon received a text message instructing him to drive to a car park at nearby Box Hill. Tyler had warned him there would probably be a watcher at the station, so Bradon waited until after pulling away to relay the message to Tyler, who was still en-route. Neither man had known where Box Hill was, and both had to consult maps on their SATNAVs. To give Tyler a chance to get ahead, Bradon said he would travel there slowly.

Tyler threw his car into third gear, braked for the next bend, then accelerated hard, the exhilarating roar or the engine filling his ears. The road climbed. On either side, trees largely still leafless from winter, cast flickering shadows across the tarmac.

Suddenly he burst into a clearing where Box Hill should be. To his right was a low building. Seconds later, there was an entrance to his left for car parking that zigzagged out of sight among trees. He swung in fast, bumping across the rutted surface in a plume of dust and grit, and swerved into the bay of spaces farthest from the road. There was no sign of Bradon's Mercedes.

There was a scattering of other cars that were already parked despite the hour, no doubt those of early morning dog walkers. One of the vehicles, though, would have been left there by Argus.

Tyler tried to think like the blackmailer. If things were the other way round, he would already be here with a pair of binoculars to check how things panned out. On the assumption he was now being watched, Tyler got out casually, zipped up his jacket, and shrugged the day pack that held his camera and a bottle of water on to his back. Without looking at the other cars, he walked towards the footpath that disappeared between the trees, ignoring the sign that sternly asked if he'd paid the parking fee and displayed the ticket. He tried to appear relaxed. *Look straight ahead. Ignore the feeling of eyes boring into you.*

Memories of Bosnia flashed before him. His unit had been deployed in the nineties to gather intel for the UN on suspected atrocities occurring during the civil war. Images of slowly crossing a cobbled square towards a church filled his mind, causing his stomach to clench. Wearing civilian clothes, undercover, no weapon, yet suspecting a sniper's bullet might punch through his skull at any second added to the anxious feeling of being watched.

Despite the cold morning, sweat trickled down his back. As soon as he was deeper into tree cover, he broke into a run. There was little chance of being able to spot Argus, but Tyler wanted at least a brief reconnoitre before Bradon arrived in case things went wrong.

He cut left along a narrower trail and started to circumnavigate the car park. A wood pigeon fluttered away in fright, but otherwise the only sounds apart from his footfalls were those of tree boughs tapping together in the wind.

It took twenty minutes to complete the circuit and be back within sight of his BMW. Tyler's breathing was still heavy from the run as he took up position among the trees. He was relieved to still be ahead of Bradon – already he could hear a car approaching. A moment later, Bradon's black Mercedes cautiously turned on to the dirt track. The game was on.

The car glided to a halt in the middle of a bay of a dozen empty spaces, each marked by a horizontal wooden log. Tyler crouched low in the undergrowth and shuffled his position for a clearer view. Bradon cut the engine but sat there, Tyler guessed waiting for further instructions. Argus had to be watching. Tyler scanned the hills and trees for him, but could see no hint of the blackmailer.

Sudden movement made Tyler snap his attention back to the Mercedes. Bradon was climbing out, his overcoat pulled tight around him against the wind. He looked haggard as he walked to the next bay and stood in the mouth studying the three cars. The wind swept off the expanse of hills and whipped the dust in the car park into a series of little eddies. He shook his head slowly and tried the next bay. Two cars there. Tyler thought he saw Bradon nod.

The businessman moved out of sight again, and Tyler shuffled through the undergrowth, reaching a better position in time to see him approach a blue Fiesta. Bradon reached for the boot, found it unlocked, and pulled a bulging Jiffy bag from his coat pocket and tossed it inside. Without a glance elsewhere, he slammed the boot and marched back to his car, anger clearly visible in the tightly clenched jaw. Moments later, Bradon fired up the engine, and the Mercedes swept out of the car park and its sound slowly died in the distance.

Just you and me now.

Tyler cautiously slipped the rucksack from his back, laying it in front of him and easing out his camera, careful that his movements were slow and wouldn't draw a watcher's attention. He took a round of shots of the Fiesta, then laid the SLR on top of his bag and settled back to wait.

Fifteen minutes passed. A mouse or rat scuttled through nearby undergrowth, but otherwise, the wind-rustled leaves were his only companions.

The harsh whine of a small car engine carried to him as it

climbed the hill in too low a gear. Tyler heard it slow, caught sight of red bodywork as it crawled into the first parking area. He cautiously moved a few feet to his left and photographed the car and its occupant, not that he imagined the elderly lady in pink wellies and Barbour raincoat who climbed out with a small Scottie dog was likely to be the blackmailer. She and her dog headed straight to a footpath and were soon out of sight, although Tyler could still hear the animal yapping from a distance.

His mobile vibrated – a text – and he saw it was from Sandra. He hesitated. What spiteful wisecrack had his wife thought up this time? He should just ignore it, but he opened it anyway. *Hi Mr Icy-Heart. Only fourteen days to go before I'm rid of your miserable face. Celebration time!* He stabbed the delete key so hard that he almost dropped the phone. The woman should get her head seen to.

Another ten minutes passed. Suddenly, there was movement in the trees opposite, and Tyler was totally alert. A young man – late twenties maybe – left the footpath. He was panting and rubbing sweat from his forehead as if he'd just finished a steep climb or a run. Was this Argus, or just someone out for a jog?

The man looked round as though he, too, was searching, then crossed to the middle bay and approached the blue Fiesta. He stopped near the boot and rested, hands on hips like a recovering runner.

Tyler focused the 500 mm Canon lens on the young man. 'Hello Argus,' he muttered to himself as he clicked the shutter. Short sandy hair glistened with sweat, a little goatee, blue eyes, youthful pale skin …. Tyler clicked away from his vantage point.

Through the viewfinder, he watched the blackmailer straighten up and pull on gloves. He was a wiry five feet ten and wore a grey top and navy trousers. Dark sweat patches had spread under his arms and across his chest. Tyler held down the shutter key, and the SLR clunked away capturing multiple images.

With a nervous glance over his shoulder, the blackmailer bent to the rear wheel arch and pulled something from it before getting into the driver's seat. A moment later, the Fiesta did a hesitant 3-point turn and headed slowly down the steep hill towards the A24.

The second it was out of sight, Tyler ran for the footpath. Afraid Argus had left an accomplice behind to check for a tail, Tyler slowed as he emerged from the trees and walked more casually to his car. He placed his day bag on the passenger seat and drove in the direction the target had gone.

He caught up to the Fiesta with ease and followed it down into Dorking through roads choked with morning traffic, and then on into the countryside. The blackmailer did nothing to check for a tail – none of the fancy double backs or sudden stops that Tyler had expected. Arrogant overconfidence it seemed. Well, it would be Argus' downfall.

Tyler's car kit rang. 'Sarge, it's Stu.'

'Hi mate. Your girlfriend got something for me on that car registration?' Tyler had given him the details he'd got from Bradon about the last car Argus had used. Stu, who'd been an explosives expert in the SAS, had left at the same time as Tyler and joined a security firm. More importantly, Stu's partner worked in the police force.

'Sal didn't really want to do it. You know, confidentiality and all that crap. Anyway, what she would say is that those plates were nicked from a different vehicle. Some geezer in Ilford got back from holiday and didn't notice it till the next day, stupid pisshead. She wants to know why you're asking.'

'Just something I stumbled across. I agreed to help someone out.'

'I thought you were totally dedicated to writing thrillers these days. No cloak-and-dagger stuff.'

'Slight diversion, that's all.'

The Fiesta indicated left as they approached a roundabout. Tyler followed, one car between them.

'I've got something else for you,' Stu said.

'Oh yeah?'

'You said it was a white Golf. She thought you might like to know one got stolen at about the same time, a few streets away from where the number plates were taken. She wants to know what's going on, Sarge.'

'It's kinda confidential at the minute. You know how it is. Let her know I'll tell her as soon as I can.' He heard the sigh down the phone, knew what an ear-bashing Stu would be in for. He'd met Sal a few times – a large girl who looked like she could break every bone in your body with a single squeeze. 'Can I push my luck a bit further?'

There was another sigh, louder this time. 'Go on.'

'I've got another registration that needs checking.' From memory, he recited the number of the car he was following and gave its description. 'If she could manage that as well, it would be great.'

'She won't like it.'

Tyler hung up with a promise that he would let them know what it was about in a couple of days. He felt disappointed she hadn't provided much that helped, but he couldn't realistically have hoped for a lot more.

It had looked as if Argus had been heading for Guildford, but the Fiesta now turned on to a smaller road signed for Albury. Tyler turned after it, dropping back.

A few miles farther on, the Fiesta pulled into a deserted lay-by surrounded by dense trees. A few of the tall bushes that arched over the kerbstones showed early splashes of purple blooms. Weeds grew through cracks in the concrete, and the solitary dented bin clearly hadn't been emptied in months, its lid stuck open over the cartons and bottles.

Why was he stopping? Tyler swept past, but as soon as the next bend hid him from view, he braked to a halt on the overgrown verge. He grabbed his camera and darted across the road into the trees, forcing his way through knee-high nettles and cow-parsley until he could make out the lay-by between the trunks. The blue Fiesta was still there with Argus at the wheel. Tyler hurriedly snapped a couple of photos, one wide angle and one zoomed in to clearly show his face. Argus must be waiting for an accomplice.

Traffic here was almost non-existent, and anything that

came down the road was clearly audible a mile away. No-one was going to arrive without Tyler knowing.

He knelt in the damp grass behind a clump of brambles and waited. Five minutes passed and Argus didn't move, just stared through the windscreen and occasionally picked his nose. Behind Tyler, birds sung. The wind that had whipped up Box Hill was absent here – no more than a gentle rustle above his head.

Six minutes, seven, then the rumble of a diesel carried from the direction of Farley Green village. It sounded like a small lorry travelling fast, its engine screaming.

Moments later, a dented Ford Transit barrelled round the corner doing sixty, then braked sharply. Tyler captured two shots and ducked back as the van shuddered to a halt on his side of the road and blocked his view of Argus. Both front doors flew open. Two men exited – bald heads, T-shirts and jeans. Tyler raised the camera. These had to be the guys the blackmailer was waiting for.

They charged into the woods towards Tyler, and Tyler realised he'd been wrong – it wasn't Argus these two had come to meet. They'd come for *him*.

CHAPTER FIVE

At the same moment, Trish McGowan hesitantly stepped into Sylver & McGowan Interiors. The normally smooth skin round her hazel eyes was pale with fatigue. One of her ears still had a plaster where the wound refused to heal, matched by one on her cheek. No makeup today, not that she often wore much. The first thing that struck her was the smell – damp concrete and something acrid that was probably burnt plastic. She screwed up her button nose and froze in the doorway before letting out a long sigh. The windows were still boarded, but the shaft of sunlight from the front door showed enough of the shop's interior. *I'm sorry Flo, this was all my fault.* She closed her eyes, wanted to cry.

Beth Field was at her shoulder. 'The electricity's back on,' Field said and flicked on the overhead lighting. 'A gorgeous hunk of an electrician sorted it all out on Friday. Pity you missed him.' She grinned, but Trish merely nodded, not being in the mood for laughs.

Field pulled the door shut and laid a hand on Trish's

arm. 'It's not as bad as it looks,' she said. 'We'll soon have everything back up and running.'

Trish fought back tears and nodded firmly. *At least I've still got both arms and legs to make it happen.* She gritted her teeth. No way was she going to allow one stupid mistake twelve months ago to destroy everything she and her aunt had built up.

She took a deep breath of tainted air. 'Let's see the worst out back.'

'Are you sure about this? You were only discharged half an hour ago.'

'Of course, I'm sure.'

When she was two steps short of the back office, there was a crash from the other side of the closed door, and Trish's legs locked in panic. *He's come back already.* She listened intently but all she could hear over the cars outside was the whistle that was still in her ears. She stared at the charred door, waiting for it to open.

Beth was a few steps behind. 'You all right?'

Trish breathed out. 'Fine.' It must have been something falling over when the floorboards moved. The three-hundred-year-old building was creaky at the best of times and the poor girl had just taken quite a beating.

'We can do this later, you know. We can …'

'No,' Trish said firmly. 'I want to see everything and then get to grips with repairs straightaway.' She took a deep breath, strode forward and snatched at the handle.

It stuck. For a second, she imagined him on the other side holding it firm. She tugged, and the door squealed and flew open. Of course, no one was there. She felt a flush redden her cheeks.

The boarded window left the room dim, and it took her a moment to recognize what she was looking at. Tears moistened her eyes, and she quickly brushed them away before Field noticed. Her desk stood crookedly below the window, its surface charred and gritty, the paint on its legs peeling. Her designer lamp had been reduced to a blackened metal arm that was on the floor in the corner, its flex missing. She couldn't see the monitor anywhere, and the computer was on its side under the desk with its case a mass of bubbled paint. Under foot, the carpet had all but gone – just a few patches of the underlying mesh stuck to the charred boards.

If I'd been sitting there ...Trish's legs started to shake, and she grabbed the doorframe for support. Images exploded in her memory: the bleaching whiteness, the total silence, the panic ...

'You don't look very well,' Field said. 'Are you really sure you're ready for this?'

'Of course I am,' Trish snapped, then tried to smile and added more softly, 'Sorry. I'm just a bit jumpy.' She needed a cigarette.

'Look, why don't you come and spend a few days with me while your nerves settle? And in the evenings, we can plan out exactly how to get everything straight.' Field hovered in the doorway. 'Let's go back to the main shop. It's less of a mess in there.'

Trish followed. 'It's very kind of you to offer. I appreciate it but it's not necessary.'

'Really? It'll give us both company.'

'It's just that ...' Trish stopped.

Field looked at her sympathetically. 'It's nothing to be embarrassed about, needing time to recover. It's natural. How about staying over for a few days?'

Oh hell, it would be good to tell someone. It burst out in a tumble of words. 'The thing is I'm scared someone's trying to kill me.'

Field hesitated briefly while she took in what Trish had said, then offered an encouraging smile. 'You're just suffering from shock. You've been through a lot.'

Trish shook her head. 'There's more to it than that.'

'Like what?'

Trish just continued to slowly shake her head.

'Then go to the police.'

'I can't. I just can't.'

'Why not?'

'I can't say. Okay? But there are reasons.'

'Trish?'

'Sorry. Just ignore me. I'm probably being stupid. As you say, it's just shock making me paranoid.'

'Why would anyone want to kill you?'

'Just forget I said it. I was being stupid.' They walked solemnly back to the main shop, Trish's legs still barely supporting her. She fingered the rolls of material that someone had restacked against the wall. A beautiful roll of lilac satin had a dark stain across one corner. A cold lump of anger started to grow in her stomach. He wasn't going to ruin this for her. This shop was Flo's memory come to life.

Trish straightened an imitation Victorian mirror and brushed grit from the ornate frame. Field gently put an arm round her and smiled at their reflections. 'We'll do it,' she said, giving Trish a slight squeeze.

Trish brushed the pink and green locks of hair from her eyes and rubbed away the last tear. 'We will,' she said with determination. She put her head on one side and studied her friend, the similar length hair, a round face much like her own. They were both about the same height as well, although Trish was slightly slimmer. 'You know, if it wasn't for my coloured streaks, we might look like sisters.' She forced a smile. 'And thanks for the invite. Perhaps just a day or so while my nerves calm down. That'll be great.'

CHAPTER SIX

Tyler faced the two thugs. They entered the woods, heading for him. One, tall with a beer belly – slow but strong. The other: short, wiry, fast, but less muscular. Metal glinted in Shorty's hand. A knife. Six inches long.

Tyler straightened and moved his legs apart for better balance. Adrenaline poured into his bloodstream as he concentrated on the pair, preparing for their attack. They hesitated twenty yards away. Tyler wasn't running; clearly not what they'd expected.

Shorty came first. Wary, but his blade gave him confidence.

The scrunch of leaves and twigs under his feet was loud. Tyler relaxed his shoulders. There was nothing around he could use as a weapon.

Shorty suddenly moved in fast.

Tyler dodged to one side as the knife sliced the air. He tried to kick out but missed. The camera swung wildly from his neck, briefly putting him off balance. Shorty spun round, lunged again.

Fatty hung back.

Tyler jumped sideways, chopped down at the wrist but caught Shorty's arm instead. The knife didn't drop. Shorty spun around and with anger in his eyes, sized up his prey. Tyler's SAS training that had been drummed into them, the hand-to-hand combat practice, all came surging back. He circled slowly to his left, keeping the other thug in view. Time to strike. As Shorty tensed his muscles to lunge again, Tyler landed a powerful blow to the side of the man's head. There was a thud of flesh and bone. Shorty staggered back. Tyler grabbed the knife hand, twisted viciously, yanked the arm back until he heard cartilage and tendons tear. Shorty yelled, dropped the knife. Tyler powered his left fist hard into Shorty's stomach. Shorty buckled forward with a gasp, and Tyler grabbed his head, slamming it down into his rapidly rising knee, smashing Shorty's face. Nasal cartilage crunched, followed by a grunt of pain.

Shorty went limp and fell. His partner was already moving forward, exhibiting only brute force, and no skill. He charged Tyler like an animal.

Tyler jumped aside. Where had the knife gone? *Can't see it.*

Fatty threw a punch. Fists like slabs of meat. Tyler dodged, his camera swinging. Tyler grabbed an arm but it was shaken off. Fatty swung another punch. Missed. Suddenly, he threw himself at Tyler, snarling, arms reaching for him.

Tyler stumbled as he tried to avoid the lunge, felt a blow

hammer into the side of his head. Ears hissing, knees sagging. Through greyed vision, he saw hands reach for his throat. Tyler tried to raise a hand to knock them away but it was like moving through water.

A vice tightened across his windpipe.

Training overcame the instinct to claw at the hand. Instead, he thrust two rigid fingers into his attacker's eyeballs. Tyler felt them sink into softness. A cry. A momentary release of pressure.

Suck in air while you can. Lungs on fire. Vision grey and blurred.

Tyler stiffened the fingers of his left hand and drove them into his attacker's windpipe with all his remaining force. The head jerked backwards. Tyler grabbed one of Fatty's fingers and yanked it back until he heard the snap of bone.

As Fatty gasped for breath, Tyler pulled himself free. Fatty writhed like a wounded bull. Tyler sidestepped the flailing figure, grabbed his massive head, and drove it hard into a tree trunk.

Fatty sagged but kept his feet. Tyler grabbed him, viciously hammered his head again and again into the tree until he fell limp. Fatty slid down the oak, collapsed into the leaves at its base that were spattered with blood.

Shorty stirred. Tyler spun, coughing, panting for breath. Where the hell was Argus? Tyler sprinted back to the road while rubbing his throat. His vision cleared as he charged through the trees.

His attackers' van stood at the kerb, doors open, blocking

his view of the lay-by where the Fiesta had been parked.

He ran round the front of the van. The lay-by was empty.

Tyler was on the road now, tarmac underfoot. Argus' car had been facing up hill. Probably gone that way. No sound of an engine above the hammering in his own ears.

Tyler sprinted to the next bend and scoured the view past his own car for the Fiesta. An avenue of rhododendrons stretched up the hill into the distance, but there was no sign of Argus.

He rested for a moment, drawing in the sweet air. His windpipe still stung from his encounter with the two thugs. There was a towrope in his car that he could use to secure the thugs for questioning. As he started to jog towards the BMW to fetch it, Tyler heard the rattle of the van's engine starting. One rev and the diesel roared.

No!

He sprinted for his car, rammed the key into the ignition. Tyler u-turned and accelerated to where the Transit had been, but the B-road was empty by the time he cleared the bend.

Foot rammed to the floor, he tore after them. Where the hell had they gone? Cross-roads. Slammed on the brakes. His big car shuddered to a halt. No sign of them either way. Mental toss of a coin.

Straight on, engine roaring. A small car coming the other way passed in a blur, otherwise nothing. Two miles of empty road, then houses and a village store. He glanced at the side roads as he passed but there was no white van. He slowed to scan other side streets and drives. Nothing. He left the built-up neighbourhood and re-entered areas of farmland. He pulled over, two wheels on the grass verge, and sat with engine idling. He hammered the steering wheel. What now? Argus gone, money gone, thugs gone.

He gently rubbed at his throat – very tender but no lasting damage. How the hell had Argus spotted him and known to call in his thugs? It was possible the blackmailer had realised he was being tailed, but Tyler didn't think that was the case. If he ever found the pair again, maybe he'd get an answer.

Tyler turned his car and slowly retraced his route while scanning every side road and driveway. A few white vans went about their business but not the one he wanted. None of them had a red sticker on the windscreen and a rusting dent across its driver's door.

He parked in the lay-by Argus had used and crossed the road on foot into the trees where they'd come for him. He searched for ten minutes in the hope of finding some clue to who they were, but there was nothing except the kicked-around leaves where they'd fought. He checked his camera, but the image he'd quickly captured of the van was blurred. He hadn't even managed to get a registration number.

What the hell was he going to tell Bradon?

CHAPTER SEVEN

Three days later, Trish McGowan was putting a carrier bag of food on the mat and closing the door to Beth's flat behind her. She winced as the damaged arm muscles complained.

It was strange there was no reply. It was still early, and Beth hadn't said she was going out. She called again towards the lounge. 'Beth, I managed to get everything except that wicked chocolate ice cream. I'm afraid they'd sold out.'

No answer. Trish slipped off her shoes and carried the groceries to the kitchen. 'Beth?' She crossed to the lounge in bare feet, pushed open the door. At first glance she thought it empty. Already she was half-turned back to the hall.

Then she saw her friend curled on the floor.

'Beth? You okay?' She rushed across. Beth must have fainted. Trish bent beside her. Vague memories of first aid they'd been taught at school – roll into recovery position.

Trish laid a hand on her friend's shoulder and gasped. Blood soaked the back of her jumper. There was a cloying nauseating smell that made Trish gag, but she forced herself to lean forward. *Where's all the blood coming come?* Her own fingers were now red and slippery. Before she could help herself, she had rubbed them on the carpet in revulsion. She rolled Beth further on to her side. A glistening crimson stain oozed across the pile.

She had to staunch the flow.

Trish staggered to the kitchen, snatched a towel and half ran, half stumbled back. She gritted her teeth, not wanting to look, heart thumping hard.

Quickly, Trish pulled at her friend's top ready to push the towel against the source of the bleeding. She gasped at the bloody slash in her back across the kidneys. This was no accident.

A sudden creak came from the far side of the room. She jumped violently. The French doors moved in the wind, and for the first time, she realised they were ajar. It was then she noticed shards of glass across the carpet. A cold clamp gripped her chest as she took it in. Someone had smashed the window, reached through, turned the key that Beth always kept in the lock.

She forced the towel hard against the wound. It was no use.

We need a paramedic.

Where was her bloody mobile? She lurched back to the kitchen, putting a hand on the wall to steady herself, leaving a brown smudge across the tiles. She grabbed her handbag and ran back while pulling out the phone. She started to stab the screen, her fingers sliding across glass that was now sticky with blood.

She knelt beside Beth and suddenly froze with her finger hovering above the mobile. The realisation hit her. It had taken time, but now it struck like a cudgel blow: it hadn't been a burglar; *he came for me*. Only recently, Beth and she had joked about how similar they looked, apart from Trish's fringe of coloured hair. And from the back …

Tears of panic blurred her vision. *It's my fault. Beth, please don't be dead.*

She had to get help but if she became entangled with the police, the whole story with Wendell would come out and she'd have her own questions to face. It would be the end of the shop. All that her aunt had built up and handed to her would be destroyed.

Use Beth's phone. That can't lead back to me. Trish looked frantically for the Apple she'd seen her friend use, spotted it on the coffee table only a meter from Beth's hand. Trish dropped her own and grabbed it, quickly stabbing nine-nine-nine.

'Ambulance please. Quick,' she shouted as soon as it connected.

'Can I have your name and location, please?' A woman's professional voice.

'Just get an ambulance. My friend's dying.'

'Can I have your name please, miss?'

'No. It doesn't matter. Get an ambulance.'

'I need your name first.'

Trish hesitated. 'Bethany Field,' she said quickly and gave the address. 'Now get me a bloody ambulance.'

'One moment.'

Beth might not have a moment. The voice was so damned calm.

A pause, then: 'A unit is on the way to you. It'll be there very quickly, so don't worry. Now, please stay on the line. What state's your friend in?'

Trish shook her head and hung up, letting the phone drop to the floor.

She knelt beside her friend, pushed the sodden cloth against the wound. 'An ambulance is coming,' she said softly. 'Just hang on Beth. I'll stay with you as long as I can. You'll be fine.'

Beth's mobile started ringing. Trish ignored it. It vibrated on the carpet until it went to voicemail.

She raced to the front door, unlatched it, left it ajar for a paramedic, then ran back with her shoes, and flung her mobile into her bag ready to flee. She again knelt with the towel pressed against Beth's back. The blood that seeped through it slowly dried on her hands.

Five minutes of waiting. Trish felt faint, looked away from the blood that soaked Beth's top. *Don't die, Beth. Don't die.*

A siren cut through the silence. Beyond the curtains she glimpsed the fluorescent panels of a paramedic's car. Door slamming, running feet. Trish grabbed her bag. 'I'm so sorry, Beth. I can't stay. I'd have too many questions to answer. An ambulance is here now. They'll look after you.' She let the bloody towel slide down her friend's back.

With tears wet against her cheeks, she raced across the

broken glass, out through the French doors, and darted across the small garden to the gate that led to a footpath. There was no-one around to witness her leaving. She wanted to keep running but forced her shaking legs to slow to a normal pace, just in case.

Light-headedness started to engulf her as she crossed the deserted playing field and pushed through the iron gate back to the street. Trish held on to the stone wall to keep herself upright.

She was a fair way up the road, but could still see Beth's house. An ambulance was now parked behind the paramedic's sleek car. Its rear doors were wide, a ramp already down to the road. As she hesitated, a police car swept past her with lights flashing.

Trish turned quickly away, and her pulse raced as she steadily walked the remaining fifty metres to her car and dropped into the driver's seat.

She had driven no more than a few hundred yards before her whole body started to shake so uncontrollably that she had to pull in to the kerb. She would never eradicate the memory of that great slash in Beth's back. Trish tightly gripped the steering wheel and closed her eyes. *Oh Beth, I'm so sorry.*

Eventually the shaking passed, to be replaced by tears that brimmed in her eyes as she cried until her whole chest ached. She sucked in deep breaths once it finally subsided and reached for tissues from her handbag. Her mind began to clear. Trish fumbled for a cigarette, lit it shakily, and closed her eyes. She knew what she had to do.

There was only one way to end this whole business now, and that was to try to contact Argus. She restarted the engine and headed for the main road.

CHAPTER EIGHT

Craig Tyler had returned to his work on BDE's history. There seemed little he could do right now about Argus.

He was in the log cabin he'd built behind his house in Hereford – an alternative bolt-hole to his writing cottage in the Welsh mountains. An overloaded bookcase stood in one corner beside a rattling fan heater that spewed warmth towards his feet. The panelled walls displayed framed cover-prints from his thrillers. A dark rectangle on the wood showed where a wedding photo had once hung.

He sat at the large scratch-built desk surrounded by transcripts of the interviews he'd held with BDE staff. On the floor beside him stood a stack of faded company newsletters dating back twenty years. He'd only been at the desk half an hour when the phone call came that would finally change things in his favour.

Tyler had been reading through his transcripts with growing despair. If he wasn't careful, the history book would be nothing more than a vapid list of facts. He had to find something – some theme to run through it – to keep it alive. The newsletters had held a few random glimpses of interest – articles about optimistic product launches and new innovations in production, alongside photos from parties for haggard-looking engineers and managers who'd finally retired. He would track some of them down, he decided. They might have a different slant on things to the current employees, all of whom had been cautious when they'd spoken to him.

The company's biggest investment in recent years was easily the development of an unmanned aerial vehicle – a UAV – codenamed 'Dragonfly'. It was the latest in drone technology. They had been in their infancy during his time in the Service – he'd witnessed them in Bosnia gathering intel' on targets' movements – but they'd come a long way since then. He thought of the debacle the Ministry of Defence had suffered with Watchkeeper – hundreds of millions over-budget and years late. Dragonfly was smaller and cheaper, but it was privately funded, so an overspend of even a fraction of that amount could push a company of BDE's size into administration.

He flipped open his laptop and typed *BDE Dragonfly UAV* into Google. He frowned when it returned a clutch of newspaper articles all from four years ago – one in the local press, three from papers around Farnborough and Aldershot, even one in The Times.

Tyler had just opened the first Farnborough one when his mobile buzzed. It was Stu. 'Hi Sarge. I've got something for you. You remember that vehicle registration you asked

Sal to check?'

'Go on.'

'Well, it was nicked like the last one. Again, the owner didn't notice it missing. Looks like whoever's doing this is careful who they target – it ain't looking like random theft. Anyway, thing is it turned up again. It was left almost exactly where it had been taken from in Stratford.'

'Burnt out?'

'Not at all. It's like you'd never know it had been taken. The owner probably wouldn't have realised if you hadn't called it in. The local cops did a quick dust for prints but didn't turn up nothing but those of the owner. As it's just a stolen car that's been returned, they're doing naff all more than that. They ain't going to do detailed forensics like if it was a murder or something.'

'I thought you had something useful.'

'I'm getting there. Thing is, they noticed a smear of something fresh on the driver's seat, decided they'd send it for analysis to see what it was. It came back this morning. The police ain't following up on it, but Sal thought you might be interested. Said if you got anything from it to let her know.'

'Spit it out, mate. What was it?'

'She described it as an aliphatic resin compound.'

'What the hell's that?'

'Some type of wood glue apparently, but it's a bit specialist. Used for furniture repairs. Thing is, that smear was pretty fresh. It almost certainly came from the clothes of your driver.'

'So, he's some sort of furniture restorer by trade?'

'Looks like.'

'Did she say how easy that glue is to get hold of?'

'Well, you can get it online simple enough, but not in your local B & Q. It ain't the kind of stuff you'd use for DIY – you'd just use PVA for that, you know the white stuff you can get in a tube anywhere, even in a pound store. This glue, though, you'd only find on the high street in a specialist shop.'

'Okay. Thanks mate. Anything else?'

'Na. That's all. But she still wants to know what you've got into.'

'Sorry Stu. Give me a few days.'

After the call, Tyler lay back and stuck his feet on the edge of the desk, thinking. From what Sal had said, it was clear Argus targeted car owners who were away, stealing keys only when no one would notice. That would demand a lot of up-front surveillance and suggested Argus lived or worked nearby. Tyler swung his feet to the floor and opened a fresh tab on his laptop's browser, putting aside his search on Dragonfly and pulling up a roadmap. The midpoint between Ilford and Stratford was close to Forest Gate Rail Station, and he mentally drew a circle centred on it with a ten-mile radius. Argus probably spent a lot of time inside that circle.

The Yellow Pages website soon provided four screens of furniture repairers and restorers in the area. He printed the list, locked the cabin door, and hurried back to the house for his car keys, forgetting the newspaper article he'd been about to read on Dragonfly.

CHAPTER NINE

All she could think about was Beth. Trish drove home on some sort of autopilot, and as she pulled into the drive, she grabbed the phone from her bag. The shock at seeing smears of blood across the screen almost made her drop it. Trish tried to ignore them while she Googled a number for the local hospital. She felt nauseous.

She cleared her throat as it rang. 'A friend has just been admitted via A & E. Could you tell me if she's alright, please?' Her voice quivered as she gave Beth's name. While she waited, her heart pounded so hard she thought she might collapse.

'We have no-one here by that name.'

Perhaps it was too soon. Maybe they'd spent time at the house stopping the bleeding before moving her or something.

On legs that could barely carry her along the path, she tottered to the house and let herself in. Her agonized brain noticed the details in the pristine hallway: walnut floor,

Coral Reef SW6606 paint on one wall, balanced by Balboa Mist on the others, two carefully positioned mirrors, the painting of Buttermere she'd made when her aunt had shut the shop for a holiday in the Lake District to celebrate Trish finishing art school.

She dropped onto the bottom step of the stairs and scanned through her mobile for the messages she'd received from Argus. She called the first number with trembling hands, then tried the others with a growing sense of panic. Each time she got the same message – *the dialled number didn't exist.*

She kicked off her shoes and ran upstairs to the spare room that doubled as an office and booted her laptop, then sent a message to the three email addresses Argus had used. Swiftly she received automated responses– *user not known.*

Desperation, panic, loneliness, all bubbled-up inside her. She chewed her bottom lip, but wasn't going to allow herself to cry – she was nearly thirty, not six.

Out loud, sounding like her aunt, she said, 'You got yourself into this shit, Trish. Now it's time to get yourself out before anyone else gets hurt.'

Trish glanced at her watch. When could she ring again about Beth?

Suddenly, there was the sound of a car slowing outside. She held her breath, aware again of the incessant whistle in her ears. She crept to the window, stood to one side out of sight, and moved the curtain enough to peer through a crack. She recognized the car as her next-door neighbour's Vauxhall and breathed out slowly.

Trish let the curtain swing back. She couldn't live like this, scared by every sound.

Find Argus, force him to help – it was the only way she could think of to get Wendell off her case and get her life back. And if she couldn't phone or email, the only thing left was to find him in person. And there was only one place she knew to try.

Being away would also mean she would be out of Wendell's sight when he discovered she was still alive – an added bonus. Trish found a couple of holdalls and started to pack.

Grabbing her tent from the box room, she paused beside a threadbare soft-toy rabbit – the only memento of her childhood – and patted its once-fluffy head. 'I'll be away a while,' she told it with her voice breaking. 'But don't worry. I'll be back soon.'

CHAPTER TEN

Tyler reached London later that morning ready to check out furniture repairers. He entered the first shop on the list, setting an ancient mechanical bell jangling above the door. Smells of wood and leather hung in the dusty air. Price-tagged furniture was dotted round the walls – a leather wing-backed chair sat between an upholstered chaise longue and an ebony dressing table that was so polished he could see his reflection scowling back at him.

A balding man in brown overalls shuffled through the far door and smiled to show a missing front tooth. 'Good afternoon, sir.'

'Hi.' Tyler had rehearsed his approach on the way over. 'Is the young man here today?'

A frown formed in the furrows of his leathery skin. 'I'm sorry, but it's only me and my brother who work here. And neither of us are exactly young.' He laughed, a cracked dry sound.

'Sorry. My mistake.' Tyler took a step closer. 'Actually,

I've got a bit of a strange request.'

Suspicion etched itself into the man's features. Tyler took a slip of paper from his trousers and turned it to the shopkeeper, who perched some large spectacles on his nose. Tyler asked, 'Do you use this?' He hesitated over his pronunciation. '… aliphatic glue?'

The old man straightened up from squinting at the paper and removed his glasses. 'Of-course. It's key in furniture restoration. We don't quite use it by the gallon, but we have plenty of it out back.'

Tyler nodded, returning the paper to his pocket and replacing it with a print of the photo he'd taken of Argus. 'Have you seen this man here at all?'

The glasses went back on to view the picture, but he soon shook his head. 'Don't think so. I certainly don't recognize him. Are you a private investigator or something?'

'Sort of. Are there any other furniture repairers round here?'

He pursed his lips, silent for a moment. 'There's a place over in Woolwich, down near the old docks, close to that big old chimney thing. Do you know it?'

He didn't, but it sounded like one of the places already on his list. Tyler turned to go.

'What's he done? Murder or something? Is the glue some sort of clue?'

'Kinda,' Tyler said as he let himself out of the dusty shop, leaving the bell to jangle wildly.

He managed to visit four more repair shops. Traffic, as always around London, was slow, noisy, and frustrating. He hated driving in town.

Tyler pulled up near the small factory unit in a cluster of grubby buildings. He yawned and stretched. So far it had been a boring day of visiting shop after shop, and the novelty of playing detective had already worn off. No-one had recognized his photo of Argus.

He trudged inside, met by the same aroma of leather, sawn timber, and polish, a mix of smells he'd begun to hate. Like all the others, the slightly rundown shop was unattended as he stepped inside and let the door clang shut behind him. Tyler surveyed the collection of furniture that was stacked three pieces deep round the walls. To his left was a globe suspended in an antique oak frame. He spun it absentmindedly, remembering the places he'd been posted over the years – the Falklands, Syria, Iraq … His fingers stroked their outline. Libya: that had been bad – so damned hot. That's where Terry had been shot in the face by a jihadist.

A bony man appeared in the internal doorway wearing faded jeans and a stained red jumper. 'Can I help you?'

Tyler released the globe, leaving it to spin as he went into his well-practiced routine, receiving the same familiar shakes of the head. The hunt was not going as well as he'd hoped. He was starting to turn back to the door when a thought struck him. Stu had told him aliphatic glue was used in furniture repair and he'd taken it as gospel. He stopped with his hand resting on the handle. 'Aliphatic glue isn't used anywhere else, is it? I mean other than in furniture repair?'

The shopkeeper sniffed and rubbed the back of his hand across his nose. 'Dunno, really.' He scratched his thinning hair. 'Mind you, I think they use it in model making. You know, those large ships and planes people make with remote controls that geeks like to muck around with.'

Tyler's sullen mood lifted. 'They use it in the construction?'

'I think so.'

'Can you buy it from model-making shops?'

'Guess so. Probably not from all of them, but from specialist ones I suppose.'

'Are there any model shops round here?'

He shrugged bony shoulders and set his baggy jumper flapping around his arms. 'Not my thing, mate. Don't know.'

Tyler sat in his car using his mobile to search the internet, and finally added five model shops to his existing list. Maybe Argus didn't work at a furniture restoration shop at all. Perhaps he was an enthusiastic model maker instead. Tyler phoned each in turn from outside the factory building and asked if they stocked aliphatic glue, which eliminated three of them. With renewed enthusiasm, he headed north, back across the river.

***

Tyler's luck came in as the first high street shopkeepers started pulling down metal shutters for the end of the day's trading. Second model shop on the list.

It was the oldest and most cramped establishment he had ever seen, just off the North Circular Road and only just inside his search zone. It smelt of dust. Floor to ceiling display units ran along all four walls. One of them even stood half-way across the High Street window. Each was crammed with a miscellany of shapes and colours of boxes, some new and crisp, others yellowed with age. They finished a foot from the ceiling, but the tops were lined with more cardboard boxes, most of them unlabelled.

On a table just inside the door, a tiny diesel locomotive dragged a carriage at great speed round a circular track. Its high-pitched whine was almost painful. It raced past miniature plastic houses and stationary cars on perfectly black streets.

At the back of the shop was a glass-topped counter with a dozen model planes suspended on fishing line above it. They ranged from a flimsy bi-plane to an American F-18 fighter with guided missiles under its wings. He recognized a modern, 5th-generation F-35 Lightning II. He'd seen those flying during joint exercises with the Yanks.

Tyler absorbed all this in the few seconds before his eyes rested on the middle-aged man who sat behind the counter. Bottle-top glasses perched on his nose beneath unruly black hair. He looked up from a magazine. 'Good evening.' A cheery not-a-care-in-the-world kind of voice. It must be nice to be like that.

Tyler forced a friendly smile and stepped closer. In a conspiratorial voice he said, 'I'm trying to track down a particular model maker and I wondered if he ever came in here.' Tyler held out the now rather creased photo of Argus.

The shopkeeper put his head to one side and nodded. 'I

think I recognize him. A fairly regular customer.'

Tyler's heart skipped. 'Do you know his name?'

A shake of the head. 'Afraid not. I think he's a member of the Leytonstone RC club, though. You might find him there.'

'RC?'

'Remote control. He flies a scale model Chipmunk with RAF roundels, I think.'

'Where can I find him? Do they meet somewhere?'

In answer, the shopkeeper pushed back his stool and went to the shop window, where he lifted out an A2 pinboard and spun it round for Tyler to see. 'There we are,' he said after a second and tapped a curling postcard. 'Leytonstone RC Club meets ten o'clock every Sunday morning. If you're lucky, you should find him there tomorrow.'

CHAPTER ELEVEN

Trish McGowan turned towards Guildford, leaving the crawling traffic of the M25 and eventually driving through quieter roads as the shadows lengthened and threatened the onset of dusk. Coming here was the only way she could think of reaching Argus.

Oaks and rhododendron bushes encroached on the verges with splashes of purple blooms. She almost missed the final turn, spotted it at the last minute, braked sharply, and swung through the narrow opening on to the stony track. The blankets she'd put on the back seat tumbled into the footwell.

She remembered the first time she'd come here, and her stomach churned. But she had to come back. She bit at her lower lip.

The trees closed in on either side of the track, and thin branches tapped at the windows as if trying to get at her. Tiny saplings that had grown up along the way clawed at the doors and side panels. She jolted through potholes, the car's suspension squeaking. Eventually, the track turned and widened into overgrown gardens, and she saw the ruins of the derelict manor ahead.

She reversed her Mini as far into the trees as she could manage and cut the engine. Everywhere was silent. Before getting out, she again phoned the hospital. Same response – no-one admitted with that name. *Where had they taken Beth?* With heart pounding, she called Cliff's mobile. 'D'you know anything about Beth? Where she is and stuff.'

'No. I assumed she was with you.' He paused. 'How are you getting on?' It sounded like he was in a pub. She could hear muffled music and chatter in the background.

'I'm okay. Look, I need to be away for a few days. Can I get you to look after the repairs? If you can't get hold of me, just go ahead and make any necessary decisions.'

'Sure.'

Another thought struck her. 'Do you have a number for Beth's parents? I had one in the shop files but they went up in smoke.'

'I might have. Hold on.' She heard him tapping at his phone. 'Yes. I'll text it to you.'

Trish made excuses for getting quickly off the line then called their number. It rang for ages, and her fingers were tingling with nerves by the time she finally heard a soft male voice. Beth's father at a guess. She'd met him once but couldn't remember the face, just a memory of neat greying hair and steel-rimmed glasses. 'Mr Field?'

A cautious acknowledgement.

'This is Trish McGowan. Beth works for me at the shop.'

She was sure there was a sharp intake of breath at the other end. She continued slowly, 'I wondered if you knew where she was.'

'She's...' There was a small gulp, a pause. 'She's dead.' The voice quivered.

It was like a blow to the head. He was saying something else but she didn't hear. Tears brimmed in her eyes. *What have I done?* 'I...' she began, but her voice caught.

'Sorry,' Beth's father stammered. 'I can't ... I can't talk right now. It's too much. Perhaps later. Please. I'm sorry, I have to go.'

He disconnected, and Trish sat there stunned. Her ears started to whistle again.

How long she stayed in the car she couldn't remember later. 'Beth, I'm sorry,' she whispered to the passenger seat. 'It was all my fault.' Trish screwed her eyes tightly shut, trying to stop the tears, but all she could see was Beth's body, the puckered slash in her back, the spreading stain. *What have I done?* She repeatedly pummelled the steering wheel with her fists. *Why?* She opened her eyes to rid herself of the image, instead focussing on the gnarled tree trunks through the windscreen, the knee-high blades of grass, the scattering of last year's leaves that she could just make out in the fading light. *I'm so sorry Beth.*

She opened the door, let the cool air sweep across her face. She wiped her cheeks. Wendell had to be stopped. Getting Argus to help seemed a vain hope, but what else had she got left?

Which meant finding the man who didn't want to be

found. And this was the one place she knew he might come.

Trish climbed out and stood unsteadily in the grass. She found an old branch that had a few twigs still attached, and used it to rub away the tyre tracks and brush the leaves back as best she could. There was no way it would pass close scrutiny, but a casual glance would miss the marks her car had left.

She wiped her eyes and blew her nose. She breathed deeply, tasted the cool air, sucked in the smells of rotting leaves and damp soil. Birds fluttered in the trees with occasional calls as they settled for the night. She looked back towards her mini. Daisy's yellow paintwork was fairly well hidden. She just wished now she hadn't bought such a brightly coloured car.

Trish stood at the start of what had once been the formal area of grounds, where the drive joined a grand sweep of gravel, now thick with weeds. The stone façade of the boarded-up mansion was just visible behind a large cedar, its details hard to distinguish in the failing light. In front of it stood a cracked fountain with a rusting metal pipe protruding from the top.

It was too late to check out the grounds this evening. Just pitch the tent and investigate in daylight.

***

She woke shortly after sunrise with light shining through the tent fabric. After using the basic latrine she had dug some distance away, she pushed between the dense trees and undergrowth and started to circumnavigate the long-abandoned grounds. The early morning air was cold, and she was grateful for her thick coat.

Check out the area. Find vantage points, learn my way around.

With every step, Beth's father's words repeated in her memory. 'She's dead.'

Branches quickly formed a canopy above her head. She pushed on through long grass and drifts of leaves, forcing aside saplings. A startled squirrel darted away and up a trunk out of sight.

Trish tripped over the first one by accident. Her shoe caught the thin, black wire that stretched ominously across her path beneath the leaves. She stumbled and lost balance, grabbed at a tree but scraped skin from her hands and fell awkwardly. Her ribs burned, still sore from the explosion that had thrown her across the courtyard.

She crouched to study what she'd fallen over. A trip wire, maybe? Her heart lurched. She imagined alarms sounding. She freed her foot and inspected the thin cable. A light tug lifted more of it out of the soil. It seemed to be running in a straight line from the house. She followed it, pulling it from the ground as she went. This wasn't a trip wire. She furrowed her brow and followed it into denser undergrowth.

Just when the public road started to come into view between the trees, she found the end clipped to the bottom of a massive oak. She ran her fingers across the gnarls of bark, following the wire up the trunk. Mounted just above head height facing the road was a small security camera.

Argus' way to see who approached the derelict building, maybe? Trish couldn't tell if it was on. She stood on tip-toe behind it and tried to shake it free, but it was firmly fixed. Had he seen her arrive? Hairs rose on the nape of her neck.

A moment's hesitation before she turned and followed the wire back towards the house, continuing to tug it from the ground as she went. Across the drive, sand and gravel pinged into the air as she pulled at it, until the wire finally disappeared into grass on the other side. She was close to the old house now, her access blocked by a barricade of two-metre-high panels of chain link fencing mounted into concrete sleepers. A sign hung crookedly from one of them, held by a single rusting clip. In faded red characters, it read: *Dangerous structure. Keep out!* The wire dipped beneath the fence.

She brushed her hair from her face and looked up at the derelict building. She had hoped never to return and it set nerves fluttering in her stomach. Boarded doors and windows, broken downpipes with jagged ends that dripped rainwater into puddles, small plants in the gutters, a handful of roof slates lying broken around the perimeter.

Trish released the wire and wiped her hands on her jeans. She followed the fence round the side of the house to where it met a small outbuilding half way along. She had checked it out when she'd first come here last year, concluding it was an old gardener's store – empty, dank, and scented by animals.

The chain-link fence passed half a metre from its back wall, and she squeezed into the gap between its crumbling bricks and the fence as she'd been instructed before. The deep shadows down the back reeked of damp and decay.

Nothing had changed. Trish edged along until she found the place the two barriers weren't joined and pushed them apart enough to slip through.

She hurried back to where the wire dipped beneath the fence and continued to pull it from the ground, tracing it to where it disappeared under a boarded-up door. She squatted and studied it more carefully. Puzzled, she grabbed one of the broken slates and used it to dig away the soil. Five more cables lay just beneath the surface. She hooked a finger under the whole set and tugged them from the ground. They fanned out in all directions.

Over the next hour, Trish traced each of them, finding cameras in an arc around this stretch of the grounds' perimeter. She guessed there would be others covering the rest. She looked up at the mansion's crumbling façade. How many other glass eyes were hidden high up monitoring the grounds? She shuddered. If Argus was watching, he would know she was here and that she had found his cameras. But maybe that was good. Perhaps it would bring him to her.

The sun was rising above the tree line. She badly wanted to know what those wires were doing on the other side of the door. She bit at her lip, undecided, then marched back to the door and landed a series of hard kicks against the wooden sheet that was nailed across it. It didn't as much as creak.

Trish went round the ground-floor windows one by one, trying to prise away the plywood, but everything remained firm.

On the far side of the house, she found what had been a

tradesman's entrance. Momentary hope surged through her when she saw it wasn't boarded-up, but any optimism was dashed when she yanked the brass handle and found the door stood as impregnable as everything else. Strange, though, how the handle and locks didn't look tarnished. She repeatedly kicked the door as hard as she could, but nothing budged.

She stared upwards, wondering if she could climb to a higher window. She rattled an ancient downpipe and was rewarded by a shower of rust and grit. No way was she going to risk that. Trish circled the house again, continuing to pull at the boards over each window as she passed, but nothing moved even a millimetre. Back near the break in the fence, she eyed-up a small panel that was nailed at floor level to the side of the building. She knew what it was – the wood covered most of a larger hole but didn't quite reach the ground, leaving an open slot along the bottom. This was where she'd been forced to come before, made to push a padded envelope through that hole.

It had probably once been a coal chute that dropped into a cellar. Perhaps if she could get the panel away ... She had dismissed it earlier because of its small size, but maybe ...

She squatted, grasped the wood, able to get both hands into the hole with a good grip on the bottom of the panel. She pulled in a series of short jerks, and it separated by a few millimetres before jamming. She sat among the weeds and old leaves, put both feet against the brickwork, and pulled as hard as she could. Trish cursed her weak muscles.

Finally, rusty nails creaked and squealed a little more.

Encouraged, she tugged harder. Suddenly it gave way and sent her backwards. The board flew from her hands and bounced in the dirt before clattering against the chain link fence. Her fingers stung from the effort on the rough wood. In front of her, the old coal chute led into darkness. The hole looked tiny. She was slim – "skinny" her aunt had called her – but even so ...

She brushed away the cobwebs from the opening and peered into the cellar. She could make out nothing. If she went down there, she didn't think she'd ever get back, even if she landed safely. But she wanted to follow those wires. Surveillance cameras meant Argus.

Once more she squeezed through the fence and ran to her Mini. She quickly downed a pre-packed sandwich she'd bought the day before, and was soon hurrying back with a torch in her pocket. Trish carried a stack of tent poles and a guy rope in one hand and a first aid kit in the other. She had been annoyed at having to dismantle the tent – it had been a pain to erect last night in the near dark – but perhaps she could sleep inside the building tonight.

Dropping her load on the ground, she used the torch to peer into the cellar. The beam dimly picked out a dusty floor two or three metres below. A few lumps of coal lay there with a scattering of dead leaves that had blown in through the opening. She used a couple of bandages to lash all six poles together to strengthen them. They would sit nicely across the hole and ought to be strong enough to support her eight-stone, five weight.

Trish tied one end of the guy rope tightly round the

poles. It didn't look very long by the time it was secured, but it would have to do. Her hands shook when she tossed the cord's free end into the dark.

She lay face-down in the leaves and wriggled backwards into the opening, pulling the poles after her and hoping they would jam across the hole. Her breath was coming now in gasps.

Gripping the rope firmly in one hand and holding the edge of the sill in the other, she slowly lowered herself into the blackness.

CHAPTER TWELVE

Tyler had stayed overnight at a Travel Lodge and driven to Leytonstone by ten o'clock. There was only one car park, and when he arrived it was already wedged with cars, many with boots open. Clusters of men hovered at the start of the field, and the grey sky above them was already whining with model aircraft.

On either side of the road, a large expanse of scrubby yellow grass disappeared in all directions. A few gorse bushes and spindly trees edged the road. Two blocks of concrete flats were visible in the distance, standing slightly apart in the remnants of early morning mist like a massive pair of gateposts rising out of the grass. It was amazing to think he was in the middle of London.

Tyler squeezed his BMW into a far corner of the car park and stayed behind the wheel. Three groups of men stood at the edge of the field with bulky jackets protecting them from the chilly morning, watching model aircraft skim and bank above the wide expanse of grass. Tyler noted a total absence of women.

Argus was in the middle group of five men. Argus and two others held remote controls with long aerials, while the others watched and joked, occasionally gesturing at the sky. Planes took off and landed on a narrow strip someone had mowed into the grass. A balding man in his fifties had a model of a Tornado. From the screaming howl it made as it tore into the air, it could have had an actual jet engine. Tyler remembered the genuine article from the Gulf war. They were noisy bastards.

Tyler wound down the window slightly, enjoying the cold air against his face. The windscreen had steamed up, and he rubbed a small patch clear to give a forward view.

An hour later, Argus landed his Chipmunk for the final time, lovingly scooped it up and, with a few waves and shouts from friends, headed for his car.

When the silver Renault Clio headed north towards the A12 a few minutes later, Tyler followed. On the back window was a faded orange sticker – *One life. Live it hard.*

Argus seemed oblivious to his tail. No anti-surveillance tricks, but then why should he think there was a risk of being followed? Tyler tailed the Clio to a side street on the edge of Hackney borough. Argus left his car near a school and headed to the bustling main road on foot with the plane cradled like a baby, holding its wings vertical. Tyler managed to find a space farther up the road. He ignored the sign about permit holders and hurried after Argus in time to see him disappear into a block of flats. Tyler dashed after his quarry.

Argus hadn't used the entry system, and Tyler guessed it only locked at night. The door to the flats was glass with a fine internal wire mesh, and he could see straight through to a similar door on the other side. In case Argus had planned another ambush, Tyler sprinted round the side of the building, crossed a small square of grass, and charged through the rear door. He let it crash shut behind him and, without stopping, took the first flight of concrete steps two at a time. *Never remain in the funnel zone of a doorway; know your exits* – the old mantra from a forgotten life.

He stopped briefly on the first landing, panting slightly. It smelt of disinfectant and stale cigarette smoke and reminded him of barracks. Someone had left a bicycle propped against the wall near the stairs.

From above him came the grate of a key in a lock over the rumble of traffic. Careful not to run, Tyler hurried up the flight of steps, his footfalls echoing off the bare concrete walls. Each floor had four doors, one on each corner of the stairwell. Tyler didn't break step as he reached the second floor. In the periphery of his vision, he saw Argus' back disappearing through the doorway of number nine before the door clicked shut.

In case Argus was watching through the peephole, Tyler avoided looking directly at the door, continued instead to the third floor where he waited the best part of a minute with his hands in his pockets. He pretended to be looking idly out of the window, but his ears strained for any movement on the floor below.

Convinced there was no further sound, Tyler quietly

retraced his steps to the ground floor and dodged through a gap in the traffic to the other side of the street. A few yards away were two bus shelters, and he slouched on one of the bright red seats to watch. From here, he could see through the flats' door and monitor both entrances.

There was just one set of stairs with an out-of-order lift, and there'd been no sign of a fire exit. If the stairwell caught fire, he guessed all they could do was jump from their balconies. There was no way Argus could leave without being seen.

Tyler just had to wait for his chance to get inside, which meant seeing Argus walk out that door. It would be okay to sit in the street for the first half hour. After that, he would need somewhere less conspicuous.

One question still remained in his head, something that didn't feel right in Bradon's story: how had Argus laid hands on this childhood book in the first place? It didn't make sense and it bothered him. Either there was something he wasn't being told or something Bradon had lied about.

He settled in the cold metal seat amid the noise and bustle of the high street and waited.

CHAPTER THIRTEEN

Trish screwed up her nose at the overpowering smell of the dampness. She left the guy rope hanging in the shaft of sunlight and headed for an arch that seemed to be the only exit from the cellar. Her torch beam swept across dusty remnants of coal that crunched underfoot.

The sounds of birds faded with every step as she ventured farther into the darkness, heart pounding. It reminded her of when her parents had taken her into the Cheddar Gorge caves – their last holiday before *The Tragedy*. Their guide had turned off the lighting, and Trish had squealed and wrapped herself around her dad's arm.

Through the arch, she found the other room was also an empty shell. Yellow and brown moulds clung to an outer wall with beads of moisture that glistened in the torchlight and dribbled into a narrow stain on the floor. She shuddered and tried not to think about rats.

Between the two rooms, her beam picked out dusty steps of worn stone that led upwards into total blackness.

She breathed deeply, trying to control the panic that threatened to well up while she climbed. She steadied herself on the wall and felt its ancient bricks cold and damp against her hand.

At the top, she paused and swept the beam down a long corridor with flaking cream painted walls and bare floorboards. A bundle of cables lay along the base of the wall, as thick as her arm and tied together every meter with electrical tape. It snaked through an open door farther along.

She followed it towards the doorway, the floor creaking with every step. More cables came from the other direction, presumably feeds from other cameras at the back. Taking a deep breath that tasted of mould, Trish stepped across the threshold.

Her torch illuminated a stack of electronic equipment on a table in the middle of the room. All the cables converged there, joined to a row of connectors that partly obscured a cluster of knobs and tiny buttons. On top of the stack sat a blank monitor; nothing seemed switched on.

She nodded, understanding. It was like a control room. A three-legged stool stood at the table, and she imagined Argus sitting here, watching all the approaches. She remembered the previous times she'd come to this building, and shuddered. He would have been here, studying her while she squeezed through the chain-link fence and pushed the package of money through that slot. Bastard.

Trish swept the torch beam round the room.

The equipment seemed to be powered from a generator. It stood in front of a cobweb-draped fireplace with a can of petrol beside it. She briefly thought about slopping fuel over everything and lighting a match. Tempting, but it wouldn't help.

Taped to the generator's rusty casing was a Sony mobile phone with a handful of coloured wires sprouting from its connector. She stepped over to it and stroked her finger across the screen.

It sprung into life, and Trish's heart lurched. She jumped back, imagining all the equipment waking up as if she'd accidentally roused a monster from sleep. Nothing happened. She breathed out, and the Sony's screen went black again. He had to be using it as a remote control, a way to fire-up the generator. And also, perhaps, stream video from the cameras.

What Trish wanted was a way to talk to Argus, and she wondered about the phone. If Argus called it to power up the equipment and monitor the video, there should be a number in its call log, one that wasn't instantly discarded after each message. When she stroked the screen again, she saw it demanded a PIN. No go.

She sighed and perched on the stool, tried to think logically. Absentmindedly, she pulled a packet of Lambert & Butlers from her pocket and lit a cigarette. *How do I provoke him to come without making it obvious I'm here?*

Argus accessed this equipment remotely to check the house and grounds before he approached to make any collections. Once here, he could sit on this stool and study the whole area...

Slowly a plan gelled. She stepped forward and held

down the phone's power button. The phone switched off with a buzz. She nodded to herself. All she needed now was the guts to make that plan happen.

CHAPTER FOURTEEN

Tyler had moved position three times while watching Argus' flat, and now sat part way up the handful of concrete steps that led to a shop's fire door. It was set back a few paces from the road in the shadows between a coffee shop and a run-down taxi office.

His chance came after two hours of waiting. He saw Argus leave from the front entrance and walk casually in the direction of his car. How long he would be away, though, was anyone's guess. Tyler lacked the resources he'd had in the SAS – other operatives watching the different approaches, radio links, thorough intel. It could be a quick trip to a corner shop for a pint of milk. *I'll give myself twenty minutes, no longer.* Even that was possibly pushing his luck – his search of Argus' flat would need to be fast but thorough. He pulled on a pair of gloves. Ready.

Tyler had brought with him a short crowbar that had sat uncomfortably inside his coat pocket since leaving his car. He now withdrew it and pushed it up his sleeve, hiding the cold metal tip in his hand before getting up.

A minute later, he was on the second floor of the building. Doing this quietly wasn't going to be easy, so best just to get it over and done quickly. Assuming the flat was empty, of course, without a flatmate. He rang the bell and waited. No sound of movement.

Tyler slid the tip of the crowbar far enough out of his sleeve to force its chisel-like wedge into the gap by the lock. The door was a sloppy fit. One hard push against the bar, forcing it as far as it would go without splintering the wood. It creaked. When the frame was about to break, he rammed his shoulder into the door. It shuddered, then burst open with a crash that echoed round the stairwell. He quickly stepped inside and, ducking under a model aircraft that dangled from the ceiling, pushed the door shut behind him and propped the brush mat against it to hold it closed.

He kept an eye at the peephole for a few seconds for any inquisitive neighbour, but there was no movement anywhere.

Tyler set to work.

A small flat – one bedroom with a scattering of clothes draped over a painted wooden chair, a kitchen with piles of dirty plates stacked at the sink, and a long thin lounge-diner with a settee and a computer desk at one end and a round dining table with one plastic chair at the other. Four more model planes hung suspended from the ceiling on cords. A fifth was nearly finished on the edge of the table near a laptop. The larger one he'd been flying rested on the floor.

He saw the laptop and thought its contents might be

useful. He took it.

More important – where would you hide a valuable diary?

Tyler ripped the only two pictures from the wall in case of a safe – one of a spitfire against an unreal blue sky, and the other of a B2 stealth bomber – and let them drop to the floor, where the glass of one of them shattered.

In the kitchenette, he swept the tins and packets from each cupboard on to the floor and peered to the back. He ripped the kickboards away and checked beneath the cabinets with a torch from his pocket. Nothing but drifts of dust and spiders' webs. His hands were sweating inside his gloves.

In the bathroom, Tyler used the screwdriver on his penknife to free the bath panel so he could search behind it. Nothing. The bedroom wardrobe had three cardboard boxes in the bottom below the hanging clothes. Tyler pulled them out and up-ended them. A jumble of trainers, table tennis bats and ping-pong balls, toiletries, and a few unopened packets of socks scattered at his feet. No sign of a forty-five-year-old childhood diary.

Fourteen minutes gone already.

Tyler pulled the chest of drawers away from the wall, looked behind it, then yanked each drawer clear of the carcass and checked for anything taped to their backs or undersides.

Sixteen minutes gone. Back to the lounge. Lift the TV from the cheap unit it stood on and tip the unit over. Pull out the drawer, check anywhere a book could be taped.

Nothing.

The drawer had been full of papers. Tyler noticed one with the Lloyds Bank logo, and he fanned out a handful of statements across the carpet. Apart from his monthly salary – which wasn't very much – there were no large deposits. The money must go through a different account, but there was no sign of other statements. Tyler was about to get up when he realised with a shock that he recognised one of the names among the transactions. He frowned, but there was no time to think about it now.

He daren't stay any longer.

After checking the peephole, he quickly left the flat and walked swiftly back to his car. Argus' Clio was still absent.

Tyler drove fast, releasing his anger into the car's horn whenever the traffic ground to a halt. It shouldn't have been a surprise the diary hadn't been there. An accomplished blackmailer would keep it safe elsewhere, perhaps even in a bank's safe deposit box. But it had been worth a try. Maybe the laptop that now sat on the back seat would surrender a clue.

One thing stuck in his mind was Argus' lack of money. Not just the bank statement, but the whole flat. Cheap furniture you could buy from any large store or supermarket, worn settee, a small Bush TV... Bradon had already paid him tens of thousands, so where had it gone?

At least he now knew where Argus lived and who he was – the bank statements had showed him to be Matthew Casey. He finally had something positive to show Bradon, rather than his string of failures. Now all he needed was a plan to find the diary.

Time to get some intel' collection going, he decided. And he knew just the man who could help. Tyler made a quick phone call from his car, then stopped off at a corner shop that was a drop-off point for a courier. He packaged Argus' laptop using a whole roll of bubble wrap he bought over the counter, and addressed it.

He just hoped what he'd asked for in his phone call wouldn't take too long.

***

Two days later, Tyler stood in Bradon's office, its view across the hills masked by mist. An occasional raindrop tapped on the large windows. 'You haven't lived up to expectations have you,' Bradon snapped. He glared at Tyler. 'I've received another blackmail threat.'

Tyler's face muscles tensed at the insult. 'I —' He stopped, realising it wasn't worth the breath to argue.

He had been avoiding Bradon's calls ever since Argus' thugs had stopped him from following the money. This morning when the businessman had phoned and roused him from his hangover-ridden sleep on the settee, Tyler had answered. Now that he had good progress to report, he need put it off no more, but Bradon allowed him no chance to share the news. They were to meet straightaway, Bradon demanded and flatly refused to discuss anything over the phone.

Bradon now glowered from behind his desk. 'You promised to bring back both my money and my diary but you seem to have failed on both counts. And now I've got this in the morning's post demanding a penalty payment for what he's calling "punishment".' Bradon yanked open his top drawer and almost threw an envelope at him that was jaggedly ripped open along the top.

Tyler sank into the seat opposite Bradon's desk. How could he have fallen down on a task as simple as following one padded envelope? Ex-SAS. Had he forgotten years of training and experience so quickly? Well, it wouldn't happen again. Argus, the little runt, would pay a heavy price for making him look dumb.

A Watford postmark. Probably little more than twenty miles from Argus' flat. A single sheet of paper – computer printed – demanded fifteen thousand in response to Craig's botched attempt to follow the money. Tyler felt his face smart as he read the three lines of text.

He returned it, and Bradon thrust it back into his desk drawer in annoyance. Tyler waited, then said quietly, 'Although I've not got your money back yet, it won't take much longer because I now know Argus' identity, his address, and his car registration. And I'm having his laptop examined at this moment. I call that pretty good progress.'

Bradon's head snapped back up in surprise. 'Is it anyone I know?'

'A lad called Matthew Casey. Late twenties probably. Lives in a flat in London.'

Bradon pursed his lips. 'It doesn't immediately ring a bell.'

'Do you want me to take the information to the police? Have him arrested for blackmail?'

A brisk shake of the head. 'Too much risk of it all coming out into the open. I want my money and my diary back, Craig, and I'm relying on you to get them.' A moment's silence, just the growing patter of rain, then Tyler said, 'One thing about this that still doesn't square in my mind is how Argus got your diary in the first place.'

He shrugged. 'Don't know.'

'But you're confident he has actually got it?'

'Oh yes. He sent me photocopies.'

'But how could he get something from your childhood? It doesn't make sense.'

'Look, I really don't know.' Bradon's dark eyes flashed with a mix of anger and frustration. 'As I said last time you asked, I assume it got lost in a house move at some point. Perhaps a box it was in got left in a lorry and some removals guy read it. But how this chap got it I don't know. Anything's possible.'

It didn't seem very likely, but Tyler wasn't going to argue it yet. 'Maybe. Okay, so what about motive?'

'I've presumed it was purely money.'

'Possibly.' Not that the contents of Argus' flat had struck Tyler as those of someone with plenty of cash. 'Could there be a political motive? Draining your money so you can't campaign for office?' It seemed unlikely because Argus lived well outside the ward Bradon would be competing for, but he had to ask.

Vigorous shake of the head. 'A political enemy would simply publicise excerpts from my diary. As easy and as spiteful as that. That's what many politicians are like, I'm afraid.'

Tyler paused. 'In that case I reckon I know the motive, and I don't think it's only about the money. There's something about Matthew Casey I haven't told you yet.'

Bradon frowned. 'Which is?'

'He works for you.'

His bushy eyebrows flicked upwards in surprise. 'You sure?'

'Positive. I saw his bank statements. He gets a monthly salary from Bradon Defence Electronics. I need you to get your HR department to dig out everything about him they've got. Has he had any annual appraisals that might have got his back up? What's been his reaction to pay reviews? Have there been any disciplinary issues? Any promotion he was expecting but didn't get? Anything they can find. And perhaps a quiet word with his line manager – what do they think about Matthew Casey? But don't let Matthew know we're asking about him. There has to be a motive there somewhere. Working here is the key; I'm sure of it.'

Bradon nodded and jotted a note on a pad. He straightened up. 'This is your last chance, Craig. Nail that bastard, recover my cash and get that damned diary back. Failure is not an option I'm giving you. You understand?'

Tyler bristled. Had that been a hint of a threat? He pointed to the desk drawer. 'Are you paying that demand?'

Bradon shifted awkwardly in his chair, which creaked beneath him. 'You've not left me much choice have you. Of course I'm bloody going to pay it. But you've got to ensure it's the last time. Right?'

'Sure. I'll pick him up when he leaves his flat. This time he won't get away.'

More rain lashed against the windows. It sounded like distant gunfire.

CHAPTER FIFTEEN

Tyler pulled up outside a row of uncared-for terraced houses in Manchester later that week. Leaving his BMW between an ancient Ford Escort and a rusty white van with a flat tyre, he kicked his way through the soggy pages of newspapers and junk food containers that littered the path. He hoped his car would still be intact when he got back.

The front door's blue paint was faded and flaking, and a strip of paper had been taped to the frame to tell visitors the bell wasn't working. He rapped loudly and waited.

Tyler was about to knock again when the chain rattled and the door jerked open. Tommy had to be sixty by now. Wiry white hair was pulled back into a short ponytail. Untrimmed beard and moustache formed a wild cloud around a drawn, grey face. His faded black T-shirt simultaneously restrained a large belly and advertised a heavy metal tour from 2003. He sniffed, checked the street nervously over Tyler's shoulder, and stood back to let him in without a word.

A mix of stale cooking and damp hung in the hallway. It mingled with lemon air freshener, which Tyler guessed was an attempt to mask whatever Tommy had been smoking.

Tommy started to close the door. He sniffed again. 'You all right, Craig? It was a bit of a surprise when you phoned out the blue the other day. You and the missus okay?' The door jammed, and he kicked it hard at the bottom.

'The wretched woman's divorcing me.'

'Shit man. What's that? Number four?'

'Third.'

'Not unusual in your line of work.'

'Ex-line of work.'

Tommy shrugged. 'At least you ain't got kids.'

There was no answer to that. He'd seen mates with their ten-year-olds running around, playing-out adventures with toy cars. Starting a family with Sandra had appealed to him once. Maybe children would have made the difference between them, but it had never happened.

Tommy pushed past in bare feet along the dingy hallway. Over his shoulder he asked, 'You want a mug of tea or something?' What Tyler wanted was to learn what was on the laptop, but knew his friend well enough to understand he would have to do this social ritual first.

They settled at the kitchen table, which Tommy quickly cleared of dirty plates, and chatted a bit. Eventually, Tommy wiped the side of his hand across his moustache. 'You want to see what's on that laptop then?'

He led the way upstairs over creaking floorboards to the back bedroom. The curtains were closed and it was lit by a single bulb glowing inside a tasselled shade. The floral wallpaper was peeling away at the top and looked like it had hung there since the eighties. On one long desk sat a row of large computers, their monitors were all off, but hard-drive lights blinked busily. Tommy had probably flicked off the monitors before he'd answered the door so Tyler wouldn't see what they were doing – he didn't care; not his business. Tommy was probably hacking into GCHQ again.

The room was hot, and Tyler soon felt sweat pricking his skin. Argus' laptop sat on the edge of the desk with the lid partly open. Tyler nodded towards it. 'How d'you get on?'

Tommy sniffed. 'It weren't hard. I've taken off the password so you can look at it yourself. There ain't any hidden stuff or encrypted files or nothing. It's pretty boring.'

Disappointment sank into Tyler's stomach. He'd imagined a blackmailer's client list and accounts. 'Let me have a look.'

Tyler swung it round to face him and explored the files, then slammed down the lid. Nothing.

Tommy held out a memory stick, his face expressionless. 'I also did a low-level inspection of the hard drive and recovered some stuff that had been deleted. I put them on here.'

Tyler snatched it and shoved it into the USB port. Twenty or so files.

He opened them one by one.

'Why the hell didn't you give me this stuff at the start?' A Word document – the latest message sent to Bradon. Next file down – Bradon's home address; the proof he needed. He carried on through the rest, hoping to find other victims' details but nothing else was relevant. 'Well done, Tommy.' He grinned and slapped the old man on the back. 'That's what I wanted to see.'

Tommy lifted a cardboard box from the floor without replying and balanced it beside the laptop. 'I got the rest of the stuff you wanted. I think it's all here.' He pulled out what looked like a normal computer cable and handed it to Tyler. 'That's for sniffing email, documents and stuff like that – anything that's done on the computer it's connected to basically. Works like a standard USB lead but buried in the connector housing is a kind of microcomputer that will send copies of everything that's done to a server.'

Tommy laid it on the laptop and held up two short mains extension leads. 'I've also got you a pair of these. Standard radio bugs. Just make sure the sockets you plug 'em into are switched on.' Tommy laughed briefly. 'You wouldn't believe how dumb some people are. I've also thrown in a couple of compact fluorescent light bulbs and some LED bulbs with bugs inside. Again, stick 'em into something that looks like it's going to get used a lot, or the batteries'll go flat.'

He lifted out a die-cast box. 'They transmit to this. It'll store a month of data if you need. Just one thing...' He prodded a foot-long wire that dangled from the box's side like a bootlace. 'If you stick it in a car boot out of sight, for heaven's sake remember to stick this aerial through and on to the backseat or something. Otherwise, you'll pick up zip.'

Tommy held out one last item that looked a bit like a torch. 'Take this as well. It's a scanner. You can use it to check the bugs you've put in place are all functioning before you leave.'

Tyler nodded and counted out notes from his wallet. There wouldn't be a receipt, and he wondered how much Bradon would gripe about that.

As he drove away, he wondered – as he had several times over the last few days – whether it would quicker just to snatch Casey and interrogate him until he said where the diary was, but what if he had an accomplice who would disappear with it at the first sign of trouble? No, Tyler had to know more first.

All he needed now was an inconspicuous way to get back into Argus' flat. He was still thinking about that when his mobile rang. It routed to his car kit. 'Craig, this is Art Bradon. Can I talk?'

'Sure. I'm alone.'

'I've got all the data you wanted on Matthew Casey. He's been with us seven years, works on our other site in Enfield. Feedback is that he's a good lad. Pretty conscientious, good at his job. He's one of our electronics technicians. Taken quite a lot of sick leave over the last twelve months but not enough to give particular cause for concern. His annual reviews have been good, certainly nothing there to have got his back up. Seems to get on well with everybody. Reasonable pay rises, no cause for him to complain, anyway. There were two years when people got no increase, but that was the same for everyone. We had to make a few redundancies four years ago and we couldn't raise salaries at the same time. Everyone understood that. Basically, Craig, there's no evidence of anything for a revenge motive against me.'

'Well, he must have one. I've just been going through his laptop and found the last threat he sent you and your home address on his hard drive.' Tyler paused as he negotiated a roundabout. 'There has to be a motive there. It's too much of a coincidence that he works for you otherwise. Have another look, can you?'

There was a sigh. 'Okay. I'll read the file myself this time. I'll get it sent over. I don't think I can show it to you – you know, confidentiality and all that – but I'll study every word of it.'

'And nothing from his line manager?'

'Other than the increased sick leave, no. What really worries me is that he's working on our most important project. I'm tempted to dismiss him, or at least get him off that particular work.'

'No. Don't do that,' Tyler said quickly. 'He doesn't realise we know who he is. We need to keep it that way.' Argus would have no reason to suspect the break-in was related.

'I'll think about it. But this is a vital project for us and we've got some critical flight trials coming up over the next few weeks. If he really does have something in for me then I don't want him involved in those.'

'Then we'll have to work fast.'

Tyler went back to planning the best way to get back into

Casey's flat.

In the end, Tyler didn't get a chance to plant the bugs. Events escalated too quickly out of his control.

Half an hour later as he was heading south on the M40, just past Oxford, Bradon phoned again. It was four-thirty, traffic already heavy. 'Argus has been in contact by text again. He's got a car ready. Wants me to do the same thing as last time – put the money in the boot and walk away. Six thirty this evening. Make sure you get there and, this time, nail the bastard.'

CHAPTER SIXTEEN

It was to be a black Ford Sierra. Matt Casey felt his guts twist as he read the text message while still at work. The initial collection was always the scariest part but today things were worse. The break-in had haunted him all day and kept him awake last night. It made him cold inside, and he couldn't shake the memory of climbing the stairs to see his door ajar with its lock broken. That five seconds had continually replayed in his mind's eye, and he reckoned he'd managed no more than an hour's useful work all day. Too many electronic circuit boards needing modifications piled up untouched on the rack above his bench.

Casey left the office as early as he dared. With the final preparations – more accurately, panic mode – underway at BDE ready for Dragonfly II's flight trials with the MOD, everyone was expected to work late. 'I'm sorry. I can't. Not tonight,' he kept saying when asked. 'My flat was done over. I've got to sort it out.' It was true. But it was also a useful excuse. He needed to fetch the Ford at five and get it to today's collection point.

Leaving his Renault in the company car park, he took a crammed London bus to collect the stolen Sierra, alighting nearby and perching on a low wall for several minutes until he'd convinced himself there were no men in dark suits watching it and no suspicious vehicles.

He pulled the key from the wheel arch and drove south out of London and into the countryside. For most of the journey, traffic was hell, bumper to bumper with red-faced commuters. Once, he thought he was being followed, but soon lost sight of it and told himself not to be paranoid.

Eventually, he was waiting nervously in the quiet lay-by, repeating his routine.

If it hadn't been for Alicia, he would never have got into this. He sighed. He still missed her. Five minutes passed, then a further ten. It never took this long.

He scratched at his goatee through his gloves. Much longer and it would be getting dark. Already, long shadows from the trees stretched across the road. He found himself tapping the wheel. He changed station on the stereo, skipped boring news reports, ended up with local Guilford Radio.

But he wasn't listening. His mind kept drifting back to the break in. He shut his eyes, trying to calm down.

What should he do if the message never arrived? Go there anyway? Turn around and abandon the trip? He looked at his watch again. He would give himself another ten minutes and then head to the house, message or not.

A few seconds later, his phone buzzed with a text:

"Now."

Breathing out deeply, Casey turned the key and pulled back out on to the last stretch of road to the house. Half a mile later, he swung on to the narrow track between the rhododendrons.

The car had an iffy gear box that had given him grief the whole journey. The gears grated loudly as he forced it into second for the potholed track. Not what you wanted when you were trying to be inconspicuous.

This was the bit of the journey that always un-nerved him, when the trees and bushes closed in around him, and the track funnelled to no wider than the car. Branches tapped the bodywork as he approached the final bend. Something scraped at the exhaust pipe. There were puddles in the pot-holes from the earlier rain, and the car bounced in and out of them with a splash.

Then the house was in front of him. He glanced at the mansion's once grand façade. Against the evening sky, its creamy bricks looked drab, streaked black with neglect. The boarded-up windows made it look a giant's face with the eyes and teeth pulled out.

He turned the car at the crumbling remains of an urn-like fountain that had a rusty pipe sticking vertically out of a puddle of rainwater. Casey brought the Ford to a halt facing the way he'd come in, and cut the engine.

***

Trish McGowan heard the car slow and the grinding of its gears when it turned on to the track. She bit her lip. This was it. *Oh dear God, help me go through with this.*

She ran back through the wood while the car crawled up the potholed drive. She had selected a good vantage point earlier – a tall oak that gave a view to the front of the house but with branches low enough for an easy climb. The trees around it – some evergreen – gave sufficient cover; she was confident she wouldn't be spotted.

Panting from the run, she reached up to the first bough and heaved herself up. *I really should get fitter.* Every nerve in her body felt taught. Her stomach churned and she feared she might be sick.

Be firm, Tishie. The voice of her aunt floated through her memory. It was what she'd been told when her parents had died. *I'll help you, Tishie. You and me, we'll get through this together because you're a fighter and always have been.*

'I'm a fighter. I will survive,' she repeated as she climbed higher. She didn't feel like one. Her breath was coming in short gasps and her legs were trembling so much that at one point she nearly fell. *You're strong Tishie. You can overcome the world if you want to.* Her aunt had been great. The car engine became louder.

She steadied herself on the branch, standing on one and firmly gripping the rough surface of the one above. Around her, the birds quickly settled and sung once more. She peered through the foliage in time to see a black car circle the remains of the Victorian fountain and come to a halt.

She had timed every move she would make. Now, she just wondered if it really would work.

At least he'd come – first step: tick.

Whether she could force him to get Wendell off her back

was another question.

The engine cut and Trish realised she'd been holding her breath. She strained to catch her first sight of Argus.

A sandy-haired man climbed out of the car. He looked about her own age. Strong and athletic and wearing dark trousers and a navy fleece. Quite good looking, she admitted. *Right, Argus, time for you to sort out this mess for me.* She glared at him as he slammed the driver's door. 'You bastard,' she hissed under her breath. 'Now you're going to help me for a change.'

Trish dropped softly to the ground. She had already cleared a path through the trees, brushing away the sticks and leaves to make her approach as silent as possible. Now, she jogged down it and came out close to the old gardener's store. If her timing was right, he should just be going through the gap in the fence now. She had loosely tied some lengths of wire to the top of the fence panel, and eventually she heard them jangle as Argus squeezed through.

She crossed to the back of the small building and waited. Her deep breathing sounded deafening. She tried to reduce her chest heaving, afraid he would hear, scared she might cough.

The scuff of his feet receded. Her legs started to shake and she allowed herself to slide down the wall to sit on the dusty ground with her back to it, and hugged her knees. She had to do this. It was the only way to get her life back.

I'd love a cigarette right now.

Trish figured that Argus needed to find out why he'd been unable to communicate with his equipment. He would have to walk round to the side door, unlock it, let himself in, then walk down the corridor. Nineteen seconds. When he found the phone, he would just assume it had switched itself off – they did that sometimes if hers was anything to go by. Trish had left no sign she'd been there, and thought she'd done a good job of putting the wood back over the hole. She imagined him turning the phone back on and checking its battery level. Hopefully he would then shrug and come back.

There would be at least a minute before his return, and Trish was confident she would not be seen if he went as far as monitoring his cameras. She was certain she was in a blind spot.

The large plank she had selected from the handful that lay abandoned in the old store now leant against the wall nearby. She pulled it to her. The previous day she had carefully removed the splinters with her penknife, and smoothed the corners of the end she would hold. Barely twenty seconds passed before the wires she'd hung from the fence jangled again and sent her heart lurching. That had been quick. He couldn't possibly have got up to his control room in that time. He must be coming back for something. She jumped up and gripped the plank.

This was her only chance. And it wouldn't exist for more than a few seconds.

Trish stepped from her hiding place. He was two metres ahead. She took a step forward and smashed the wood down as hard as she dared into the back of his skull.

CHAPTER SEVENTEEN

The man she thought of as "Argus" fell face-down at the base of the fence. The force of Trish's blow ripped the plank from her grasp and sent it spinning into the air. It crashed into the shed wall, and pain burned her palms and fingertips. She scrabbled for her weapon, raised it again, but he didn't move. She hovered at a safe distance. Was he feigning, waiting for her to get close, ready to grab her? Her breathing came in shallow gasps. Keeping the wood raised, Trish edged closer. Her arms started to shake violently.

He lay in the gap between the fence and the back wall. She'd bought a bundle of the largest zip-ties she could find from a local hardware store. Without taking her eyes off the body, she leant the wood against the wall, fumbled the bag from her pocket and tore into the plastic. She cautiously reached for his feet and pulled them together. The ties weren't long enough to reach round both ankles so she joined two together and pulled the combination tight around his legs with a satisfying click-click. She grabbed his wrists and zip-tied them as well. Trish squinted at the ties, then gave them one more pull. They dug into his flesh, and she instantly felt guilty. *Don't be stupid*, she told herself. *He'd do the same to you without the slightest hesitation.*

She leant over him and tried to roll him on to his back, but the body kept flopping back. Straining, and with her back pressed against the wall, she eventually succeeded. A few leaves and a scattering of soil clung to his cheek. He had a handsome face. Shame it belonged to such a bastard. She grabbed him under the arms and started to drag him towards the shed. He moaned but didn't stir.

Trish had to stop four or five times. He seemed so heavy. Her chest heaved with the effort, and her back ached. Every time her face went close to his, she smelt a hint of pleasant aftershave.

Sweat was trickling between her breasts and across her brow when she finally managed to prop him awkwardly against the wall inside the gardener's store. She wanted to rest – her arm and leg muscles burned – but he could come round any moment now, and she needed him well secured by then. Who would have dreamt it could be so difficult to move an unconscious body? Trish heaved him as close to a sitting position as she could manage and tied rope round his body, securing it to metal rings she'd bought from a hardware store earlier in the week and firmly attached to the wall.

His eyelids fluttered when she tightened the final knot. The white of his eyes briefly seemed to glow in the dim interior of the outhouse. She jumped back, alarmed, but he again slipped into unconsciousness.

She quickly retrieved the plank from where she'd dropped it. Still breathing heavily, she flopped down against the wall opposite him to wait and lit a cigarette with trembling hands.

She studied his face. The last rays of evening light sliced across the room from the partly open door, making patterns across his legs and catching the tiny particles of dust that danced in the air.

The man stirred again, moving his head slowly side-to-side. She had been preparing for this moment, rehearsed repeatedly what she would say. Now that it was reality, her stomach tightened and her mouth turned as dry as dust. He muttered something and opened his eyes, winced and shut them again, mumbling something she didn't catch.

**

Matt Casey's head felt as if he'd been hit by a steamroller. He tried to open his eyes again. Everything was blurred. A rectangle of light glowed opposite him. A doorway, maybe? Where was he? He couldn't remember. Suddenly, fragments flooded back: pushing the envelope of money into the basement, squeezing back through the gap in the fence, then...

He squinted at a fuzzy shape that moved in front of him. A woman's voice. He blinked, trying to clear his vision, saw a wild-faced woman about his own age glaring down at him.

**

Trish stood, but kept well back, brandishing her weapon in

one hand. She took another breath of her cigarette to steady her nerves. 'You need to help me,' she said, relieved her voice remained firm and loud. She knew she had to appear confident.

'Uh?' Casey's eyes flickered open and locked on hers.

'You need to help me,' she repeated.

He mumbled something, then licked his lips, slowly looking around, clearly confused. Eventually, he said, 'Who are you?'

'I'm Trish McGowan from Sylver& McGowan Interiors.'

He frowned. 'I ... I don't think I know ...'

'Then think harder,' she snapped. 'You do know me.'

Casey tried to push himself up but the rope held him. He looked at his wrists and ankles. He tried to flex his legs, but the zip-ties held his feet firmly together. The confusion in his face switched to anger, and Trish gripped the plank tighter. He stared at her intently. 'What's going on?'

'You're staying there until I can make you understand.'

'Understand what?' He pulled on the ropes.

'I almost got killed by a bomb because you're forcing me to blackmail Kurt Wendell, and now a close friend has —'

'Stop,' he interrupted, and tried to raise an arm. 'You must be mistaking me for someone else. Now get these things off me.'

'Don't give me that crap. I know you're Argus.'

'Argus?' There was sudden fear in his blue eyes. 'I don't know what you're talking about.' His voice quavered.

'Crap. You made me send blackmail letters to Kurt Wendell and because of that, he's trying to kill me. And my best friend ...' He fought with the rope, but it was holding firm. Her voice faltered. To cover it up, she poked the plank towards him, and he instinctively shied back. 'He's already murdered a friend of mine thinking it was me, and I'm running for my life. You're going to sort it out.' Trish jabbed the wood towards his face. 'You're going to contact him and explain it's not my fault.'

He shut his eyes and shook his head. His face was chalky white. 'I honestly don't know what you're talking about. I've never heard of this Kurt Wendell or whatever his name is.'

Trish stepped forward, anger burning. 'You understand every word, you bastard,' she yelled. 'You got my friend killed. You'd better admit it or I'm going to bloody pulp your head until you do.'

'I don't know...' He yanked harder at the rope.

'You're Argus. Admit it,' she screamed.

'I'm not.'

'Rubbish, rubbish, rubbish,' she yelled, turned and stormed out, slamming the door behind her. She hadn't expected him to admit it right away, but this was going to be tougher than she'd expected. She felt tears of frustration and exhaustion welling up inside her, and took a deep breath of the damp evening air. Her cigarette had burned close to the stub. She took a final puff and ground it out under foot. *Count to ten and go back in again.*

She'd only got to three when a hand clamped tightly across her mouth and snapped her head back. Before she could move, cold metal pricked her throat.

A man's voice whispered in her ear. 'Are you having

fun?'

CHAPTER EIGHTEEN

Trish clawed at the hand that clamped her mouth but the grip was too strong. The knife pricked harder into her skin. She kicked and squirmed, tried to scream. Her heels caught his legs but he never flinched. He pulled her further back until she was off balance, revealing more of her throat.

It was probably the same knife he'd used on Beth, she thought. Trish imagined her friend's blood dried on the blade.

She tried to bite, tasted his skin – slightly oily – but couldn't force her jaws apart.

He was lifting her off her feet, pulling her backwards. She flailed wildly. Suddenly she was falling. She landed, thudding on to one hip. She immediately felt a knee rammed into her stomach, forcing her down. *Dear God, help. He's about to kill me. Or is he going to rape me first?* She swung her head wildly from side to side, trying to free herself from his hand. Wendell would take his final revenge. 'It's not me. I'm not Argus,' she tried to scream. 'Argus is in there. He's the one who's behind it, not me. Please, you've got to understand.' It came out as a muffled blur of words.

'Shut up,' the voice hissed. His face was so close she felt his breath against her ear and a brush of stubble against her cheek. The blade scratched at her windpipe. 'Calm down missy. If you calm down, I'll release you.'

Yeah, right. Is that what he'd said that to Beth?

She ferociously shook her head, tried to scream. Her head barely moved under his vice-like grip. Trish thought she heard him sigh.

It would all be over soon. She tried to relax, let her body go limp. Perhaps there would be less pain that way.

She screwed up her eyes and waited. Her breath was coming in short gasps. There was a moment's silence before the voice whispered, 'I'm going to let you go in a second, but I want you to stay quiet and not move. Is that understood?'

Trish nodded slightly and felt the hand release from her mouth. The metal remained pricking against her neck but the pressure became less. She stayed motionless, eyes tightly shut.

'Don't move,' he said, and the blade was gone. She heard her assailant shuffle back a couple of steps. She desperately wanted to rub her throat but didn't dare move. 'Okay. Now slowly sit up.'

Cautiously she pushed herself up and sat in the grass facing him. She had never seen Wendell before. With a name like that she had assumed he was German, although his address had been in Windsor, a town a little west of London. This man looked and sounded British. His hair was short and dark, framing a tough, sun-tanned face. Emotionless dark eyes studied her. He nodded slightly, as if satisfied she was no threat. Perhaps this wasn't Wendell.

His voice came in a whisper that she could only just hear over the whine that had returned to her ears. 'What are you doing here?' He nodded towards the gardener's store without taking his eyes off her. 'And who's in there?'

Trish was about to explain but stopped herself. Instead, she asked, 'Who are you?'

He shook his head slowly. 'The fact I'm holding all the cards means I get to ask the questions. What are you doing here?' There was a sudden hardness in his voice that made her guts twist tighter. Even if this wasn't Wendell, she had no doubt he wouldn't hesitate to kill her. His cold stare made her shiver.

'I …' she began, then cleared her throat and tried again while vigorously rubbing her neck. 'What the hell are you doing waving a knife around? The police'll be very interested when I tell them.'

'Don't screw around with me. Who have you got in there and why?' When she didn't answer, he sighed. 'Look missy. Let's set the rules out here. I've got the weapon and I'm far stronger than you are. Answer my questions and everything will be fine. If you don't …' He shrugged.

She pouted stubbornly. *Could he be a colleague of Argus' come to help*? 'Tell me one thing first, just to set my mind at rest.'

He nodded with a slight sigh.

'Do you know who I am, and do you know Kurt

Wendell?' She studied his eyes, searching for lies.

'That's two questions. But as far as I can remember, I've never seen you before and I've absolutely no idea who you are. And I've not heard the name Kurt Wendell before either.'

She breathed out deeply. 'And your question in return?'

'Who's in that building and why?'

'He's a blackmailer.' She paused. 'And I need his help.' *Shut up! What am I saying?* Her brain was slowly catching up. This guy could be here to kill Argus. He looked tough enough for a hired assassin. And if he did that, she would never get Argus' help with Wendell. She would be on the run forever. Ridiculously, that meant she now had to protect Argus. 'He's got some really important information in his head that I need,' she said quickly; then added, 'It's very valuable data.'

He nodded thoughtfully. 'Okay. I believe you,' he said at last. 'Thing is, I want to talk to him as well.'

'Are you ...' She stopped herself quickly. She had been about to ask if he intended to kill Argus. 'Can I ask why?'

'Nope.'

'But I don't want to be locked out of things, yeah? I need him to do something for me.'

'What does he need to do?'

'That's private.'

He raised the knife again until it pointed between her eyes. 'This says you can share it with me.'

Her body tensed, but she said firmly, 'No.'

He shrugged. 'I don't care anyway. Let's go and talk to

him, shall we?' He motioned with his head towards the hut door. 'You first.'

Shakily, she stood and brushed herself down before turning back to the outbuilding. The door with its peeling white paint and rotting wood stood ajar where she'd tried to slam it earlier. Trish reached for the handle.

The door suddenly crashed outwards, smashing her knuckles, slamming into her chest and sending her stumbling backwards.

Casey exploded from the gap. His outstretched hand struck her on the shoulder and sent her reeling. She gasped as she struggled to keep balance.

Casey swerved to his right to avoid the heavily-built man who had stood a few feet behind Trish, but who now moved surprisingly fast. Casey's hands were still tied.

Trish's assailant smashed a fist into the side of Casey's head, pitching him sideways. He grunted when his knees thudded into the ground. With both hands tied, he had little chance of protecting himself.

The man with the knife now took a single step towards him, grabbed him by the hair, and smashed his face down into the dirt. The man knelt with one knee in the small of Casey's back and turned to Trish. 'You get inside the hut and sit against the far wall where I can see you.'

'I don't think ...' she started but tailed off when she saw the raw violence in his eyes. She scowled but stepped inside, finding her legs could barely carry her. Trish dropped against the wall close to where the rope lay in the dirt together with the zip-ties he'd managed to slide off his ankles. Her arms started shaking and she folded them tightly across her chest.

The assailant hauled Casey to his feet. There was blood across the side of Casey's head and trickling from his nose. Mud was streaked across one cheek. The stranger marched him back into the hut and re-tied him.

Trish sat glowering at her assailant. Argus was *her* prize. And who was this guy anyway?

'Now Argus,' he said. This time you've no-one to protect you, and I need answers.'

***

Craig Tyler took a step back and surveyed his two captives. He wondered who the woman was. She looked mid-twenties, a wild and unkempt look, a fringe of hair with vivid green, blue, and purple streaks dropped across one eye and she pushed it back. Behind it she was pretty – strong high cheek bones, smooth skin.

He'd arrived in time to watch her drag Casey's unconscious body into the little hut. What the hell was this woman up to? She had described Argus as a blackmailer. Was she another of his victims? Or were the pair of them criminals, perhaps arguing over profits?

Without taking his eyes off them, Tyler pulled the door shut behind him. It creaked on its hinges but this time remained closed. He stood to one side so that anyone rushing the entrance couldn't take him down in the same move.

Tyler pointed the knife at the centre of Argus' forehead. The face was pale. Blood from his nose dripped into his lap.

Without your two thugs for protection, you're nothing.

'I'll get to the point. You've got something I want back for my employer. If I get it, you'll go free.'

The woman flinched. 'No way. He's not going to just walk out of here. I need him to help me.'

Tyler swung the knife towards her. 'You shut it.'

Tyler was in a foul mood. He'd received another text from Sandra while he'd been tailing Argus from his place of work. *Hi Darling, my solicitor tells me papers are in the post. So looking forward to getting your emotionless wreck out of my life. Kiss kiss!!* He could hear the sarcastic sneer of her words. One more and he would block her number, he promised himself.

Tyler glared at the woman sitting hunched beside Argus. For a second he thought she was about to leap at him like a she-cat, but she stayed put. She was going to be a pain. Perhaps he'd have done better to tie her as well.

Argus said in a weak voice, 'Look, I'm not Argus. Really, I'm not. I'm being blackmailed by him. I'm only here because he made me deliver a package.' A dam that had been holding in all the secrecy seemed to burst. The words rapidly tumbled out. 'I just had to collect a car, right? There was money in the boot, and I was told when to collect the car and where to drive it to. I just followed his instructions and brought it here, that's all. I put the money in the old house over there.' He jerked one arm vaguely towards the main building. 'You've got to believe me. If I didn't do it, he said he'd release details about … about something stupid I did. I had no choice. Really, you've got to believe me.'

The woman's eyes gleamed. 'That's exactly what happened to me.' She turned to Casey. 'But how do we know you're telling the truth?'

Casey looked from her to Tyler and back again. 'You two have to believe me,' he pleaded. 'I just delivered the money as I was told. I've no idea who Argus is.'

'Sure,' Tyler said sarcastically. 'What about your two thugs who tried to beat me up?'

Casey looked genuinely surprised. 'I don't know what you mean.'

'Last week I followed you when you collected a blackmail payment. You waited in a lay-by a mile down the road from here. A van pulled up and your two thugs tried to beat the shit out of me. They didn't succeed by the way, as you can see.'

There was a flicker of recognition in Casey's face. 'I know where you mean,' he said slowly, 'but I was told to wait there. I remember the van because of how it was driven, but just as it arrived, I got a text to tell me it was time to get up here and deliver the money, so I left. I don't know anything about that van. Honest.'

It might be true. And he didn't look like Tyler imagined a blackmailer would. He was just a normal twenty-something year old lad. It would also explain the lack of evident wealth in his flat.

The sound of a diesel engine suddenly carried through the trees to the hut. A powerful car or off-roader. Tyler stiffened. The others could hear it now. The young man swung his head urgently to face Tyler. 'That'll be him. He'll have come for the money.'

CHAPTER NINETEEN

'Stay here,' Tyler yelled to the girl and sprinted from the hut. He charged into the woods behind the house. Briars snagged his clothes, and a branch whipped his face. The sound of the engine was moving quickly to his right, already heading away from the building. A brief flash of brown bodywork between the trees, then the air fell silent. It had looked like a large SUV; no chance to recognize its make.

Tyler slowed to a jog until he found the narrow track it had followed. Deep tyre marks rutted the soil. He kicked the nearest tree trunk. How the hell was he going to explain this to Bradon? *Sorry, I just lost all your life savings for you.* A few years as a writer and he'd lost his touch. He gritted his teeth. Argus would pay for this.

Clear your head Craig, do this logically.

He had just crouched to examine the tracks when sudden crashing from the undergrowth made him spin round. The girl pushed through the branches, panting. 'You don't half run fast,' she gasped, and leant forward with hands on hips.

'You went off like a rocket.'

'I told you to stay in the hut,' he yelled.

'Did you get a look at it?'

Who does she think she is? He took a deep breath and waved a hand towards the tyre marks. 'That's all.'

'Ooh,' she said sarcastically and crouched beside him. 'Just like Enid Blyton's *Secret Seven* isn't it, copying down tyre treads. Have you got a notebook?'

He clenched his fist, itching to teach a lesson with it. If she and Casey were both involved with Argus, maybe they were his route to the real blackmailer. Without replying, he pulled out his mobile and photographed the tread pattern with his hand beside it for scale, then stood. 'Come on. Let's get back and see what your bloke can tell us. You go in front.'

The girl hurried back through the trees. Tyler kept close behind her. 'If your mate was simply delivering money, then Argus just got in without us knowing, grabbed it and disappeared. I want to know where your mate left it.'

'He's not my mate,' she called over her shoulder. 'But he'll have pushed the package through the old coal chute. That's what I had to do. There's a door the other side of the house that's got new locks rather than being boarded up like the rest. I guess Argus went in and out through there.'

'Show me,' Tyler snapped.

They burst from the trees. The woman pushed between the gardener's building and the fencing, and through a gap in the chain-link panels. She led him to the side of the decaying mansion and a few moments later stood panting at a closed door. As she had described, it had two new Yale locks.

He noticed scuffs in the grass near the fencing barrier, as though two panels had been separated at that point and then pushed back together.

Tyler thudded the heel of his boot into the door. It shuddered but stayed firm. He took a step back and did it again. He was annoyed he didn't still have the crowbar with him he'd used on Casey's flat. Third, fourth attack and it was loosening. The girl stood back. Finally, the door flew open with a splintering crack causing dust to fly into the air. A latch clattered across the stone floor.

'You first,' he said and stood aside.

She hesitated, then stepped obediently into the gloom, pulling the torch from her pocket. Its beam probed the darkness, and she indicated the stairs. 'Down to the basement and the room with the coal chute is the one on your left.'

'You go in front but give me the torch,' he said, snatching it before she could respond. He gave her a push farther into the corridor and shone the torch on the stairs that disappeared into darkness. 'Lead the way.'

Tyler followed her down the uneven concrete steps and into a room where a feeble shaft of light dropped from a slot high on the outside wall. She stopped just inside the doorway and pointed up at it. 'I had to drop the money through there and then leave. I guess that's what he had to do as well.'

Tyler swept the torch across the floor. It was covered in a

layer of black grit and a scattering of dry leaves. He stepped cautiously into the room, pushing her ahead of him and shining the light at the base of the wall where anything would have landed. There were plenty of scuffs in the grit just there.

'How d'you know about the inside of this place?' he asked.

'I broke in through that hole and explored.'

'What else is in the house?'

'It's wired with CCTV,' she said, turning to face him. 'Or at least it was.' She grinned. 'I powered it down. I expected it to make Argus come to see what had gone wrong. That was my plan. I think the system was designed to send the video out on a phone. I guess it was so he could check no-one was around before he collected his money.'

An electronics technician would be able to set that up, he told himself. That's what Casey did for a living. 'Anything else?'

'Not that I found.'

'Show me the CCTV.'

She stomped back up the stairs in silence and pointed into one of the dark rooms that smelt of damp. Tyler played the torch over a stack of equipment in the middle of the room. 'Go in,' Tyler prompted.

He followed her. The equipment was off.

'There's a mobile phone connected to the generator,' she said. 'I turned it off so he couldn't power stuff up remotely.'

She's smart. He traced the bunches of cables to the wall using the light from her torch. 'D'you know where they go?'

'To cameras around the grounds mainly. I found a couple inside the house, one of them in the basement watching the coal chute, but most of them give a view all over the grounds.'

Neat. Maybe there was even one monitoring the road where he'd been ambushed. Maybe that's how the blackmailer had known to call in his thugs. 'Let's get back to your mate,' he said.

They emerged back into the grounds a few moments later. The air tasted fresh after the dank interior. The moon had risen above the trees, and the breeze already carried the chill of night. They squeezed back through the fence, Tyler still using the torch to light their way.

The beam bobbed across her back and legs, and he admired the curves of her body. She looked good. When they reached the hut, she hesitated.

'Go in,' he commanded and stood back. He rested a hand on the hunting knife in its scabbard strapped to his belt. She paused, then cautiously pulled open the door. It creaked on rusty hinges.

Casey had vomited while they'd been away, and a slick of it now ran across the uneven concrete floor and collected against the wall. The room stank, and the woman hovered in the doorway with a hand across her nose and mouth. 'Go and sit beside him,' Tyler demanded.

'What? With that smell?'

Casey was watching them nervously. He was very pale.

Interrogation time, and the sick would be an advantage, put them both on edge. Provided it didn't mean Casey was suffering a severe concussion or an internal brain haemorrhage where the girl had tried to crack his skull. 'Sit down,' he yelled at her, and she obeyed, sitting as far from the trickle of vomit as she could.

Tyler squatted in front of the lad. 'How's your vision?'

'What d'you mean?'

'It anything blurred?'

'No.' He started to shake his head but winced and stopped. 'My head just hurts like hell.'

'Look at me,' Tyler demanded, and Casey focussed on his face. 'I'm not blurred at all?'

'No,' Casey said impatiently. 'I said. I'm fine … bar a splitting headache.'

Tyler swung the torch beam into his eyes. He looked alright, other than the chalky-white of his skin. Blood from his nose was drying in a slick across the chin.

Tyler nodded and stayed crouching in front of his prisoner. 'Tell me about Art Bradon.' He kept the beam in the lad's face, and Casey screwed up his eyes.

'I don't know …'

Tyler slapped him hard across on cheek and his head snapped sideways. 'Tell me about Art Bradon,' Tyler spat.

'I … I had to send him a letter. He's the head of the company I work for.'

'Go on.'

'I don't know what it said, but …'

'Why don't you know?'

'It was in an envelope. I just put that inside another that I addressed and posted.'

The woman straightened. 'That was the same for me,' she said.

'Shut up,' Tyler snapped.

'It's just …'

'Shut it.' She was getting annoying. He turned back to Casey. 'What next?'

'I got a message to go and collect a car from a car park and then drive it here. I had to take a package from the boot, put it in the house, and drive back.'

'How did Argus contact you?'

'Sometimes through an email at work, sometimes with a text message.'

'Did you ever reply to his emails?'

'I tried, but they always bounced back as unknown. And they were different email addresses each time.'

'What if you need to contact him?'

'I can't. I haven't got a way.'

'What about the number for the texts?'

'Same. It never worked. Just "number not in use". And it was a different one every time.'

The girl shifted. 'I tried mine as well and had the same problem.'

'I told you to button it.' He stood over her, feet apart. 'You say another word and I'll break something.'

She nodded in silence, and he returned to Casey. 'Tell me about yourself.'

'I've got nothing to hide. I'm Matt Casey. I'm an electronics technician at a company called Bradon Defence Electronics and I live in Hackney. What else d'you want? I'm not Argus.'

Tyler sighed. It made sense. When Argus blackmailed people like these two who had no money, he instead turned them into pawns to blackmail wealthier targets like Bradon. It gave him safety.

He wondered how many more pawns Argus had around the country. Tyler turned the torch beam on the girl. 'And how d'you fit in?'

'Oh, I can talk now, can I?'

He quickly took a step towards her and she raised a hand to protect herself. 'Okay, okay. I'm Trish McGowan from Sylver and McGowan Interiors. Like him, I was blackmailed to pass on messages to other people, collect their money and dump it here.'

'So why did you tamper with that CCTV and try to smash his head in?'

'I didn't try to smash it in. It's just I thought he was Argus and I need Argus to help me. This was the only way I could think of to make Argus listen to me.'

'Why d'you need to talk to him so importantly?'

''Cause someone's trying to kill me.' Her voice caught and he thought for a moment she was going to cry. 'I had to pass threats to an arms dealer called Kurt Wendell. He must have discovered who I was and come after me because he thought I was the blackmailer. I've tried to email him and tell him it's not me who's behind it, but I guess he doesn't believe me or doesn't think it makes a difference or something. I wanted to get Argus to help me. It was the only thing left I could think of.'

'How d'you know he's an arms dealer?'

'Because unlike Muppet over there, I read the letters before passing them on.'

Tyler stood and went outside, standing with his back to the hut wall and looking up at the stars that had started to twinkle high above. They both seemed to be telling the truth. He sucked in the fresh air, glad to be out of the acrid stench of Matt's vomit.

His mind made up, he went back inside. Trish McGowan was kneeling beside Casey, but turned as Tyler approached. 'I don't think he's very well,' she said. 'Might I have …' she tailed off. 'Could I have given him a serious injury?'

'My head's splitting,' Casey snapped.

McGowan turned on him. 'You got into this yourself. Don't blame me for the consequences.'

'You could have just talked to me. You didn't have to stove my head in.'

'I thought you were Argus. What d'you expect?'

Tyler bellowed, 'Shut up. You're like a pair of bloody children.' He turned to Trish. 'Untie him and bring him outside.'

'You believe me?' Casey asked with an evident mix of relief and surprise.

'Yes,' Tyler sighed. 'Get outside and get some fresh air. The girl can help you.'

'I've got a name,' she muttered, but Tyler ignored her and shone the torch on the knots. Trish slowly unpicked them.

Casey stumbled out of the door, using the wall for

support, and sat down outside with his back to the wall. He was shivering. Tyler leant forward and used his knife to slice the zip-ties from his wrists.

'So, none of us are any further on, are we,' Tyler said to no-one in particular. He thought of Bradon and the money that had just been taken. *He won't be running for any local elections now.* That lifelong ambition had just gone in the waste bin … thanks to Tyler's incompetence.

He suddenly realised Trish was talking. He spun to face her. 'What now?'

'I think I've just realised how we could find Argus. Thing is, it'll need all three of us to work together. Is that practical?' She swept a lock of green hair back out of her eyes and stared straight at him. 'Looks like we're all at a loss individually. Are you man enough to form a team?'

His jaw muscles clenched at the challenge. He took a deep breath. 'Come on then, Miss Marple. What are you planning that's going to be so successful?'

CHAPTER TWENTY

'I want nothing to do with this,' Casey shouted and turned to leave, but Tyler grabbed his wrist. Casey tried to shake himself free. 'I've got to get rid of that stinking car. It's nicked.'

'Tough.'

They'd been sitting huddled in a circle in one of the rooms of the mouldering house. They had found some old crates, and Trish had fetched a stack of blankets and a battery-powered lantern from her car. The light sent their shadows dancing across the peeling walls.

Trish said, 'For heaven's sake, Matt, we've got to work together. Don't you see that? We all need the same thing.'

'You and he need the same thing. Not me. If I cross Argus, he'll tell what I've done, and I'll get fired. He ain't going to forgive me for today as it is. I can't afford to antagonize him anymore.'

'What about me?' Trish screamed. 'I've got one of his victims trying to kill me because he thinks I'm the blackmailer. D'you know what it's like to find your best friend knifed to death by mistake? He's trying to kill me.'

He swung to face her. 'That's your stupid mess. I was doing alright before tonight. Who knows what's going to happen to me now.'

'But can't you see? It might be easy for you now but what if *you* get told to send blackmail messages to someone like Wendell? Then you'll end up in the firing line like me.' She paused, saw him hesitating. 'Working together is our best chance to put a stop to it all.' She looked at Tyler for support but he said nothing. She cleared her throat. 'I've been thinking. My plan had been to come here and persuade Argus to get Wendell off me. Thing is, I'm realising I could have the same problem with his next victim and then the next. I'll be looking over my shoulder for the rest of my life. But I reckon I could use the situation to solve the problem forever. If I can find Argus and then tell Wendell who he is and where he lives, Wendell will put an end to Argus for us.'

It sounded so callous spoken out loud. What was she turning into? She looked at the pair of them, but it was hard to see their expressions. No-one spoke for a few moments as they absorbed what she'd said. Trish's stomach tightened in the silence. 'Come on guys, please help with this. It'll help all of us.'

Tyler laughed and applauded. She looked at him sharply. Was he making fun of her? To her surprise, he nodded. 'I'll help you on one condition.'

'What's that?'

'That I get to talk to Argus when we find him before you let your rabid dog loose.'

'Deal.' They both turned to Casey, who was looking down at the floor.

He seemed to sense them staring at him and looked up. 'We're just a bunch of untrained nobodies. What can we do?'

Tyler shook his head. 'You might be, but I'm not. I was an SAS sergeant for some years.'

Casey snorted. 'Yeah, right.'

'Why the hell d'you think I'm here?' he snapped. 'I fought in Libya, Syria and Iraq, as well as in UK operations, and I've been hired by someone you're blackmailing to make it stop.'

'Someone I'm blackmailing?'

He ignored the question. 'I followed you here from where you work to make you give back the evidence against my client. It's just that she beat me to it.' He glared at the younger man. 'I'm your professional. And the girl's right – you'll be in the same boat as her at some point if we don't stop Argus.'

Casey didn't answer but started to sit back down. Briefly, the light shone across his face. He looked alarmingly pale, and Trish's stomach churned at the thought she might have done serious damage with her blow. She'd heard somewhere about internal bruising, how it swelled the brain, how the patient could die days later. She had offered him some Ibuprofen from her handbag when she'd untied him, and he had gratefully swallowed a couple.

Trish said, 'We all have a bit of knowledge about Argus

even if we don't realise it. There must be something common between you and me and this ...' She suddenly realised she didn't know the SAS sergeant's name. She turned to him. 'What are you called?'

'Craig Tyler.'

'Okay. So, with our pooled knowledge we should be able to find him.'

Casey nodded slowly. 'What are you suggesting?'

She felt their eyes on her in the dimly lit room. 'We've got to be honest with each other. It's the only way – we need to share all we know about him to find what we all have in common.' Neither Casey nor Tyler replied. 'Okay, let me share what I know,' she began and paused for effect, gratified when both pairs of eyes bore into her. 'A few years ago, I did something stupid in my business – I run an interior design shop near Beaconsfield – and Argus blackmailed me because of what I was doing. The thing is, the only way Argus could have known about it would be if I'd done a quote for him. It was only sitting here all day thinking about it all that I realised what the connection was.'

'So, what did you do to get blackmailed?' Casey asked.

She hesitated, ignoring his question. 'Don't you see? His name must be on my quotations list.' She looked around at them excitedly.

'And where do we get that list?'

'Well ...' she paused and sighed. 'It's all on a big spreadsheet that I had on my computer.'

'Had?' Tyler asked.

Trish felt a surge of panic tighten her chest. The blast of

the bomb, the brilliant white, the sight of the charred, melted, computer all flashed through her mind and the words suddenly wouldn't come. 'I … My shop …' She cleared her throat and realised her hands were shaking. She clenched them together in her lap. 'Wendell blew up my shop trying to kill me.' She faltered again, embarrassed by the way her voice had become unsteady. 'Thing is, my computer's now a melted heap.'

'Oh great,' Tyler snapped, waving his arms in obvious exasperation. 'So that's a really great plan then, isn't it.'

'There'll be a backup of the file. Cliff, who helps in the shop, he looked after all the IT stuff. He kept going on about on-line cloud backups. We should still be able to retrieve a copy.'

Casey said, 'You should be able to log on from anywhere. That's the whole point. You might even be able to do it from your mobile.'

Tyler turned back to Trish and held out his phone. 'Try it.'

She didn't move. 'I don't know how to. Cliff did it all.'

'So?'

She hesitated. 'I can call him. See if he can help.'

'So go on.'

She took out her own phone and switched it on. It had been off since she'd first got here to preserve the battery and it now pinged repeatedly as various texts arrived. She noticed the last one said her voicemail had seven messages.

She dialled.

'Trish, where have you been?' Cliff asked the moment he

recognized her. She heard music being switched off in the background. 'Are you alright? I've been trying to reach you. D'you know what happened to Beth? You were staying at her place, weren't you? And then the police and everything... I was so worried. What happened? You did know about Beth, didn't you? Sorry, I ...'

'I'm fine, really. Sorry for not calling. It's all been rather confusing.'

'What's going on?'

'It's nothing to worry about. It's getting sorted.'

'Come on Trish. I can help. And the police want to talk to you.'

She chewed her lip in silence for a moment. 'Look, I'll come over to see you as soon as I can. Right now, I need to access a file that used to be on my PC. You arranged for everything to be backed-up, right?'

'Sure.'

'How do I get it?'

'I can text you the details if you like. But it would be easier if you come over here and I get it up on my PC.'

'Can you just send me details of how to log-on, and I'll sort it.'

'Of course. I'll do it straight away. But we need to talk, Trish. Especially with Beth... And the loss adjustor came yesterday to inspect the shop. And then the police kept asking if I knew where you were.'

'I really can't talk now. Please text me details of how to get the files. Sorry.' Trish hung up before Cliff could say more. She imagined his stunned face at the other end and felt guilty.

Tyler asked, 'How many names and addresses are there?'

About ten quotes a month; that's a hundred and twenty a year. 'Maybe three hundred or so.'

Casey snorted. 'So how long's it going to take to check that lot?'

She swung round to face him. 'You got a better idea?'

'It just doesn't sound realistic.'

'With three of us, it's only a hundred each, and they're all fairly close together. What else can we do? I don't see how we can narrow it down further.'

Her phone buzzed with a text. She opened it and turned to Tyler. 'You got something to write with?'

He pulled a dog-eared notebook and a pen from an inside pocket of his coat, tore out a page for her, and handed it to her with the pen. She quickly jotted down the details Cliff had sent, then turned her phone back off. She'd seen too many films when someone was tracked by their mobile phone signal, and Cliff had said the police wanted to speak to her.

'Can we do it on your phone?' she asked Tyler. 'Someone might be trying to track mine.' He looked at her quizzically, but he just shrugged and took the note from her.

While he started to access the website, Trish asked, 'Do either of you two have anything else that might help? We need to find a common factor between the three of us.'

Tyler shifted awkwardly and looked up. 'I caught a glimpse of the car Argus was driving just now. That might help a bit.'

'Why the hell didn't you tell us you'd seen it?'

'I just caught a glimpse of the back of it. No more than a blur. I couldn't even tell you what make it was.'

'You should have said ....'

He raised a hand. 'It was a large brown car, okay? It was possibly an SUV or something. I really don't know anything more.'

'Really?' Trish stared into his eyes, but could see little in the semi-darkness. She turned to Casey, 'So what's your story? What have you learnt about Argus?'

'I don't think I've got anything useful like that.' He looked from one to the other 'Look, I did something stupid at work and Argus somehow found out.'

'But how did he find out?' Tyler asked. 'One of the keys to his identity has to be that he was in a position to gain knowledge about your activities as well as hers and my client's.'

Casey shrugged and paused. 'I've absolutely no idea how Argus found out about what I did,' he said at last.

Trish sighed. 'Just tell us the whole story.'

'Alright. How far do I go back because it's quite complicated? I was sucked into it in stages.'

'Give us the whole thing. How he found you in the first place is probably the most important.'

'It was one Friday lunchtime. I was in the pub with my workmates and I was moaning about how hideously in debt I was. Someone must have overheard me because that afternoon I got an email out of the blue offering me some evening work doing electronic component assembly at home. All legit and it paid really well. It was only after I'd been doing that for a while that the bloke emailed me again to say a one-off job had come up that would pay a whole lot more. Argus couldn't have known about it.'

'And you never saw the guy who offered you the work?'

Casey shook his head. 'A courier always brought the kit to me and collected the finished goods. I never saw him. We just communicated over email.'

'And then?'

Casey had stopped and seemed to be prising dirt from under his fingernails. Without looking up, he muttered, 'Well, I did the extra job. It was stupid, but I needed the money. It...' he stumbled over his words. 'I was horrified when I realised I'd been tricked into making one of our products seriously malfunction.' He continued to pick at his nails. 'Then, a week later, I got an email from Argus saying he knew what I'd done.' Casey finally looked into Trish's eyes and waved his arms in despair. 'I've absolutely no idea how he knew.'

Trish nodded slowly. She could guess how he felt. She turned to Tyler. 'And your client?'

'An old diary. He has no idea how it fell into Argus' hands.'

They continued to talk, probing each other's stories well into the night as Friday turned into Saturday. In the end, when the lantern's battery was low, and its light had dimmed to a meagre yellow glow, Trish said, 'It looks like the best lead is to go round to all my addresses and see if we can't find that brown SUV.'

Tyler had downloaded the file and they'd scanned down the spreadsheet together. Two hundred and seventy-eight addresses in about a thirty-mile radius.

'I'll get an A-to-Z of the area first thing in the morning,' Tyler said. 'We can mark them all up and then carve it into three sectors. We all stay here overnight.'

'I can only help over the weekend,' Casey said. 'I've got to be back at work on Monday. We're really busy at the moment getting ready for some demos and I can't afford not to be there.' Trish scowled at him but said nothing. Casey turned to Tyler. 'And what about me returning that car? The longer I hang on to it, the more likely it is the owner's going to report it missing.'

Tyler said firmly, 'First light. And I'll come with you so you don't do a runner.'

Trish yawned and rubbed her eyes, suddenly realising how tired she was.

Half an hour later as she finally slipped into her sleeping bag and listened to the others shuffling around in the dark under spare blankets fetched from her car, she felt strangely comforted. Although she sensed she could never fully trust this new partnership, it was good to feel she was no longer alone.

Trish lay in the dark for a long time, imagining what she might find if she ever made it inside Argus' house. She finally fell asleep thinking about Beth.

CHAPTER TWENTY-ONE

Casey snatched his mobile from the passenger seat. His pulse throbbed in his neck while he waited for Trish to answer. 'I think I've found it,' he whispered.

Sunday afternoon. He'd been driving around since six that morning, house after house, total tedium. At least he had his own car back. Having returned the stolen one the previous night it was a relief to be rid of it.

The sky was grey with high cloud cover, and there was no breeze through his open driver's window. He was parked opposite a large detached house – fifty seventh on his share of the list. Builders' scaffolding clung to one side above stacks of bricks and a couple of piles of sand. Although Sunday, they were still working, and the rumble of a small cement mixer carried to where he was parked.

A large metallic bronze Volvo stood in front of the double garage.

Trish's excited voice exploded in his ear. 'Brilliant. Where?'

He gave the address. 'Your list says the quote was for a Ms Argyle.'

'Have you checked the tyre tread?'

'Course not. I can't just wander up and start checking the car, can I. There's builders around.'

'I'm coming over.'

'Should I call Craig?'

A slight pause. 'Not yet. Let's check it out together first.' The line went dead.

He stared at the back of the SUV, his nerves tightening. *What the hell am I doing here, right where Argus might see me?* Was helping Trish to put an end to the blackmailer really the right thing to do? He wondered how she was so calm about it and slowly shook his head. Perhaps they were right. If he worked for Argus forever, maybe he would end up like Trish with someone trying to murder him as well. By now his stomach was bubbling from worry. He shut his eyes, lay back in his seat and resisted the temptation to just drive away. It took Trish twenty minutes to reach him.

She yanked open the passenger door of his car and threw herself inside, the hint of a recent cigarette clinging to her. He wrinkled his nose but said nothing. Her face was taut with tension.

'I remember quoting for this,' she said. 'I wonder who got the job. It was a right snooty woman who wanted an interior designer for that new extension, but I really got the impression I wasn't upper class enough for her. "It's a new reception for my regular soirees",' she mimicked in a good impression of the queen, and Casey couldn't help smiling despite his nervousness. 'It was all ankle-deep luxury carpet and expensive paintings and ornaments. Not a great deal of taste.'

'So how are we going to approach him? You can't just knock on the door and say, "Excuse me, are you Argus?"'

'No,' she said thoughtfully. 'But let's see if anyone's in anyway. Come on. And take a good look at the tyres on the way past.'

Before he could answer, she was out and crossing the quiet street. He hurried to catch up, and dropped into step. They both slowed as they reached the car. Trish suddenly stopped and bent to fiddle with her shoe before continuing to the door and ringing the bell. As the chimes rang out deep within the house, she moved her face closer to his and whispered, 'Dead match, I'm sure. There's also mud splashed up around the wheel arch.' He caught the pleasant scent of her perfume. He couldn't remember her wearing it before as she always seemed to smell of cigarette smoke.

He was wondering if she'd put it on for his benefit when a tall skinny woman opened the door. Nostrils of a long nose flared as she examined the pair on her doorstep. 'Yes?'

'Hello Ms Argyle. I'm from Sylver and McGowan Interiors. We quoted on some design work for you last year. I noticed the builders haven't finished yet, so I thought I'd drop by to check if you'd found someone good to do the interior.'

'Yes, thank you.' Argyle glanced warily at Matt. 'I have arranged for a London company to start next month as soon as the builders are out. Sorry.'

'That's okay. Do you mind if I ask why we lost out?'

'I really can't remember. It was a long time ago. Goodbye.' She shut the door without allowing Trish a reply.

He wondered if Argus had been there, lurking in the background. What if the blackmailer had recognised him and wondered why the two of them were together? Casey hadn't seen anyone else, but as they turned and walked silently back down the drive, it felt like eyes were staring at him. His muscles tensed.

As soon as they were on the road, Trish said, 'D'you think we can break in?'

He looked at her sharply. 'They've got an alarm. How the hell are we going to do that?' He'd noticed the box earlier while he'd been watching the house.

'Haven't you ever had builders in?' We've often worked on houses where trades are still finishing off – they always leave the flipping doors wide open, whatever you tell them. We can probably just walk straight in.'

'The builders'll see us.'

'So, we say we're her children or something. She's old enough to be our mum.'

He replied with a non-committal snort. It was crazy.

She rounded on him. 'How else do we find proof this is Argus' place? Sure, we found a car that *might* be the one he got away in parked where I've given a quote, but we need to be sure. What if it's just coincidence and they have a similar make of car?' She paused. 'We'll have to wait till they go out.'

In the end, they waited just over two hours.

The bronze SUV hesitated at the kerb with Argyle alone behind the wheel. She glanced both ways, not seeing them, then swung out and headed towards Chalfont St Peter. The workmen were still on site.

Trish whispered, 'She must have her builders on some sort of penalty clause.' He nodded as he watched her car disappear round a bend, and let out a deep breath. She glanced at him. 'Let's look round inside.'

'What if there's someone else still in the house? What if Argus is there?'

She shrugged. 'We'll just have to find out, won't we.' She wrenched open her door. 'Come on,' Trish called and ran across the road towards the front of the house. Casey locked the car and hurried after her. By the time he caught up, she had already rung the bell and was waiting.

After a minute, she shook her head. 'No one inside.'

'So how do we get in?'

'Back door?' Trish pursed her lips. 'If I remember right, the extension was going to wrap around the back corner to make an L-shaped lounge, and there was a patio door in the original bit.'

'So, we just walk round the back?'

'Why not? We can probably get there by going down the side of the garages. That way we don't go past the builders.'

Casey took a deep breath. His stomach churned. *This'll be the first time I've broken the law*, he thought, then corrected himself – other than what Argus had forced him to do.

Trish darted to the garage block and disappeared. Casey took one look to where the cement mixer was still churning, and ran after her into the dank shade beside the building, screwing up his noise at the pungent odour of cat piss. Trish was just ahead, peering round the back of the garage. He really didn't want to be here. He could feel his legs trembling.

Over her shoulder he could see a neat lawn stretching away in front of them towards an octagonal summerhouse. To their right, the new extension jutted out into the grass. The windows still had plastic film over the frames, and on the earth below them lay little mounds of discarded mortar and a few chopped bricks. An unseen radio was bellowing out the local radio station over the top of the rumble of their mixer.

'Now,' Trish hissed and disappeared towards the new section of house. Casey sprinted after her. She grabbed the handle of a patio door that led into the main building, slid it open, and darted inside. He followed and pushed the door shut as quietly as he could. The music faded slightly. She winked at him. 'Easy.'

They stood in a lounge from which the carpet had been removed. The smell of damp plaster hung in the air, and furniture stood under a large dust sheet against one of the bare walls. Light fittings had been stripped to bare bulbs. Used builders' tools were stacked in one corner.

'This way,' Trish called, yanked open the door to the rest of the house and ran through without stopping. They hesitated on the wooden floor of a hall. 'Let's start upstairs.' She took them two at a time.

She was panting at the top. 'Pick a room and see what

you can find, I guess.'

Trish disappeared through the first open doorway, and Casey headed into the next room to his left, still worried the house might not be empty.

It looked like a spare room – single bed without sheets or duvet, small cupboard, chair. Everything looked unused. Back to the landing and into next room – laid out like an office. What the hell was he looking for? Business cards with "Blackmailer" written on them?

A desk stood below the window, all very neat – laptop, switched off but lid open, notebook, answer phone, an expensive fountain pen. Beside it, a bookcase lined with books and a dozen files.

Casey was turning to the desk when Trish swept in. 'I've been through the bedrooms and bathrooms. There's no sign that anyone else lives here other than Ms Argyle. No husband or children. I'm beginning to think she's Argus. She's certainly creepy enough.'

He tried to recall what had given him the impression that Argus was male. He left the desk for Trish and turned to the row of files, all labelled alphabetically. He reached out for the first but a man's voice made him jump violently. 'Hi Doll, it's me.'

Shit. He spun round, heart thumping. Trish was leaning over the desk operating the answer machine. The voice continued, middle-aged, deep and resonant. 'Looks like I can get tickets for the Royal Ballet in June. They're doing Don Quixote. Let me know if you fancy it. See you later.'

Trish looked up. 'That's the only message. Who was it?

Some fancy man?' Casey shrugged and lifted down the first folder. Trish flicked through the pages of the desk diary, then bustled out.

The ring binder Casey held was full of invoices. He tried the next one. It held the same things. It appeared as though Ms Argyle was a medical sales rep.

A scream made Casey spin round and dash to the door.

Trish stood transfixed ten feet from him. He couldn't see what she was staring at. 'Trish?'

She didn't move.

CHAPTER TWENTY-TWO

Trish had frozen near the top of the stairs. Casey tried to look past her. 'Trish? What's the matter?'

'Come and look at this,' she whispered. Casey stepped cautiously on to the landing and saw she was studying a picture. His heart was still thumping from the shock of her scream. He stared at the artwork, and Trish asked, 'Do you know what this is?'

The print was mix of drab browns and greens, with a single slash of red in the middle from a woman's dress. A peacock fanned its tail beside her.

'No.'

Casey didn't see the severed head at first, until he realised the man's corpse slumped in the foreground was sliced at the neck. A maid balanced the head on her knee for her mistress to examine. Why both women had their tits hanging out he couldn't imagine.

'That's a print of a Rubens,' she said softly. 'It depicts the story of Argus, who had a hundred eyes. In Greek mythology, he was murdered and his eyes were used to decorate the peacock's feathers.'

Casey moved nearer to study the picture. He was so close to Trish that he could feel the warmth from her body. 'Argus?'

Trish nodded. They straightened up, and her eyes glowed with excitement. 'I think we have our proof.'

Casey took a last look at the picture and thought that it was not the sort of thing he'd hang on his wall. 'How d'you know all that stuff?'

'I did an art degree. We got taught about the works of all the famous artists.'

'So how come you didn't realise earlier where our blackmailer got his name from?'

'*Her* name,' Trish corrected. 'And it was only when I saw this picture that I remembered. Sorry for being so stupid. I did art, not Greek mythology.'

Casey muttered, 'Hundreds of eyes watching everywhere. Just like Argus. A good name for him – sorry, her – to choose.' He exhaled deeply. 'So, what now? It's freaking me out just standing here. What if she comes back?'

'Well at least we now know for sure Ms Argyle is Argus, what with this and the car. For my part, I want to persuade her to do something about Kurt Wendell.'

'How?'

Without answering, Trish spun on her heels and hurried back into the office. She tore a sheet from the notebook on Argus' desk. 'How about like this?' She uncapped the fountain pen and scrawled in large letters, *Argus, Kurt*

Wendell is trying to kill me. I need your help. Please contact me ASAP, and left her email address. She placed it square in the middle of the desk. 'Now let's get out of here.'

Trish cautiously led the way down the stairs and ran quietly out into the garden. He caught her up at the back of the garage. She paused to check the way was clear before darting down the drive and back across the road. She stood gasping for breath beside his car and reached for a cigarette.

'We should call Craig,' he said.

'Let's just get out of here first in case she sees us on her way back,' she panted. 'Craig is probably back at the house by now anyway.'

***

The three of them met up again at the old house in the room they had adopted as an operational centre. 'Anything?' Tyler asked the moment they entered the dingy space.

Trish was just ahead of Casey and answered first. 'Yes. Ms Antonia Argyle in High Ridge Road. She lives alone, no sign of family. Early fifties and she's a right old cow. We reckon her day job is a medical sales rep. And the car on the drive's a large sort of bronze coloured beast with very familiar treads.'

'Volvo XC90,' Casey added. 'Top of the range.'

Trish continued. 'And she has an interesting framed print on her landing wall.' She paused for effect. 'It's from a painting by Rubens and features Argus, who in Greek mythology had a hundred eyes.'

Tyler raised his eyebrows. 'Pretty conclusive combination. How did you get in to see it?'

'The builders are still there, so we sneaked in through an open door when she went out.'

He pulled a face. 'If security's that lax, I guess she doesn't keep the blackmail material in the house. Did you get much of a look round?

'We went round most of the upstairs. She has a kind of office up there, but, you're right, we couldn't find anything even vaguely related to blackmail.'

'Perhaps I'll take a look myself anyway,' Tyler said. 'I've got an appointment tonight but if I go right now, I can fit it in first. What's the address?'

Should she give it? What was he planning to do? After a slight hesitation, she recited it from memory. Tyler scooped up his keys from the upturned crate they'd been using for a table and hurried out.

Trish remained silent until she heard the engine start, then pulled out her phone and switched it back on.

'I thought you were trying to stay off-grid,' Casey said.

It was a risk she had to take. 'I want another go at contacting Wendell. I've emailed him before and even written once to explain it's not me who's responsible, but he ignored me. Maybe now that I can tell him I know who Argus really is and where to find her...' She ignored the message that popped up to remind her of her voicemails. 'Give me a hand creating an email for Kurt Wendell.'

'Why not just leave it all to Argus? You left her that note.'

'Because she probably won't do anything. I mean, why should she? But if I can contact Wendell, maybe I can get him to go after her instead of me.'

'Or both of you.'

She glared at him. He still didn't seem a hundred percent committed to this. 'What else can I do?'

'Doesn't Wendell think you're dead anyway?'

'I imagine Beth's death will be all over the papers. He must know by now it wasn't me.' She tapped at her phone, licking her lips in silence. After a few moments, she handed over her mobile. 'What d'you think?'

Casey read aloud.

> *Dear Kurt Wendell,*
>
> *I've been blackmailed to forward demands to you over the past few months from someone code-named 'Argus'. It is not me blackmailing you but I'm a victim as much as you. I'm not surprised you're trying to get rid of me, but please believe me when I say that I am NOT the blackmailer. I now know Argus' true identity and address. If I give you those, will you agree to leave me alone?*
>
> *Thanks,*
>
> *Trish McGowan.*

Casey frowned and handed it back. 'Do you really think that'll work?'

'Don't know, but I've got to do something. Otherwise, next time he comes for me, I mightn't be so lucky.'

Poor Beth. A lump formed in her chest. *Poor innocent Beth.* Without another word she sent the email.

***

An hour later, Tyler entered Argyle's house through the same route the others had taken. There was no sign of the bronze Volvo but the builders were still there. Dedicated, Tyler thought. In his experience, tradesmen knocked off by three if the owner wasn't around, especially on Sundays.

As he crossed to the stairs, he passed a table in the hall on top of which lay a small bunch of keys. He hesitated, then scooped them up and dropped them in his pocket. They might be useful in the future.

He climbed to the landing and found the home office that the others had mentioned. When he had searched Casey's place, he'd had no qualms about making a mess – enjoyed using it to intimidate Casey in the hope the pressure would force him to make a slip. Here, though, he wasn't so sure. Better, perhaps, to remain unseen, especially as he was confident what he was after wasn't in the house. He just wanted to get a feel for what she was like.

He had seen the print Trish had spoken about. An ugly old-fashioned scene in an out-of-date frame.

Tyler started with the files on the bookcase, flicking through each in turn. As the others had said, she was a medical sales rep. The question that remained was how the hell she'd found out about Casey and Bradon.

Faintly in the background he could hear the workmen's radio, and there was an occasional clatter from the scaffolding, but he would hear if the car returned.

He moved to the desk and immediately saw a scrawled note sitting prominently in the middle. *Argus, Kurt Wendell is trying to kill me. I need your help. Please contact me ASAP. Trish McGowan.* He scrunched the sheet into a ball and thrust it into his pocket. He couldn't allow Argus to know they'd uncovered her identity. The last thing he could afford was for the blackmailer to close up shop and disappear.

***

Every half hour, Trish switched her phone back on, checked for email, and quickly turned it back off. Each time, her mouth went dry.

Just as Tyler was leaving Argyle's house, she powered it up again. This time it chirped briefly. One email. Every muscle tensed as she looked at the screen. Wendell had replied.

CHAPTER TWENTY-THREE

'You sure this is right?' Casey asked. He squinted at the map on the car's sat-nav screen. 'This can't be the car park Wendell wanted to meet us in.'

They were sitting in Trish's mini, parked among trees. Her knuckles were white from tightly gripping the wheel. 'It's the only one,' she said firmly.

Wendell had refused to discuss anything over email or phone, insisting instead that they meet immediately. Agreeing to come was a hell of risk. Only days before, he'd been trying to kill her, now she was waiting to meet him in a remote car park with no-one around. She bit at her lip and reminded herself that she had convinced him that she had valuable information, and so he wouldn't kill her; that he'd want to talk instead. Even so, she felt her legs shaking.

It had been nearly impossible to persuade Casey to come with her. He kept saying he had to be heading home ready for work in the morning, but eventually he'd given in.

It had to be less than an hour before nightfall now. She slowly shook her head. 'It doesn't look like he's coming,' she mumbled.

'I'll take a look round,' Casey said, but Trish grabbed his arm.

'Don't. Please stay here. Perhaps he just wants to make us split up. Maybe that's what he's waiting for.' Her stomach was in knots.

'So, we do what?' He raised his voice and shook off her grip. 'Just wait? How long have we got to hang around? I've got a long drive home tonight.'

'I don't know,' she shouted back. She lowered the window and looked around, straining for the sound of a car. There was nothing. Dark trees formed an almost impenetrable barrier to their left; to their right, open fields rose on a gentle incline with hedges and farm fences dividing them into random squares. A few sheep grazed at the top of the slope.

She lit a cigarette and blew smoke out of the window. The hillside gradually darkened. No cars appeared on the narrow road.

After another ten minutes, Casey said, 'Perhaps he's chickened out.' He angled his watch to catch the last of the light. 'Sorry, but I've really got to go back.'

'We can't leave.' She felt panic rise in her chest.

'I've got no choice. We're really busy at work getting ready for some demo flights. I've got to be there.'

'Well thanks for your support,' she snapped. A sudden thought struck her. 'Maybe he's changed his mind because he wasn't expecting two of us.' An ice lump formed in her chest. If that was why Wendell hadn't showed, it meant he'd seen them arrive and maybe he was still watching them now. She looked around again, peering into the gloom. No sign of anybody, but the hairs on her neck bristled.

'Or this was just a ruse to get us out of the house,' Casey said.

'Why?'

'Who knows? So he can plant bugs or something?'

'But he doesn't know we're there.'

He stared straight at her. 'Are you sure?'

She suddenly felt sick. Had she fallen for a trick? Her face flushed. 'All right, he's not coming so let's get back.'

She twisted the key and violently drove back out on to the road. She gritted her teeth. *Damn you, Wendell.*

They were at the end of what was effectively a long cul-de-sac that wound its way to this final car park. Up ahead, she could see the road narrowing at an old stone bridge. All was clear beyond, so she kept going fast, only braking at the last moment as they approached the hump. She knew her anger showed in her driving, but didn't care.

As they closed on it, there was a loud crack somewhere to Trish's right. The car suddenly veered wildly, and an ear-splitting whine screamed from its front wheel. She fought to steer back but it was out of control. Going too fast, they hit the kerb with a massive jolt. The car spun. *Brake.* A smell of burning rubber. The bridge loomed sideways-on. A heartbeat later, the wing smashed into stone.

Air bags exploded around them with thunder-claps

while glass shattered and metal buckled. The car was flung back. The airbag smothered her, and the seatbelt bit at her shoulder. She lost all orientation as the car careened out of control. Another crash as they hit something else and the car pitched forwards.

Cold and dark. The car came to rest at a sickening downwards angle. There was water around her feet. *Dear God, we're drowning.*

Panic rose within her. *Must get out. Come on, Trish, move.* She wrenched at the handle, flung the door open but couldn't move. *Seat belt – release the bloody seat belt.* She unclipped it and threw herself out. She slipped in mud and grabbed the car for support. Viciously cold water swirled up to her knees and made her gasp. The back of her mini sat on the river bank, the car's bonnet submerged.

She reached back in and snatched her handbag from the floor behind her seat where it had fallen, then realised Casey hadn't climbed out. 'Matt?'

His head moved slightly. He was clearly dazed. 'Shit. What happened?' he mumbled.

She grabbed his arm and shook him hard. 'We're half in the stinking river. Get out before you drown.'

Seconds later, he was scrabbling at his door. 'It won't budge,' he yelled. 'I'm coming your way.' Casey unfastened his safety belt and crawled across with a grunt and splashed into the water, ending up right next to Trish.

Miraculously, neither of them seemed hurt. Trish hauled herself up the bank through the churned grass and mud, and examined the damage to her beloved mini. The car rested at a steep angle, nose deep in the swirling water. From what she could make out, the front wing was now mangled metal. Through the side window, the airbags looked like ghostly deflated balloons.

She felt sick. Her beloved Daisy ... Her little yellow Mini....

Casey was wildly scanning the fields and trees around them. 'Did you hear that bang just before we left the road?' he said. 'D'you think it was a gun shot?'

She stopped abruptly at his words and spun to face him. 'Are you serious?'

'I think so.'

She tried to remember but panic was jumbling her thoughts. They peered into the gloom, scouring the incline to their right for signs of movement.

It was Trish who saw him first. Her heart lurched and she grabbed Casey's arm. She pointed across the fields, momentarily unable to get a word out.

A figure was jogging down the slope towards them, barely a hundred metres away and keeping close to the hedge. His dark clothes made him almost invisible. He was tall and skinny with a head that seemed to sink into his torso without a neck.

He carried something long, and it took her a second to realise what it was.

A rifle.

CHAPTER TWENTY-FOUR

Twenty miles away, Tyler had reached his appointment at the Four Oaks Care Home. Charles Aston's retirement party had made three pages in the first edition of BDE's newsletter, and Tyler had been delighted when he discovered the old man was still alive.

Tyler sipped a milky tea from a cup garishly decorated with yellow flowers, and examined the old man propped in the chair opposite him. Ninety if he was a day. Charles Aston's liver spotted face smiled weakly at him. The voice recorder on Tyler's mobile was running, with the phone sitting on a doily-topped table close to the old man. The lounge was almost empty – just one woman snoring gently in a corner in front of a TV with the sound turned down.

'I was at Bradon's, man and boy,' Aston said. 'Started at sixteen on the factory floor and worked my way up. Ended up as the Production Manager.'

Tyler nodded. 'I read the article about your retirement party that was in a company newsletter from twenty years ago.'

'Wow. How did you get that?'

'Art Bradon's secretary found a complete set for me. That's why I wanted to talk to you about this history book Art's asked me to write. You're one of the few people outside the immediate family who has seen the company from the outset.'

Aston nodded, his eyes distant.

Tyler prompted, 'Did it change much over the years?'

'It grew larger and took on bigger projects, but the Bradons always managed to keep it feeling like a small family-owned business. They were nice to work for.' He paused, momentarily lost in his memories. 'It wasn't always BDE of-course.'

Tyler raised an eyebrow. 'Really?'

He nodded. 'The original company was founded straight after the war by Art's grandfather, George Metcalf. I think it was called something like ...' He paused, trying to remember. 'Metcalf Engineering, or something like that.'

'Strange. Art told me it was formed in 1970.'

'Ah.' Aston waved a bony finger in the air. 'There was a big family bust up at the end of the sixties, and the company split in two. One half became BDE.' He grimaced. 'I can remember it clearly. There was an awful row in the boardroom – we could hear them shouting at each other from the factory. We got to hear the rumours later. Someone was stepping down from the board, and George Metcalf decided it was the right time to bring in his son, Austin, even though he was only just out of Oxford. Christine –

that's one of George's daughters – was already a member, but she was a good ten years older. Anyway, Christine had married a guy called Ed Bradon, and she insisted that if Austin was joining the board, so should her husband. She argued that he was also family. But old George absolutely refused and insisted on having his son but not Ed. There was an almighty bust up – the shouting went on for ages. It ended with Christine leaving the board and setting up her own company with her husband. That's where Bradon Defence Electronics came from. Art was their son and joined the company in the early eighties straight from university.'

Aston paused, wheezing slightly, and took a sip of tea. His hand was shaking, and some of it spilt on his already-stained cardigan but he didn't seem to notice. 'Christine approached a small group of us afterwards and asked if we would join her and Ed. Offered us promotion and a good pay raise. We all knew she was a fantastic manager and most of us defected with her. George rebranded what he had left as Metcalf Systems & Aeronautics, MSA for short.'

'Were they both successful after the split?'

'Sure. It was a good time for the defence industry, what with the Cold War and all. Both did well. Mind you, there was a hell of a lot of competition between the two companies. Rumour had it that Metcalf's would always bid for any business that BDE was going for just to spite them. Kind of trying to prove they were still the stronger, but Ed and Christine were great at business and BDE flourished. Sadly, though, it's said that the two halves of the family never spoke again, and Austin Metcalf and Ed Bradon became bitter enemies.' He sipped more tea and put the cup back with a rattle.

'Metcalf's half was never as stable,' he continued. 'They nearly collapsed in the mid- seventies. They had a big family misfortune, and George's other daughter went off the rails. They lost focus while it was all going on and the company almost went under because of a lack of leadership during that time.'

'Misfortune?'

'About Harriet's baby and the fire.'

'Harriet?' Tyler frowned. 'I don't think I've heard of her.' Tyler doubted it was relevant to BDE but it might provide colourful background. It was worth letting him ramble on.

'They don't tend to talk about it. Harriet lost her baby daughter in a house fire a few years after the companies split. She went right off the rails and had a mental breakdown. They say she blamed herself for the baby's death. It was so sad – she ended up committing suicide. George was totally devastated, losing his youngest daughter and granddaughter in one go, and MSA wobbled badly without his normal firm grip. But it recovered in the end.'

'Was the blaze an accident?'

'The inquest brought in a verdict of accidental death on the baby and concluded some candles that Harriet had left unattended in the lounge had set fire to the curtains. There were plenty of rumours, of course, but they were only silly tales.'

Tyler nodded slowly. 'So, coming back to BDE, are they any other titbits you can give me to spice the story up a bit?'

Aston sighed. 'Well, there was the crash of Dragonfly I, of course. That was after my time – only a few years ago – but everyone was talking about it. Do you know about that?'

Tyler remembered the name. Several people had spoken about the project, including Bradon himself, but there had been no mention of a crash.'

'Tell me.'

'Dragonfly I was their first UAV. All the latest technology. A bit of a showpiece for what BDE could do. It crashed at a big demo at the Farnborough Air Show. All the bad publicity set the company back several years. In fact, they nearly collapsed. Made about thirty members of staff redundant.' Tyler remembered the newspaper articles he had come across and made a mental note to read them when he finally got home.

'What was the cause?'

'No one ever found out from what I heard, although as I said, I'd retired by then so I don't know the full story. Their engineers would have done a detailed post-mortem, but I never heard that they'd satisfactorily got to the bottom of it. The craft just suddenly went out of control during the demonstration and nose-dived. It was lucky no-one was killed. Art felt awful about it apparently, took it personally, felt it was all his own fault.'

Tyler nodded slowly. 'But it looks like the company recovered okay.'

Aston brightened. 'Oh yes. They've invested loads in its successor, Dragonfly II. To be honest I'd be a bit worried they've invested too much. If they don't get good sales for this, it could be the end of the company.'

'How strong's the competition?'

'There's a couple of big boys in this field. It's hard to fight against the large conglomerates, but I think BDE probably has an edge technically.' He laughed a rattling chuckle. 'Mind you, they probably see MSA as their most important competitor. Not because MSA's product is better but because it's run by Art's uncle. The rivalry has simply moved down a generation. It's a shame. I guess they learnt it from their parents.'

'Two halves on a family both in the same business doesn't sound like a path to harmony.'

Aston grimaced. 'Bitter rivals.'

They talked a little more before Aston's stories dried up. Tyler reached over and scooped up his phone. He pulled out a notebook and scribbled down his mobile number before tearing the page out and leaving it on the table. 'If you remember anything else that might be good for the book, just give me a call.'

The old man held out a limp hand for Tyler to shake. 'Thanks for coming, sir. I don't get many visitors in this place and it's nice to chat.' He suddenly looked drawn and tired and closed his eyes. Tyler sighed. He would hate to end up in a place like this. He'd rather die young than slowly fade out in a home.

Tyler tried to shrug off his maudlin feelings as he stuck the key back in the ignition of his BMW. It was nearly dark. He didn't fancy another night back at the old house, but he still didn't trust Casey and McGowan. He wondered what they'd been doing in his absence.

CHAPTER TWENTY-FIVE

Trish scrambled to her feet and darted to the old stone bridge to use it as cover. Her feet crunched on broken glass and shattered plastic. She crossed the bridge in a low crouching run with Matt close behind. Heart thumping, and keeping her head down, she charged off the road into rough grass on the other side, vaulted a low fence, and stumbled into the cover of trees.

Her eyes soon adjusted to the gloom. Underfoot was uneven but firm, with tufts of coarse grass and loose leaves. She zigzagged between the trunks, the wet trousers flapping against her legs and her feet squelching in her trainers.

Soon her lungs were burning and she coughed. Over her shoulder, she saw Casey close behind, and then Wendell charged into the trees a long way back, rifle in hand.

Trish's breath was coming in gasps. Casey overtook her, then suddenly stumbled and fell, sprawling headlong into the leaves. Trish swerved round him, almost losing her own footing.

Glancing back, she saw him scramble to his feet. Her heart was hammering. Her chest ached, and the back of her throat was sore as she sucked in air. A stitch stabbed into her side. *Ignore it. Keep going.* She felt a rhythm briefly develop, legs and arms in unison, powering forward through the trees, but she couldn't keep it up.

Breath rasped in her throat. Again, she coughed loudly. The stitch intensified. Casey was at her shoulder again, but there was no sign of Wendell. Trish gasped, 'I can't ...'

The trees and undergrowth were so thick here that Wendell could go right past and not notice them. She stopped and leant forward with hands on knees, and Casey skidded to a halt beside her. Trish felt as though her heart was trying to hammer its way out of her chest. She coughed again and spat a ball of phlegm into the leaves.

Casey stared back into the gloom. 'We might have lost him,' he whispered.

They crouched together in the leaves, and their breathing slowly steadied. Soon it would be too dark to see where they were going.

After another minute, he gently laid a hand on her arm. 'Are you ready to move?' he whispered with his mouth close to her ear.

Trish felt a tingle when he touched her. She nodded stiffly. 'I don't know what to do about my car,' she said. 'I can't leave poor Daisy like that, but I'm afraid if we go back to sort her out now, Wendell will be waiting for us.'

'There's nothing you can do yourself anyway. It'll need a tow-truck. Was there anything you need from the boot?'

'Just a few spare clothes and a bit of food. Nothing urgent.'

'In that case, leave your car for now and call a garage to collect it as soon as you can.'

'You're right. Okay, if we can find a landmark somewhere, we can get Craig to collect us if he's back yet.'

Casey fumbled in his pocket. 'Let's see a map ... if I can find my phone.'

He thrust his hand in the other pocket, then increasingly frantically patted down the rest of his clothes. 'I've lost my phone.' He stood, again checking each pocket in turn. 'I must have dropped it when I fell over.'

'We'll never find it in this light.'

'Hell.' He continued to pat wildly at his jacket and trousers. 'Can you ring it? We can retrace our steps and listen for it.'

'What, and walk straight back into Kurt Wendell? You've got to be kidding.' She pulled out her own phone, switched it on, and opened its maps. Casey leant in close. His warm breath caressed her cheek.

'There'll be no GPS because of the trees,' he warned, 'but you should be able to locate the bridge.'

A moment later, she had scrolled across the map to where they'd been ambushed, then zoomed out. 'If we can carry on in a straight line, we'll break out at this road here...' She pointed at the map, then scanned along the road in both directions. 'Here's a pub,' she said at last. If Craig's back, we can call him and get him to pick us up there.'

It was so dark in the wood now that she could barely see

where to walk. Cautiously, she switched on the phone's flashlight and used it to guide their feet, keeping its beam low so it couldn't be seen from a distance. 'This way,' she said and started forward again.

Her stomach churned with nerves. With every step, she expected Wendell to loom out of the blackness and grab her.

***

'What the hell were you doing talking to Wendell?' Tyler exploded. He swore loudly, waving his arms in disbelief. 'I thought he was your arms dealer victim.'

It was half an hour since Trish and Casey had finally emerged from the woods, and they were now standing in the pub car park by Tyler's car, away from the lights and chatter that spilled out of the building. Three young men who stood near the door smoking glanced at Tyler, then continued with their own discussion.

'Wendell's not *my* victim – he's Argus',' Trish said. 'And why shouldn't I contact him? If I can make him understand I'm not the source of the blackmail, he'll leave me alone.'

'Don't you get it?' Tyler said, lowering his voice to an urgent hiss. 'If he kills Argus, I might never recover what I need for my client.'

'So, it's all about you! Stuff the rest of us. Is that it?'

Tyler shook his head violently, then continued in a slightly calmer tone. 'You've got to see the bigger picture. Besides, why should Wendell let you go free anyway? You know what he's being blackmailed for. More than likely, he'll still consider you a threat and take you out anyway.'

'I don't see why.'

Casey interrupted. 'But if we point this arms dealer in Argus' direction and he kills her, that'll stop all of us being blackmailed. We'll be free.'

'Precisely,' Trish said. 'It's got to be the best route.'

'No, it's not,' Tyler shouted, then took a breath and said more quietly, 'Look, if you do survive but haven't recovered the blackmail material Argus has on you, what makes you think it'll all be over? Wendell will be searching for whatever evidence Argus has on him and if he comes across the stuff against you two at the same time, what's to stop your German friend picking up where Argus left off and becoming a blackmailer himself? Everyone will be worse off.'

There was silence. She hadn't thought of that. She felt Tyler's eyes boring into her.

'We should get out of here,' Tyler said. 'We shouldn't hang around if there's a maniac in the neighbourhood.'

Trish nodded and turned to his BMW. To Casey she said, 'I can sort poor Daisy out over the phone, but what are you going to do about your mobile?'

'I ought to go back when it's light to try to find it.'

Tyler swung to face him over the roof of the car. 'What's up with your phone?' he snapped.

'I must have dropped it. I fell over when we were in the woods.'

'Shit. Any chance her arms dealer could have picked it up?'

Casey shrugged. 'I don't know,' he stammered. 'I suppose so. Why?'

'Did you use its sat nav?'

'Yes.'

'To drive to the derelict mansion the other day?'

'Yes. So what?'

'Then if Wendell now has your phone, he can see from your sat nav history where you've been. Is the mobile locked with a PIN or anything?'

Casey shook his head.

'Then you've effectively shown Wendell exactly where to find us.'

CHAPTER TWENTY-SIX

They approached the old mansion with caution. Tyler's BMW purred to a halt in the mouth of the track, out of sight of the house, and he cut the headlights. 'Wait here,' Tyler whispered and quietly slipped out of the car and disappeared into the night.

'I don't like this,' Trish whispered. 'I feel like a sitting target.'

Casey quietly muttered something in reply that she didn't catch.

Five minutes passed before Tyler let himself back in. 'No sign of him yet,' he said and restarted the engine. 'So, let's clear out as quickly as we can.'

In the tense drive back from the pub, they had discussed options. 'It's no longer safe for any of us to stay there,' Tyler had declared. 'I've got a cottage in Wales that I use when I'm writing. You can move in there for a bit until we get this sorted.'

'I don't need to hide,' Casey said. 'I mean, it's not me Wendell's after.'

'Face it, if he's got your phone, you're in as much risk as she is.'

'He might not even have it. It could still be lying in the middle of that wood.'

'Do you want to take that risk?'

There was silence. Trish studied Casey's face in the light from the streetlamps that swept past. As the words sunk in, he physically paled. 'But what about work?' he said after a moment.

'Take a holiday.' Tyler said over his shoulder. 'Tell them you're enjoying the Welsh mountains.'

'I won't be allowed. Everyone's working flat out to get ready for a big demo to the MOD.'

'Well, I don't think you've left yourself much choice. You shouldn't have got mixed up in this in the first place.'

To Casey's obvious irritation, it was finally decided that they would transfer across the border to Tyler's cottage. Trish wondered how much Tyler was using it as an excuse to get them out of the way so they couldn't interfere in what he was doing, but for the moment she saw no better alternative.

As soon as Tyler pulled up by the cracked fountain, they scattered. Tyler sprinted back to the road to keep a lookout, and Trish started to clear out their stuff while Casey reversed his car out of the trees and parked it, boot open, beside Tyler's. He joined her with removing items from the house. Each time Trish neared the cars with another armful, she looked nervously towards the road, half expecting to see Wendell emerge from the darkness.

Within five minutes, everything had been thrown into the boots of the two cars. As she carried down the final load, Casey ran along the drive and quickly came back with Tyler, who gave the final instructions for the journey.

Trish went with Casey, and they followed Tyler's BMW through the night, reaching his cottage at two in the morning.

They fell, fully dressed, on to bare mattresses, Casey in one room, Trish in the second, and Tyler on the lounge's put-you-up. Trish was asleep almost instantly.

She was woken hours later by sunlight. She opened the curtains and winced at the bright light of day. Morning had dawned sunny and already had a perfect cerulean sky. She was sticky and uncomfortable, wearing clothes she'd been in for several days. In the bathroom, it felt good to strip and stand under the warm shower, eyes closed, letting it pour over her head. The first job this morning was going to be finding the washing machine.

By eight, everyone was up. They sat caressing mugs of coffee round a wooden table that was scarred from decades of use. The cottage had very masculine decor, she decided after a glance round the room – a couple of black-framed pictures with brooding landscapes and not a single pop of colour anywhere. It was clear Craig's wife had never lived here. She guessed it was the sort of place where the fridge was stuffed with beers and the bin wedged with pizza boxes. She would take a look later.

Trish pulled a crumpled box of Claude & Butlers from her jeans pocket. 'Anyone mind if I smoke?'

Tyler shrugged. 'It's *your* lungs.'

She looked at Casey, but he wouldn't meet her eyes. 'Damn it,' she said and slapped the packet on to the table. 'I'll have one later. What's the plan of action? We can't just stay here forever.'

'I'm going to find out more about Argus.' Tyler said. 'Detailed intelligence is everything. I'm going to bug her house and learn her habits and routines, where she goes, who she visits, and so on. Then I'll decide what to do.'

'We're not leaving you to deal with her all by yourself. I still need to sort out Wendell, and if you do something to Argus you could easily scupper my chances.'

'Once I've recovered my client's stuff, how about I bring her here to you? It's got to be much safer for you to stay here out of sight.'

She sighed and looked at Casey, who shrugged. It was frustrating but she knew Tyler had her trapped.

'And what about me?' Casey asked. 'I'm meant to be back at work, and my boss is going to have a fit. How much longer is it going to take?'

'This sort of intelligence gathering would normally take weeks but I haven't the luxury of time. I've got to find a way to compress it into a few days. Why don't you take the week off?'

'I'm not sure I can.'

Tyler swore. 'I don't get it. You're both running for your lives. I reckon that's a tad more important than your bloody job. You don't understand this world do you.' He looked stolidly at them one after the other. He shook his head and sighed. 'You stay here, right? I'll call you ten o'clock each evening to let you know how I'm getting on.'

When neither of them answered, Tyler seemed to take that as agreement. 'Let me tell you about this cottage before I go,' he continued. 'We're pretty much cut-off here from everyone, which is great. I'll show you how the security works – I've got a set of infrared beams and motion detectors round the garden that sound an alarm if something breaches the perimeter. Occasionally I get the odd tourist or deer trying to wander through that can set it off, but that's fairly rare. There are also four CCTV cameras on the roof that show the entire grounds on the TV.'

'I'm surprised,' Trish said. 'Why so much security?'

Tyler shrugged and seemed almost embarrassed. 'When you've spent years wondering if the next bullet has your name on it, it's hard to switch back to civvy life without feeling there's always an enemy at your back.' He shook his head. 'My nerves were totally shredded, and I found the security helped. That's all.'

Trish was about to ask if all ex-SAS suffered the same paranoia when he abruptly swigged the last of his coffee and stood up. 'Just in case Wendell does somehow turn up, let me show you where to leave your car for a quick getaway. We came in the main entrance last night, but there's a small path out the side that climbs through a defile to another track higher up the slope. You can leave your car at the end of that, and then if you do need to make a quick exit, you can do it unseen from the front. Let me show you.' As he approached the door, he paused. 'There are always charged torches just here, by the way, so you can also do this after nightfall.' He pointed to where they hung.

Trish snatched her cigarettes and lit one the second she was outside. She stood there for a moment, enjoying the feel of the fresh morning air against her skin and slowly blowing smoke upwards.

Fir trees dipped away toward the back of the house, turning into a carpet of green. She could see the distant mound of what she assumed was Mount Snowdon, flanked by smaller brown-clad mountains.

Tyler led the way along an overgrown stone path, and they were soon enveloped by firs and following a shallow rut in the forest floor that looked like an animal track. Moments later, Trish heard water, and they reached a gorge where water splashed across the rocks in a series of small cascades. The air was moist and cool. Tyler jumped the stream and followed a track on the other side. As they climbed rapidly, the sound of the falling water became surprisingly loud. Grey walls of rock briefly closed in around them before they burst out onto a plateau.

Trish looked back but the cottage was hidden by trees. 'This way,' Tyler called, and she turned to catch up with the two men as they reached a wide dirt track. 'This is woodland owned by the National Park's Forestry Section,' Tyler explained. He pointed to their right. 'That way takes you back down to Penmachno village. And just round the corner behind us is an area that's used for stacking any timber they fell. You can leave your car there. If anything happens you can be up here and away in seconds and no-one will see you from the front of the cottage.'

They followed Tyler to the left and found the area he'd described, the ground dusted with decaying sawdust. 'Leave your car here just in case,' Tyler said grimly. 'Okay?'

They both nodded.

Tyler led the way back to the stream and along the narrow path, nimbly jumping from rock to rock on the descent, Trish and Casey following more slowly. When they were out of earshot, Casey asked, 'Do we really need these paranoid escape plans?'

'Of course not. But then again, I don't mind having them just in case.'

Back at the cottage, Tyler demonstrated the intruder system and how to switch the TV to monitor all four cameras. 'I'm heading back to start watching Argus straight away. Make yourselves at home.'

As soon as Tyler had left, Casey picked up the cottage's phone. Trish looked absentmindedly out of the kitchen window across the expanse of Welsh countryside. A red kite languidly circled high in the sky, and she watched its effortless movements. 'I'm not going to sit here and do nothing,' she muttered to herself. 'I'm going to dig myself out of this mess and I don't trust Craig Tyler to help.'

The question was, how?

**

Casey dialled the number from memory and made the call he'd been dreading since waking that morning. He asked for a week off.

'You know this MOD demo's almost upon us,' the voice

boomed back at him down the phone line. 'Everyone's doing overtime, working their arses off, and you're saying you're not coming in for a few days? You're a key part of this team, Matt, and we need you here. I don't see how I can sign off any holiday.'

'I know it's short notice, and I know it's a bad time, but I've got a shed load of personal problems I've just got to sort out. And Mohamed and Russell can cope with the work going through the wire-shop at the moment. I only need a few days. It's really, *really* important. And I'll work doubly hard the moment I get back.' Casey felt guilty as he put down the receiver. He ought to be there, helping the guys.

Trish took the phone from him and spent most of the next hour talking to her car insurers, then to a garage before calling her shop and discussing repairs. Casey paid little attention and browsed the paperbacks stacked on an antique dresser. There was a full set of Tyler's own works there, alongside Chris Ryan, Andy McNab and Duncan Falconer, and he idly thumbed through Tyler's *Disposal*.

When Trish finally finished, she turned to Casey with a coquettish smile. She brushed the locks of coloured hair out of her eyes. 'How d'you fancy driving me out in your car to explore? We need to get some food anyway. Have you seen the contents of his cupboards?'

He hadn't. 'Sure. It's better than being cooped up here all day getting bored, I suppose.'

'And on the way back, we can move the car up to that place Craig showed us. Just in case.'

'Really?'

'Why not? There's no harm.'

He sighed. 'It's just such a long hike back and forth.'

She tilted her head to one side. 'Please,' she pleaded.

He conceded, and her smile unexpectedly set his heart fluttering. She was so pretty.

They drove into the narrow streets of Penmachno. Finding it offered little more than a pub, they continued into Betws-y-Coed, where they mingled with tourists and bought food.

He remembered what shopping with Alicia used to be like. She could spend hours in a clothes shop, and he was surprised how quickly Trish returned with a bag and a smile. For the first time since Trish had introduced herself by hitting him over the head with a plank, he felt calm and safe once more. Perhaps it was the holiday feeling of the town. Wendell could never find him here, and Tyler, ex-SAS, would sort things out within a few days.

He couldn't have been more wrong.

***

That evening, Casey phoned his mum. He always did on a Monday night – his dutiful son routine – and she would fret if he missed it.

It proved to be a careless and near-fatal mistake.

'Is that you dear?' his mother asked. 'We've had a lot of phone trouble all day. Ringing when it shouldn't, hissing and crackling. Jim says there's probably a loose connection somewhere, but it seems better now.'

'I'm over in Wales for a bit at a friend's cottage. He's invited me for a few days.' It was largely true, but he still felt a pang of guilt at lying.

'That's nice dear. Whereabouts?'

'It's just outside a village called Penmachno.' He stumbled over the pronunciation. 'You can see Snowdon from the kitchen window.'

They chatted briefly and were about to hang up when he heard his stepfather murmur in the background. His mum relayed the message. 'Jim's just reminded me that someone was urgently trying to get hold of you on the phone yesterday evening. I don't know why he tried us. He didn't leave a name but he sounded German.'

CHAPTER TWENTY-SEVEN

Tyler was slouched in his car opposite Argus' house chewing on a tasteless cheese sandwich when his mobile rang. The voice, when he answered, wasn't one he recognised. Male. Sounded about fifty. Hint of a London accent. 'I was given your number by Charles Aston at the old folks' home. You visited him recently.'

'Uh-huh'

'He told me you were writing an official history of Bradon Defence Electronics.'

'For its upcoming anniversary. That's right.'

'Well, I used to work there. I've got a few stories you might be interested in.'

'Go on.'

'Let's meet. There's a pub on the main road just outside Great Missenden called *The Three Bells*. I can be there at nine o'clock this evening.'

'Okay. And what's your name?'

'*The Three Bells* at nine o'clock. I'll see you there,' and the line went dead.

**

The pub sparkled with lights on a stretch of main road that lacked streetlamps. Tyler swung into the dark car park an hour early. Old habits, but he never took chances. Caution was a way of life in The Service. In Afghanistan it had become as normal as breathing – in order to *keep* breathing.

Tyler picked a deserted corner from where he could see the road and both entrances to the pub. Minutes ticked slowly past. Punters arrived and left but there was nothing suspicious. No one waited in the dark, just ordinary folks enjoying an evening out.

At fifteen minutes to nine, he decided to check out the inside. As he stepped out of the car and clicked the door shut behind him, an arm wrapped round his chest and pulled him off balance. A knife pricked at his neck, and Tyler smelt cigarette-tainted breath.

Adrenaline pulsed through his veins, but Tyler forced himself not to move. Didn't want the knife opening up his throat by accident.

The voice when it came was deep and rumbling with a slight wheeze, different to the one on the phone. It gave the impression it belonged to a large overweight man. 'You're careless mate, to let me jump you like that.' Tyler said nothing. 'Why are you asking questions about companies like MSA?'

'I'm not. If you're talking about my meeting with Charles Aston, it was Bradon Defence Electronics I was asking about.' It was hard to speak with the blade so tight across his windpipe.

'Now the truth.' The knife pricked the skin.

'Look, I'm just an author. BDE's owner employed me to write the company's history. That's all.' Tyler slowly adjusted his leg positions to recover his balance. 'If you take that knife away, I'll explain.'

The blade seemed to hesitate. Perhaps he couldn't simultaneously think and hold a weapon steady. After a moment, he said, 'Tell me like this.'

Tyler sighed. 'I'm a writer. I told you. I'm collecting stories about BDE for a book to mark its fiftieth anniversary. That's all.'

'So why were you asking Charles Aston about MSA?'

'I wasn't. In passing he told me how BDE and MSA were both formed from the same company when it split. That was all. I've no interest in MSA.' *But all of a sudden now, I've become very interested.*

'And what about when you was over Guildford way, hanging about in that wood. What was you doing there?'

'What d'you mean?' Stall for time while quickly thinking of an excuse. Was this the bloke he'd fought there?

'What was you doing there?'

'I was meant to be meeting one of BDE's employees. He said he had some stuff for the book and could I meet him there.'

There was a pause. He doesn't know what to do next, Tyler thought. Just a thug hired to ask questions he didn't understand.

Tyler heard a car approaching slowly. Headlamps

washed across the hedgerow opposite. It was turning in. His assailant was momentarily distracted, slightly loosened his grip. Tyler sensed him turning to look.

In that second, Tyler dug his heels into the ground for leverage and smashed his head backwards into the man's face. He grabbed the arm with the knife and twisted viciously, then beat the hand repeatedly into the side of the BMW until the weapon dropped into the mud. The grip round his chest disappeared. Tyler spun round and hammered a fist into the stomach. A grunt. He grabbed the man's head and slammed him face-first into the car window, pinned him there with his full body weight, yanked his assailant's arm up his back.

The car pulled up at the front of the pub but Tyler ignored it. Doors slammed. Female voices chattered, and stilettos tapped across concrete.

Tyler put his mouth close to the man's ear 'What's this all about?'

No reply.

Tyler rammed a knee hard into the base of his assailant's spine. Another grunt. 'Tell me. Who sent you?'

'No one.' It was more a gasp than an answer.

Twist the arm tighter. Rewarded with a gasp of pain. 'Why are you here?' Tyler snarled in his ear.

The man sucked in air. 'Just to find out who you are, why you was asking about MSA and to tell you to stop snooping.'

'Well, I told you the truth. There's nothing more to it than that. I don't care anything about MSA. Take that message back. Now, who sent you?'

A mumble.

'Say again?'

Tyler leant forward. He didn't hear the footstep behind him. At the last second, he felt the whoosh of air as a club hammered into the back of his skull. Too late to do anything.

It sent a bolt of lightning through his head. Ears hissed. Vision tunnelled into monochrome. Tyler slumped forward into darkness.

CHAPTER TWENTY-EIGHT

The attack came at three the following morning.

The incessant wail of the alarm jerked Casey from sleep. His heart pounded while he spent a few dazed seconds trying to work out what the noise was. *Craig's intruder system!* He scrambled out of bed and grabbed clothes from the chair, rolling them into a ball while he ran for the lounge. 'Trish,' he yelled, but she was already up and powering the TV.

He forced bare feet into shoes while the grey ghostly images of the night vision cameras flicked into place one-by-one on the screen. He was praying it was only a deer when a smudgy shape in one view resolved into a tall figure that moved steadily towards the house. It seemed to have no neck, and had a rucksack on its back; there was no mistaking Wendell's outline.

'Move,' Casey screamed. They each grabbed their bundle of clothes.

He raced to the kitchen and turned the key slowly, trying

to prevent even the slightest click. Trish leaned over him and quietly slid back the bolts. Cautiously, Casey eased open the door, met instantly by cold night air that tore through his pyjamas and bit into his body. He snatched a torch from the side and led the way. Trish quietly pushed the door closed, and they darted along the narrow track. Faint moonlight lit the path, and they both kept the torches off until they were well into the trees.

Trish was right behind him. A quick glance told Casey she was still in the T-shirt and shorts she had slept in, but she had at least managed to push her feet into trainers. Their torch beams danced across the undergrowth as they raced through the woods. It looked so different in the dark that he almost missed the turn towards the stream.

He paused, wildly sweeping his torch around the trees in panic. Trish came up behind him, gasping. 'That way,' she said, waving an arm to his left. His beam showed the narrow opening through a clump of scrubby bushes, and they darted through. The sound of water spurred him on.

The cascades glowed in the moonlight. Casey jumped the stream but slipped as he landed. His hand smacked into the stone face of the gorge, and the torch flew from his hand. He heard it bounce on the rocks before it splashed into the water.

Trish landed behind him. 'You all right?'

'I've dropped my torch.'

'Leave it.'

She flicked her torch beam up the defile ahead and picked out their footing as they climbed the steep path up to the track and then ran for the car. Casey reached into his bundle of clothes and found the car keys. He was shivering, despite the climb.

He tossed the clothes on to the back seat and threw himself in, gunned the engine, and was already careening down the track before Trish had closed her door. She hugged herself to keep warm, her clothes and handbag on her lap.

Casey glanced down into the gorge as they passed the top and thought he saw the flicker of a torch in the trees. He switched on his headlights, and the car barrelled down the road with the engine screaming.

Casey fought the wheel as his Clio slipped on the loose surface and scattered grit down the hillside. The narrow track had no safety barriers, and to their right, the road fell away steeply into the valley below. To their left: solid rows of trees.

His legs were shaking, making his control of the pedals clumsy. He peered ahead for the next bend. Trish pulled out her phone, and the light from its screen lit her pale face. 'I'll have a map up in a second.'

Casey suddenly braked hard. A finger post in the road he didn't have time to read. Right, Tyler had said, he was sure, and he slewed the car in that direction. He lost control on the grit, and the back end spun away for a moment. Dust flew up in the headlights and coated the windscreen.

He had control again, and they skidded down a rutted track. It felt like the car was being shaken to pieces. Trish gripped the grab handle with one hand, trying to hold the phone steady with the other.

They bounced violently on the compacted stones and mud. 'Slow up or you'll kill us anyway,' Trish yelled above the scream of the engine.

Casey eased off. The road was empty.

'There's a T ahead,' Trish said. 'Go left and then you should be on a proper tarmac road.' The headlights picked up the junction a second later, and Casey stomped on the brakes.

In a few moments, they were running smoothly on asphalt, and Casey let out a deep breath. It was too narrow to do more than thirty or forty but at least it was a proper road.

'How the hell did he find us?' Casey asked.

'Craig?'

'No. He wouldn't have shown us that route up the stream if he'd intended to shop us.'

There was silence for a moment before Casey said, 'My phone.'

'What?'

'Kurt Wendell must have found my phone. It had my mum's number in it. He must have...' He tailed off, remembering his earlier conversation with his mother and her comment about the problems with their line all that morning. 'He bugged my mum and stepdad's phone. I'm an idiot – when I spoke to her, I described where we were. Wendell must have heard every word.' He smacked the steering wheel. 'I'm so damned stupid!'

Trish didn't reply. She bent forward, slipped off her

trainers and started to dress. She awkwardly wriggled into jeans over her shorts, pulled a top over her head and squirmed into it past the seatbelt.

Suddenly headlamps reflected in the rear mirror, approaching fast. He eased down on the accelerator, edged their speed up to fifty, and gripped the wheel tighter. Still the lights gained.

Trish sensed his reaction and looked behind. 'It can't be him.'

'I'm not taking that chance. It's coming up very fast.'

He rammed his foot to the floor, and the Clio surged forward. Trish turned back to her phone's map. 'There's a village up ahead. We might be able to lose him there.' She squinted at the display, struggling to keep it steady. 'There's a building on the right round the next bend. Turn immediately before that, then take first left.'

In a second the house loomed in the windscreen. He stamped on the brakes, and the car juddered violently. *Slow down, damn you.* At the last second, he hauled on the wheel.

With a squeal, the car turned, clipped and mounted the kerb. Something grated down the side. He spun the wheel, and the car bounced back on to the road before they swerved left into the next side street.

A glance in the mirror. Darkness. Then a moment later, headlamps again flickered behind them. Closer.

Dark houses either side now, hedges, an occasional streetlamp.

'Next right.'

A smooth turn. He rammed it into third gear, tore away.

Several cars parked ahead now. Without slowing, he swung round them.

'Keep going straight. There's a crossroads.'

Casey didn't stop, just prayed as they shot across the deserted junction.

Still headlights behind. Trish twisted briefly in her seat, then back to her phone.

'Where now?' Casey yelled.

'Don't know.'

'We've got to lose him.'

His foot was hard against the floor. The speedometer edged up further, but the lights still rapidly gained on them. They lit the interior of Casey's car. He felt vulnerable, a silhouette, a perfect target for a gunshot.

He didn't see the little van in time.

It turned out of a side road up ahead, and they were on it in seconds. Trish yelled and braced herself. Casey barely had time to react.

He stomped hard on the brakes, setting the ABS chattering as it battled to maintain control. Casey tried to swing round the van, almost made it, but the back of his Clio fishtailed.

The sound of metal grating on metal reverberated around them. The Clio bounced off the side of the van and spun helplessly. The tiny van was knocked sideways into a wall, and glass rained across the pavement before the vehicle ricocheted back into Wendell's path.

Wendell ploughed into the side of it. Casey's car stalled, coming to a halt sideways-on in the road. With horror,

Casey watched through the side window as the van jerked under the impact and then spun away. Wendell's car scraped down the side of it. A tyre shredded from one of them, sending strips of rubber spinning into the air under the streetlamp.

Casey twisted the key, and the engine roared back into life. Trish turned to peer through the window. He slammed the car into gear and accelerated hard. 'I'm not stopping. Kurt Wendell's back there and we're on his hit list. I'm not going back to meet him.'

Trish muttered something he didn't hear.

Casey kept to the speed limit and realised his arms and legs were shaking. As they crossed the Conway River a few minutes later, he saw the welcoming glow of a 24-7 petrol station. He turned into the forecourt and pulled up beside the stone-built shop. Casey cut the engine and laid back, limbs quivering. 'That was horrific,' he muttered.

He grabbed what clothes he'd managed to bring with him, and pulled them over his pyjamas, then got out to check the damage.

The air was fresh and cool. Fluorescents lights cast long shadows across the side of the car, but he could clearly see a pair of long scratches down the rear door and buckled bare metal near the wheel arch. 'At least it's driveable,' he said as he climbed back in.

He lay back and closed his eyes, still shaking. Trish was rummaging in her bag, and Casey heard her opening a cigarette packet. 'I'll step out for a quick smoke,' she said.

She never got the chance.

The roar of a powerful engine filled the cabin. Casey jerked his eyes open and twisted in his chair, blinded by light as a large car with a single working headlight swung across the back of them to block their exit before it jerked to a halt.

Before Casey's hand could even touch the handle, the door was wrenched open.

There was nowhere to run.

CHAPTER TWENTY-NINE

Trish stared in horror as the driver's door was yanked open and the barrel of a large pistol appeared in the gap. 'Hands on the wheel and do not move,' a deep voice barked, accented faintly with German. She watched Matt obey. A rope was tossed across and landed in her lap. 'Tie her hands,' he said to Matt. 'And do it very tightly.' Numbly, she held out her arms, and Casey slipped the rope round her wrists. Her mind raced. Surely the petrol station's CCTV could see what was happening? They were probably already phoning the police.

'Tighter,' Wendell demanded, and Trish felt the rope dig into her skin. 'Now both of you get out and quietly get into the front of my car. 'You will drive,' he said, indicating Matt.

Wendell stood back, and Casey slowly climbed out. He reached for the keys that dangled in the ignition, but Wendell barked, 'leave them.'

Trish's legs were shaking, and she held the door to keep herself upright as she climbed out. Desperately, she looked toward the shop but the windows were out of sight. 'Come on. Move,' Wendell called.

She hesitantly climbed into Wendell's car. It was awkward to secure the seatbelt with tied hands, but she managed it eventually. When she looked up, Casey was slipping into the driver's seat beside her. He gave her a small smile of encouragement as if to say, 'It will all be okay,' but his eyes betrayed his fear.

Wendell slid into the back seat and prodded the muzzle into the nape of Casey's neck. Casey stiffened. 'Now drive. I will instruct you where to go. Just do not forget I can kill both of you in seconds, so do not try anything stupid. You will not manage it.'

'Okay,' Casey said. The key was already in the ignition.

They turned left out of the forecourt, and Wendell said with a laugh, 'You should not have stopped somewhere so obvious. Then I would never have found you again.'

They followed the coast for a short way, then back into England and joined the motorway network heading north. Trish was so tired. She laid her head back but sleep wouldn't come. Slowly the sky lightened. Signs for Manchester and Liverpool were replaced by those for Preston and Blackpool as sunrise turned into a morning of grey skies.

Wendell's mobile suddenly trilled. Trish twisted in her seat and saw him slide it from his inside pocket, but he kept his eyes firmly on her. She shuddered at the total lack of emotion in his look and turned back. He answered the call and listened for a while before replying in English. 'I assure you it will be ready for collection where we agreed on

Friday. It has already left the factory and will be on the final leg of its journey shortly. The border crossing has all been arranged. I'm overseeing it personally.' There was a pause and he signed off. She heard the rustle of his jacket as he put the phone back.

Gradually the roads narrowed. Dry stone walls closed in on either side. He was taking them somewhere he could shoot them without being seen or heard; a place where they would lie undiscovered.

It was nearly eight in the morning by the time they arrived at a farmhouse nestled among trees in a dip in the hills. Typical Yorkshire Dales, she thought. A two storey, grey stone façade. A black and white cat watched them from the front doormat as Casey swung the car onto the gravel and came to a halt facing the house. As Casey put on the handbrake and sat back, clearly exhausted, Wendell said, 'I want to learn what you know about Argus.' Trish was surprised at how calmly her brain acknowledged the realisation that Wendell was probably only saying it because he didn't want them to panic.

'Keys,' Wendell demanded and held out his hand, palms uppermost. 'Slowly.'

Trish tensed. This could be her moment. She coiled herself, ready to lash out, but some instinct warned Wendell and he withdrew his hand. 'Put them on the arm rest and then put your hands back on the wheel,' he said steadily. Casey obeyed. 'You,' he said talking directly to Trish who was half-turned in her seat. 'You put your hands on the dash.' With a sigh, she did as she was told.

'Wait where you are,' he commanded and let himself out of the car and took up station a few metres away on Trish's side. A chill wind blew around her neck from the open door but she still felt hot and sticky. Casey had closed his eyes, laid his head back, hands still on the wheel.

This was the end, she thought. They would be marched into those trees, forced to kneel. A bullet in the back of the head. Her breath came in short gasps. Her heart hammered. They had to do something, but her mind could no longer focus. Her thoughts were jumbled. Tears pricked at her eyes. *Someone help me.*

Movement at the front door of the house made her turn. A farmer stood in the doorway. Plump, fleshy face, florid. Short sandy hair and a donkey jacket that hung open to show a belly that sagged over a thick belt.

A double-barrelled shotgun rested across his arms.

The cat had disappeared. Trish caught an almost imperceptible nod pass between the two men, and the farmer crossed to the car and waited on Casey's side with the weapon now levelled. Wendell called, 'You two into the house.'

Trish's back and legs were stiff from the long drive, and she felt drained and sick.

'In,' Wendell shouted and raised his gun more precisely to point at her chest. Her heart was beating so fast, she wasn't sure she could make it as far as the door.

The farmer had disappeared inside with Casey, and she heard them cross stone flags. She staggered after them towards the black opening of the doorway. The bleating of sheep could be heard from behind the house. Trish tried to take a deep breath, but her throat seemed to constrict. Wendell was going to kill her. Images of his knife slash in Beth's back flashed through her mind, causing tears of panic to course down her cheeks.

She crossed the gravel feeling totally numb, clutching her bag in her tied hands. Shakily, she climbed up the stone steps into the house, met by warmth and a smell of fresh bread. She glanced to her left and saw an empty kitchen. Sprays of lavender hung in bunches along the top of the window. An Aga range cooker stood centrally in the middle of white painted units. Everywhere was neat and tidy, except for what looked like the contents of Casey's pockets on a stretch of work surface. 'Empty your pockets and put your handbag on the side.'

She stepped into the kitchen, feeling the warmth wrap around her. Wearily, she dropped her bag onto the worktop. 'Nothing in my pockets,' she muttered.

'Lean against the wall.' She did so, and he ran his hands over her clothes. Remembering she wore no bra, she screwed up her eyes and tried to ignore what was happening. At least he kept his massive hands away from her privates. She heard him step back. 'Upstairs,' he snapped.

With another deep breath, she turned and followed his instruction. The stairs creaked underfoot. It was dim inside the house and it took a while for her eyes to adjust. A couple of black and white photos of The Dales in winter hung on the wall, and there was one of a collie lying in front of a field of sheep.

'Turn right,' Wendell grunted as they reached the landing.

She obeyed. Casey was already entering a room at the end of a short corridor ahead of her. The farmer stood back, shotgun pointing at the carpet to allow her to pass and follow Casey into the room.

The curtains were open to reveal a view across rolling fields. Fluffy clouds played in a blue sky, and a brown horse nuzzled the wooden gate in a distant field.

The room held two single beds with floral eiderdowns, a padded chair, a Victorian mahogany wardrobe with decorative arched top, and a matching dressing table with a mirror that had lost its silvering round the edges.

She shuffled close to Casey and they stood with their backs to the window. At least they weren't being shot yet. Wendell stood in the doorway. 'I do not have time to talk to you at length now,' he said in his accented English. 'So, I have to make arrangements with my friend here. I have some urgent meetings to attend but when I am back, I want to hear in detail what you know about Argus. For now, I will take your word that you are not Argus and that you are a victim of blackmail just as I am.' He looked directly into Trish's eyes. She shuddered at their coldness. 'Please do not give my friends any trouble. I have told them they are free to shoot or maim you if you try to escape. As you can understand I am curious but I don't particularly care what happens to you. You are free to untie Ms McGowan's hands,' he added before he spun on his heels and left. The door clicked shut, a key was turned and withdrawn, and footsteps and murmuring voices retreated down the corridor.

Casey untied her hands, and she rubbed her wrists. He gave a sympathetic smile. 'Sorry,' he said quietly, and she shrugged.

A door in one wall led to an en-suite. At least she wouldn't have to sit here with her legs crossed as she was dying for a pee. She found an avocado pedestal sink with matching bath and loo in a sea of glossy beige tiles.

She locked the bathroom door and sat on the toilet with her head buried in her hands. She could hear Casey rattling the door to the corridor. She had no doubt that once Wendell had extracted all he could from them that he would take them out into the fields and put a bullet through their brains.

She sat there for a few minutes. She could hear Casey exploring the bedroom. Eventually, she took a deep breath and stood up, glancing at her face in the mirror. *Come on Trish. Where's all that famous grit and determination gone?* She washed her hands and then her face, enjoying the cold water. As there was no towel, she dried herself on the sleeve of her top, took another deep breath, raised her eyebrows to her reflection, and went back to the bedroom.

Casey was tugging at the sash window but it wasn't budging. She came and peered out beside him. It was a storey's drop on to concrete; not a great hope even if the window did open. They heard an engine start and then tyres crunching across the gravel. Wendell was leaving.

Trish perched on the edge of a bed, watching Casey as he stared down from the window. 'Do you believe what he said?' she asked. 'About wanting to talk to us when he got back?'

He turned to face her and shrugged. 'Who knows?' He thought about it. 'Maybe. Otherwise, he would already have killed us.'

'And once we've told him all we know about Argus …?'

He looked down, wouldn't hold her eyes. 'I'll guess he'll kill us.'

She felt her stomach churning. It was what she had concluded also. Her plan to use Wendell hadn't proved such a good one. She sighed heavily. 'We don't know how long we've got until he's back, so let's see if we can break out of here.'

He idly tugged at the window again. 'How are we going to manage that?'

She jumped up and checked the dressing table, but its drawers were empty, as was the wardrobe; not even a clothes hanger. A sense of beginning panic started to run through her. She tapped at the walls. Solid. Not like the flimsy rubbish her house was made from. She stood with hands on hips. There had to be some way.

She looked up thoughtfully. 'I wonder …' She jumped on the bed and tapped at the ceiling. 'We're on the top floor, right?'

'I think so.'

'Then there are no floorboards above, just a plasterboard ceiling, so we should be able to break into the roof space.'

'... and smash our way down outside the room,' Casey completed. There was excitement in his eyes again. 'We can give it a try.'

Trish stretched out her arms to touch the plaster above her head. 'You can just make out the nail heads, so we know where the joists are.'

Casey climbed on the other bed and pushed the palm of his hands against the ceiling. He pushed hard, but it was the mattress that moved. 'We need something sharp to cut into it.'

Trish looked around. There was nothing anywhere. They could break the light bulb perhaps, use the glass like a knife, but their hands would be sliced to bits before they were even halfway through.

The drawers, three of them – the handles were small and round, but perhaps...

She jumped down and yanked a drawer open. The handle was screwed into place with a bolt head on the inside. She pushed a thumb hard against it and tried to rotate the knob, but the whole thing just spun. Bed springs creaked as Casey pushed again at the ceiling. She jerked open the second drawer and repeated the exercise. This time, she felt the knob start to unscrew. She slid her nail into the slot to hold the head more firmly and slowly unthreaded the knob. With sudden excitement, she pulled the two halves free and jumped on to the bed. She gave the bolt a couple of turns back into the knob and held it with the smooth wooden sphere in her palm, a centimetre of metal bolt protruding upwards.

Trish hammered it into the plasterboard above her head. Paint flakes scattered into her upturned face. She hammered again – same spot. A brown crater appeared. Viciously, again and again. Lumps of plasterboard cracked away, hanging loose, held by their papery coating. She tore them away, letting them fall. Hammered again.

A hole, large enough for a fist. Beyond it, blackness. A clot of loft insulation brushed her face as it tumbled past her.

Seeing what she was doing, Casey quickly constructed a similar tool from the knob of the bottom drawer, and jumped up beside her. He struck it hard into the ceiling half a metre away. Paint flakes and plasterboard rained down on them. He put both hands into the gap and pulled hard, rewarded by a large section of board coming away. Casey let it fall.

'Not so much noise,' Trish hissed.

He nodded and attacked the next section. They were soon both covered in plaster and lumps of Rock Wool. Suddenly a jagged length of board fell away and thumped onto the bed in a cloud of dust. Casey plunged bare hands into the insulation that now flopped into the hole and tore it apart. Dropping the handmade tool into his pocket, he grabbed a beam and hauled himself up into the void.

She tried to follow. It was like doing pull-ups at school. Her arm muscles strained, but she couldn't make it.

'Grab a chair,' he whispered.

Trish climbed softly from the bed and tiptoed to the dressing table. She grabbed the chair, balanced it on the bed and awkwardly kneeled on the seat. It moved as its legs dug into the mattress, and she swayed precariously. She grabbed at the ceiling for support and cautiously stood using one hand flat against the plasterboard to steady herself as she reached into the hole. Trish felt the rough wood of a beam and pulled herself up into the black loft space. The chair toppled sideways on the mattress.

Bent over and holding the trusses above her head for balance, she used her feet to feel for the joists and slowly crept away from the hole into the black. Casey's whisper came out of the darkness ahead of her. 'If we can come down in one of the other rooms rather than the landing, we've a hope of not being spotted straightaway.'

Through the roof she could hear birds calling. A cobweb clung to her face, and she brushed it away. With every step she felt her legs shaking. Any second now she might fall, disappear through the ceiling and break her neck on the floor below.

'About here do you think?' Casey whispered from somewhere up ahead.

She tried to recall what she'd seen of the farmhouse layout. 'We must be the other side of the stairs by now, so yes.'

Trish almost bumped into him, just spotted the white of his shirt collar as she reached the joist he was already balanced on. She grabbed a roof truss to steady herself as she tottered on the narrow beam.

'Ready?' Casey asked

'Go for it.'

She heard him push aside insulation. 'This might be

noisy so the second we're down, we must move fast. Down the stairs and out.'

'I want my stuff back from the kitchen.'

'Here goes.' He smashed a foot into the middle of the board.

Dust kicked up around them. Trish covered her mouth, stifling a cough.

His foot slammed down again. A jagged crack of light appeared.

He kept kicking until a section of board fell away. It dangled for a moment before dropping. Casey coughed as well, choked by the dust. 'Come on.' Casey knelt beside the hole. Gripping the joists on either side of the opening, he lowered himself through, hanging for a second before letting go and dropping from sight.

CHAPTER THIRTY

Two hundred miles south, Tyler was back at the Four Oaks Care Home, impatient, angry, and still nursing a dull ache at the back of his head. He could have phoned, but he wanted to see the expression in the old man's eyes.

The thugs had asked about his discussion with old Charles Aston, so Argus had somehow learned of his visit. Tyler was determined to find out how she knew.

They again met in the lounge, Aston in the same chair he had occupied on Tyler's previous visit, but this time the room was busier, with most of the chairs taken by women with neat grey perms and old men reading oversized newspapers. Two nurses in starched navy uniforms bustling among them with small trays.

Tyler tried to keep his voice down. He glared at Charles Aston, who seemed to shrink away from him. 'Who did you tell about my visit the other day?' Tyler snapped.

'It wasn't secret, was it?' Aston stammered in alarm with his rattling dentures adding sibilance to his words. 'I mean, you didn't say it was, did you?'

'No, but who did you tell?'

Aston shrugged his bony shoulders. 'I mentioned the book you're doing to a few people,' he said defensively. 'I told Matron, although I don't think she particularly listened. She always just lets me ramble on. And there was some bloke doing research about loneliness in care homes. I think I mentioned it to him. He was keen to know if we received enough visitors.'

So that was it. Tyler nodded. 'I left you my phone number on a bit of paper. Do you still have it?'

Embarrassment swept across Aston's face. 'I think I mislaid it. I had it on the table in my room, but when I came to put it somewhere safe, I couldn't find it. At my age you get a bit doddery and forgetful, I'm afraid.'

Tyler patted the old man's shoulder. 'No worries,' he said.

On Tyler's way out, he asked the little Irish nurse who manned reception about the researcher, but she frowned. 'I don't think we've had anyone like that for ages,' she said. Tyler signed himself out and scanned the other entries in the book, but no-one else had put Aston down as the person they were visiting.

But how had Argus known he had come here in the first place? He pondered that as he pushed through the front door towards his car. There was something he was missing. His hand was on the car's door lever when he changed his mind, went to the boot, and reached into the box Tommy had given him. He pulled out the scanner, switched it on, and slowly walked round the BMW with it. This wasn't what he'd been given it for, but he couldn't see why it wouldn't work.

It remained silent. Tyler shrugged and was about to put it back when it beeped once. He stopped and held it closer to the bodywork while working his way towards the back of the car. A second bleep, louder. When Tyler bent and wiped the scanner along the rear bumper, it lit up so brightly it almost jumped from his hand. Poking his fingers up behind the plastic near the wheel arch, Tyler felt something the size of a matchbox and prised it free – a tracker.

So *that* was how Argus knew about the visit. He bounced it in his hands a few times, thinking back. Argus must have attached it while Tyler was watching Matt Casey sitting in the lay-by. A precaution in case her thugs didn't manage their job.

Tyler was about to smash it when he changed his mind. He quickly glanced at the windows to ensure no-one was watching, then bent to the neighbouring car and pushed it into the gap behind the front bumper. It was unlikely the adhesive would hold for long, but it would be enough.

He grinned broadly as he pulled out of the car park and started the journey to Argyle's house. He had a plan on how to retrieve that diary and he was confident it was going to work.

***

He found a space close to the house, but out of sight of the front windows, and slipped on a pair of headphones. As soon as he'd returned from Wales the previous day, he had driven here and found her car missing. Once the builders were again busy, he had slipped into the house using the stolen keys and distributed the bugs he'd collected from Tommy, originally intended for Casey's flat. He knew there were a few dead spots around the place, but he'd done what he could to minimize them.

It was time to set things running.

He adjusted the volume. To a passer-by, it would look as if he was enjoying music from his phone. This time, she was in – from the headphones came an occasional rustle of paper, then the tap as Argus laid down her pen. Opera warbled at low volume in the background.

It was time. Tyler took off the headphones, picked up his mobile, and set it to hide his outgoing number before dialling Argus' house. It was answered on the third ring.

Tyler said, 'Good morning, Argus. I believe you have an old diary that's worth a lot of money to someone. I want to buy it from you and I'm offering forty thousand pounds.' He had no intention of paying of course, but he'd carefully picked a figure that would sound realistic yet still highly tempting.

There was silence. At the other end, the woman cleared her throat. 'I think there's been a mistake. You must have the wrong number.'

'No, Argus. I'm speaking to the right person.'

'You've dialled wrongly.'

'I don't think so. I'll be at your house tomorrow at this time and I'll bring cash with me. You can show me the diary, and assuming it's genuine, the money is yours. It's a good offer.' He hung up before she could reply and quickly slipped the headphones back on.

Through them, he heard the opera being switched off and soft footfalls as she paced back and forth. It took her five minutes to decide, then Tyler heard her pick up the phone and tap in a number. There was a pause. Just a shame he hadn't bugged her phone line too, but there was rarely any point to it these days – too many people just used mobiles. Tyler shut his eyes, imagining the scene in her office room.

'Hello darling. It's me. Have you got a moment?' She sounded nervous, unsure.

A pause, then, 'Well, I've had a really strange phone call and I don't know what to do. I thought it was a wrong number, but he was insistent it wasn't and he said he's going to come here tomorrow.' Another silence. 'He kept using the name *Argus* and going on about a diary.' A longer pause. 'He offered me forty thousand pounds for it. I'm scared, Hugo. Do you think I should call the police?'

Tyler frowned as he scribbled the name *Hugo* into his notebook and put a large question mark beside it. But why talk about going to the police? he wondered.

The reply was obviously short because almost instantly she asked, 'Why not?' Another frustrating silence. 'Okay darling. That's a good idea. I'll do that. Thanks. I feel so much better already.' She put the phone down and left the room.

An hour later, Tyler heard her come down the stairs and put something heavy on the hall floor. There was a rattle of keys and the opening of the front door. Moments later, a car engine started, and her large Volvo swept past him and away up the road.

Tyler followed with a grin. The bait had been taken. He was sure she was about to lead him to the diary. He pulled out of the parking space and followed, searching through his phone contacts with one hand as he drove. Eventually he found the one he wanted, a number he hadn't used for a long time. When he got through, he said simply, 'I need a gun. And I need it within twenty-four hours.' It was time to step up the pace.

CHAPTER THIRTY-ONE

Tyler had still been in the Four Oaks Care Home when Trish had cautiously lowered herself through the hole in the ceiling. She dangled briefly from the rafters before dropping nimbly into the room below.

They'd come down in a musty box room. A yellowing mattress was propped against one wall. Standing against another was a wooden chair with a broken leg, and a bookcase of faded paperbacks, all thick with dust. Casey already had the door open a crack and was peering through. He turned to her. 'Ready?'

She nodded, and Casey quickly pushed the door wide and darted into the corridor. He paused at the top of the stairs and cautiously made his way down. Trish followed close behind, straining to catch the slightest sound. The stairs creaked, and they froze for a second before Casey gently took the next step.

She could see the front door at the foot of the stairs, inviting. She hardly dared breathe.

At the bottom, Casey peered round the door into the kitchen before darting inside. Trish followed seconds later and found him standing at the worktop sweeping his confiscated items back into his pockets. Trish snatched her bag, darted to the front door, hesitated on the step to quickly scan the yard, then sprinted from the building. Her feet scrunched loudly on the gravel, and she could hear Casey at her heels.

They sprinted for the back of a row of barns – the only cover close to the house – and disappeared into the shadows between them. The corrugated-iron walls towered above them to form a narrow canyon down which they ran. It had become a dumping ground, and they dodged piles of old animal-feed bags, discarded pallets, and rotten wood posts. They could hide among this lot, she thought, as she nearly slipped on a corner of an abandoned tarpaulin.

They stopped at the far end of the buildings, panting. This side, the barns formed a horseshoe around a concrete yard, facing a track that disappeared into the distance between drystone walls that flanked a patchwork of fields. Sheep grazed lazily in the sun. 'Across those fields,' Trish whispered. 'I don't think you can see them from the house.'

Casey sprinted from cover. She darted after him, powering across the concrete towards the fields and their freedom.

At the end of the yard, they veered away from the track towards the first drystone wall. A shout from behind them bellowed across the concrete. A deep man's voice, thick with a Yorkshire accent: 'Stay right there and don't move.' She glanced over her shoulder to see the farmer standing in the mouth of one of the barns raising a double-barrelled shotgun.

Casey was nearly at the stone wall a few metres ahead of her. He threw himself over and dropped from sight. She was four strides behind.

'You stop or I'll shoot the pair of you.'

She had almost reached it when the gunshot echoed round the yard. The face of the wall in front of here exploded into splinters. Weeds at its base were shredded by buckshot.

'Stay there and you won't get hurt,' came the shout from behind her.

One more stride. The second shot came as she scrambled over. The vertical stones on top were sharp, digging into her hands and legs as she threw her body over and landed close to Casey's crouching figure.

Shot peppered the wall where she'd been a split-second before. She was panting hard.

They took off along the line of the wall, doubled over to keep out of sight, Casey leading as they ran parallel to the road. She imagined the farmer reloading his weapon and striding after them. Fifty yards ahead, another wall blocked their way, dividing the field into two. Until they reached it, all the farmer had to do was enter the field behind them and he would have a clear shot.

The ground was uneven, making it hard to run. She glanced over her shoulder, couldn't see him yet.

Casey reached the next wall, vaulted over, and

disappeared. Trish's lungs burned. She gasped for air. Nearly there. She grabbed the top of the wall, but the stone came away in her hands. She grabbed another, used it to haul herself up, then rolled over the wall and dropped into the grass beyond. Buckshot peppered the stones where she'd just been.

Casey was already a good distance ahead to her left keeping close to the wall that headed away from the track. She sucked in a deep breath and raced after him. Mustn't stop, she chanted and tried to ignore the growing pain in her chest. The wall they were following stopped when it reached a row of trees, the field boundary marked by another drystone wall, grey and miserable, barring the way ahead. Casey was now only a few metres from it. Watching him instead of her feet, she tripped, and her knee crashed into hard earth. She tumbled sideways, and her shoulder smashed into the wall. She gasped, tried to push herself her, but pain burned in her ankle.

Suddenly a hand grabbed her wrist and pulled her up. Casey must have seen her fall and turned back. He supported her, almost dragged her towards the next wall.

Those wasted seconds had allowed their pursuer to gain on them, and another shout followed them up the gentle incline. It was hard to make out what he was calling because he was out of breath.

They reached the final wall. Trish grabbed the cold stone on top and hauled herself over. Casey was doing the same beside her when the shotgun boomed again. Stone chips flew into the air around them, and Casey cried out as he threw himself over and tumbled into the grass in the cover of the wall.

He lay for a second, clutching his leg, then pushed himself up with a grimace. He reached out again for Trish's hand. 'Can you run?'

'I think so.'

'Into the trees.' They stumbled into the shadows of oak and birch. Quickly, the trees engulfed them, muffling sound as they ran into its dark interior. It was colder, and the air was full of the smell of damp leaves.

Trish gritted her teeth against the pain that burned in her ankle and the stitch that worsened in her side. She slowed, squeezing her side with one hand. 'Slow down,' she gasped. 'I can't keep up.'

Casey looked desperately behind them. 'Just a bit deeper into the trees,' he pleaded and pulled her on.

It was another minute before he finally stopped. They stood with hands on hips, bowed forwards, gasping for air.

She peered back through the trunks. No sign of their pursuer. Casey pulled up his trouser leg, and Trish was startled to see blood smeared across the skin. He rubbed it. 'Did you get hit?' Trish asked in alarm.

'It's only scratches from bits of flying stone. You ready to go on?'

Trish straightened and was about to answer when a loud, angry howl of an engine filled the air and cut her short. She looked behind them. 'What the hell's that?'

'I dunno,' said Casey, 'but we've got to keep going.'

Once more they ran between the trees, but Trish's stitch

grew to a vicious pain in her side. 'I can't do this,' Trish panted after a minute. 'Leave me behind. You go and tell Craig what's happened, get his help.' She just wanted to lie down.

'Don't be stupid. We're in this together.'

The engine roar grew louder, and Casey swore. Trish followed his gaze and caught a glimpse of a quad bike hurtling towards them through the trees.

'Get to a denser area. Quick,' Casey cried and turned sharply to their right, gripping her hand as she followed.

They crouched in the densest section of undergrowth they could find, panting. Ferns, grass, and brambles hid them. The quad bike seemed to be circling. Several times, she caught sight of its black and red chassis through the trees.

'We're trapped,' she whispered. 'The moment we break out of here, he'll be on us in seconds with that thing.' The howl of the engine filled her head.

'Maybe,' he said thoughtfully. 'Unless we un-mount him.'

'What d'you mean?'

'I'm not sure. Wait here. I'll be back in a second.' Casey released her hand and silently disappeared the way they'd come. The engine was quieter now as the farmer reached the point on his circle farthest from them. Moments later, Casey was back. 'I think I've got it,' he said. His eyes glinted. 'Come with me. And be totally silent.'

She followed, keeping low, testing each foot for noise before transferring her weight. Not that anyone would hear them over the racket of that engine. Still the quad bike circled menacingly a short distance away. He doesn't know where we are, she thought.

Casey crouched beside her and whispered, 'There's a long branch over there. Between the two of us we can easily move it across a track. If we can get him down here in some way, we can use it to knock him off.'

'Are you mad?'

He put his fingers to his lips. The growl of the engine was louder now, coming up slowly from the right. 'Get right down and stay still.'

She lay flat in the leaves and closed her eyes, smelt the decaying vegetation, heard the quad bike pass close by and continue on its circle as it searched them out. A vulture circling its prey.

'Okay. This way,' Casey said as soon as it had passed. He darted forward and grabbed a fallen branch. It looked nearly three metres long, thick and heavy. 'Give me a hand.'

They hauled it across a gap between two trees and piled leaves over it. Casey said, 'We'll shout or something to get him down through this gap in the trees. There's plenty of undergrowth either side we can hide in. As he comes past, we'll lift it up, one of us either side, hold it like a bar. It'll take him right off. We can jump on the bike and be gone before he knows what happened.'

'How are we going to get him down here?' The engine was at its quietest now at the farthest point from them. It would be twenty seconds before it was close again.

'My jacket's bright,' he said and pulled it off. He ran

down the path and hung it over a bush so that its blue material stood out clearly. 'You get over to that side out of sight, and I'll take the other. I'll get his attention and as soon as I signal, we'll both lift our ends to chest height. Okay?'

She nodded and looked round wildly for the best place to hide, choosing to duck behind a dense bush. Trish crouched low - fingers curled round her end of the log. The quad bike roared closer. She bit her lip. Her heart pounded in her chest.

The heavy throb of the engine filled the woods.

She couldn't see where Casey had hidden himself, and when he let out a long yell, she jumped violently. At the same moment, Casey hurled a handful of stones along the track so that they clattered through the bushes around his jacket and made the foliage quiver.

The response was instant. The engine revved. From her hiding place, Trish saw its black and red body like some giant insect as it turned and powered towards them. From her hiding place, she could see the driver's face, grim, his eyes focussed on Casey's jacket.

Trish tensed. Any moment now. She shifted her legs ready and tightened her grip on the wood. The engine's roar throbbed in her rib cage.

Over the din she heard Casey shout, 'Now.' She felt the bough being lifted at its far end. She jumped to her feet and jerked her end upwards. The driver swung his head towards her; alarm and confusion filled his face.

He had just started to raise the shotgun when he ploughed into the raised branch.

CHAPTER THIRTY-TWO

The impact from the strike ripped the rotting bough from Trish's hands. The wood shattered. Pieces of the branch flew into the air around their pursuer and scattered into the undergrowth. The blow knocked the rider backwards, sending him sprawling across the narrow track. The engine cut, and the quad bike crashed into undergrowth.

Casey was already up and running towards it. 'Come on,' he yelled as he heaved the quad bike upright. The farmer's body was slumped on the ground like an abandoned scarecrow. She glanced at it then ran to join Casey. There was no sign of where the shotgun had landed.

The engine coughed into life, and Casey revved it hard. 'On the back,' he screamed over its roar. She jumped on behind him and clung to his waist. When they swept past where Casey had thrown his coat, he grabbed it with one hand and accelerated away.

She buried her face in his back as they raced between the trees. Wind howled past her. They bounced across the rough ground, and Trish opened her eyes a crack in time to see them burst out of the wood into an area of scrubby grass. A pair of horses in the adjacent field shied at the disturbance and galloped away in fright.

There was a road ahead, and they tore towards it but another drystone wall barred their way. Trish turned, but for now there was no sign of the farmer. Casey drove parallel to the wall until they found a gate, and seconds later they were roaring along tarmac. It was a risk to use the road, she knew. If the farmer used his Range Rover, he would quickly find them, but the road was necessary if they were to put distance between them and their pursuer. She also reckoned any police car that saw them would instantly pull them over, especially with their lack of helmets. Were these things even legal on the highway?

They drove for two miles and abandoned the quad bike on the edge of Hornby where the fields gave way to rows of stone houses. 'Let's see if we can find a bus to get us out of here,' Casey said while they hurried along the footpath. Trish's ears still rang from the engine's roar.

They reached an A-road that sliced through the rows of creamy-stone buildings. Cars rumbled in both directions over a bridge, and in the distance, they could see a church tower. They headed towards it in the hope it marked the village centre. A couple of minutes later, they found a general stores in a row of terraced houses. A bus stop stood outside.

They crowded round the faded timetable, their faces close. 'There's a bus all the way to Lancaster,' Casey said excitedly. He glanced at his watch. 'It'll come through in ten minutes.'

'I'll grab something to eat and drink from the shop,' Trish said. 'You wait here in case it comes early. I'll be as quick as I can.' She checked her handbag and was relieved to see Wendell hadn't taken her purse or credit cards.

By the time she emerged clutching a bag of provisions, Casey was pacing up and down outside. He took the proffered roll with a word of thanks. They kept their backs to the road, pretending to study the notices in the window but watching for the bus in the reflections. They both fidgeted nervously.

'I'm worrying about my car,' Matt muttered between bites.' I don't know what's going to happen to it.'

'It leaves us both transport-less at the moment,' Trish said round a mouthful of ham. Her mind reeled as she remembered Daisy bonnet-down in the river.

'So, what do we do now?' She shook her head in despair. 'We're on the run without cars and nowhere left to hide.'

He didn't answer immediately. 'We're going to have to rely on Craig. He's the professional.'

'I just don't trust him.'

'But he's the only person we've got. We can't go to the police so what else can we do?'

A line of slow-moving cars passed, caught behind a cyclist, and she hid her face, heart pounding. It felt as though everyone was staring at the back of her head. *Come on bus, get us out of here. I can't stand much more of this.*

Once the cars passed, she said, 'Any ideas on how to

hide from Wendell in the meantime?'

Casey nodded. 'I've been thinking about that. My team at work is heading up towards the Lake District to demonstrate our UAV to the Ministry of Defence. That's got to be a good a place to hide. We'll be staying in a hotel near an RAF site. Why don't you come with me while Craig sorts everything else? We'll be safe up there.'

At that moment, the bus hissed to a stop, and they clambered onboard. Trish let out a deep sigh of relief as she sunk into a seat at the back with Casey. She twisted her head to take a final look in the direction they'd come, and was relieved to see the road behind was empty.

Casey said, 'So why don't I ring my boss, tell him I'm cutting my holiday short, and ask to join the demo after all? I can offer to head up there under my own steam.'

She nodded slowly. It sounded as good an idea as any. 'Do you want to borrow my phone, then?'

Casey nodded and wiped his hands on his jeans.

A few minutes later it was all arranged. She couldn't help but smile when Casey told his boss that he'd been thinking about what he'd said before about how important the trials were and so had managed to cut his holiday short in order to be free to help. When he'd finished, he turned back to Trish.

'The team's staying at the River Side Hotel in a place called Gilsland. It's north-east of the Lakes.' He handing back the phone. 'They'll arrange a room for me starting this evening. I obviously couldn't ask them about one for you. We'll just have to sort that when we get there and hope there's one free.'

'Okay. Now for Craig Tyler,' she said and called his number. He answered on the third ring and, when she described what had happened in Wales, he started to swear so loudly that she could well imagine him as the SAS sergeant he'd once been.

After a brief conversation, she ended the call and switched the phone back off. 'Not happy,' she said simply, 'But he says he *might* help us with Wendell after he's got that diary back.' Not exactly the gallant hero she'd hoped for. She laid back and closed her eyes, suddenly exhausted. She realised she'd managed barely six hours' sleep over the past two days.

At least she would be safe wherever this place was Casey had mentioned. She didn't realise she was heading closer to the centre of the trouble than she'd been before.

***

The River Side Hotel, according to the leaflet Trish found in her room, sat "on the banks of the tranquil River Irthing close to historic Hadrian's Wall and within an easy drive of the Lake District National Park." It had originally been "a splendid Georgian manor house built in 1821" but from what they'd seen on their way in, its pair of single-storey extensions, large conservatory, and brick built "health and wellness centre" had turned it into a typical modern sprawl drained of any original character.

Standing at her bedroom window, she looked down at a neatly manicured lawn. It was fringed by trees and stretched to a distant hedgerow and what she guessed was the river that gave the hotel its name. The grassy hills beyond glowed yellow in the early evening sunlight. Maybe while Matt was busy at the RAF base, she would do some painting if she could find art supplies somewhere.

She showered and changed into the new clothes she'd bought along with toiletries and make-up when they'd changed busses at Lancaster. She could never have imagined how much better it felt to be clean. Once she was happy her hair was correctly arranged again, and had applied a little concealer and the lightest touch of eyeliner and mascara, she went along the corridor and tapped lightly at Casey's door.

He, too, had changed into the freshly purchased clothes. He looked good in slim jeans and a dark sweat-shirt.

'When's everyone else from your company getting here?' she asked once he'd shut the door behind her.

'They're here already. I saw some of them milling around the bar when we registered.' She hesitated, feeling the need for a drink and a meal but not wanting to embarrass Matt by turning up with him. That would raise too many awkward questions and lewd remarks. It was clear Matt was having similar concerns. 'Shall we just go and look at the restaurant menu?' he suggested. 'I don't need to meet up with everybody yet.'

The sounds in her stomach told her the restaurant would be a great idea.

A few minutes later they were crossing the modern reception of marble and dark wood between palms that grew in polished chrome planters. It was then that the shouting started. A pair of raised male voices boomed from the bustling bar area that she could see through a large archway. They could easily be heard from reception and she couldn't help but slow up to listen. One of them yelled, 'What the hell are you doing staying here?'

'Come on. You knew full well we were going to be at the trials too. Where else d'you expect us to stay around here?'

'You're only going for this contract to spite us. Haven't you ever grown up?'

'You got something to be afraid of? Scared we're going to better you again?'

Trish heard a titter at her side and turned to see one of the cleaning staff beside her. 'Grown men acting like kids,' she said to Trish with a raised eyebrow. 'But it's good for entertainment.'

The voices faded into murmurs as Casey and Trish continued down the corridor. 'What was that all about?' Trish asked.

'That was our CEO. I don't know who the other guy was but from the sound of it, maybe someone from a company called MSA. We guessed they were also tendering a bid. It's run by the uncle of our boss, but they're bitter rivals. It's said the only reason MSA got into drones in the first place was because we were designing them and they just wanted to beat us.'

'Are they really that childish?'

'Guess so.' They'd reached the restaurant, and Trish cast an eye across the menu that stood on a dais in the middle of the floor. How could they charge so much? 'I'm not paying that,' she said in disgust. 'It's ridiculous. You're alright –

you're on an expense ticket now.' She paused. 'I'll get something back in the village.'

'I don't need to eat here. I'll come with you to find somewhere better.'

'I'll be fine. You need to meet up with your colleagues anyway. I'll see you later.' She turned and headed back through reception. The arguing seemed to have stopped.

She strode down the road in the surprisingly warm evening air towards the short terrace of buildings that masqueraded as a high street. She hadn't paid much attention to them when they'd arrived and suddenly wondered if she was going to end up hungry. She tried the sleepy little pub, but the barman told her they didn't serve food in the evening. The nearby baker's shop had blinds down over its window, but a little farther along, she found a small tourist café that was still open. It was not cordon-bleu and certainly a different league to what Matt would be enjoying.

Trish sat on a wobbly plastic seat in the window and propped her elbows on a tea-stained Formica table.

She'd only taken two bites of the burger when she saw it.

Her guts clenched, and she dropped the bun back on her plate. She had idly picked up a copy of the *Daily Mail* that someone had left on an adjacent chair. She had turned to page two but now stared in horror at the photograph half way down.

Hands shaking, she read the text above it, then fled from the café.

CHAPTER THIRTY-THREE

'What the hell do I do now?' Trish was almost in tears, her mind spinning. She had run straight to her hotel room and thrown herself face down on the bed, not daring to look for Matt in the bar or restaurant. Every ten minutes, she had jumped up and used the bedside phone to call to his room until he eventually answered and she had raced down the corridor to meet him. Now, she paced frantically up and down in front of his bedroom window, feeling as if everything was trying to crush her head.

Casey looked up from the newspaper she'd thrust into his hands. He stared at her. 'You're wanted for murder?'

Trish hadn't managed to read more than the first few lines. She nodded, biting her lip to stop it quivering. 'Cliff said the police wanted to talk to me, but I didn't realise .... I found Beth stabbed and called the ambulance. I waited with her, but the second it arrived, I legged it. What else could I do? If I'd stayed, the police would have questioned me and all the stuff about blackmail would have come out. I just couldn't face that.' Tears choked her voice and she took a deep breath. Images flashed in her memory – Beth's blood-soaked top, the gaping wound in her back, Trish's hands smeared red ....

Casey dropped the newspaper on the bed. 'And they think *you* did it?'

'They must have discovered I was there and put two and two together.' There was the broken glass from the French doors, of course. Why hadn't that showed them there was a third person there?

'You could give yourself in and say you've only just seen this newspaper article.'

'I can't, can I,' she shouted in frustration and started to pace again. 'I can't get out of this.' She shook her head and wiped tears from her cheeks. 'I'm totally trapped.' She dropped into the chair and closed her eyes. 'If the police are looking for me, they'll probably be watching my credit card transactions and even tracking my mobile.' She remembered the calls they had made on the bus and was glad it had remained switched off since. 'I'll have to check out in case they start studying hotel registers but I can't pay without using my card. I don't know what to do ...' Thank God reception hadn't insisted on taking a card swipe when she had checked in. She swallowed hard. 'I don't know where they got that photo, but it means I've got to make myself look different.'

'I suppose you could alter your hair in some way. That would help. Those coloured streaks are very noticeable.'

Trish realised she was subconsciously winding them round her fingers. The three colours that defined her:

Serpentine Green, Lagoon Blue, and Purple Haze. Her mum would have freaked at her dying her hair and forbidden it, but Aunt Flo had been cool. 'I can't – I've had those for years ever since Mum and Dad ... They're part of me.'

'So what? If you want to make yourself look different, you'll have to. I could trim your hair for you into a bob if you want and dye it all black.'

'Black?' She glared at him in horror. 'And do you know how difficult it is to cut hair properly? Have you ever done it before?'

'No, but it's better than leaving it as it is.'

She was about to argue but knew he was right. *Be decisive*, she told herself. 'All right. Let's do it. But what about my room?'

'I'll lend you the money. I'll get some cash from an ATM.'

She forced a smile. 'Thanks. I'll pay you back as soon as this is all over.' But how could it ever be over? She hung her head in her hands.

Without looking up, she said, 'Sometimes I feel ... in my darkest moments ... like at night when I was camping out at the old house in the hope of Argus showing up, I imagine it must be something about me that brings death.' He started to interrupt but she carried on, silencing him. 'My parents died when I was a child. D'you remember the London bombings in 2005?' She looked up briefly. He was staring at her intently. 'Mum and Dad were on that train ...' Her voice faltered. 'They were on the underground heading to the Royal Opera House for some sort of meeting when it went off; they were both musicians. Then there was Aunt Flo – she had breast cancer. She hated screening and wouldn't go, didn't think it would happen to her. By the time she found the lump and summoned up enough courage to see the doctor it was too late.' She swallowed back tears. 'She was great, my aunt. She took me in when Mum and Dad died. I was totally off the rails, got into all sorts of trouble at school, but she always had such patience with me. Now she's gone too. And now Beth. I just wonder ... everyone I love seems to die.' She paused, staring at the swirling pattern on the carpet. 'When I was camping at the house, I honestly thought about getting a hose and sitting in my car with the engine running, you know... but, well, I kinda pulled myself together in the morning.'

'Those deaths were all just coincidence,' Casey said softly.

'Really?' Trish shrugged, picking at her nails. 'But it doesn't seem fair, does it.'

There was nothing he could say to that. She wanted a hug, wished Matt would come over and put his arms round her, to give comfort.

Neither of them said anything for a bit, and it was Casey who eventually broke the silence. 'I'll get some cash so you can check out.' He paused and she looked up at him. He seemed embarrassed. Hesitantly, he said, 'You can share my room if you want.'

Trish nodded slowly and sniffed. 'Can I? I'll take the floor.' She paused. 'Would you mind getting some stuff for my hair while you're out, before I change my mind?'

Casey arrived back an hour later with a carrier bag, by which time she was feeling more composed. Where the hell had he managed to get that lot? He must have used a taxi. He lifted out scissors and a box of hair dye and laid them on the bed, then handed her a pair of black-rimmed reading glasses. 'I don't know if you'll be able to see through them but they were only a couple of quid. They were the weakest I could get.' He had also brought fruit and pre-packed sandwiches, and handed her some crisp ten-pound notes to pay for her room.

'Hair first?' he asked.

She nodded submissively. 'As soon as it's done, I can safely check out. She moved the chair into the middle of the room and pulled a towel tight round her shoulders. 'Just don't take much off,' she added nervously. She closed her eyes and heard the first snip of the scissors.

Ten minutes later, she went into the bathroom and locked the door, avoiding looking in the mirror. She washed her hair, dyed it, then dyed it a second time for luck. Eventually she took a deep breath and turned to the mirror. Every muscle was tense. The face that stared back at her was not Trish McGowan's, but that of a miserable dowdy thirty-year old. The cut wasn't quite level and was far too short, and the fringe hadn't dyed properly – while the rest of her hair was now deep ebony, what had once been coloured had turned a mouldy brown.

She shrugged and stuck out her tongue at the reflection before turning away and once more fighting back tears. But it would do. At least she would not easily be recognized.

Trish checked out apologetically at the front desk. 'Something urgent has come up and I've got to rush home tonight so I can't stay after all.' She was asked to pay the one night's charge anyway, but she didn't argue. The last thing she wanted was to draw attention to herself or have to discuss it with the manager.

The glasses made everything slightly blurred, but she felt safe hiding behind them. Her confidence had partly returned when she headed back to Casey's room. The receptionist had showed no recognition or alarm at seeing her.

Trish didn't know it, but that confidence wasn't even going to last twenty-four hours.

***

Craig Tyler stretched awkwardly in the front seat of his car. The corner he had chosen in the Travel Lodge car park was still dark, although a watery sun now peeped above the roof of the neighbouring McDonald's. He was parked in the elbow created by the motel's L-shape, hidden from the 24-7 lights of the drive-through.

Argus' large Volvo hadn't moved overnight. Thick dew coated the bodywork and clouded its windows. From where Tyler sat in his driver's seat, he could make out the motel's front door and Argyle's car. It had dropped to six degrees overnight, but he hadn't cared.

He touched his watch to illuminate its face. Nearly 6:00 A.M. He wondered if Argus had called his bluff. Was she going to ignore his offer? Only three hours to the rendezvous. For the first time, doubts crept into his mind, and with them, the nerves tightened in his stomach. Perhaps he'd been naive to presume his call would send her rushing to where she kept the diary.

He had stuck with her continuously since she'd left the house the previous morning. She had done what he guessed was a normal day for a medical sales rep – a half-hour visit to the gated modern office block of a pharmaceutical company in Bristol followed by a long tea break in a Sainsbury's cafe during which she flicked through a sheaf of printed papers before driving to a Chippenham business park, where she disappeared inside a glass and stainless steel block for an hour. But rather than return home, she had then checked in at this Travel Lodge on the edge of Warminster.

Had she perhaps arranged for someone to do the negotiation on her behalf? He doubted it. His view of the psychology of a blackmailer was that they worked alone – secretive and insular people.

He wasn't sure which way to jump – stay with Argus to see what she did next or go back to her house in time to check it out before the rendezvous? But what if doing that meant missing whatever Argus was about to do? He banged the wheel in frustration; either course of action could be wrong. This is when he could have done with help from the others, but after Trish's call the previous day, he knew that wasn't going to happen.

Half an hour later, he impatiently checked his watch again. Two more minutes, then he would go. A short man in his mid-thirties pushed through the doors and hurried across the road to the McDonald's but otherwise there was no movement anywhere.

Angrily, Tyler twisted the ignition key, flicked the wipers, and cranked up the ventilation to clear the screen before he swung out of the car park at speed. Damn her. He would have to head to the house in case she had arranged for someone else to strike a deal. It seemed unlikely, but having set up the meeting he had to see it through. Of course, it could now be a trap, with Argus keeping clear while her thugs tried to deal with him again. Well, they hadn't succeeded last time.

He pushed his foot firmer on the accelerator, and the needle climbed to ninety.

It took him an hour and a half, and he arrived well in advance of the planned meeting. He slowed and tucked into a space fifty yards from Argyle's house. He cut the engine and sat in silence for a moment, checking the other cars, the street, the house fronts. He pulled the receiver from the glove box and pushed a bud into one ear. The audio hummed slightly, and he switched between the bugs he'd left in the house. One of them provided the resonant tick of a clock, but nothing suggested anyone was inside.

He listened for five minutes, keeping an eye on the road around him at the same time. Assured there was nothing out of the ordinary for a residential street this early in the morning, he pushed the equipment back into the glove box and stepped on to the pavement to breath fresh spring air.

A silver Ford Sierra passed. It didn't slow, the driver didn't glance his way; just a commuter on his way to work.

Without hurry, Tyler glanced over his shoulder and walked away from Argyle's house. His eyes darted, checking every car as he passed, every house window for anyone watching. There was nobody about.

He crossed the road and walked steadily back, doing the same. Past Argyle's house – apparently deserted – and beyond. No sign yet of the builders. The street was clear.

The weight of the Sig Sauer handgun in his pocket was comforting. Tyler had been lucky to get it so quickly but had been forced to accept what his contact had been able to get with almost no notice. Tyler had left off watching the Travel Lodge shortly before midnight and driven to a grubby flat on the edge of Bristol to collect it and had been back by two in the morning. He had no intention of firing the thing, but the sight of a gun was always effective at encouraging co-operation, especially in those untrained for warfare like a dumb medical rep cum blackmailer.

At the end of the street, he turned and headed back, more briskly now. A flicker of nerves rippled through his stomach as he walked purposefully up the drive of Argyle's seemingly empty house. He slid one hand into his pocket and curled it round the weapon.

As he'd done previously, he headed down the side of the garage to the neat lawn at the back. He paused, listening. A pair of blackbirds squawked at each other on the edge of a recently weeded flowerbed, and a pair of collared doves cooed from the upper branches of a fir.

Keeping close to the brickwork, he started along the back of the house, peered in at the first window, then the next.

Confident that no one was inside, he took out the bunch of keys he'd taken during his earlier visit and tried several in the lock of the patio door until he found one that turned. Hoping the intruder alarm was still off for the builders, Tyler silently eased the door open. He slid the gun from his pocket and stepped into the room.

Quickly and soundlessly, he reconnoitred both floors before taking up position at the small table in the kitchen, gun laid close to hand on the otherwise empty surface. He had a view of the drive through half-open blinds.

An occasional car swept past the house but nothing slowed or turned in. At one point, the central heating started up, and a gentle whistle of water ran through the pipes. Tyler sat motionless. His eyelids drooped, and he got up and made himself an instant coffee and found some biscuits in the cupboard. He sipped the drink and nibbled a fig roll while he waited. It helped him stay alert.

The kitchen clock ticked inexorably forward, and Tyler sighed. He wanted to be gone by the time the builders arrived. He puzzled why no one had showed. Was she calling his bluff? It was a shame he didn't have her mobile number or he would have called, kept up the pressure.

He wondered if she gave it on her answerphone message or if any of her business cards were in the office; he didn't remember seeing any last time. He picked up the pistol, leaving the empty mug on the table, and jogged upstairs. The answerphone's outgoing message turned out to be the standard one pre-installed on the machine, and he could find no business cards. Pity.

He glanced at his watch and headed back downstairs and let himself out the way he'd entered, locking it behind him. He didn't care the kitchen table betrayed his visit.

When he reached the front of the garage wall, he put the gun back in his pocket, although he kept one hand on it while he cautiously peered round towards the front of the house. Seeing all was clear, he stepped from cover and strode out of the drive.

Why hadn't the stupid woman taken his bait? Surely his offer was too tempting to ignore. Maybe this was a prelude to bargaining on price.

His eyes darted left and right; his ears strained for any unusual sound. There was nothing out of place. The patina of dew that still lingered on all the parked cars suggested none had recently arrived, and there was no-one on foot. He stopped at his car, rummaging through his pocket for the key fob.

As he unlocked the BMW, he felt a whoosh of air behind him. Before Tyler could do anything but register the movement, pain exploded in his skull and he toppled forwards into darkness.

**

Matt Casey's confidence that they would be safe here at the MOD demonstrations was shattered during breakfast. He stood at the row of heated stainless-steel dishes in the hotel restaurant ladling scrambled egg on to a plate when someone called out from a table a few metres away. Instinctively, Casey turned towards the source of the shout.

The words registered, and he froze. A large broad-shouldered man was gesturing towards one of the kitchen staff from a nearby table. His large double chin wobbled. He had thinning black hair and wore a suit jacket over an open-necked pink shirt. 'Hey doll,' he bellowed. 'Over here a moment darling.'

Casey knew that voice. More than that, he knew the phrase. Where the hell had he heard it? The nerves that suddenly gripped his stomach told him it had bad connotations.

'Hey doll.' The man waved again.

Casey studied him more closely. An ID badge dangled round his fat neck but it wasn't one of theirs, and he was too far away to read it.

Then Casey remembered where he'd heard that phrase and almost dropped the serving spoon.

CHAPTER THIRTY-FOUR

With legs feeling they were about to give way Casey carried his tray to an empty table. He dropped shakily onto the seat and stared at the man's back, his heart hammering. That voice – that "Hey doll" phrase – echoed in his memory. It had been on the answerphone at Argus' house. This was Argus' friend, and it couldn't be coincidence. What the hell was going on?

No one knew Casey was coming here, so Argus couldn't have sent him after them. It felt like the tangled ends of a dozen threads were dangling in front of him and he couldn't tease them apart. *Why is he here?*

At that moment, another suit took a seat at the same table. He was noticeably older than Argus' friend, plump, with neatly trimmed white hair above a round face and tidy beard. 'Morning Hugo.' Argus' friend nodded in acknowledgement, and the newcomer carefully laid out his knife and fork and unfolded a napkin.

Hugo. At least Casey now knew his first name.

A sudden voice beside Casey made him jump. 'Can I join you?' It was another of BDE's employees, the team's project manager. Casey nodded distractedly, and a waitress appeared and poured coffee into a fresh cup. When she'd gone, Casey gestured with his fork towards the two men. 'Do you know who they are?'

The manager frowned. 'Isn't that the head of MSA?' He was referring to the man who had just sat down.

'And the one with his back to us? I think he's called Hugo something.' At that moment, Argus' friend stood and headed towards the buffet, and they saw him in side profile.

'Hang on, let's see.' The project manager pulled out an iPhone and after a few taps said, 'There we go. It's Hugo Metcalf, their CFO.' He turned the screen for Casey to see. There on MSA's company website was the unsmiling podgy face, his name, and professional biography.

So many dangling threads.

Casey quickly stuffed his breakfast and excused himself, then almost ran from the restaurant.

When he burst into his room, Trish was gathering the pillows from the floor where she had insisted on sleeping. She looked up in alarm.

'Down in the restaurant ...,' he panted. 'You remember there was a message on Argus' answering machine, some bloke talking about tickets he'd got for somewhere.' She nodded. 'Well, the guy who left that message is sitting downstairs at breakfast and I found out who it is.'

Fear swept across her face. 'You sure?'

'Totally. It's the Chief Financial Officer of MSA, our big

rival. The voice, the phrases he uses, they're identical. He's definitely Argus' friend or lover or whatever. That's got to be how Argus knew enough to blackmail me.' He felt a sudden hatred for the fat little man he now knew as Hugo Metcalf.

Trish frowned 'I don't understand.'

'I'm still not entirely sure myself, but he has a lot more in common with me and what happened than Argus ever did. I've never been able to understand how she knew what I'd done but now it's starting to make more sense. He told her about it.'

'Sorry, Matt, but I'm still not with you. Because I don't know what you did to get yourself blackmailed, I'm not following the link with this MSA bloke.' She studied him, head to one side, looking more beautiful than ever.

'Well ...' Casey swallowed nervously. *Go on Matt, tell her.* Where to start? With the crash itself? No, it all started with Alicia – begin with her. Casey perched on the edge of the bed and intently studied his trainers. 'Several years ago, I got myself into a lot of debt. I had a girlfriend from a posh family that had loads of money and – I was stupid, right – but I felt I had to live like she was used to. So, I spent massive amounts taking her out, going to expensive dos, giving her ridiculously lavish presents ...' He sighed. 'I built up so much debt that I just couldn't pay it off, and when I stopped buying her presents and suggested we stayed in rather than going out, she started to say I didn't love her anymore.' His voice cracked slightly. 'We had loads of arguments and eventually broke up. I suppose we were never a good match but I didn't see it. You know how it is.'

He briefly glanced up. Her face was so sad. She watched him with soft caring eyes, and he felt his insides flutter. Her hair was nicer now without the colour. Its removal seemed to have taken down some sort of barrier. He wanted to say, 'I think I love you, Trish. You're different,' but instead, he looked away again.

'But how did you end up entangled with Argus?' she prompted gently.

He sighed. 'Well, I got offered that evening work that I told you about but it was only paying off what I owed quite gradually. Then he told me he had something else for me that would earn a really big fee. All I had to do was to let him have a copy of the flight control software program from our UAV and then load a different one that he would give me just before it flew at a demonstration. He told me all it would do was monitor the flight performance for them, nothing else.

'I hesitated, of course. I knew it was some sort of industrial spying, but he said he'd give me five thousand quid, and I was still so short of money that I said, "okay." I was dumb, right, but I never guessed what the consequences would be. Just before it flew at Farnborough – you know, the military air show – I changed the software for him, and the UAV crashed during the demonstration. This Hugo Metcalf would have been there and seen it happen.' He sensed her stiffen, and he quickly added, 'No one was hurt, thank God, but it was such bad publicity we didn't sell Dragonfly to anyone and the company ended up making loads of people redundant. It was horrid. It was such an awful atmosphere at work. And I knew it was all my fault.'

'And that's what you were blackmailed about?'

Casey nodded. 'I received an email from Argus a week later saying she knew what I'd done. I just panicked and deleted it afraid someone might see it. Then I started to worry that I was meant to do something and hadn't read it properly. I got in a bit of a state.'

Trish nodded. 'I know what you mean. I was the same.'

For the first time, Casey realised she did truly understand. Trish was the only person who knew exactly how he felt. 'I got another email precisely a week later. Argus said she would keep quiet about it if I would simply pass a letter for her to my CEO. It seemed such an innocent thing to do.' Craig shook his head in despair.

Trish added, '… and it was only when you also had to collect the money later that you realised you were now blackmailing your boss on Argus' behalf.'

He looked up and their eyes locked. 'Exactly.'

'But how did this guy know it was your fault?'

'That's the bit I haven't worked out yet, but him finding out seems a lot more believable than Argus working it out by herself. The only way I can think of is that he found out from the bloke who paid me. It's a small industry. Most people know each other at their level.'

'Did you get any clues about who got you to do it?'

Casey shook his head. 'He signed his letters "Tom" but I've no idea if that was his real name. A box of parts would arrive at my flat via courier every Saturday morning together with a cash payment, and the finished boards I'd done were taken away at the same time. I never met the guy who commissioned the work. Now I wonder if the whole thing was set up just to get me to trust him before he asked me to change the software.'

They fell silent, lost in thought, before Trish eventually said, 'It would be good to know how involved this Hugo bloke actually is. As you say, he probably just innocently let it slip - like a bit of gossip, but what if there's more to it than that? What if he's an active partner in the blackmail?'

'Shit. So, there could be two of them?'

'Argus could be a name for a partnership, not just one person.' She looked up, eyes burning. 'So, if I do use Kurt Wendell to stop Argus, it's no good if he just gets rid of the woman because if Hugo *is* heavily involved, Hugo will simply take over and carry on.'

'You're still going to try to use Wendell? After all that happened?' His muscles clenched at the thought.

Trish nodded thoughtfully.

'You realise you're racking up the body count, don't you. Is that really the right thing to do? You know what Wendell's like. I not sure I'd want that on my conscience.'

She glared at him. 'It's okay for you,' she said bitterly, 'but unless I can persuade Wendell it's not me he needs to stop, I'm going to end up a dead woman.'

He raised a hand. 'Okay, okay. It just feels ...'

'What else can I do?'

Casey said nothing. He suddenly felt a protectiveness toward her. After a pause, Trish said, 'At least let's find out how heavily involved Hugo is. Then decide what to do'

'How?'

'We could search his room. See if we can find anything to tell us.'

Casey thought for a moment. 'Maybe while he's out at the trials. He'll be there first thing for meetings, but us minions don't need to arrive till half ten today ... but we don't even know his room number, let alone how to get in.'

She grinned and raised her eyebrows. 'Not at the minute, but I think I've got a plan.'

CHAPTER THIRTY-FIVE

Half an hour later, Trish was crossing and uncrossing her legs in a chair by the first-floor lifts. Her mouth felt as dry as old leather.

The corridor ran both ways in front of her, and bedrooms continued beyond the propped-open fire doors. Whenever anyone walked past, they glanced at her. Despite the change of hair and addition of glasses, they might still recognize her, and she kept her face averted. But where else could she wait? It was certainly safer here than where Matt was, just outside the main entrance. He watched in case Hugo Metcalf's car returned to the car park. If it did, Matt would have time to race through reception and up to the first floor to get her out. Keeping her mobile off was proving a pain.

Trish had sat there ten minutes now, waiting for the right moment to go into Metcalf's room ever since Matt had seen Metcalf leave the hotel in his Jaguar. She so needed a ciggie. Trish looked at her watch again. *Come on.*

Matt had learned Metcalf's room number from the two

sheets of paper the restaurant staff used to tick off guests as they entered for breakfast. 'Just say you don't think they crossed you off when you came down earlier so that you can get a look at the list,' Trish had suggested. 'That'll show his room number.'

Now she sat where she could see Metcalf's door – room 127 – awaiting her chance. The cleaners slowly worked their way towards her.

Her stomach churned. If she got caught doing this…

It was another fifteen minutes before the cleaning trolley rattled past where she sat. Trish tensed. There were two of them, one pushing the trolley loaded high with towels and toiletries, the other carrying a bucket of sprays and cloths. They entered Metcalf's room and propped the door open while they worked.

Five minutes later, they re-appeared. Trish came instantly to her feet, walking fast down the corridor towards them. She had to get the timing right as there would only be the one chance.

The cleaner bent to pick up the bucket from where it held the door. With a slight creak, the door started to swing closed.

Two firm strides more.

With a smile at the woman who was about to move to the adjacent room, Trish caught the door. 'Morning,' Trish said cheerfully. 'Have you finished?'

The cleaner simply smiled back. Perhaps she didn't speak English.

'Thank you.' Trish stepped into Metcalf's room and let

the door click shut behind her. She took a deep breath.

The bedroom had the same layout as Matt's and identical furniture.

Every muscle was tense. *Get on with it as fast you can and get out.* She pulled off the reading glasses and thrust them into her pocket. Bedside cabinet first.

Top drawer – a tatty Frederick Forsyth paperback, loose reading glasses, a handful of coins. Shelf beneath – hotel supplied New Testament, seemingly un-touched. Nothing else.

Wardrobe. She pulled open the door. Coat, suit, a few shirts hanging. A cabin bag stood beneath. She slid it out, knelt in front of it. Not locked. She wrinkled her nose – used underwear, a screwed-up shirt. Beneath then, a few scraps of paper – old till receipts, as though he'd emptied his wallet into it, and half a dozen folded A4 sheets that curled at the corners. She flicked through them. Meeting minutes – nothing of interest – three sales invoices for lines of items she didn't understand. The last one was a copy of a warehouse rental agreement.

In case any of them proved relevant, she flattened them on the carpet and pulled out her phone. She powered it up and instantly switched it into flight-mode so it wouldn't be seen on the mobile network. She used its camera to photograph each sheet before tossing them back. She flicked quickly through the till receipts – restaurant, petrol …

Trish froze as her eyes caught the details on the next one. She fumbled with her phone, hand shaking, and double-checked her incoming call history.

Shit. She pocketed the receipt. They had been wrong. Hugo Metcalf wasn't just Argus' lover, he was Argus himself.

Trish threw everything back into the wardrobe and got out quick. She ran back down the corridor and burst through the doors towards reception. Had to find Matt.

***

Casey jumped, startled at her sudden appearance. 'What's happened?'

'We need to talk,' she panted and pulled him away from the doors. She dragged him to a corner of the car park, away from where anyone might recognise her. 'Look at this,' she said as soon as they came to a halt. Her hands were shaking as she held out a till receipt.

He studied it briefly. 'It's for a pay-as-you-go SIM card. So what?'

In reply, she pulled out her own mobile, tapped the screen a few times and turned it round for him to see. 'That's the last text message I got from Argus. Compare the numbers.'

They matched.

A white Range Rover pulled into the car park and made a slow orbit, searching for a parking space. She lowered her voice. 'He used a different number virtually every time he contacted me. I guess he binned the SIMs after each set of messages and bought new ones so that he couldn't be traced. This is the last one he used.'

A businessman in suit and tie headed in their direction, and Trish turned her back to him. He unlocked a Ford Focus and drove away.

Casey frowned. 'This is getting so confusing. Are you suggesting it's Hugo Metcalf who's Argus?'

Trish nodded and leant closer, her blue eyes sparkling. 'I've had another thought as well. You said you don't know who it was that approached you to do that work in the first place, right? Could it have been Hugo Metcalf?'

Casey frowned. 'I suppose so,' he said slowly. 'I never got to see him. But why —'

'You told me Hugo Metcalf is the CFO of your company's biggest rival, right?'

'A *very* big rival. They're both family businesses and the owners are uncle and nephew. Rumour has it they had a bust-up years ago and have been bitter enemies ever since.'

'What if it was Hugo Metcalf who got you to change the software in your UAV and cause it to crash?' Before he could answer, she continued urgently. 'Could MSA be so anti- you guys that they would go as far as sabotaging your prototype?'

'Maybe not the company itself, but perhaps Hugo Metcalf …. He's son of the owner, and the family feud could have passed down a generation.'

'And perhaps that rivalry led him to use you for the sabotage.' Casey flinched at the word, but she was right; that's what it had been. 'And then he makes the most of it and blackmails you for what he'd persuaded you to do. One and the same person. That would explain how Hugo Metcalf knew what you'd done – he's the one that persuaded you to do it.'

It made sense. He felt anger burning. How could he have been so stupid to be manipulated like that?

'We've got to tell Craig about this,' Trish said. 'He's concentrating on the woman, but this could change everything. We don't actually know how deeply she's involved. That picture in her house – maybe Hugo Metcalf saw it there and it inspired him to use *Argus* as his alias. Maybe she's got nothing to do with it after all.'

'But the car …?'

'It was her car alright, but what does that prove? He could have borrowed it to avoid being recognised himself.'

Casey nodded slowly. 'We'll call Craig.' He pulled out the new phone he'd bought when they'd stopped off at Lancaster to change busses. His mind was in turmoil. It was like being in a thick fog, seeing vague shapes he recognized yet unable to see the whole scene. The phone rang for what felt like ages before going to his answering service. Casey left a detailed message for Tyler and violently stabbed at the "End" button. Where the hell was Craig when they needed him?

CHAPTER THIRTY-SIX

While Trish McGowan was in Metcalf's hotel room, the car carrying Tyler had been travelling slowly down an unmade road. The jolts brought Tyler groggily to consciousness. He didn't move, just slowly let his senses return. The throb of pain pulsed in his skull. The back of his head radiated agony.

Cautiously, he tried to move, found his wrists and ankles tied with rope – he flexed them but they didn't budge. He slowly opened his right eye and saw he was slumped in the passenger seat of his own car. They seemed to be crossing farmland, and what he could see of the sky still held the watery blue of morning. The sun's position suggested they were currently heading north-west.

The vehicle slowed further, and he guessed they were nearing their destination. He wondered if Argyle – Argus – would be waiting for him at the end of the track. He wanted to look round, see who else was in the car, but didn't want to make it obvious he was conscious. He explored the knots at his wrist further. He tensed and relaxed the muscles, fingers probing the thin rope.

The car pulled into a yard surrounded by dilapidated farm buildings, the kind of places built to house farm machinery or hay. One was missing its roof, on another the rusted metal sheets had collapsed and were now overgrown with ivy, but the one they stopped outside looked almost serviceable. At least it still had a functional roof and the wooden slatted walls were largely intact.

Tyler closed his eyes again and waited motionless. The engine cut and everywhere fell eerily quiet before the driver got out and Tyler could hear him walking round the car towards him.

His door clicked open. 'Get out. I didn't hit you that hard. 'It was a thin voice with a rough London accent. Tyler didn't move. Let them think he was weaker than he actually was.

There was a pause and a sigh. 'C'mon Dave. Give me a hand with this bastard.' It sounded like the guy who'd tried to jump him at the pub.

The car rocked, and Tyler heard the rear door open. Seconds later, two pairs of hands grabbed him under the shoulders and hauled him from his seat. He let his feet hit the ground as they pulled him clear, and allowed his heels to drag across the concrete. One of them was puffing from the exertion, reeking of a mix of BO and stale cigarette smoke that smelt like an old bonfire. His friend had breath that stank of beer.

They paused, and Tyler heard the barn door being

kicked aside. It rasped against the concrete. Every minute he felt stronger, more alert, although the pain continued to throb like hell at the back of his head. They dragged him inside and let go. Tyler toppled sideways like a lifeless doll.

'Bring him to. We can't wait all day.' Tyler felt a half-hearted kick in his side and obligingly moaned and twisted his body.

A second voice, deeper, and with the same London accent. 'Wake up bastard.' A second kick struck him harder. Tyler grunted loudly and curled into a foetal position.

The voice again from across the room: 'Can you hear me?'

Tyler pushed himself into a sitting position. His head was pounding. 'Stuff you.'

Away from the light that spilled across the floor from the open barn door, the interior was dim. Feeble shafts of morning sunlight seeped through cracks between the timbers of the walls. Piles of bird droppings were just visible beneath the beams supporting the roof, but the rest of the building receded into darkness. The bloke who'd kicked him – known as Dave – had backed away. His shaven head glistened with sweat. His jeans and trainers were splashed with paint.

His partner stood backlit in the doorway, younger, with dark curls escaping from under a beanie. 'Why are you offering a lot of money to buy a book?' So, this was definitely a response to his offer.

'Where's Argus? I'm only negotiating with Argus directly, not through some lackey.'

Interesting there was no look of puzzlement at the name "Argus". They knew exactly who he was referring to. Dave stepped forward and kicked Tyler in the ribs. Tyler rolled with it and it didn't break anything. 'Why were you offering so much for that book?' Interesting he didn't refer to it as a diary. Perhaps they didn't know. They clearly weren't that chummy with Argus.

'I like old books. Now get Argus in here so we can talk. I want to see it first so I know it's genuine.'

'Tell us why you're offering so much. What are you going to do with it?'

'We seem to be going round in circles here. I'm offering a lot of money if it's genuine, but I want to see it first.'

Dave was about to say something else when Beanie-Boy cut in. 'So how d'you know about it?'

From his position on the floor, Tyler attempted a shrug. 'Just some gossip I picked up. Y'know, some bloke in the pub shooting his mouth off more than he should.' As he spoke, he continually flexed and relaxed his wrists, each time rotating them slightly to bring his fingers closer to the knots.

'So how d'you get interested in High Ridge Road?'

He decided he could tell the truth about that one but said nothing. No point in making it too easy for them. Dave glowered at him. 'You deaf?'

Tyler pulled a face that was meant to say, 'I don't want to tell you about it,' but wasn't sure if it was successful. Dave took a step forward, shoulders tensed, and Tyler added, 'It was the car that gave it away.'

'Car?'

'Yeah, you know, big metal thing with four wheels.' Dave kicked out at him but was too slow, and Tyler twisted away easily so that the boot glanced off his hip. He gasped exaggeratedly. 'I meant I saw the same big Volvo at the derelict mansion and followed it back to High Ridge Road.' Dave nodded slowly. There was no question about "the derelict mansion" so these thugs obviously knew Argus used the old house, although maybe not what for. He didn't reckon Argus would tell them how much money was getting deposited there. 'D'you know what Argus uses that old house for?'

Dave shrugged. 'Not my business.'

'Lots of money.' Tyler noticed Beanie-Boy lean a bit closer, and Tyler dropped his voice conspiratorially. 'I mean tens of thousands of pounds each time. Someone drops it off there and it's just lying around, sometimes for days before Argus collects it.'

Dave's eyes glinted in the dim light, but he added less convincingly, 'As I said. Not my business.'

Tyler shrugged. 'Fine.'

It seemed like Argus wasn't coming to this meeting after all.

'But what I do wanna know is what you know about Argus.'

'Nothing really. I know where she lives, what car she drives, and that she uses that old house for money deposits. Nothing else.' He wasn't telling them anything they didn't already know.

Confusion briefly flashed across Dave's face, then he shrugged as though it wasn't relevant. He turned and walked over to Beanie-Boy and they bent their heads together. Tyler worked faster on his wrists while the pair weren't watching, fingertips teasing the rope ends. He felt them begin to loosen.

The two guys laughed, and Dave took the few steps back towards him and squatted. He probably meant it to be intimidating but it just brought the vulnerable part of his body close to Tyler's professional hands. If he could finish getting the rope off now, this was his opportunity.

Tyler could see the lines around his eyes. He must be late forties, older than he'd first appeared. Dave said, 'Tell me more about this book you want … so there's no misunderstanding.' His breath stank.

One end of the rope was finally moving, and Tyler's fingertips slowly eased the knot apart.

Dave put his face closer still, only inches away. 'You deaf? Why's that book so damn special?'

Tyler felt the rope loosen. He collected a glob of saliva and spat it in Dave's face. It struck his nose, and the creamy mucous dribbled down one side.

Dave lashed out, but from his crouched position the punch had little force. Tyler had been waiting for it and twisted his head away. It barely grazed his cheek. While Dave recovered his balance, Tyler adjusted to a kneeling position so that the knots holding his ankles were out of sight behind him. The barn was sufficiently dim inside that there was a chance he might be able to work on them without the thug realising. He just needed to free his hands.

Dave wiped the spittle away with his sleeve and bent down again. He didn't seem to notice Tyler had moved. Anger burned in his grey eyes.

The rope loosened further. Keeping his eyes locked with Dave's, Tyler teased the last loop apart and felt it slide down his wrist. Dave's face was now so close he couldn't see Tyler reaching down his back for the knots at his ankles. The man's bulk blocked Beanie-Boy's view.

Dave's stale breath washed over Tyler. 'You think you're clever don't you, but you don't want to mess with us.'

Tyler laughed. 'What gangster movie did you learn that line from?' With small unseen movements in the gloom, he picked more rapidly at the rope round his ankles, not moving any other part of his body. He kept his eyes locked with his captor's, holding his attention. He'd have to be quick now. His fingers were sweating and slipped on the knots. He dug his nails deeper into the fibres for grip. *Come on.*

Blood vessels in Dave's temples pulsed. 'I'll teach you to mouth-off.'

Beanie-Boy, sensing a fight, took a step towards them. The change of angle must have been enough for him suddenly to see what Tyler was trying to do. He yelled a warning. Dave turned towards Beanie-Boy in surprise. Tyler yanked at the ropes, twisting his ankles, feeling the skin burn. Dave swore and began to stand but was too slow. In that instant, Tyler's feet came free. He leant back, then headbutted Dave hard in the face. The nose broke. Blood erupted and streamed down Dave's face. His hands instinctively went up towards the damage. Tyler sprung up, but his leg almost collapsed from cramp. He regained balance and kicked him under the jaw. The head snapped back and Dave swayed backwards. Tyler gave himself space and landed another boot as hard as he could into the man's temples. A gasp was all Dave could manage before he collapsed sideways.

Out of the corner of his eye he saw Beanie-Boy hesitate then dart for the door. Tyler lurched towards him, stumbling stiffly as he ran into the courtyard.

Beanie-boy hesitated a few yards away, looking at Tyler's car, then to his right across the field to distant trees. Tyler was as close to the car as he. Beanie-Boy made up his mind and sprinted away across the grass towards the boundary hedgerow, six feet of bramble and holly laced with the remnants of a barbed-wire fence.

He was fast, quickly putting distance between them. Tyler sprinted after him as best he could. The uneven ground made it hard to maintain a rhythm.

Beanie-Boy suddenly darted to the right, reached the hedge, and disappeared.

A few seconds later, with his legs moving more freely, Tyler found the break in the brambles and barbed wire Beanie-Boy had used. He jumped through the narrow gap and burst on to a rutted lane.

His quarry had gone straight over, up the bank the other side and pushed through a row of elder that formed the other boundary. Panting hard, Tyler darted across the lane and jumped up the bank after him. A strip of grass stretched left to right, dappled by sunlight. Beyond it lay the dark of a wood into which Beanie-Boy was disappearing.

Tyler sprinted after him, arms pumping hard. The cool of the trees quickly closed around him. No sign of Beanie-Boy.

He staggered to a halt among the dense trunks, ferns and rough grass, listening intently. Above the pounding of his heart, he heard a twig break over to his left.

Eyes already adjusting to the dark, he briefly caught sight of a blur of movement among the trees and darted after it, crashing through the low undergrowth. Spots of sunlight randomly speckled the ground where it broke through the canopy. The trunks became slowly denser, slowing him down as he careened between them. He'd lost sight of Beanie-Boy. He stopped again, listening.

Nothing.

He turned his head slightly, scanning for sound but the wood was silent. Was Beanie-Boy waiting too, paused up ahead listening for him?

Cautiously, Tyler took another step forward, careful to avoid anything that might betray his position. Silently, he crept forward in the direction he'd last seen the target. Every step, he paused, checking all around in case Beanie-Boy was trying to circle round behind him. His phone vibrated in his pocket, but he ignored it.

For five minutes, he cautiously stepped from tree to tree, but his quarry had disappeared. Slowly he turned and retraced his steps, still careful to make no sound, his SAS training for silent movement kicking back in. He paused to check over his shoulder for any sign of his target. Once out of the wood, he broke into a jog. He had lost Beanie-Boy, but there was still Dave. Tyler wanted to learn what their instructions had been. As he neared the cluster of low buildings across the field, he saw his mistake.

His car had gone.

He raced to where it had been. There was a splatter of blood across the concrete leading from where they'd fought. When he checked the building, he found it empty.

CHAPTER THIRTY-SEVEN

Trish's luck ran out at lunchtime.

Her stomach had forced her from the sanctuary of Casey's room for a sandwich. Room service prices were a joke, and she wasn't going to face the risk of returning to the café, so had ended up as the only person sitting on a high stool at the bar. She would be alright, she told herself. She wore those stupid glasses again and she wouldn't be recognised.

She was thinking about Beth's murder when she was jerked back to the present by two bulky policemen in fluorescent jackets who entered the foyer and headed for the reception desk. Trish couldn't help but turn and look when she heard the electric door hiss open and shut. She froze with a paper serviette in her hand, about to wipe her mouth.

The policemen had stopped at the desk and were speaking quietly to the receptionist, who pointed Trish's way. The policeman turned to follow her direction. Trish looked away quickly, but too late.

Run. No choice but run. There were double glass doors to her left that led to the gardens. She fled towards them.

'Hey, excuse me,' one of them called. Trish's hip caught the back of an upright chair and sent it crashing into a table as she ran across the reception area. 'Wait there please, miss.'

Five metres to the double doors. No one in the way. She flung them open, darted over the patio and away across the grass.

Trish glanced over her shoulder. One of the cops was already through the doors, raising his radio to his mouth. She couldn't see the second one.

Trish sucked in breath and sprinted. She was younger than he, but knew she wasn't very fit. She had walked the grounds before, remembered how it ended at the trees with a gate to the river bank. Bad route – get on that footpath and she could easily be cut off with nowhere to go.

To her left: more buildings, still part of the hotel. Safer to go that way – more directions to run. She changed course, glanced behind. The policeman concentrated on running. Still no sign of his colleague.

Her lungs burnt. She sprinted through a cluster of trees where the grass was less well trimmed. In front of her now was a row of single-storey flat roofed buildings. Staff quarters maybe. Trish ran parallel to them but knew she couldn't keep going much longer. Her legs seemed to weigh a ton. She was nearing the corner of the building, could see a car park stretching out beyond.

Suddenly the second cop appeared round the edge in

front of her, panting, face red. For a second their eyes locked. Trish skidded to a stop. She spun round. Behind her the first policeman, grim-faced, headed towards her, slowing to a jog when he saw she was trapped.

Nowhere to go.

She sprinted for the side of the single-storey building and jumped, grabbed the edge of its flat roof with both hands and hauled herself up until she could get one foot on to a windowsill. Her trainer gripped its surface, and she pushed herself higher until her chin was above the edge of the roof. She swung her free leg on to it and rolled herself up and over on to the sharp gravel and clumps of moss. Her lungs and legs were screaming with pain.

The small stones dug into her knees and hands as she scrambled up. The two cops shouted to each other.

The roof was only the width of two rooms but long and it stretched away in front of her. The premises formed a T-shape and she was on the stem. At the far end where it met the rest of the building, it became three storeys and the wall blocked her path. She staggered towards it anyway. Over the edge of the roof to her right, she briefly saw one of the policemen racing round the perimeter, then lost sight of him. Trish was about to veer left to the edge to climb down when she realised a window was ajar in the wall that loomed ahead of her.

With renewed energy, she darted towards it, chest heaving, mouth open, sucking in air. It was a top-hung casement open just a few centimetres. She slid a hand inside to release the stay and hauled the window open. She launched herself through and tumbled into a chair that stood beneath.

Small room – single bed, wardrobe, desk, TV. No one around. The window crashed shut behind her. Trish raced to the door, twisted the catch, and wrenched it open.

A corridor dimly lit by fluorescents, vinyl on the floor rather than carpet – definitely staff, not guests. She dashed towards a fire door at the end. Her trainers squealed on the hard floor and echoed round the walls. Trish barged through the door and found a stairwell. She grabbed the handrail for support and ran down the stairs, skidding round the first turn. Light spilled from a frosted glass door at the bottom.

She had only a half-dozen steps to go when a shadow blocked the light.

Trish grabbed the rail, pulled herself to a stop, turned, and ran back up.

The door swung open, and she heard an out-of-breath male voice call, 'She's on the stairs.' In her mind's eye, she saw him using the radio. She couldn't go on. Her legs were heavy, the muscles burning with fatigue as she forced herself back towards the first floor. Her chest heaved.

She should give up, surrender.

From behind her came the pounding of boots, heavy panting.

Trish reached the landing and pushed through the door on to the corridor where she'd been minutes before. With a jolt she realised the door to the room she'd entered had clicked shut, and knew she was trapped.

She flattened herself against the wall beside the stairwell entrance, panting loudly. Blood hammered in her ears. Boots clattered on the stairs, and the door swung open towards her. Trish grabbed the handle and without thinking used all her remaining power to ram it hard back into the policeman as he charged through the opening. It caught him off guard, smashed into his shoulder, sending him sprawling. From somewhere she found a reserve of energy and tore back to the ground floor, praying the second cop wasn't there.

She burst into the cool air and ran haltingly toward the car park. As she ran between the cars, the stitch in her side became intense. Ahead was the field she'd been in earlier. She jumped the low wall that bordered it and dashed into the handful of trees. Her lungs exploded with a cough and she staggered to a halt behind an oak, coughing violently, hands on knees. This was futile. She couldn't run on.

CHAPTER THIRTY-EIGHT

Craig Tyler had left the small cluster of buildings on foot and was heading back along the dusty track to the main road. He would need transport first and then he would remake contact with Argus, repeat his offer and again insist on seeing the diary to check its authenticity. Now he had a measure for her level of protection, he knew what he had to deal with and it wasn't much.

He pulled out his mobile to call a taxi and saw he had a voice message waiting. At least the two thugs hadn't emptied his pockets. They'd taken his pistol but nothing else. That had been one-and-a-half grand totally wasted.

Tyler dialled his answering service. 'Where are you, Craig?' It was Matt Casey. 'This is really important. Trish and I have found some stuff that shows it's a guy called Hugo Metcalf who's been doing the blackmailing. She found details of one of the SIMs that was used to send messages to her.' Hugo – that was interesting. That was the name of whoever Argyle had called immediately after Tyler had made contact.

The message continued, Casey sounding almost out of breath. 'We're not sure what to do next. We're at the River Side Hotel in Gilsland, and Hugo Metcalf is here too in room 127. Things are becoming clearer. Give us a call.'

There was no point in trying Matt's mobile because the clumsy kid had lost it. He tried Trish's several times but it seemed to be switched off, and he instead called back the number Tyler had phoned from. It turned out to be the hotel, but when he was put through to Casey's room there was no answer.

So now he had a choice – either go haring up to where Matt and Trish were and follow their lead with Hugo, or try to relocate Argyle. He didn't know how long she planned to be away from home, so finding her again would take time.

He reached the road, checked his phone's sat nav to see where he was, and headed left along a narrow grass verge. There was light rain in the air, and he hunched his shoulders against it while he browsed the internet for a local taxi company and then called them. His car had broken drown, he told them, and he was walking in the direction of Great Missenden. Could they pick him up?

By the time the taxi driver found him, Tyler had made up his mind. He would head north at full speed, see what he could get from Hugo Metcalf while simultaneously keeping the pressure on Argyle by leaving messages on the answer phone in High Ridge Road.

An hour later, he was driving a two-year old Ford Focus hire car with a full tank, heading for the M40 and, ultimately, the Pennines. On the way, he planned how he would deal with Hugo Metcalf.

The journey took nearly six hours, including a brief stop for a pee and to buy a barely edible pork pie with a carton of chips and a Red Bull. Finally, he crossed from Cumbria into Northumbria and located the hotel without difficulty, leaving his hire car in the nearly empty car park.

The building's electric door swished open, and he found himself in a large marbled reception area. At the far end he could see through an arch to a bar, the long sweep of mahogany deserted. The whole place was dead at four in the afternoon.

A male receptionist in a pale blue suit and gleaming white teeth smiled in greeting. 'Good afternoon. May I help?'

Tyler still wore the jeans and fleece he'd been in when the thugs had clobbered him and he wondered what kind of picture he presented. Tyler had ensured the fleece was now zipped to hide the splatter of Dave's blood. He'd done his best to smooth down his hair but knew he probably looked a fright. 'Could you tell me if the group from Bradon Defence Electronics is back yet?'

The receptionist shook his head, his blond hair swishing gracefully like he was in a shampoo ad. 'I don't believe I've seen them yet.'

'In that case do you have some paper I could use?'

'Of course, sir.' He withdrew a pad and pen from a shelf beneath the desk and laid them on the countertop, his glowing smile never waning.

Tyler scribbled a note for Casey to tell him he'd arrived. He folded it in two, wrote Casey's name on the back, and handed it to the receptionist. 'Can you ensure Mr Matt Casey gets that as soon as he returns, please?'

Tyler turned away and headed to the bar. There was no one there, but a few seconds after he propped his elbows on the wood, a stern East European woman appeared through the door. He ordered a pint, paid in cash, and pushed through the doors to the patio with glass in hand. He needed to find a quiet place where he could meet Hugo Metcalf.

There was a paved area with wooden chairs and tables, then a long lawn edged on the left by trees and, at the end, by a tall laurel hedge. He took another slug of his drink – it felt good after the long drive – and carried it down the lawn.

Set into the far hedge was a gate and, when he pushed through it, he found the hotel grounds backed on to a river with a narrow footpath down each side. He returned to the lawn and stood under the trees for a few minutes, sinking the last of his pint while making final touches to his plan.

When he returned to the hotel, he slapped the empty glass down on the bar as he passed and walked through to reception. Taking another sheet from the ever-smiling receptionist, he carefully worded a note for Metcalf – *We must discuss Argus urgently. Events are unfolding. I need to speak now. Head through the grounds towards the river and I'll meet you near the far gate at 6:00pm.* He walked to the first floor, found Metcalf's room, and pushed it under the door.

Now he just had to wait. Inevitably, Tyler ended up back at the bar with another pint at his elbow. He called Trish's mobile but it was still off.

Slowly, the hotel became busier, and additional staff appeared at reception. A second girl with a constantly sad expression helped at the bar as it slowly filled. The clientele were mainly young men in casual dress with ID badges on chains that dangled from their necks and occasionally clinked against their glasses.

He noticed that one group clustered round a couple of tables by the door were MSA employees. Then, minutes later, another group arrived with blue badges entitled Bradon Defence Electronics. Tyler scanned the faces and caught sight of Casey's short blond hair crossing the foyer. Tyler pushed his way through the growing crowd and followed. He didn't call out as he saw no point in advertising that they knew each other. Casey gripped Tyler's note in one hand.

Tyler caught up with him as he reached the second floor and fell into step alongside. 'I decided to come and see Hugo Metcalf for myself. Where's Trish?'

'She's having to stay in my room. You won't believe what's happened.' He explained about the newspaper headline.

'Shit. That's trouble.'

Casey unlocked his room and stopped, surprised, just inside. 'Trish? You there?' He knocked on the bathroom door and pushed it open, then shrugged. 'Guess she got bored of being cooped up.'

'Tell me what you know about Hugo Metcalf.' They sat on the edge of the bed and Tyler listened intently. Casey concluding by asking, 'What's the best way forward?'

'Well, I'm going to get a meeting the Hugo Metcalf.' Tyler glanced at his watch. 'Actually, I should be heading out there now. I'll let you know how I get on.'

Minutes later, Tyler pushed through the crowd in the bar and out into the garden, past the smokers who loitered on the patio, and took up position out of sight among the trees at the end of the lawn. It was half an hour to go and he couldn't be certain Metcalf had even got the message. His mobile buzzed like a trapped wasp, and he pulled it out. Another message from the missus, soon to be ex-. He put his phone away without opening it.

The low sun was becoming no more than a glow on the horizon, and a chill started to fill the early-evening air. Other than the occasional babble of voices and music that escaped the hotel as punters stepped out for a smoke, everywhere was quiet. Even the A69 seemed silent from here.

Tyler glanced at his watch. It was well gone six.

Yet no one came.

It reminded him of watching a hotel in Sierra Leone from the end of its garden, waiting to snatch a terrorist, but their 'intel' had been wrong, and the lad never showed. The difference was the smell – there it had stunk of piss and rotting vegetables, whereas the air here smelt sweet with last year's leaves.

Suddenly, the faint click of the patio door carried down to the garden, and Tyler watched a man step on to the patio. His broad shoulders made it look as though he took up the whole doorway, and Tyler caught sight of a fat face and prominent ears.

The man quickly surveyed the lawn then strode towards where Tyler was hidden, each foot stomping into the ground with obvious annoyance. This had to be Hugo Metcalf. Tyler scanned the patio and the rear of the hotel in case anyone was watching Metcalf's back, but the blackmailer seemed to be alone.

He was close enough now for Tyler to hear the leather soles swish through the grass and the rustle of a coat, but Tyler stayed hidden among the trees. Metcalf approached the hedge at the end of the grounds and the gate that led to the riverside path. He stopped to peer over the boundary left and right and then turned and stared into the copse where Tyler waited. Tyler remained perfectly still in the deep shadows.

The gate creaked open, then clanked loudly shut behind him, and Tyler took a step forward, quickly scanning the garden for any movement before hurrying silently towards the hedge. He could hear Metcalf's feet on the gravel path the other side shuffling back and forth.

Metcalf tutted impatiently. More scrubbing of his shoes before a determined spinning on his heels and the crunch of footsteps back to the gate. It squeaked open, and Metcalf reappeared.

Tyler remained against the hedge and said quietly, 'Over here, Argus.'

Metcalf swung round and glared at Tyler. 'Was it you who sent me that stupid note?' He took a step closer.

'It was me, yes, but it wasn't "stupid". I've been sent to

talk to you about Argus.'

'I don't know what you're talking about.'

'My employer wants his diary back. He's already paid you a lot of money and he don't appreciate being stuffed for more. I've come to collect the diary from you.'

'What diary? What money?' His voice cracked with nerves.

Tyler smiled but didn't reply, allowing the silence to answer for him.

He could feel the tension as seconds passed. Eventually Metcalf said, 'If you've got nothing more to say, I'll go back to the hotel.'

'Argus, I've still got a *lot* to say. And you'd better wait around to hear it.' Tyler moved to block Metcalf's return to the buildings. 'I was talking to your mistress the other day. Very nice lady. Does your wife know about her, by the way?' No reply. Tyler continued, 'Using young Matt Casey as a cut-out for your blackmail was a good try, but I've got to him, too. I've got all the details. You give me the diary back, together with the cash you were paid, and you'll hear no more from me. I'll just disappear from your life. That would be the best for you, Argus.'

Metcalf suddenly turned and flung himself at the gate, wrenched it open and ran, yanking it shut behind him with a clang. Tyler was after him and through the gate in seconds, but the blackmailer was surprisingly quick for such a large man.

He could hear the river lapping against stones on the edge of the bank. The last pale rays of the sun glinted orange across its surface. Metcalf sprinted left along the narrow footpath, and Tyler darted after him. Tall panelled fencing blocked off several gardens to their left while thick hedges bordered others. There was no way off the path.

Suddenly Metcalf tripped and staggered sideways towards the water. Now on uneven grass, he lost his footing entirely. Tyler reached him and tried to catch his arm, but Metcalf tumbled over the shallow bank and went down hard into the river.

Without hesitation, Tyler went in after him. Cold water lapped at his waist and Tyler gasped. Metcalf was already on his feet and staggering towards deeper water as if to try to swim away. Tyler reached out and grabbed him. 'Now you bastard,' Tyler yelled. With both hands round Metcalf's fat neck, he forced his head below the inky surface. Metcalf thrashed, scrabbling at Tyler's hands. Ten seconds, then he hauled him up. Metcalf gasped, coughing.

Without letting go, Tyler snarled, 'Where's the diary?'

'I don't know—' but his words were choked off as Tyler pushed him back under the water. Metcalf kicked out while clawing furiously at Tyler's grip.

Fifteen seconds this time, then hauled him up. 'The diary.'

Metcalf suddenly swung his right arm, and something hard cracked into the side of Tyler's head. His ears whistled. He briefly loosened his grip, and Metcalf wrenched himself free. He raised his arm again, and Tyler saw him holding a stone he must have picked up from the riverbed. Metcalf started to swing it a second time towards Tyler's head, but

Tyler ducked back, felt air sweep past his face. He grabbed the arm, twisted it hard, and Metcalf screamed, dropping the rock with a splash.

One step forward and Tyler grabbed him round the neck and thrust his head back deep into the river. He was angry now, forced him down hard till his own arms were outstretched, could feel the current tugging his clothes. He wanted to hold him under till he died, but a nagging voice screamed in his head for Tyler to let him go – he needed answers.

Fifteen seconds ... twenty. Metcalf thrashed, churning up the water around them. Tyler had water-boarded an Al-Qaeda fighter once. Ten times they'd held him back and poured water down his open throat. He'd spoken in the end.

Tyler pulled him up. 'Where is it?' Metcalf spat water, coughing, choking. A strange gurgling noise came from this throat and he vomited into the river. 'Where?' Tyler repeated.

'Antonia,' he gasped then broke into a violent bought of coughing.

Tyler held him steadily by the neck. 'Antonia?'

'The diary... It's in Antonia's garage. Please—'

Metcalf's words turned into a gurgle as Tyler thrust his head back into the water and counted to fifteen. The fight was draining from Argus now. Tyler hauled him up and twisted him so their faces were close. Metcalf gagged for air, mouth wide, gasping. Tyler yelled, 'Who's Antonia?'

There was no hesitation in him now. No desire to go under again. 'She's my friend,' he said and coughed violently, spluttering in Tyler's face. 'In High Ridge Road. The diary's in her garage ... under the floor in a raised workshop area. It's there with the last two payments, honestly. Look, you can have them all.' The man's eyes showed sheer terror.

Cowards. That's what blackmailers were, Tyler thought. They got their kicks from a distance but were right shitters when they got caught. Tyler looked up and down the bank. They were still alone. 'Does she know it's there?'

'No. She doesn't know anything about this stuff. Honest.'

'But she collected the money from that derelict old mansion.'

'No. That was me. I borrowed her car. That's all. She knows nothing about this whole thing, I swear. Leave her alone.' He burst into another fit of coughing. Tyler rammed his face down into the murky water again. The river frothed around him as Metcalf tried to fight back. It splashed across Tyler's face, through his hair. He hauled him up again, and Metcalf gasped for air. 'Stop,' he spluttered. 'Please. I'm telling you what you want.'

'How much does she know?'

'Nothing.' He coughed, but the rest was choked off as Tyler rammed his face deep into the river. He scanned up and down the footpath. He was pushing his luck being here this long. The churning water glowed white. Tyler pulled him up.

Metcalf gasped, gagging and coughing. 'Please mate, you've got to believe me. Honestly, it's all true.'

'Don't "mate" me,' Tyler hissed in his ear, 'and it had

better be true or you're going to wish you'd never started this.' He gripped Metcalf's shoulder tightly, digging his fingers through the wet fabric of the coat. 'Anything else to tell me first before it's too late?'

'No.' He shook his head violently. Tyler stood, the river lapping round his thighs, and hauled Metcalf to his feet. Water dripped from their clothes.

'Then we'll go and get it.'

'We?'

'You're coming with me. We'll see if you've been lying.'

Tyler started to turn to the bank. A wind cut through his wet clothes and he could feel Metcalf shivering beneath his grip. Tyler tried to pull the other man after him, but Metcalf didn't move. 'Look,' Metcalf said, 'I've got an important meeting here this evening. I can't miss it. You don't really need me —'

The words changed into a scream as Tyler grabbed his arm and twisted. 'You're coming with me,' he hissed. 'Just to be sure.'

Tyler twisted the arm viciously, and Metcalf vomited a thin brown mucous into the water that floated across the ripples. He spat, gasping for air. 'My arm,' he moaned and twisted his head, seeing something over Tyler's left shoulder.

A distant call carried down the path on the near bank. 'Are you both okay?'

Still gripping Metcalf's shoulder tightly, Tyler turned to see a tall man in his thirties with a hiking jacket and rucksack hurrying towards them.

Tyler shouted back, 'There's been a bit of an accident, but he's okay. We'll be alright thanks.'

'Shall I call an ambulance?'

'He insists he doesn't need one.'

Tyler felt Metcalf squirming under his grip, then suddenly twist and pull free. Tyler spun round. Metcalf was wading away through the water to the other bank.

Shit. Metcalf quickly opened the gap between them. With a witness, Tyler could do nothing more. He let him go and waded back to the bank and clambered up on to the path where the hiker stood. Metcalf had nearly reached the other side and was looking back.

The walker hurried up to him. 'Goodness, you're soaked. What happened?'

'I think he twisted his ankle and went into the river.'

'Is he alright?'

'I think so.' They watched as Metcalf staggered across the loose stones to the other path, glanced at them, then hurried away. 'He was a weird fellow,' Tyler added and tried to brush himself down. 'I need to go and get dry.' The hiker smiled as Tyler jogged back to the gate.

It was a gamble now. He could head back south to High Ridge Road or go after Metcalf, but Metcalf had already disappeared from sight, and Tyler reckoned he would have little chance of finding him now. He thought he'd been telling the truth, but the risk was that Metcalf could quickly be on a phone to his mistress or one of his thugs to get them to move the diary. It would take Tyler hours to get back down there.

He hesitated just inside the hotel grounds, then made up his mind. He would go south ... and hope Metcalf hadn't lied.

CHAPTER THIRTY-NINE

Matt Casey felt hollow inside. He left the bedroom curtains open, although the sun had finally dropped below the treetops. Trish was gone, and he had no idea what had happened to her. His guts twisted at the thought Wendell had caught up with her. Why else wasn't she here? Maybe she was already lying in a hastily dug grave. *And I never said how I felt about her.*

He hadn't eaten and now felt sick. After Tyler had left, he'd called Trish's mobile on the off-chance she had it powered, but it had still been off. He had checked all the hotel's public areas with a growing sense of helplessness. He'd ended up in the bar, where three of his colleagues were sitting with pints at a round table. They'd waved him over. 'We missed all the fun while we were out today,' one of them said, a spotty electronics geek. 'Apparently the cops were here. Some sort of manhunt. There was a big chase right through the hotel.'

Casey stared at him, his chest constricting. 'How d'you

know that?' he managed to ask. He felt weak.

Someone else added, 'He was trying to chat up the receptionist.'

'What if?' The geek turned back to Casey. 'She said the police were here for ages.'

'Did they get whoever they were looking for?' Casey's voice caught as he asked, and he wondered if they'd noticed.

'She didn't know.'

Casey had extricated himself and sidled up to the reception desk, his mouth dry. 'Have there been any messages for me? Room 214.'

She checked and shook her head. 'Sorry sir.'

As casually as he could manage, he said, 'I hear you had some sort of manhunt going on here today. Did the police find whoever they were looking for?'

A professional smile. 'I don't know. They were here a long time, but I didn't see them go.'

Casey nodded. 'I guess it'll be in the papers tomorrow.' He had trudged up the stairs to his room on legs that felt like lead.

Now, he was still standing at the bedroom window, staring blankly out at the darkness. Trish was great. Clever, gutsy, really attractive. He imagined pulling her into an embrace, holding her tight. *Trish, I hope you're alright wherever you are.* He tried playing with his new phone to take his mind off things, scanning through the screens and customising the settings, but it didn't help.

The gentle tap on his door ten minutes later made him jump violently. It had been so quiet he wondered if he'd imagined it. He cocked his head to one side. It came again and he raced to the door and pressed his eye to the peephole. The corridor was dim but the dishevelled shape was definitely Trish. She was looking nervously left and right.

He wrenched open the door and drew her in, quickly slamming the door behind her. Casey hugged her tight, feeling her cold cheeks against his. 'You're frozen,' he said and stepped back. 'What happened? I heard about the police. Was it you they were after?'

She smiled faintly. 'I'm fine. Can I use your loo, though?'

'Of course.' He moved into the bedroom to let her pass. 'Tell me what happened,' he called through the door.

'Just give me a sec. We need to talk about the stuff I found in Hugo Metcalf's room. I've been thinking more about it.'

'You sound so cool about what happened. How did you get away?'

'I've spent the whole afternoon and evening up a tree. I guess someone recognized me from that newspaper photo despite everything we did. I was terrified at one point when a police van with dogs came up the drive but they seemed to be searching outside the grounds.'

The flushing of the toilet prevented any further conversation. She emerged a few moments later. 'Anyway, where's Craig?' she asked. 'Did he make it?'

'He was here when I got back from the trials but he hurried out for a meeting with Hugo Metcalf. I've not seen him since. I tried to call him once but his phone went to voicemail.' He realised she was shivering. 'You're cold,' he said, and pulled the duvet off the bed and gently draped it round her shoulders. 'Here, have this. I'll make you some coffee.'

She dropped wearily on to the edge of the bed while he crossed to the tray on the side and flicked on the kettle. The maid had left a tiny complimentary pack of biscuits, and he threw it across to her. 'Are you hungry?'

'Thanks.' She tore open the cellophane. 'I hit a policeman in order to escape,' she said. 'I feel so bad about it. What if I really hurt him?'

As he made a coffee, he said over his shoulder, 'Why didn't you phone me or something, let me know what had happened?'

'To start with, I was too terrified to do anything. I didn't dare make a noise. Then once everyone had left, I thought about it but reckoned they would be monitoring the mobile networks for any sign of my number, so I thought I'd better not use it.'

He handed her the drink and Trish cupped both hands round the mug with the duvet draped across her shoulders. She reminded him of those photos of refugees rescued by the Red Cross. He sat beside her and put an arm round her to keep her warm. She leaned toward him.

They were silent for a moment before Matt said, 'You mentioned something about wanting to tell me more about the stuff in Hugo Metcalf's room.'

She nodded vigorously. 'Yeah. I kept thinking about some papers that were with that till receipt. They didn't seem relevant at first so I ignored them, but having spent all day running this whole thing round and round in my head, I started wondering.' She pulled away from him and took out her phone. 'I've been keeping this in airplane mode, but I photographed everything. Most of the other papers were just business invoices, but I'm positive one of them was for a rental near here and I keep coming back to it and wondering if it's relevant.'

Trish dropped the duvet and stood, putting her coffee on the bedside unit. She sat back down and their shoulders touched as they both watched the phone display.

Seconds later, she had the pictures up on the screen, and scrolled through them until she found the one she wanted. 'Look at this,' she said and enlarged it. What would Hugo Metcalf want with a very short-term rent of a warehouse near here? Do you think it's significant?' She looked at him for an answer, her eyes sparkling with excitement.

Her face was so close that he felt her breath across his cheek, setting his heart pounding. He swallowed, looked away, back to her phone. 'It can't be anything to do with the demos we're all up here for. These UAVs have military level security, and that includes any spare components. MSA has got a secure area on the RAF base like the rest of us. Nothing's allowed outside of that.'

'So could it be anything to do with his blackmailing schemes?'

Casey nodded slowly. 'I certainly can't see it being business related.'

She flicked through the other photos, but the rest looked

like just legit company invoices. 'Can you try Craig again? I'm starting to feel out of my depth.'

Casey picked up his mobile from where he'd dropped it on the bed. This time, Tyler answered and it was clear he was driving. Trish leant close to listen. 'Where are you, Craig?' Casey asked.

'Something's come up and I've had to turn round.'

Casey sighed. 'Did you get to meet Hugo Metcalf?'

'Just briefly. I don't think it helps much, though.'

'Well, we've got some more news here. First of all, Trish is safe.'

'That's good.' He didn't sound particularly bothered.

'The other thing is that there was a receipt in Hugo Metcalf's room that suggests he's temporarily renting a warehouse near here.'

'So?'

'We think we should go and have a look at it to see what he's storing there. It might be related to the blackmail.'

'Sorry mate, I won't be back until tomorrow lunchtime at the absolute earliest. You'll have to wait till I get back.' There was a pause. 'I've got to go. I'm driving. I'll be in touch.'

The call was cut, and Trish and Casey looked at each other. Trish shook her head. 'I've said all along he's got his own agenda. I noticed he didn't say *why* he suddenly had to head back.'

'Well, I know what *I* want to do,' Casey said. 'I want to take a look at that warehouse. And I'm not going to wait for Craig.'

CHAPTER FORTY

It was nearly ten that evening by the time Trish and Casey found the warehouse in a dark corner of the industrial estate. An odour of acetate hung on the night air, carried from one of the adjacent factories. They were all grim, dark buildings, a mix of brick and rusting metal.

It had taken a long time to get a hire car. Casey had phoned everywhere local, many of whom were shut, but eventually found one who'd been prepared to drop a car off that evening at the hotel. It hadn't been cheap, and Casey wasn't sure he could really afford it.

They parked out of sight near a pair of dumpsters and crept into the gloom. Light from street lamps on the main road didn't penetrate that far into the cul-de-sac, and Trish pulled a torch from her bag.

Unit five was identified by a faded numeral stencilled on its brickwork, and an estate agent had nailed a "Let" sign to the wall. A gust of wind sent some loose newspaper pages across the concrete until they stuck round a drain pipe, flapping like a dying bird. Casey shivered.

They peered in through a barred window but could see nothing. Farther along was a wooden door held shut by a padlock. Trish's torch beam picked out the peeling surface, and Casey twisted the handle and gave the door a shake. The hasp keeping it closed rattled and didn't look particularly strong. 'Wait here. I'll get something.' He ran back to the car, hoping it was sufficiently old fashioned still to have a spare tyre. Under the boot liner, he found the long metal handle from the jack and was soon brandishing it at Trish's side. 'Stand back.'

He jammed the metal into the gap behind the hasp and levered hard against the frame. With a screech, screws tore from the wood and scattered across the concrete. The padlock and the loop that had held it clattered to the ground, sending an echo bouncing off the surrounding walls. *What am I doing?* Casey asked himself. *I'm not a criminal.* It brought him up with a start. What Argus had made him do meant he probably already was.

He pulled open the door and then rubbed the handle clean with his coat sleeve. 'Better not touch anything,' he whispered.

Trish's torch beam picked out a dusty rectangular room the size of a small sports hall, and he sighed loudly. 'It's empty.' To the left were rows of tall metal racks arrayed like a library. They were thick with dust and held a haphazard collection of battered cardboard boxes, some open and on their sides. He pulled a couple down, but found them empty. Above their heads loomed a ceiling-mounted gantry and crane with chains that hung lifeless out of reach. Dangling cobwebs glistened as she swept her torch across it.

Beyond the racks along the outside wall were three offices with glass windows on to the main area. Casey pushed open the first door and peered in with Trish at his shoulder holding the torch. Just one old table in the middle, thick with grit and dust. A mouse darted away from the beam of light.

They stepped back, and Trish swung the torch around the rest of the factory. At the far end, the light reflected off translucent plastic ribbons that hung vertically to form a barrier. Their scratched surfaces glowed pale in the torch beam. Casey pushed through them into a larger part of the warehouse. He held the plastic strips aside for Trish to join him, and she slowly swung the light across the space. What they saw made Casey freeze.

'What is it?' Trish gasped.

'A partly dismantled UAV.' She stepped forward and swept the torch beam along its matt grey sides. 'That's the main fuselage,' Casey said as the beam lit the individual items. 'That's a radar dome. The landing gear is over there and those are the electric motors. And I think that crate probably contains its batteries.' Next to it sat the hemispherical camera housing, looking like an oversized space helmet with round tinted apertures that glowed in the torchlight like alien eyes. The beam completed its scan of the room, resting finally on the wings that lay in sections along the side wall, propped against wooden batons.

'Wow. It's large,' Trish said, and they slowly walked

round it. It wasn't one of BDE's, but Casey recognized it nonetheless. The shape of the body and the splay of the wing tips were characteristic of an MSA design. He'd seen one fully assembled on the runway the day before at the RAF base.

They stopped near the tail fin. It sat at an angle because of the craft's absent wheels, looking as if the drone had crashed. Memories Casey had spent months trying to suppress flashed painfully in his mind. He had stood with the engineers in a ring round the wreckage of their UAV like mourners at a graveside. The tail fin had stood proud, still upright despite the tangled fuselage. He went cold at the memory. They were the last trials he had attended, when he'd been tricked into changing the flight software.

Casey felt the same clenching in his stomach as he had felt when he'd seen their drone suddenly dip its nose and plummet downwards. He could still hear the sudden gasp from the engineers beside him, followed by spectators' screams as it had dived towards them, air whistling from its wings.

Casey clenched his teeth. MSA had made that happen – or Metcalf at least – and BDE's orders had suddenly vaporised as a result. Thirty of their workforce had been laid off. He'd been there for that, feeling the guilt and shame.

Maybe fate was handing him an opportunity for recompense. 'That's one of MSA's,' Casey said at last when he realised Trish was staring at him. 'And it shouldn't be here.'

'A spare maybe in case something goes wrong at the

demos?'

'No.' He shook his head violently. 'You don't understand the security. If this is for the MOD, there's no way it should be here in an unsecured site like this. This is something unofficial.' Anger rose in his chest. 'Maybe they're cheating at the trials and this ...' He tailed off. 'But I don't see how this would help them ....' Then he remembered what Wendell had said on his phone call while they were in the car. 'You said Wendell's an arms dealer, right?'

'I think so. That's certainly the impression I got from the blackmail letters.'

'That phone call he received in the car, could it have been from Hugo Metcalf? Could Metcalf be arranging to illegally sell him a UAV? He could have used the trials as an excuse to get two crafts out of their factory, and then secretly diverted one here.'

'But why all this subterfuge? Why not just sell it normally?'

'Because there are many countries you wouldn't be allowed to sell it to. If North Korea wanted one, for instance, they wouldn't be allowed to have it. They're embargoed for military stuff like this.'

'So, Kurt Wendell and Hugo Metcalf are doing an illegal arms deal?'

'It could be,' Casey said. 'My guess is that this is where Wendell was heading, ready for a meeting with Hugo Metcalf to check this UAV before the sale.'

'And Wendell doesn't know it's Argus he'll be talking to, does he.' She was talking fast now, excitedly. 'Wendell will be stitching himself up good and proper because Hugo Metcalf's going to play it both ways – first selling it illegally to Wendell to make a fat profit for MSA, and then he'll come back under the guise of Argus and blackmail Wendell even more for illegal arms trading and get another pile of money for himself.'

'So, the bastard wins twice,' Casey muttered and gritted his teeth. 'That's what he did to me, isn't it. He got me to do something wrong, and then turned up as Argus and blackmailed me for it.' He bunched his fists.

'But you know what?' Trish said and waved her torch beam in excitement. 'We could use this to break Argus. I mean, if we somehow let Wendell know what Metcalf's up to, Wendell will turn on him. He didn't hesitate to try to get rid of me, did he.'

'It'll be like putting two tigers in a ring and giving one a poke,' Casey said. 'How do you know we won't end up being mauled in the process?'

'We'd have to be careful but it would get Argus out of our hair for good.'

Casey fell silent for a moment before stroking the smooth top of the tail fin. 'Whatever we do, this beasty shouldn't be here. We've got to tell someone about it.'

'We can't,' she snapped back. 'If we do that, we'll have to explain how we knew about this warehouse and we'll have to admit to breaking into Metcalf's room. And then they'll ask why we targeted his particular room, and the whole blackmail thing will come out. I'm not doing that.' She paused. 'And, anyway, I'm staying out of it. The police are looking for me, remember?'

'So, what the hell do you suggest we do? We can't just ignore it.'

Trish bit her nails. 'I'm trying to think. What about an anonymous tip-off?'

'Maybe. If we tell the authorities that both men are on their way here, they can lay in wait and round up the pair when they turn up. Put them both behind bars. Won't that solve everything for us? We could tell the police anonymously.'

'I guess ...' she said. 'I'd probably feel better about that. I'll confess that setting them up so Wendell kills Metcalf does give me the shivers. Made me feel like I'm turning into one of them.' Casey was about to reply when he realised she was still thinking, so stayed silent, not wanting to break her train of thought. Eventually, she frowned and shook her head. 'Are the police going to take an anonymous tip-off seriously enough to respond quickly? I mean, Wendell's probably going to be here tonight.'

He sighed. 'Yeah, you're probably right. The police won't hurry if it sounds like a hoax.' Casey's guts twisted at the thought that Wendell could appear any minute. 'Perhaps we'd better get out of here and think about what we're going to do on the way back.'

She nodded. 'I'd feel a lot happier with Craig's expertise at our side.'

'Come on then. We'll try to call him again on the way. He might have some contacts who could convince the police to act.' They pushed back through the plastic strips and were soon driving back to the hotel.

Trish used Casey's new phone to call Tyler, and this time he answered. She switched it to speaker so Casey could hear. The light from the display made her face glow. She's so pretty, Casey thought but resisted the impulse to reach out and take hold of her free hand. The twists in the road ahead meant she would need both hands on the wheel.

'We've got a lot to tell you,' Trish said.

'Go on.' It was clear Tyler was driving too. She relayed what they'd found.

'Do you think it's anything to do with the MOD trials Matt's at?'

Casey shouted over the road noise. 'I don't think so. I can't see how it would help them to have another one here.'

Trish was nodding. 'We reckon it's most likely an illegal arms sale to Kurt Wendell. Our guess is that he'll do the deal and then come back hiding behind the name of Argus to blackmail Wendell for buying it.'

Tyler came back choppy over the mobile link. 'Won't Kurt Wendell get suspicious of how Argus found out and put two and two together?'

Casey concentrated on driving the unlit winding road, leaving the conversation to Trish. 'Maybe,' she said, 'but Argus is clever. He's probably done this sort of thing before.' Casey felt himself blush.

'You could try going to the MOD about it rather than the police,' Tyler suggested. 'That might get a better result. In fact, if Matt can get someone high up in BDE to talk to them, then they'll take it seriously and they'll act quickly, especially if they think it's a security breach. That's more likely to work than you trying to tell someone yourself. I could phone Art Bradon but I'm a bit tied-up right now and you're both there on the ground.'

'Can't you phone one of your old contacts from the SAS? They'd have enough clout with the police.'

There was a pause and Casey thought they'd lost the call. Eventually, Tyler said, 'Right this second, I'm in the middle of something else and I can't afford to get caught up in loads of phone calls. Besides, I'm not sure I've got the best contacts for that. The pair of you are right there and if you can get authorities to act via BDE, it should be effective enough.'

'The only thing is, we'll need to think up an excuse how we knew about it,' Trish said.

'Definitely. The MOD Plod will want to understand your involvement.'

'That's what's worrying me. That's why we wanted to do it anonymously.'

'I'm sure you'll think of something.' And Tyler ended the call.

They drove on in silence. Casey was wondering how to explain away what they'd discovered, but however much he tried, he still hadn't thought of a decent excuse by the time they reached the hotel.

The car park was wedged solid as if the bar was offering free drinks. He jumped out, leaving the engine running. 'Find a space in the overflow, will you? We haven't a second to lose,' and without another word, he tossed her his room card and dashed into the hotel.

CHAPTER FORTY-ONE

Tyler hung up as he turned into High Ridge Road. Argyle's place was in darkness, and he parked opposite the empty drive. He scanned the surrounding houses for twitching curtains. He saw none. Having adjusted the car's interior light so it wouldn't come on, he slipped from the car. The night air was surprisingly cold, but totally still and silent.

There was enough light from the street to see the tarpaulin-covered cement mixer and pile of sand but the double garage was no more than a dark shape to the left. Its door was a standard up-and-over affair, and the flat end of the crowbar he'd brought with him had the catch released in seconds. Cautiously, he raised the door, wincing when it squealed on its runners. He eased it up just enough to duck inside, then gently pulled it down behind him, leaving it open just a crack.

A throbbing headache was developing where Metcalf had clouted him with the stone. The double-dose of Paracetamol he'd taken at a service station wasn't doing much. He flicked on his torch and swept its beam around inside the garage. 'Under a raised workshop area,' Argus had said, but Tyler was greeted by a pair of adult bikes, a lawn mower, and a jumble of spades and forks standing along one wall. An ancient workbench piled high with old paint tins stood in a corner, and a rusting bed frame was propped beside it. A large chest freezer hummed gently, and a stack of paint tins and a step ladder rested among cobwebs against the other wall. Had Metcalf been lying?

Tyler moved into the centre of the garage and slowly swept the torch around again. He let it linger on a stack of cardboard boxes in front of the workbench and realised they hid the fact there was a small dais behind them, no more than six inches tall. He investigated further. The bench with its chipped and paint-splashed top was bolted to the raised area and was stacked high with dusty paint tins, a few hand tools, and a roll of decaying carpet.

Tyler slid away the boxes. Many of them were empty and disintegrating with the dampness. Those that weren't just held a single tin of paint. The patina of dust and grit on top of them was smudged, and the couple of spiders' webs that clung to their sides were clean and fresh.

With growing excitement, Tyler knelt to examine the chipboard panels that formed the raised floor. The screws in one of the boards were freshly burred, and the rough metal glinted in the beam. 'Yes,' he muttered out loud.

Tyler searched through the tools on top of the bench for a screwdriver. With racing pulse, he removed the screws, tossed the wood aside, and peered into the void.

Three large jiffy bags, each sealed with a single line of tape, unaddressed. He was a bit surprised there wasn't more. If these were all Bradon's, where was the stuff from his other victims? Trish, Matt and Wendell? Perhaps what he had on them wasn't physical like a diary. He fingered the bags. The first two felt as if they held money, but the third was what he wanted. It held something slim and hard. A notebook.

As Tyler picked at the tape, the door runners squealed behind him and the whole room burst into light. Tyler spun, still crouching. Through squinting eyes, he saw a handgun levelled at his stomach, held steady in a fat hand.

Tyler stood slowly, clutching the envelopes, eyes adjusting quickly.

From about twelve feet away, he faced the heavily built thug he knew as Dave, the guy he'd headbutted. From this distance, sadly, his nose didn't look too bad.

Tyler felt adrenaline thundering through him, quickening his heart, setting his fingers tingling. Dave took a step forward. 'You stay right there or I'll put a bullet through you.'

'I'm not moving.' He recognised the gun as his own Sig Sauer P226. It was good to see it again, but not from this end. 'D'you know how to use that thing?'

Dave grinned. 'You want to try me?'

Running footsteps outside. Tyler tensed his muscles, ready to dive for the weapon if Dave was distracted, but the bald man's glare never left Tyler.

Out of the corner of his eye, Tyler saw Beanie-Boy duck

under the door. It seemed the two came as a pair. Tyler glanced quickly at him – pockmarked skin, black leather jacket, and still with his hat firmly on his head. The man was panting as he came to a halt beside Dave. 'Sorry mate,' he grunted. 'I only just saw your text.' Local then, thought Tyler. There had been no sound of a car.

The two of them glared at Tyler.

'What have you been told to do?' Tyler asked.

Dave took the lead as he had at the warehouse. 'What are you holding?'

Tyler shrugged. 'What's it to you?'

'Hand them over.'

'Look,' Tyler said, putting his head to one side, trying to look as unthreatening as he could, which he knew at over six feet tall and being heavily built was not easy. 'There's a load of money here. Thousands. All I want is a little book that's of no value to you. You let me keep the book and we'll split the money. Here. Have a look.' Tyler tossed the fattest package towards them. Dave flinched at the movement, and for a second Tyler thought he might shoot.

It landed on the concrete between the two men. 'Check it,' Dave said to his friend without taking his eyes off Tyler. Beanie-Boy picked it up and tore off the tape. He pulled out a handful of twenties and laughed. 'There's loads here.'

Dave held his gun steadily on Tyler. 'Why don't I just kill you and take the whole lot anyway?'

Tyler sighed dramatically. 'Because then Argus will know it's you who got it. If we share it and you let me go, you can say that by the time you got here I was gone. He'll blame me and assume I took the lot.'

'I could shoot you and say the same' He was obviously keen on the shooting bit.

'If you fire that thing in here, you'll have all the neighbours coming round to see what's going on. Argus will soon learn you shot me and will want to know where the money went. It won't work. But if you let me walk out of here, you'll be rich, and he'll never know.'

Beanie-Boy glanced at his friend hopefully. 'There's got to be ten grand here,' he said and waved a handful of notes towards him.

Dave thought about it. Obviously, a painful process. Eventually he said, 'Give us the other ones.'

'This is only an old book. It's no use to you.' Tyler held up the smaller of the two packages. It was clearly not stuffed with cash.

'The other one.'

'One each.'

Dave brought the gun up slightly, aimed more at Tyler's head. 'Give us the other one.' Tyler tossed the padded envelope of money towards him. Keeping the gun trained on Tyler, Dave bent and picked up the package. 'Show us that last one.'

'It's only a book'

'I wanna see.'

With a sigh, Tyler held it out towards him, showing the slimness of the package.

'Give it here.'

'I said it's only a bloody book! It's no use to you.'

'So why d'you need it?'

'It was stolen from a mate. He wants it back.'

Dave screwed up his ugly face. 'Na. Give it here.'

'It's no value to you at all.'

In answer, Dave thrust the packet he already held into his coat's large outer pocket and gripped the gun in both hands. His finger curled tighter. 'I'll decide that. Now give it.'

Tyler studied his face, the steadiness of his hands, then tossed the jiffy bag towards him, letting it fall midway on the concrete.

Dave moved cautiously to one side. Without taking his eyes off Tyler, he said to Beanie-Boy, 'Pick it up and let's go.'

His accomplice did as he was instructed and retreated, pushing it into Dave's outstretched hand. Dave thrust it into his pocket with the other package and backed slowly towards the garage door. Beanie-Boy had already turned and disappeared through the gap.

Tyler's heart was pounding. He knew if they were going to shoot him it would be now. He tensed, poised to dive to one side if the gun finger tightened further. Dave paused in the doorway and reached for the light switch with his free hand. The room went dark.

In that instance, Tyler dropped to the floor but there was no shot. The only sound was their footfall across the drive.

Tyler picked up the heavy crowbar from where he'd left it and hurried silently after them.

CHAPTER FORTY-TWO

The bar was busy when Casey hurried into the hotel. It was packed almost exclusively by young men in shirt sleeves, some still with ID badges swinging from the necks as they drank. The hubbub of voices drowned an obscure music track that was playing from hidden speakers. He guessed the crowd represented the other companies here for the trials, but he caught sight of the man he was looking for at the far end of the bar and pushed his way across.

Casey reckoned Art Bradon, his CEO, was in his early sixties, skinny and drawn-looking as if a heap of problems weighed on those scrawny shoulders. Casey knew him by sight from the quarterly company presentations he gave, although Casey had never spoken to him. Bradon was sipping whiskey and chatting to one of their engineers. Casey hovered nearby and soon caught Bradon's eye. Bradon smiled. 'Let me get you a drink,' he offered immediately. 'Beer?'

'No thanks,' Casey said quickly, 'but I did wonder if you

could spare a moment for me to ask you something.'

'Of course. Fire away.'

Casey looked awkwardly at the engineer, who took the hint and downed the last of his drink. 'You go ahead. I need an early night anyway.'

Bradon kept his intense eyes on Casey as though sizing him up. 'So, what can I do for you?'

He'd rehearsed this but now it came to voicing it out loud his stomach tightened. 'I think I've stumbled across an issue with one of our competitors,' he said in a lowered voice.

Bradon put down his tumbler and looked at him cautiously. 'What d'you mean?'

'Well, these are all potential MOD projects, so aren't they all meant to be under strict security?' Bradon nodded. 'Well, I came across one of our competitors' crafts in an unsecured warehouse just outside the town.'

'Whose?'

'I think it's one of MSA's.'

Bradon's cheeks flushed. 'They're trying something on again,' he snapped. 'I never trusted those bastards.' Suddenly the genial grandfather-like figure had gone. Instead, dark eyes burned into Casey's. 'How did you see it?'

The question he'd dreaded. He shifted his weight from one foot to the other and looked down at the edge of the countertop. Subconsciously, he ran a finger along its scratched edge. 'I bumped into someone on the way up here who'd rented a warehouse. I was kind of curious so went to have a look.'

'Really?' It was clear Bradon didn't believe him. Not surprising.

'Yes,' he said and looked straight at his CEO, determined to keep eye contact. 'I thought if I told the MOD about it, they might not take me seriously, but if it came from someone like you, you'd have so much more clout.'

There was silence for a moment. *He might not believe my crappy story, but he wants to know more.* Bradon stood and tried to peer across the heads of everyone in the bar. He was a good six-feet tall. Suddenly he snapped, 'Come with me,' and marched through the crowd that parted for him.

'Austin,' he called as he approached a round table with three men in suits. The one in the middle looked up sharply, and Casey recognised him as the man who'd been with Hugo Metcalf at breakfast, the head of MSA and Art Bradon's uncle. He was heavily built with a fleshy face, in his late seventies with neat white hair and tidily trimmed beard and moustache. Bradon said brusquely, 'I need a word. Now.'

Casey hung back, not recognizing the two other men with him.

The man locked eyes with Bradon and when he spoke, his words were smooth with a distinct upper-class plum. 'Evening Arthur. Have you come to harass me again like you did yesterday?'

'No. I just need a few words. Perhaps best in private.'

His watery eyes glanced briefly at Casey, apparently dismissed him, and turned back to Bradon. 'I suppose I can spare you five minutes. Let's go outside.' He turned to his two colleagues. 'Excuse me, gentlemen. I'll be back in a moment.' He stood and followed Bradon, who was already marching into the lobby. Casey trailed behind them.

They stopped abruptly in a quiet corner of the lobby, and Bradon spun round. 'So, what's going on? Are you trying to pull a fast one again?'

Austin raised his hands to stop him. 'I don't know what you're talking about. If that's all you're going to say, I'll return to my team.' He started to turn away, but Bradon grabbed his arm. 'Why have you got one of your UAVs in an off-site warehouse? Hiding it away for no-one to see. What are you up to?'

Austin's face was mix of surprise and anger. 'Don't be so ridiculous. Why the hell would we do that?'

'That's what I'm hoping you'll tell me.'

'You're imagining stuff again. Perhaps you're going senile. That always did run in your side of the family.'

'If you don't explain why it's there, I'll have no choice but to inform the MOD Plod.'

Austin sighed heavily. 'Look, our craft is secured in the hangar at Spadeadam just like yours. Let me spell it out to your dull brain.' He spoke slowly as though to a child, emphasising each word. 'We have no UAV hidden away in any warehouse anywhere. Okay?' He shook his arm free of Bradon's grip and glared at him while brushing his sleeve smooth. 'Are we finished with this nonsense?'

'No.' He nodded towards Casey. 'This is one of my team,' Bradon said, and Austin seemed to notice him for the first time. 'Describe what you saw.'

Casey's throat went dry. 'Well, there's a warehouse nearby with a UAV inside. And it does look like one of yours. I might be wrong, I suppose. Perhaps I was mistaken as to the manufacturer.'

Austin pursed his lips and glared at Casey before turning back to Bradon. 'Show me,' he said suddenly. 'I don't believe a word of this. We can drive there now and end this stupidity. I think you've finally gone insane listening to such nonsense.'

Bradon hesitated, glanced at Casey and then nodded. 'Alright. Let's go now.' Under his breath, he whispered to Casey, 'You'd better be right about this, son, or the old fool's going to make a right meal out of it. That's Austin Metcalf, MSA's owner.'

Metcalf? The family links suddenly hit Casey hard, almost made him come to a halt. Casey remembered something he'd once read in the trade press. Like Bradon Defence Electronics, MSA was still a family business, father at the head, offspring and their spouses in senior positions. Was the man he was following Hugo Metcalf's father? His age was about right.

The trio marched from the hotel, and Austin's Jaguar was soon purring up the road towards Meadow View Industrial Estate with Casey in the front, navigating. They parked where Casey had left his hire car earlier that evening, and the two men followed him silently on foot to the broken door. Casey took out the torch he'd borrowed from Trish. 'We need to go through this first bit and it's in the other room.'

They had barely entered the premises – were still at the start of the rows of shelves – when Casey froze as the sight of light glowing from beyond the plastic partition. His heart hammered, and he instantly cut the torch and spun round with a finger to his lips. 'There's someone here,' he whispered.

He crept forward, noting indistinguishable men's voices. Having the other two behind him gave him a strange confidence. Casey flattened himself against the end wall and peered through the vertical slats of plastic. Every muscle was taut.

He could just make out the top of two heads on the far side of the fuselage. The view was blurred, like seeing through a steamed-up window. Now he was close, he recognized Wendell's voice. 'It can be across the border in nine days' time and at the rendezvous two days after that. That's the point at which I'll be paid and I can transfer your payment then.'

'Hold on, that's not what we agreed. I need the full amount before I can release it to you.' The second voice was that of the man on the answer phone – Hugo Metcalf. Argus.

'Then what I pay drops by fifty percent.'

They were walking slowly round the UAV, examining it as they spoke. Metcalf stopped at the nose of the craft and spun to face Wendell, stabbing a finger at him. 'That is not the way to do business. We had an agreement.'

'And I cannot release the balance until I have received payment myself, which I will get when I hand this over. I'm just a broker.'

'You agreed to pay eight point six million dollars. And that agreement stands. If you can't transfer the final payment now, then this craft goes back where it came from and I'll go to another customer.'

Casey was suddenly aware of movement beside him. Austin pushed past him and burst through the partition, overcoat flapping around him. 'Hugo, what the hell are you playing at? This shouldn't be here.'

The two men spun to face him. Wendell stiffened and thrust his hand into a coat pocket. *Shit, he's got a gun*, Casey thought. Metcalf took a step round the front of the UAV. 'Dad, why are you here?' He sounded puzzled, but that quickly changed to anger. 'What's this to do with you anyway?'

'What's it to do with me? It's still my company don't forget, at least for now. What the hell do you think you're doing? Do the rest of the board know about this?'

'It's some extra business, helping bring in more revenue. Something *you* were never very good at.'

Austin took a step closer until he was only inches from his son. 'This is not the way to do it. We're a reputable and trusted company. We always have been and I will not let you endanger a reputation that we've spent years building.' He turned to Wendell for the first time. 'And whoever you are, you'd better leave. This sale is off.'

Wendell shook his head. 'Signed and sealed. Anyway, who are you?'

'Austin Metcalf. Owner and chairman of MSA. I have

ultimate control and I'm stopping this ridiculous action. Sorry, but you'd better leave. There's clearly been an error of judgment somewhere in my company that I need to resolve.'

Metcalf's right arm was in a cloth sling but he grabbed at his father's jacket with the other. 'Don't be so stupid. No one will find out. And it's much needed revenue. You know how much we need that.'

'It's amoral. And anyway, how are you going to hide it in the books? The auditors will spot it immediately.'

'Don't be naive. Of course there's a way to hide it. And the company needs this extra money.'

'Not like this it doesn't.'

Wendell raised his voice. 'The deal's done anyway so you're too late. Now leave us alone, old man. Go back to your Zimmer frame and leave us to conduct our business.'

Austin Metcalf straightened his back. 'You don't talk to me like that. This deal is off. Now clear out.' He started to turn back to his son. 'We'd better get this craft secured.'

Wendell's blow caught him by surprise. The butt of the heavy pistol he'd pulled from his coat cracked into the side of Austin's head. The old man staggered into his son. Metcalf tried to catch him but failed. Austin fell forward, head catching the fuselage, and he slumped on to the concrete. Metcalf bent over his father, shaking his shoulder. 'Dad. Are you okay?' There was no reply and Metcalf spun to face the arms dealer. 'You bastard. Why d'you do that? You could have killed him.' Ashen faced, he turned back to Austin, who wasn't moving.

'The stupid old fool should not have interfered with me.

If he tries again, I warn you I'll put a bullet in his skull,' Wendell barked.

Metcalf suddenly lunged forward, wildly chopping at the gun hand. Wendell quickly stepped sideways to avoid him and threw a heavy punch with his free hand that smashed into Metcalf's cheek. Metcalf staggered but caught his balance. He swore and ran at Wendell, flailing wildly with his one able arm. Wendell jumped back, waited a beat, then with steady precision hammered his fist into Metcalf's face. It stopped him like he'd run into a bus. Metcalf staggered for a moment before toppling sideways into the fuselage. He grabbed at its smooth metallic surface in vain for support and slumped to the floor.

Wendell took a step forward and kicked him hard in the ribs. Metcalf grunted and curled into a ball. Wendell stood over him, panting slightly. 'Don't be so stupid again,' he snapped. 'We should not be brawling like children. We have a professional deal.'

Metcalf said nothing.

'How did the old fool get here anyway?'

'I don't know,' Metcalf muttered and hauled himself to his feet using the UAV as support. 'He certainly didn't follow me.' Metcalf crouched over his father.

From their hiding place behind the plastic partition, Casey took a step quietly back and tapped Bradon lightly on the arm. He put his mouth to his boss' ear. 'We'd better go and get help.'

As they started to turn away, Wendell caught sight of their movement. He yelled something in German, and as

Casey glanced back at them, he saw two men burst through a door behind Wendell.

'Come on.' Casey grabbed Bradon's arm. 'Run.' The arms dealer was shouting commands in German, and his men pushed through the partition, sending the strips of plastic flapping wildly. Torch beams sliced through the darkness around Casey. Long shadows lurched across the brickwork. Casey sprinted for the moonlight beyond the broken back door. Hands grabbed at his coat. Behind him he heard a scuffle and Bradon grunt.

Casey pulled free and dodged round the shelving unit. Running footsteps echoed in the empty space. Casey veered back towards the doorway but a dark figure stepped swiftly from his left and got a grip on his shoulder. Casey lunged for the door, managed to pull it wide.

Cold night air swept in but two hands had him now, pulling him back. Casey grabbed at one of them, trying to prise the fingers away, but they were too strong. They dragged him to a halt. Casey kicked out, caught nothing but air. Hands grabbed his arms and hauled him back into the building.

The German tied him to a steel ladder that was bolted to the wall and gave access to the machinery in the ceiling. Bradon was beside him, equally trussed. Casey could hear heavy items scuffing across the concrete in the other room. The UAV was being moved.

Through the plastic slats, he watched the main roller open. Faint moonlight crept across the floor, and he caught sight of the back of a massive lorry with a large blue lightning flash painted across its rear doors before someone hauled them open.

Wendell dragged Hugo's father towards the others, similarly bound, Austin's feet scarping across the ground. In the dark, Casey couldn't see if he was conscious. Casey said, 'Kurt, if you untie me, I can tell you all about Argus. I know who he is and how he managed to blackmail you.'

Wendell ignored him. Casey tried again. 'He also knows about this deal and he's going to blackmail you for this too.'

Wendell dumped Austin's limp body in silence against the other wall and tied him to another ladder that ran vertically to the ceiling. Wendell held a torch in his teeth as he tightened the rope. Austin moaned. At least he wasn't dead.

'I can prove it to you,' Casey said. 'Just untie me first.'

Wendell shone the torch directly into Casey's face and after a hesitation said, 'I see my friend didn't do a great job of looking after you. Where's the woman?'

'Headed back to her shop.'

Wendell barked a string of instructions in German, and one of his lackeys hurried past them and out through the broken rear door. Wendell turned back to Casey. 'You're right. I am interested to learn more about Argus, but I can deal with him myself. I don't need your interference.'

'But I know who Argus is. I also know how he's managed to find out about what's going on here.'

Hugo Metcalf stepped into the room behind Wendell, rubbing his temple.

Wendell stared straight at Casey. 'So, tell me. If I believe you, I'll let you go.'

Casey felt all eyes in the room bore into him. He sensed an intense glare from Metcalf, although it was hard to be certain. 'I ...' Casey began, but found he couldn't. He remembered what Wendell had done to Trish's friend and then how he'd tried to kill him and Trish. If he explained about Metcalf – if he persuaded Wendell of the truth – he knew Wendell wouldn't hesitate to put a knife through Metcalf's heart. He would do it right here in front of them.

Casey couldn't do that, not with Metcalf's father only feet away. 'I ...' he mumbled again and looked down. 'No, I don't know.'

Metcalf's silhouette seemed to relax. Wendell said nothing but turned to leave.

'What are you going to do to us?' Casey asked.

Wendell ignored the question, pushed his way back through the partition, calling out again in German. Bradon watched him go. 'They're loading the UAV to sell it to God knows who. Some embargoed foreign power, no doubt.'

Casey could just make out Austin struggling to sit up. Bradon noticed him too and called across to him. 'Are you alright, Austin?'

'Been better,' he grunted as he pushed himself up. 'Why's my son doing this?'

Bradon paused. 'The younger generation's not the same as us. They have no sense of right and wrong or of responsibility.'

'True enough.' It was said with a painful sigh. 'It'll bring my company into total disrepute. I can't allow that.'

'I don't think you're being given much choice.'

Casey used his fingertips to prod the knots that secured his wrists but they were well secured. He tried tugging the rope up and down the metal upright as far as it would go, but it just rubbed his skin raw. He thought he felt a trickle of blood.

Suddenly the sound of the lorry's rear door clanging shut echoed through the building, and the shutters whined slowly down. Wendell pushed back through the plastic strips with the two heavily built men just behind him, one of the pair carrying something large in one hand that he put down in the middle of the room. Casey stared at it, trying to make out its form in the near darkness. A can of some sort.

The men separated. It was clear they'd already discussed what to do, and set about their tasks in silence. Wendell swept the cardboard boxes off the closest shelf and let them scatter across the floor. He reached up, did the same on the other shelves and then piled the assortment of boxes against the wall to Casey's left.

He heard the other guys dragging furniture from the small offices, heard the legs scraping on the floor. They stacked them near Wendell's growing cardboard pile.

With a sickening jolt Casey realised what they were doing. They were making a pyre. The object in the middle of the room was fuel to get it started. The old building with its wooden timbers would go up like a bonfire on Guy Fawkes' Day. He yanked harder at the ropes, increasingly frantic. Nothing moved.

'You can't burn us,' he heard himself shouting. 'You

can't.'

More chairs joined the piles, then a pair of wooden tables. From somewhere, Wendell had found two old crates that he dragged across and left at Casey's feet.

Suddenly Metcalf appeared in the shadows, grabbed at Wendell's shoulder. 'You don't need to do this,' he yelled. 'It'll achieve nothing.'

Wendell spun to face him, knocking away his arm. 'It's nothing to do with you. You can go.'

'That's my father. This is plain murder.'

'I don't care. I've a job to do.'

Metcalf shoved him with his good hand, sending Wendell stumbling against the pile of boxes. Metcalf stepped forward and grabbed for Wendell's coat. He pushed the German hard against the wall.

Wendell twisted free and landed a fist into the pit of Metcalf's stomach, causing him to double up with a groan. Wendell stepped round him and shoved his way back through the partition, calling something in German.

Metcalf staggered after him. 'Come back here,' he shouted and ran through the partition. Wendell heard him, pirouetted round and punched Metcalf hard in the face as he burst through the plastic strips.

Metcalf's head snapped back and he seemed to sag mid-stride. Without hesitation, Wendell hammered a second blow into his skull. Casey heard the thud of fist against bone and saw Metcalf collapse backwards and crash to the ground. Metcalf started to push himself up on his knees but couldn't support himself. Wendell grasped Metcalf's face, one large hand on each cheek, and smashed the back of his head into the wall with his full force.

The fleshy thud and crack made Casey wince and turn away. Wendell dragged the limp body into the middle of the room and left him against the shelves, coming back a moment later with more rope with which he bound Metcalf's hands to the upright

One of the men bent to the can and unscrewed it before hefting it to chest height.

A second later the gurgle of liquid turned Casey frantic. He fought to pull free as it slopped over the tables and dripped on to floorboards. Petrol fumes stung his eyes, bit into the back of his throat and nostrils. A shout in German, then a flash of light, followed by a whoosh of flame. Blue tongues darted across the floor. The cardboard ignited in a burst of yellow. Casey pulled back his legs so his knees were under his chin. He tried to push himself up and yanked at the ropes to no avail.

Smoke smarted his eyes, sending tears down his cheeks. A wave of heat suddenly swept across his face. He choked, frantically pulling at the ropes, ignoring the pain that tore through his wrists. Bradon was shouting. A foul smell of burning petrol billowed around him, and he retched. The knots held firm.

He knew in that moment that he was going to die.

CHAPTER FORTY-THREE

Tyler cautiously emerged from the cover of the garage with heart thumping, still clutching the crowbar. The sound of his assailants running was just audible over the drone of traffic from the bypass.

Keeping close to the hedge, Tyler stopped at the end of the drive. He watched them from the deep shadows, very aware they had the gun. Dave checked once over his shoulder before disappearing round a corner.

The second they were out of sight, Tyler broke from his cover and sprinted after them, his trainers making almost no sound. He paused where the road veered sharply to the right. Their footfall was slower now. He peered round the edge of a fence to the next section of road. The two men had slowed to a jog, panting. Dave glanced behind them again as though sensing Tyler's presence, but Tyler had ducked back in time.

Tyler gave them a few seconds before continuing cautiously, staying close to the hedges and walls to merge with the shadows. They were walking now with heads close together as they talked. Twice they both looked backwards but continued, re-assured they weren't being tailed.

Did they really think he was just going to let them go? What they should have done was left him unable to follow, broken one of his legs maybe, but they were amateurs. Perhaps they'd been afraid to come too close after what he had done to them last time.

They walked for about a mile. The streets had slowly gone down-market, first becoming groups of neat Victorian semis before finally turning into terraces of brown pebble-dashed council houses. Gardens became overgrown and littered with castoffs – a set of tyres lay discarded in one, another had a rusting fridge, and another a stained settee with weeds growing round it. The cars that now packed both kerbsides were older with faded paintwork and missing wing mirrors. Dave and Beanie-Boy eventually turned into a drive between a row of unkempt conifers.

Tyler jogged forward and heard the clunk of a front door lock, followed moments later by it clicking shut behind them. Tyler stopped at the barrier of conifers that hid the house and pushed apart some of the branches to peer through. A light glowed through the glass of a front door with peeling red paint. He squeezed into the trees so his shadow merged into them and waited, holding the crowbar against his chest. The branches scraped his neck and hands.

He was beginning to wonder if they lived together when the door reopened and Beanie-Boy emerged. Tyler guessed they'd been dividing their spoils. The door clicked shut behind him and two bolts scraped closed.

Tyler stayed buried in the conifers. The sound of Beanie-Boy's footfall changed as he left the garden and headed along the footpath. Tyler gave him ten seconds then silently stepped from his hiding place and followed, the crowbar in one hand.

In the far distance, the road ended at a T-junction, and occasional headlamps showed a small amount of traffic. Tyler couldn't allow him to get that far – safer to take him here in the shadows. Tyler gained on him fast. Beanie-Boy seemed to have ear-buds in now, listening to music. He was oblivious when Tyler swung the crowbar full force into the side of Beanie-Boy's head. With no more than a grunt, he collapsed sideways.

Tyler quickly turned him over and checked his pockets. One of the padded envelopes was inside. He took it and was about to hurry away when another idea crossed his mind. He bent down and plucked the hat from Beanie-Boy's head before walking rapidly back the way he had come.

By the time he reached the house, the hall light was off, but there was a glow from farther inside, so Tyler assumed Dave was in one of the back rooms. Tyler retraced his steps to the start of the terraced row and darted into a narrow alley that he had noticed earlier and guessed would lead to the rear of the properties. He emerged as he'd hoped on to a single-lane dirt track with no lighting. In the dim moonlight, he could make out a square of dilapidated garages and a line of fences bordering the rear of the houses. Occasional windows were lighted, some curtained, some bare. The bass notes of a pop song throbbed from one of them and the smell of pizza drifted from another. He was soon at the rickety fence that bordered Dave's house. There was no rear gate, and he couldn't easily climb it, but the adjacent garden was bordered only by a scraggly hedge. Tyler forced his way through it with ease and was able to squeeze behind a rusty child's swing and into Dave's garden via another half-dead hedge. He crossed a strip of what might have been called a lawn but for its knee-high weeds. A ground floor window at the back of the house was brightly lit, and Tyler could see the colourful flicker of a television screen.

He crept forward, keeping to the edge of the garden. As he got closer, he could see it was a kitchen with chipped melamine cupboards and a TV mounted to one wall showing a football match. The target sat with his back to the window, smoking. Tyler flattened himself against the back of the house and edged to the window for a better view, still gripping the crowbar.

On a square kitchen table that was draped with a cloth of bright orange plastic lay the remaining two envelopes alongside a mobile and two mugs. There was no sign of the gun. Tyler ran his finger along the joint between window and frame. It wouldn't be difficult to get in when he was ready.

Tyler was patient, but he didn't know how much time he had before Beanie-Boy regained consciousness. He thought it likely the man would head back here.

Five minutes passed. Through the closed window, Tyler could hear excited match commentary over the roar of the crowd. The game reached half-time, the TV picture changed to the suits and ties of commentators, and Dave got up and headed for another room.

Tyler stuck his crowbar into the gap round the window and quickly forced it open. The TV's noisy replay of a goal masked any sound. Tyler jumped on to the ledge and down into the kitchen, snatched the envelopes, and was back on the sill in seconds and jumping down on to the grass.

He paused just long enough to reach back inside and drop Beanie-Boy's hat near the broken window before running back the way he'd come, grinning.

CHAPTER FORTY-FOUR

Casey was coughing violently as the noxious smoke filled his lungs and stung his eyes. Heat scorched his face. Crackles and hisses came from all around. He tried to push himself up, but the rope slid only a few inches before hitting the next rung of the ladder. Pulling as hard as he could, he tried to yank the ironwork from the wall, but it remained firm. He hammered his foot into the lower rung in the vain hope it might break, but it didn't even start to bend.

Casey could hear the others choking in the swirling smoke. Suddenly the side of one of the crates collapsed. In horror, he saw a sheet of yellow flame burst upwards, fanned by the falling wood, before a blanket of thick smoke swept over him and blocked his view. His eyes stung and he screwed them shut.

Bradon was yelling for help. Casey tried to do so as well but choked. Pungent fumes burned the back of his throat. Another part of the crate fell, and he opened his eyes a crack to witness a jet of flame and sparks roar towards the ceiling.

Austin Metcalf was coughing violently, and Casey could hear him frantically pulling his ropes against the metal.

Suddenly fingers brushed his. There was panting beside him, and someone was pulling at his knots. An unsteady beam of light glowed through the smoke. 'They're too tight. Damn it, I can't.'

'Trish. Thank God. You've—' Casey's lungs heaved and he burst into a fit of choking.

'I've got a penknife. Don't move your hands.' She was coughing now too. Her breath swept across this check as she hacked at the rope.

The door to the closest office suddenly burst into flames. Yellow tongues darted across the wood.

Then he was free, and they stumbled together through the smoke to Bradon. He had slumped to the ground, choking. Flames leapt and crackled around the offices. The thin plywood walls that partitioned them were alight now, paint peeling as tiny tongues of flame licked the surface. 'You deal with him. I'll try to free the old man,' Casey yelled. Trying to hold his breath, he staggered towards the far wall, sweat prickling his skin. The smoke continually parted and closed round him like thick curtains.

One of the office walls collapsed with a deafening crash and sent a blanket of dense smoke and sparks sweeping across the room. Casey turned his face away but a wall of heat scorched his cheeks. Flames everywhere darted higher as the wave of air fed the fire. It briefly swept aside the smoke, and he saw Austin Metcalf in the light of the flames slumped against the wall, the man's attempts to escape his restraints now little more than feeble twitches. The man's fleshy face was puffy and his watery eyes were wide with terror and despair. He saw Casey and tried to call out, but collapsed choking.

Casey staggered to him, feeling his own lungs giving out under the strain. He pulled the man forward and reached for the ropes. It was too dark. He had lost the torch somewhere in the commotion. He worked by touch, trying to pull at the knots but nothing moved.

Suddenly both Bradon and Trish were beside him. Trish pushed Casey away and hacked at the rope with her penknife. Casey was feeling faint and gripped the ladder. He needed air or he would pass out.

The old man was free seconds later. Casey and Bradon grabbed one arm each and hauled him to his feet. 'Now get out,' Casey called to Trish before another bought of coughing racked his body.

'Where's the door?' Trish screamed back. 'I can't see a bloody thing.'

'To our right.'

They struggled with Austin's near unconscious body to the door and burst into the night air. Behind them, another internal partition collapsed and sent a whoosh of flame towards the ceiling.

They paused for a moment, sucking in the cool air, but still coughing badly. Casey hawked phlegm onto the concrete.

'My son,' Austin gasped, pulling away from them. 'Hugo's still in there.'

Casey had forgotten Hugo Metcalf had been inside. Austin stumbled back to the door from which dense smoke now billowed, but Bradon grabbed his arm. 'It's suicide.'

Casey darted past him. Trish yelled at him, 'Don't,' but he took a deep lung full of air, grabbed her torch and penknife before she could resist and plunged back into the inferno.

Flames cast flickering patterns all around. Smoke obscured his path, then briefly parted in front of him. What office walls remained seemed to glow orange. Crackling and hissing filled his ears. Metal creaked as it buckled in the heat. Then the smoke reclosed around him and he could see nothing. He squinted ahead as he stepped farther into the warehouse, waving the torch beam to no avail. His eyes streamed and his lungs strained as he fought to hold his breath.

For a few seconds there was an eerie silence. A waft of air briefly dispersed the smoke, and he saw Hugo Metcalf, hair matted with blood, slumped at the base of the shelves. Casey had managed one step towards him when there was a sudden creaking in the roof. Lumps of mortar and grit rained down on Casey. A rumble filled the room, and a massive wooden support fell. It crashed into the shelves, knocking them sideways, smashing them apart. There was a grinding of steel far above his head. Metal screeched as it distorted, and one end of the beam started to fall. Casey stared in horror as it dropped, the steel crushing Metcalf's skull. Flames encircled the body, briefly danced on the suit, then flared around it and enveloped the corpse.

Casey's lungs burst into a choking cough. He sucked in smoke that burned his throat. He squinted through watering eyes, feeling lightheaded as his chest heaved. It felt like a vice was clamping his lungs. He tried to turn.

Suddenly an arm grabbed his and violently pulled him away. He staggered, nearly fell. He turned and his torchlight picked out Bradon with a handkerchief held across his face. Trish was at his shoulder with her silk scarf tied across nose and mouth. They caught Casey as his knees buckled. Above them, the roof creaked ominously.

The pair dragged him coughing and retching towards the exit. Glass shattered and the final interior wall fell. More sparks jetted towards them, and little orange flames flickered on its remains before bursting into life and roaring upwards with a terrifying whoomph.

Casey felt himself being hauled from the building, then cold air across this face. He sat for a moment, doubled up, clutching his chest as he retched violently. The image of the huge lump of metal crushing Hugo Metcalf's skull filled his mind.

Someone suddenly grabbed his arm, was shaking it. A voice startled him into full consciousness, and he realised he was on the cold concrete a few yards from the burning warehouse. Austin was kneeling beside him. 'My son?'

Casey shook his head and his voice quivered. 'I'm sorry, I wasn't able to ... He's ... The roof collapsed on top of him.'

Austin's face crumpled, and the old man closed his eyes, shaking his head, then pushed himself up and stumbled towards the door out of which now poured thick black smoke. He muttered something Casey couldn't catch.

A section of roof collapsed, sending a jet of smoke into the night sky. The window flickered red.

Bradon was talking on his mobile. No one seemed to notice the old man tottering as though drunken towards the door. Suddenly realising what he was about to do, Casey bounded after him, coughing as he did. He grabbed at Austin's raincoat, but it slipped from his fingers.

Orange tongues licked around the doorframe. Austin found sudden strength, strode purposefully towards it, broke into a stumbling run. Casey got a firm grip on his arm and tried to drag him away. Austin half turned. 'He's still in there,' he screamed and tried to pull free. He was surprisingly strong.

Casey gripped his arm tighter. 'You'll kill yourself if you go back in there. It's an inferno.'

'It's my son.' Austin broke into a paroxysm of coughing and stopped struggling. Another part of the roof fell with a screech. Corrugated iron tumbled into the building and a jet of flame burst through the doorway.

Austin fell to his knees, wheezing. Casey crouched beside him. 'I'm sorry.' He tried to sound soothing.

Trish knelt beside them. 'Your boss is calling the fire brigade before the surrounding units go up.' She dropped her voice to a whisper in Casey's ear. 'And we think the old man needs a doctor. He looks terrible.'

Casey looked at the ashen face and watering eyes that seemed to have receded into their sockets. Austin Metcalf said quietly, almost to himself, 'Hugo must have been really taken in by that arms dealer. The guy must have spun an amazing yarn to con him into agreeing to that sale.' Neither Casey nor Trish answered.

Casey stood, keeping a hand lightly on Austin's shoulder. 'Let's get farther back to safety.' Casey realised his own legs were shaking. Austin nodded dumbly. He stood hesitantly and allowed them to lead him towards Bradon.

Casey turned to Trish. 'Thank God you came. We'd all be ... well, you know ...'

Trish removed her scarf. 'I saw you all disappearing from the hotel and I guessed you'd be heading up here. I just didn't want to be left out.'

Casey smiled. 'Thanks. And now we'd better get out of here, or you at least. I take it you borrowed the hire car?'

She nodded and started to turn away. Before he realised what he was doing, Casey leant forward and kissed her fully on the mouth. She kissed him back, then grinned, gave him a warm smile, and jogged to where she'd left the car.

Bradon finished his phone call, and he and Austin Metcalf started talking animatedly between coughs. Both men were nodding vigorously. Bradon turned to Casey. 'We've got to stop that UAV getting out of the country. If it goes to terrorists or enemy forces, it could get used against our own troops. If that happens and it's discovered they're using a craft designed and built in the UK, who knows what shit would hit the fan. Austin's focussed on his family right now, but we agree his company couldn't survive the uproar if that happened. He'd lose it all in addition to his son tonight. We need to get their UAV back.'

Austin nodded violently. He tried to speak, but his words collapsed into a choke. Bradon supported Austin's forearm to steady him. Bradon's reaction surprised Casey – the two companies were bitter rivals. This was Bradon's chance to get one over on them yet he wanted to help them.

Bradon said, 'The police will be here in a moment with the fire brigade. I'll explain about that lorry. They'll soon find it.'

Casey said quickly, 'I've got a better idea. I mean, we can't even give them its registration. They'll spend forever searching CCTV pictures, but we can help if we get back to the base before that lorry gets too far.'

Bradon frowned, then realised what Casey was getting at. 'Can you control Dragonfly II?'

'Of course I can.'

'Then come on. I'll call the MOD on the way.' He turned to Austin. 'We'll find that lorry. You sit here and wait for the fire brigade and ambulance. Just keep trying to clear your lungs. Help will arrive in a minute.' Austin nodded in a daze.

'We can use my hire car,' Casey said and shouted for Trish to wait.

She already had the engine running when they reached her. Casey threw himself into the passenger seat. 'We need to get to the RAF base. I'll guide you.' Bradon took the back, and the car roared out of Meadow View Industrial Estate with a skid on some loose grit, and headed for Spadeadam. Casey turned to Trish. 'You won't be allowed into the base, so you might as well go back to the hotel after you've dropped us.'

'The hell I will.'

'But they won't let you in.'

'I don't care. I'm not going to get forced out of this. Anyway, you'll need this car to get you back to the hotel.'

This was no time for arguing. Casey gave directions, and they left the warehouse a flickering beacon behind them.

CHAPTER FORTY-FIVE

Their car swept past dark fields and hedgerows. Bradon was already on his mobile, eventually talking animatedly to an Air Vice-Marshall whose name Casey didn't catch. Casey shut his eyes and saw flames roaring around him, heard hissing and crackles. He tried to concentrate on what Bradon was saying instead, trying to shove the terrifying images from his mind.

When Bradon had finished, he leant forward between the seats. 'Right, looks like the MOD are going to treat it as an urgent security issue. They'll liaise with the traffic police on road cameras and work with us on Dragonfly II.'

Casey's pulse quickened. He would be flying her as part of a real-life operation. 'That's brilliant, but I didn't like leaving Mr Metcalf behind like that,' he said. 'I'm not sure he fully understands what happened to his son.'

'I don't like it either, but we couldn't hang around. Austin was right that we can't allow his UAV to leave the country, but there was no way I could get him to abandon his ill-begotten vigil. Anyway, the fire brigade will be there by now and they'll take care of him.'

Casey nodded and turned back in his seat to stare through the windscreen. He still couldn't get over the way Bradon was prepared to ignore the bitter rivalry and help MSA. He wanted to ask why but felt it wasn't a question he had any right to raise. They swept down the empty main road, with headlamps bleaching white the hedges and rows of skeletal trees. Trish was handling the car like a pro, pushing it hard on the straights, probably better than he could, especially with the way he was feeling.

Fifteen minutes later, they swung round the final bend in the country road, and RAF Spadeadam was spread out dark and quiet before them. The gatehouse's lights glowed at the end of the winding B-road. The curls of razor wire topping the chain link fence glinted in their headlights as they approached the red and white barriers that barred the entrance.

Trish quickly pulled the black-framed reading glasses from her bag and perched them on her nose before staring straight ahead through the windscreen. She gripped the wheel tightly.

Both car windows purred down, and Bradon leant out of the rear one and thrust his pass at the guard. 'We phoned earlier. It's urgent we see the Station Commander.'

The uniformed RAF man stepped towards them and swept a torch beam round the car's interior, resting it on each face. Casey pulled his pass from round his neck and held it out, thankful he hadn't bothered to remove it earlier.

The guard stared at Trish. 'Your pass please, miss.' He had a Scottish burr to his voice.

'She doesn't have one,' Casey replied, leaning toward the open window. 'But she's with us.'

'Sorry sir. Without an official pass she can't come on to the range.'

'But —'

From the back seat, Bradon leaned out. 'This is really urgent. We must see the Station Commander immediately.'

'Yes sir. But not the lady.'

Every second that passed, Wendell and the UAV headed farther away. 'For heaven's sake,' Casey moaned.

Trish said, 'Look, I'll wait here. You go.'

The guard nodded. 'I'll call someone to take you two gentlemen up to Station Headquarters. Meantime, Miss, you can leave your car in that lay-by.' He waved an arm to a well-lit hatched area on the other side of the road.

'Very well,' Bradon snapped. 'Just so long as we see the Station Commander straight away.'

'Someone'll be here any moment to take you over.'

Another few seconds wasted, the lorry putting more miles between them. Bradon and Casey got out, and Casey gave Trish an apologetic shrug before she wound up the windows and reversed the car. He checked his watch under the fluorescent strip that buzzed annoyingly above their heads. It was twenty minutes since Wendell had left the warehouse. Quick sums in his head. If the HGV managed forty miles per hour, it would be about thirteen miles away by now. Dragonfly II could cover that in three minutes. But in which direction?

His thoughts were interrupted by headlights that bounced up the cracked concrete track, and a jeep pulled up. Casey ran forward and threw himself on to one of the side-on bench seats in its open back. Bradon was at his heals, and they'd barely grabbed the hanging straps before the jeep lurched forward into the dark.

Casey leaned forward so Bradon could hear him over the roar of the engine. 'Why isn't MSA putting up their own craft as well?'

'It was Austin. He didn't want more people knowing what happened. He would have had to explain to their technicians why he needed them back this late, and he'd have to give more details than he wanted. He said he couldn't risk that.'

They bounced towards the cluster of buildings that were coming into view in a hollow. A single pair of street lamps dropped pools of yellow light across the tarmac outside the central two-storey building, and the jeep juddered to a halt there with a squeal of brakes.

Casey and Bradon were already up off the bench before the jeep had stopped, and they bounded out the back and up the steps to where a young man in an RAF uniform met them. The gatehouse guard must have radioed through. 'Straight up the stairs, gentlemen. Go straight in.' He held the door for them, standing smartly upright.

Bradon marched up carpeted stairs. Casey, who'd not been inside before, hurried behind. Bradon knocked once at a varnished wood door and let himself in. He turned to

Casey. 'You wait here,' and he closed the door behind him.

Casey felt his cheeks redden and wanted to argue but turned away. Top Brass inside, he guessed. He glanced at his watch. Wendell now had a twenty-five-minute lead.

Framed black and white photos of the site in previous years hung along the walls. Casey paced in front of them. Which direction should they start searching? He pulled out his phone and opened its maps, quickly finding the warehouse on the outskirts of Brampton. Wendell had said, '... across the border,' when he'd been arguing with Metcalf, and he wouldn't have meant Scotland. Therefore, Casey assumed, he must be heading for docks to take it abroad. And that probably meant Liverpool or Newcastle. He opened his internet browser, typed "Newcastle freight terminal", and soon found a freight route map but couldn't concentrate on it. He had to focus. *Come on man, just read these damned pages.* Okay, Newcastle only seemed to go to Amsterdam, which was an unlikely destination. He quickly tried the same for Liverpool and after a few moments found container routes to North Africa and through the Suez Canal.

Liverpool, then, seemed the most likely destination, which probably meant M6 south. Casey scanned his finger across the map and traced possible routes to the motorway. Straight down the A69. Simple.

He looked back at the closed door. 'Come on, come on,' he muttered between gritted teeth and bounced on the balls of his feet. Suddenly the ground floor door burst open with a waft of night air. Two uniformed men in their fifties with stern faces and many stripes above their cuffs ran up the flight of stairs. They no more than glanced at Casey before knocking at the door Bradon had entered and hurrying in.

It was another couple of minutes before it was flung wide again, and they bustled back out, raced down the stairs and disappeared into the night, the front door banging behind them. Bradon followed a few seconds later, spotted Casey and called, 'Come on. The jeep's waiting for us.'

The engine was already running when they burst from the building and threw themselves in. Without needing a word to the driver, the jeep sped into the dark.

Casey shouted to Bradon over the engine. 'From what we overheard, I think the lorry will be heading for Liverpool docks, so I reckon we ought to search in that direction.'

'Makes sense. I'll call Carlisle ATC, let them know what we're doing.' He paused. 'Just don't forget the controlled airspace round the airport. For the south runway, it stretches right across the A69.'

Casey's mouth had turned as dry as the Sahara. Could he really manage this? In prototype trials and tests, they'd done lots of searching for hidden static targets, but finding a lorry on busy roads? And what if it wasn't heading for Liverpool anyway?

The gently rolling hills of Spadeadam hid the cluster of hangars until they were almost upon them. Already, artificial lights glowed at the front and he could make out two men starting to haul open the large steel doors.

Bradon finished on his phone to Air Traffic Control and turned to Casey. 'Are you sure you can do this? Honestly now.'

'Of course,' but Casey's nerves were jangling. He was glad the darkness hid his face.

Nearly thirty minutes behind now, the gap ever widening.

Somewhere nearby a helicopter engine jumped into life, its rotors whining as they wound up to full speed before it took to the air. For a few seconds it clattered overhead, then disappeared to the West. Casey wondered if it contained the two granite-faced men who'd joined Bradon at the last minute. He was about to ask who they were when their jeep shuddered to a halt outside the massive concrete-walled hangar.

Casey ran into the huge enclosed space, calling over his shoulder to their driver. 'We'll need to hook the controller into your jeep's battery.' Bradon was beside him. Their footfall echoed round the large bay. Dragonfly II glowed under the internal fluorescent lighting, its matt silver body shimmering like snake skin.

Casey grabbed a suitcase-like box from the row of benches that arrayed the back wall and lugged it back to the jeep. Bradon was at the side of Dragonfly II, holding open a flip-down panel with one hand and tapping a pass-code into a keypad with the other.

Casey slid the case on to the vehicle's rear bench, opened the lid, and tossed a coil of wire to the driver. 'Get that connected to the power, please.'

The inside of the lid held a large monitor screen. The lower half of the case supported a black metal console with keys like a computer keyboard beneath two banks of switches, a joystick on one side of it and a roller ball for camera control on the other. Casey left the case on the seat and ran back into the building where Bradon was turning away from Dragonfly II.

Casey grabbed a long multi-section aerial from the bench, and Bradon was soon helping to extend it until it formed a long whip that they clamped to the roof fitting designed for it. Casey connected it to the control box and initiated the UAV's power-up sequence. 'Keep clear,' he shouted when the complete set of lights illuminated above the keyboard. Checking that no one stood near the tail, he started the propeller.

'Moving forward now,' he yelled towards the hangar, and the two RAF men darted away from the doors. Slowly at first, under Casey's control from the back of the jeep, Dragonfly II rolled through the hangar doors and on to the strip of concrete.

Casey's tongue flicked round his lips as he concentrated, sweeping his eyes over the various views on the monitor, the meters along the edge and its row of status indicators. Battery power was barely fifty percent, not surprising as its batteries had only been on charge since they'd left that evening, but that ought to be enough for this flight.

All cameras and radar reported healthy status. The currents drawn by the electric motor was correct. Control comms showed a zero bit error rate. GPS fix was good.

Slowly, under gentle propulsion from its large rear propeller, it slid forward. He adjusted the front night-view camera to give the best view forward, watching the colourless image of the concrete track and surrounding grass as he taxied the craft towards the runway. His heart was pounding in his chest.

Bradon climbed in beside him and watched over his shoulder as Casey lined up Dragonfly II. The strip he would take off from stretched out straight before it into the dark, lit either side by pinpricks of light to mark its edge. Wind: 5.1 knots, twenty-seven degrees. 'Don't start the run until you're well clear of their rocket test area. There's a low wall round it,' Bradon said quietly.

Casey didn't reply, gently fingering the joystick as he manoeuvred the craft along the narrow strip. Casey clicked two switches, checked the status indicators under the screen, and eased forward on the joystick.

As smoothly as a bird, Dragonfly II swept forward and silently soared into the night sky.

CHAPTER FORTY-SIX

Tyler locked the two envelopes of money into his safe before sinking into an armchair with a celebratory beer in one hand and Bradon's tatty diary in the other. The slim book had nestled in the other jiffy bag as Metcalf had said.

It wouldn't be many hours before the sun would be up but he was still too hyped to sleep. He rested his feet on the coffee table, still in his trainers.

He was curious about the little book he held. It was obviously valuable, at least to Bradon, who'd been prepared to pay many thousands to suppress its contents. A child's hand had written PRIVATE AND CONFIDENTIAL in large biro block capitals on its faux leather cover. None of his business in other words, and he was sure Bradon would not want him to read it. He opened the cover anyway.

Blue ink in a child's awkward writing covered all its pages. The flyleaf was inscribed *The private property of Arthur Edward Bradon* followed by a Surrey address. What a little prig he must have been.

The first page was dated *Tuesday 9th July, 1968*.

Tyler flicked through its pages. Something here had to be the cause of its value, but this was just the scribbling of a prepubescent schoolboy. Tyler yawned and skipped great chunks, glancing down each page. The young Bradon had faithfully kept up his diary writing; rarely had a day been missed. What caught his eye on August 12th made him stop.

He went back to the start of the section on the previous page, put down his empty glass, and read the childish hand carefully for a few minutes. He jumped up and almost ran out of the back door and down the path to his writing den. He fumbled the key in the lock, flicked on the lights, and rifled through the pages of notes on his desk until he found the transcript he'd made of his conversation with Charles Aston in the Old Folks Home. It couldn't be, could it?

Still standing, he read the whole page. He suddenly realised why there was no way Art Bradon would ever want that diary reaching the public's eyes.

CHAPTER FORTY-SEVEN

Stress and adrenaline were keeping Casey wide awake. His eyes flicked across the row of artificial instruments, watching the altimeter climb. Another twenty metres and he could bank. Its radar showed no air traffic in the area. The front-facing camera revealed no navigation lights. With a surge of exhilaration, he knew the sky was his own. He gently nudged the joystick, and Dragonfly II banked to the west.

'Are you okay handling that while we set off?' Bradon asked

'Sure.' He'd flown it enough times in the lead-up to the trials to be comfortable.

'Let's go,' Bradon called over the idling engine. The driver thrust the jeep into gear, and they tore back towards the gatehouse. Casey kept his eyes fixed on the monitor screen on which he'd opened a window with a map overlay. Dragonfly II's GPS position glowed on the map as a ghostly dot. The lorry by now, if he'd guessed right, would have reached the motorway. But what if he'd presumed wrong? What if it had headed north or maybe even turned the other way out of the industrial estate and was now on the A69 heading for Newcastle?

His fingers were sweaty on the controls. The jeep slowed, and Casey briefly glanced forward, saw the red and white site barrier rising as they neared the gatehouse. On the other side of the road, Trish was running from the car toward the jeep. Bradon leaned forward to their driver. 'Can she come with us?'

The driver hesitated. 'I'm not sure, sir. I wouldn't think so. Let me check.'

The driver used his mobile, presumably to talk to someone more senior.

Casey activated the night camera beneath the craft and adjusted the roller ball. He tapped zoom keys until it was easy to inspect vehicles on the main road below.

The jeep idled in the mouth of the road, and the barrier clanged shut behind them. Trish kept her face turned from the light so that it remained in deep shadow as she tapped on the driver's window. The driver lowered it while talking into his phone. He started to shake his head and put the phone back in his chest pocket. 'I'm sorry, miss. You're not allowed with us.'

'That's —,' Bradon began but the jeep was already lurching forward. Casey looked up from the screen and his eyes briefly locked with Trish's as the driver accelerated away. He wanted to reach out and hold her but there was a job that had to be done. He took a deep breath. He would apologize to her later.

'Get on the M6 southbound,' Casey yelled. Dragonfly II was slicing through the night sky at maximum speed towards the motorway junction just south of Carlisle. He would pick up the motorway there and methodically check southbound traffic. The police would no doubt already be monitoring camera feeds. Perhaps they would spot it first.

It would be trickier if Dragonfly II had to go near the airport – they'd had the local airspace restriction drummed into them by a heavily moustached officer before the first trial – but it could easily be avoided if it was only the motorway he needed to watch.

Bradon glanced at the instrument panel. 'How does the battery life look?'

'We've got plenty, even at this speed.' At night, the solar panels that lined its wings were of no help, but the batteries had been charged enough.

They drove past Brampton, but they still had to be ten minutes from the motorway. Traffic was light at this time of night, but the Jeep wasn't built for speed.

In the sky ahead of them, Dragonfly II ate up the miles, and the long thread of motorway lights was already visible on the monitor. Casey banked hard, then reduced air speed so that the UAV glided slowly above the M6. Its cameras auto-focussed on the vehicles, the software combining optical and IR to give one almost daylight-like image of the scene. Overlaid numbers identified the size of each vehicle as Casey centred the hair-thin cursor on them.

He'd only had one glimpse of the lorry at the warehouse.

White at the back with a blue lightning flash, but it had to be a long-load. He remembered the wings dismantled against the wall in the warehouse. Like their own model, each wing section was around ten metres long. That probably meant a 44-ton artic lorry.

As their jeep bounced over a low brick-built bridge, Bradon's mobile rang. He grunted a few times, then hung up. 'We've a couple of armed response teams coming our way.'

Casey continued to scan the light traffic heading southbound. Every time a large vehicle came into view, he slowed Dragonfly II's airspeed further to give more time to examine it, and that was wasting valuable seconds. He'd estimated Wendell would hit the docks in just over two hours.

They reached the motorway. Staring at the screen while careening down the road was making him nauseous. He slid the side window open slightly and felt cold wind whip across his cheeks. They turned down the slip road and accelerated.

On the screen, the lights of a service area flashed into view. Where was that damn lorry? Casey inspected the lorry park from high above it – saw nothing of the right size – then went back to examining the carriageway.

Five minutes later, he found it.

***

As the jeep carrying Casey and Bradon had sped away from the Spadeadam base, Trish had walked sullenly back to the car. She had briefly locked eyes with Casey as he swept past and it was clear to her that he was too engrossed in his job to care she'd been excluded. Disappointment sat heavily in her chest. 'If it wasn't for me, you'd all be dead,' she muttered.

Trish slammed the car door behind her so hard that the car rocked, and she sat for a moment in total silence. Exhaustion suddenly seemed to drain her. There was no point in going back to the hotel – she had returned the card for Matt's room – and she daren't go anywhere public while the police still wanted her.

She closed her eyes. Argus was dead, so at least she was now free from blackmail. She shuddered at the memory of the flames consuming everything with such ferocity. Maybe Casey would actually help the police catch up with Wendell and stick him behind bars. That would leave her free from his death threat as well.

She had expected to feel relief that Argus and Wendell were gone from her life – rejoicing even – but somehow, she just felt tired and sad. The way she'd suddenly been shut out of what was happening still rankled but she knew in her heart she shouldn't be blaming Matt. She felt that he liked her, particularly after his quick kiss at the warehouse, but she'd been unreasonable to expect him to find a way to keep her involved. And maybe the kiss had meant nothing.

Trish opened her eyes again and started the engine. She might as well head home. She could leave her few things in Matt's room, didn't care if she never got them back. Trish wound down the window in the hope the night air would keep her awake, and put the car into gear.

***

Casey brought Dragonfly II to its slowest speed. It almost hung in the night sky, its massive wingspan holding it like a glider. He deftly adjusted the cameras, zoomed in on the back of the lorry and locked on to it. The UAV's software would now keep the craft circling as necessary to maintain the vehicle in its sights. A vulture above its prey.

The screen showed the lorry's rear roll-up shutters, painted white with the blue lightning flash emblazoned across them.

Bradon had been on the phone again. 'They're piling MOD personnel into the area now.' He turned to Casey, 'How far behind it are we?'

'About ten miles.' Casey checked the screen. 'And the lorry's travelling at forty-seven miles per hour.'

They had been travelling at speed in the third lane, but their driver suddenly swung to the left. Sirens sounded from somewhere behind them, and Bradon twisted in his seat to look back. 'Here they come,' he said, and Casey glanced up from the screen in time to see two black Range Rovers with heavily tinted windows sweep past doing at least a hundred.

Thirty seconds later, two police cars tore past, sirens wailing, strobes flashing.

Traffic was light, and they raced past in the wake of the Range Rovers. Then the two cop cars separated. One of them slowed, moved to the centre of the road a few vehicles ahead of the jeep and started to sweep back and forth across the lanes, blocking anyone passing, slower and slower, holding back the traffic.

Their jeep, too, was forced to brake. 'That's all we need,'

the driver yelled over his shoulder. 'Not a lot more I can do for you.' They slowed further, and a few minutes later, stopped.

Bradon jumped from the back and jogged through the lines of cars. Casey's eyes remained fixed to the screen. Dragonfly II circled again.

Bradon reached the police car, was leaning in at the front window, talking animatedly. He stood with both hands on its roof, clearly angry.

A helicopter suddenly rattled overhead and swept low over them with navigation lights flashing pin-pricks in the night sky.

Casey adjusted the camera slightly. The road around the lorry was quiet now. He zoomed out further. One car – what might have been a Fiesta – slowly overtook it and edged away. Then there was nothing else on either carriageway but the lorry. The police had staunched traffic flow in both directions.

On the screen, the pair of Range Rovers swept into the bottom of the view and the helicopter appeared, keeping pace just above the lorry.

Through the windscreen in the headlights of the stationary cars, Casey saw Bradon was still arguing with the policeman. Other drivers around them, too, had got out and were wandering forward through the parked vehicles.

Through the camera high above the road and miles ahead, Casey watched the Range Rovers converge on their target like lions to the kill.

The front one drew level with the cab, tracked it for a few

moments. Casey couldn't be sure, but it looked like someone briefly leant out of the SUV's window and gesticulated to the driver. The lorry maintained a steady pace. Suddenly the Range Rover showed a short spurt of acceleration and took up position just off the front wing. The second Range Rover dropped in behind it.

The lorry was pinned to the left. The lead vehicle edged slowly towards the wing. The lorry moved left. Again, they nudged closer. The lorry's wheels kicked up a cloud of grit on the hard shoulder. The Range Rover suddenly struck the front of the cab a glancing blow. The artic briefly swerved left before the driver regained control.

Now they closed in, but this time the lorry driver swerved into their path. The lead Range Rover shuddered and veered away but was soon back and went for the kill.

It caught the cab's wing a solid blow. Something fell from the base of the cab and bounced into the road, spinning away behind them into the dark.

The juggernaut's driver fought for control. The weight of the trailer was too much, pushing forward in a straight line. Suddenly the lorry jack-knifed in a cloud of dust and smoke from its tyres. The cab swung violently one way while the trailer thrust forward under its own momentum and dragged the cab sideways with it until it came to a halt.

The helicopter hovered above it, temporarily blocking Dragonfly II's view, and Casey quickly adjusted the UAV's position. The Range Rovers skidded to a stop, one to its right, the other behind. Flak-jacketed soldiers poured out, four from each, sprinting to surround the truck. The ominous barrels of automatic weapons pointed at the cab.

Wendell had already kicked open the passenger door and was jumping down. A muzzle flash flared from a gun in his hand, followed rapidly by two more before he leapt the crash barrier, threw himself over a wooden fence, and raced across the field before the soldiers could reach him. Four of the soldiers swarmed after him, leaving the others with the lorry. The helicopter pivoted in the sky as the pilot turned to follow Wendell.

Soldiers hauled two men from the cab and forced them to the ground. One of the soldiers leant over the driver, roughly pulled his arms behind him, secured his wrists, then yanked him to his feet while the others surrounded them with levelled weapons. The police car arrived and swung across the road behind them, its strobes casting bright swirls of light across the side of the lorry.

Wendell turned as he ran and fired again, the flash of his gun a bright flare on Dragonfly II's night cameras. Wendell sprinted across the rough grass and into a clump of trees, his pursuers about twenty metres behind but gaining.

The helicopter swooped in low, and its search beam came on brightly. The heat it generated was enormous; the grass glowed white. Casey flicked to day vision in time to see Wendell crouch at the edge of the trees and fire twice. The second shot shattered the light beneath the chopper.

Camera immediately back to night mode. The glow slowly faded.

The helicopter started to rise, wary of another gunshot, but Wendell fired again. The muzzle spat twice more, and

Casey saw a brief ping of light as a bullet caught the tail rotor. Another shot – another hit – and the helicopter suddenly twisted in the air as though grabbed by a giant hand. The tail started to swing round. The pilot fought to prevent it spinning out of control.

CHAPTER FORTY-EIGHT

The helicopter pilot battled for control. Casey could imagine him fighting to disengage the main rotor before he spun out of control. The tail of the chopper suddenly seemed to sag in the air, and the machine descended jerkily into the field. There would be no more tracking from that.

Casey had lost sight of Wendell now. He increased the IR sensitivity, seeking body heat among the trees. This was what Dragonfly II was designed for.

'I can guide them to him,' Casey called to the driver, but then realised the driver knew nothing of what was happening up ahead.

At that moment, the jeep rocked and Casey turned to see Bradon climbing back in, tight-jawed with anger. 'We can't get past.'

'They've stopped the lorry but Wendell made a run for it,' Casey said quickly. 'Thing is, if we can get a comms link with the guys on the ground, I can guide them to him. Otherwise, they have little hope.'

'I'll see what I can do.' Bradon clambered forward and started talking animatedly to their driver.

Casey turned back to the screen. The arms dealer was a small purple smudge that pushed blindly through the trees. The moonlight was of little use to Wendell so deep into the wood, and his progress was slow. Casey imagined him stumbling forward, one arm in front of his face for protection against the branches.

The soldiers were using powerful torches and had spread out to form a line that slowly entered the trees. They would be cautious of another bullet from Wendell, but they travelled faster than the arms dealer was managing. Twice he stumbled but pushed on. He was increasingly veering to his left and was soon running almost parallel to the original field.

Casey zoomed out, watched the steady line of soldiers sweeping towards their target, and realised they would miss him if Wendell continued at that angle. 'They're not going to get him,' Casey shouted without looking up.

'We're working on it,' Bradon yelled from where he was hunched over with the driver.

Wendell tripped and sprawled on the ground. When he pushed himself up, he appeared to be limping. About a hundred yards ahead of Wendell, a dirt track cut through the wood. Dragonfly II's cameras picked it out in the moonlight. Casey zoomed wide and saw it led to a house. Lights and heat spilled from its windows.

The soldiers' line of torch beams swept through the trees but they were veering off course, would likely sweep past to

Wendell's right. Casey's pulsed raced. They couldn't let him escape.

Wendell reached the track and awkwardly ran along it; his limp slowing his progress. He would soon be out of sight of where the closest soldier was going to emerge.

Dragonfly II circled effortlessly high above.

Wendell was closing fast on the house. Casey adjusted the zoom again, scanned round the building. It appeared to have a carport to one side, various sheds and a large formal garden, all bathed in faint moonlight.

Wendell reached the end of the track, and two seconds later the first soldier pushed his way out of the trees, his torch beam dancing across the gravel. He hesitated. The others joined him and they split up. One ran straight ahead into the next group of trees, and the other three took the track, one towards the house and two towards the distant road.

Wendell appeared to examine the carport – from the UAV's view it looked empty – then darted to the back of the house out of sight.

Suddenly Bradon was back at Casey's side. 'We can pass on messages to the commander on the ground. It's not a direct link but the best we could do. Can you still see him?'

'He's round the back of the house,' Casey said and pointed to the tiny smudge of colour.

'Can you get a better angle?'

'Sure.' Casey took Dragonfly off autopilot and gently nudged the joystick, simultaneously adjusting the camera with his other hand. The UAV banked smoothly, heading slightly north before circling on that side of the building.

Bradon called to the driver. 'He's at the north-east corner of a house that's on the southern end of the track.'

The driver relayed the message over the radio.

Outside the jeep, the other drivers were getting impatient. A few had climbed out and stood in the road with mobiles. Casey concentrated on the screen.

Wendell was hesitating at the corner of the house as if surveying the garden in the moonlight, then sprinted awkwardly towards a small building in the middle of the lawn that Casey guessed was a summerhouse. Bradon called to the driver. 'He's left the main building and is running across the lawn.'

Wendell reached the summerhouse and darted behind it, pausing again.

Casey watched as two soldiers entered the grounds. A hundred metres behind them, the other two ran side-by-side, blurred splashes of purple and red on the monitor.

Wendell ran again, using the summerhouse to hide him from view as he headed to the end of the garden. For a moment, Casey thought he would be trapped at the boundary, but then realised Wendell had spotted a way through.

The four soldiers swarmed across the grounds after him.

Bradon called, 'He's reached the boundary fence at the far end and is crossing into the next property,' and they heard the driver relay it into his radio.

Casey adjusted the joystick, and high above their target, Dragonfly II dipped one wing and glided south. Numbers round the edge of the screen flickered as they reported constantly changing data – altitude, GPS co-ordinates, inclination, speed – but he just focussed on watching Wendell run across another stretch of lawn. Shadowy outlines of shrubs and trees blurred its perimeter. Wendell sprinted towards a large house that had a single heat source on the rear ground floor.

'He's in the next garden and heading north across the lawn towards the main building,' Bradon called, and the driver echoed it into his mic.

Casey zoomed out. There had to be an alternative route for the soldiers, some way they could cut him off. He studied the faint grey lines round the edge of the property. Beyond the house, a long drive ran to the north. Casey zoomed out further and saw it turned at a sharp angle before joining a narrow track that looped back round the garden's boundary.

The first two soldiers appeared on the lawn. Wendell had already reached the house and dodged round the side.

Casey pointed at the screen. 'If the next two guys go straight ahead when they reach the garden rather than following Wendell, I think they can get to that road. They can then follow it round towards the front of the house and cut him off. He traced his finger across the screen.

'You're right,' Bradon said and called instructions to the driver. A few seconds later, the next pair of men pushed through the hedge and cut straight across the grass as he'd suggested.

Casey adjusted the camera for a better view of the

boundary. To their right was a small gap between the end of a fence and the start of a hedge. 'Tell them to go to their right a few metres and they'll find a way through.'

A few moments later the pair had pushed through it to the road and were running along it, torches illuminating the way.

Wendell was now at the front of the house jogging away from it, his gait still impaired by a limp. To Casey's surprise, he suddenly stopped and double-backed towards the building. Casey realised the front door must be open. Heat spilled across the steps. Wendell reached it and was clearly arguing with someone on the threshold. Casey guessed the owner had spotted Wendell and come to investigate.

Wendell drew his gun and the pair disappeared inside leaving the door open. 'He's entering the property from the front,' Bradon called.

The first two soldiers had almost reached the back of the building.

Suddenly, Wendell and his captive ran back out from the front door, the arms dealer keeping a firm grip on the other man's arm as he pulled him across the drive.

Casey hadn't noticed a car that was parked among the shadows of the trees. Seconds later, its headlights flicked on and the car sped across the gravel.

'He's left the house again,' Bradon called. 'He has a hostage and they've taken a car.'

The drive had a sharp left bend half way down that took it towards the road. Casey shouted, 'The car's heading for the other two soldiers.'

Bradon leaned forward, his breath across Casey's neck as he called, 'The car will be on them in seconds.' Casey's heart was pounding.

In a blur of light, the car followed the road round the side of the boundary. Casey saw the purple smudge of two soldiers taking up position ahead of it. Suddenly muzzle flares spat in the night as their assault rifles fired, and the car swerved violently to its left and crashed into the hedge.

One of them threw a stun grenade that exploded beside the car. The whole screen briefly flared white. Wendell pushed the car door open and rolled into the ditch. Keeping low and out of sight, he edged along the gulley away from them. Torchlight flashed across the car. The owner climbed out shakily and leant against the bodywork. One of the soldiers crouched beside him, pulling him down behind the vehicle's protection.

'Wendell's in some sort of ditch behind the car,' Casey called to the jeep's driver, who instantly relayed it.

The arms dealer crept slowly along the gulley, edging away from the crashed car. 'To their right,' Casey yelled. 'To their right, only metres away. Why can't they seem him?'

The soldier advanced slowly, weapon level in front of him as Wendell's shape edged farther along in the ditch.

Suddenly they saw each other, and the soldier's torch beam illuminated Wendell's crouched figure. Wendell fired once, a bright burst from his hand gun. It missed the soldier, who released a single shot and Wendell seemed to flinch and then crumpled to one knee.

The second soldier was also there now. Both had

weapons at their shoulders aimed at their quarry while they advanced.

Wendell knelt and slowly raised both hands.

CHAPTER FORTY-NINE

A burst of exhilaration sent Casey's pulse racing. Bradon clapped him on the back. Dragonfly II continued to circle lazily above the scene. Casey yanked out his phone and called Trish but there was no answer. Eventually the network terminated the call. Nonplussed, he tried again, but received the same result.

A tremor ran through him. *Had something happened to her?* He tried a third time – still no reply – and put the phone away, puzzled.

***

Trish glanced down at the phone on the passenger seat when it rang, saw it was Matt Casey, and focussed back on the road. She still felt angry but perhaps that was just tiredness talking. She had promised to leave it on despite the risk of being tracked, but she certainly wasn't in the mood to talk right now. Besides, it was taking all her willpower just to stay awake and remain on the road. As it was, her eyes were drooping. She knew she ought to stop for a break, but if she pushed on, she would make it home before sunrise and be able to sneak in unseen. It would be so nice to be back in her own bed again.

The phone rang twice more, but she ignored it. She didn't care if it was Matt. At the moment, it was impossible for her to think about what might lay ahead.

She yawned, turned the radio up, and tried to focus on the motorway.

***

It was a sudden thump from downstairs that jerked Trish from sleep the next morning. Disorientated, she sat up in bed, startled. Daylight seeped around curtain edges. Her own bedroom. Her ears strained for another sound, but heard nothing. Silently, she slid her legs out of bed and stood barefoot on the thick rug, heart hammering in her chest.

She was sure she hadn't imagined it. In the shorts and baggy T-shirt she'd slept in, she tiptoed to the open bedroom door, paused, and slowly took the stairs. Half way down, she saw the fat A4 envelope that had been pushed through the letterbox and she let out a sigh of relief. The thump of that landing on the wooden floor and the click of the flap must have been what had woken her.

She picked it up, saw the logo on the front was her car insurer's and, still feeling wary, cautiously put her head round the lounge door. *Don't be stupid*, she told herself. *No one's there*. She padded into the kitchen diner, where the giant clock that dominated one wall showed nearly nine o'clock.

Trish tossed the envelope unopened on the oak table, dropped into a dining chair, and with elbows on the table, buried her head in her hands. *What the hell am I going to do?*

Argus was dead, but even if the Ministry of Defence had managed to stop the lorry and arrest Kurt Wendell, she still had the police questioning about Beth to face. When that happened, the fraud she'd repeatedly committed on her company's Value Added Tax returns would inevitably come to light. It would ruin her. Prison, maybe. That's what Argus had said. Over a two-month period, he had anonymously sent her newspaper clippings about people sent down for doing the very thing she had. Beth was dead because of her. The hire car was meant to be back today ... Trish's shoulders shook and tears avalanched down her face.

She sniffed and wiped the back of her hand across her face, then dried it on her top. *Get a grip.* She remembered Matt trying to call her the previous night. What if Wendell had gotten away? Was that why Matt had called – to warn her? She scooped up her phone from where she'd left it the night before on the kitchen worktop and turned it back on. Two texts, both from Matt. Her hands trembled as she opened them. *Are you ok? So worried about you. Wendell arrested :-)* She switched it back off and closed her eyes. That was something at least.

He'd signed it with a kiss. Did that mean anything?

She worried that she might have misread what he was thinking about her. After all, she'd barely seen his face as he'd been swept away in the jeep from Spadeadam and she could easily have read too much into his look; he'd been busy, after all. She knew she had to call him about the wretched hire car. *Do it now and get it over with.* Trish got up, blew her nose on a sheet of kitchen roll, and called him from the home phone. Her heart thundered in her rib cage and her mouth was dry. She was behaving like a love-struck teenager.

It was answered on the third ring. 'Trish. Thank goodness you're okay. I've been so worried. Where are you?'

'Back home. And I've got the hire car.'

'What? Why down there? Anyway, it doesn't matter. Did you get my text? We got Wendell last night. You don't need to worry anymore.'

'Don't need to worry? I'm wanted for murder,' she snapped. 'And if they don't hang that on me, I'll be imprisoned for VAT fraud. Of course I have to worry.'

'Sorry. I meant about Wendell.'

She paused, feeling guilty at having shouted at him. 'What do you want me to do about the car?'

'I'll give them a call, see if we can return it to a branch near you. I'll sort it.' He paused. 'Look, we finish here at lunchtime. Most of the group are staying on over the weekend, but I'm sure I can get someone to give me a lift to Carlisle station. I can take the train down to you and we can return the car together.'

She closed her eyes. Did he really want to see her again?

'Trish? Are you still there?'

'Yeah, sorry. That would be good. It's just ...' She heard her voice waver. 'It's just – you know – I'm worried about the police.'

'I know. Let's talk about it when I get down there. If that's alright ...? Look, I've really got to go. The guys are waiting for me. Unless I hear from you, I'll head down at lunchtime. Take care of yourself.'

She nodded to no one in particular and the line went dead.

She sighed. She wanted to get started with getting the shop straight but didn't want all Cliff's awkward questions. *Pull yourself together, woman. You're the boss. What would Aunt Flo say if she saw the state you're in?* That was the good thing about Matt. He knew her secret. She had nothing to hide when she was with him.

She opened the fridge and sniffed a bottle, screwing up her face at the revolting smell of milk gone bad.

CHAPTER FIFTY

Tyler and Bradon had arranged to meet. Tyler had phoned the previous day after reading the diary, although he hadn't mentioned knowing the contents, simply reported its recovery. Bradon's relief had been palpable down the phone line.

Bradon picked a spot well away from the hotel where there was little chance of anyone overhearing their conversation. 'Walltown Visitor Centre,' Bradon said. 'It's on the Pennine way, part of Hadrian's wall, round the corner from Spadeadam. I know it means you slogging all the way back again but any chance you could bring the diary? I've got wash-up meetings at the base so won't be back south straight away.'

Down south either meant secretaries and office workers, or the wife and kids, Tyler guessed. 'You're paying.'

It was early afternoon when they met. Other than a few grey clouds that lingered over the distant trees, the sky was clear and the sun cast strong shadows across the car park and surrounding stretch of grass. Somewhere above, birds trilled.

Tyler's rucksack was light on his back. The three items inside bounced against each other with every step. He had never seen Bradon in anything other than suit and tie, and hadn't instantly recognized him in casual trousers, walking boots, and a mac that hung open over a bottle-green fleece.

Bradon extricated himself from the picnic table where he'd been waiting. 'Let's walk,' he said brusquely. The tense jaw line betrayed his tension. *Is he worried about me and what I'm going to do with his precious diary?* Tyler wondered.

Bradon flapped an arm towards a footpath. It followed a dry-stone wall towards a rocky bluff that managed to give life to a few clumps of gorse and some stunted trees. 'Let's wander that way. Then we won't be overhead.'

Not that many people were around to hear them. Only two others cars were on the gravel apron that bordered the deserted visitor centre.

As soon as they were a few yards away, Bradon asked, 'Have you got it with you?'

'Yes. And the two packets of money.'

'Brilliant job, Craig. I knew I could trust you.'

Not what you said when the money got away first time, Tyler thought. Instead, he said, 'I used some of the notes to buy this rucksack to carry them in. You can take it.'

'There's no need —'

'If I were walking around with tens of thousands in cash, I wouldn't want to risk losing it. Take the rucksack.'

'Good point.' Bradon hesitated. 'Were you tempted to

read it?'

There was no point in lying. He glanced sideways at his employer as they walked. Bradon's face seemed to show annoyance rather than anything else. 'I confess I had a peek,' Tyler said. 'I wanted to be sure I'd grabbed the right thing.'

'Quite.'

'But obviously its contents will remain secret with me. I don't blab.'

'I was told you can apply discretion.' Bradon held out his hand. 'Can I see it?'

The pair stopped as Tyler swung the bag off his shoulders and handed Bradon the diary. He stroked its cracked and curling cover. 'It all came back to me when Austin and I were trapped in that warehouse fire, you know, the same feeling of panic. It was the heat and the smoke. Except this time it wasn't my fault.' Tyler didn't interrupt. Bradon clearly wanted to talk about it, something he'd been unable to do for sixty years. 'When I was ten ... I hadn't intended to cause the fire. My cousin Hugo and I were at Austin's house. Our Aunt Harriet was there and was meant to be looking after us. She had a baby – only three months old. Hugo had been spiteful to me as usual and I wanted to get back at him. I knew he'd spent hours on a school project, so I decided to burn his work. All of it. It was a horrid thing to do and I'm so ashamed of it now, but I never intended to cause a fire. I just put a match to his exercise book in a bin in the lounge. Harriet was a big fan of scented candles and had put a row of them and some matches on the mantelpiece while she was upstairs putting the baby to sleep or something in one of the bedrooms.

'So, I took the matches and set fire to his book, but I somehow knocked the bin over and up went the curtain. I got some water in a jug several times and tried to put it out but it was no good. In the end I just ran down the garden and hid in Hugo's den. That's where my parents found me hours later.' He hesitated - eyes distant in his childhood memory. Tyler could see the old man's jawline shake as his fingers stroked the diary. 'Harriet's baby died in the fire. I never told anyone what I'd done. They all blamed her and those stupid candles. It was put down as a tragic accident but it affected so many people. Harriet went totally balmy having lost her baby, her marriage fell apart soon after, and she ended up committing suicide. And you could probably point the finger for all of that at me.'

It tied up exactly with what old Aston had said. Bradon stared across the grass to a distant lake. 'It made the rift between our families pretty much permanent. Our fathers had never really got on. I'm surprised that I was ever allowed over there, to be honest. I wonder sometimes if, ironically, it was a sort of olive branch they held out to us to try to heal the split, but what happened just sealed our families' fates. The rift just carried on down the generations and became bitter rivalry. Everything my dad and I did at BDE, Austin tried to do better or do something to stamp us out. He always went after the same customers...'

Bradon tailed off as they started to walk again. The path's incline slowly steepened, and Bradon began to wheeze as he spoke. 'The thing is, I've never admitted to the cause of that fire. You're the first person I've spoken to about it. Ever. And it still hurts.' Tyler could see real pain in his old eyes. 'Never having confessed is what's the problem. If I'd done so, people might frown if they heard, but at least I would come out as honest. As it is, if the press got hold of this, I'll be painted as dishonest, spiteful, and a coward. There'll be no political career for me after that.'

'And Hugo Metcalf used that to his advantage.' Tyler paused. 'You do know Hugo was Argus, don't you?'

He nodded, still running a finger along the diary's ancient surface. 'I didn't, of course. Not until young Matt Casey explained what was happening and how Hugo had tried to blackmail the arms dealer.'

'But how did Hugo get the diary in the first place?'

'I guess it was at my parent's house, probably in a box in the attic. I'd forgotten all about it. When they died and it was all chucked out, I guess Hugo must have come nosing around, seeing what he could grab from the spoils.'

'What'll you do with it now?'

'Burn it, of course.' There was no hesitation. 'But carefully.'

They stopped walking again and silently admired the view back down across a slate grey lake to the trees and rocky outcrop beyond. Wind suddenly plucked at the water's surface and turned the reflection of its tiny island into a rippling green-grey smudge. The cries from a flock of birds that wheeled above them were momentarily lost in the breeze.

Tyler handed him the rucksack, and Bradon dropped the

diary back inside. 'Thank you, Craig.'

He shrugged. 'I just did what I was paid for. I'll email you my final expenses.'

***

Casey and Trish stood outside Amersham police station later that evening. Matt had insisted they eat fish and chips from a small place in the main street that had started frying early but she had left most of hers after prodding at it with a wooden fork for a while. How could she eat right now? Her stomach churned. 'How are your wrists?' she asked.

He pulled up his sleeve to examine his right hand, and she winced at the sight of the yellowing sore across the skin.

The sun, that had stubbornly remained hidden behind grey clouds, was slipping to the horizon, and the scattering of lamp posts had just switched on. The pair stood in a pedestrianised courtyard. Trees that had been planted among the concrete, rustled in the wind, and a passenger jet droned somewhere overhead above the hum of traffic. They found the police station in a jumble of two- and three-storey offices buildings with so much blank brick that they felt sinister in the falling light.

A man in his mid-thirties with an ID badge swinging from his neck bustled past in shirt sleeves without paying them any attention and entered through glazed doors under a portico supported on white metal struts. Trish felt Casey take her hand for a moment and give it a gentle squeeze. A tingle ran up her arm, and she half-turned and saw he was watching her. Concern was etched across his face. She forced a pained smile. 'Will you come in with me?'

'Of course.'

Her heart was hammering so hard she was afraid she would collapse. She had never felt worse than when she pushed on the door and it opened with a squeal. The inside reminded her of a post office, with its glass screen in the far wall separating them from a grey desk. The air smelt faintly of antiseptic.

A young uniformed officer looked up as they entered and, as they reached the desk, asked, 'Good afternoon. How can I help?' When neither of them spoke, he looked from one to the other.

Casey squeezed her hand again and let go. 'Go on,' he whispered.

She stepped forward and gripped the countertop for support. 'I ...' she began and cleared her throat. 'I think you wanted to talk to me about a friend of mine who was knifed two weeks ago. I'm Trish McGowan.'

***

Just after eight thirty on Monday morning, Casey walked hesitantly down the carpeted office corridor towards the closed door at the end. If Trish could manage it, so could he.

He hadn't been to their head office much. He was based up in Feltham, but he knew his way round well enough. To Casey's relief, Bradon's secretary hadn't yet arrived. He passed her empty desk in the adjacent recess, took a deep breath, and knocked firmly. In response to a call from within, he let himself into Bradon's office.

He'd never been in here before. It was larger than he'd expected and on the corner of the building with massive dual aspect picture windows that provided views across the hills. Lush carpet, large, immaculately tidy desk, wooden filing cabinets lining one wall, a separate small round table filled the room. Casey's CEO looked up from behind a computer screen. 'Hello Matt. What can I do for you? Quite an adventure for us all last week, wasn't it.'

Matt closed the door behind him. His throat was dry, every muscle taut. 'I wanted to let you know about something...' he began, then added, 'About a silly mistake I made.'

Bradon raised an eyebrow. 'Go on.'

When Casey spoke, his voice sounded unexpectedly high pitched. He cleared his throat. 'I was tricked into doing something I shouldn't have.' He shifted awkwardly, and Bradon waved him to the chair that faced his desk. Casey dropped into it gratefully. His legs wouldn't have supported him much longer. 'I'd like to explain.' He took Bradon's curt nod as permission to continue. 'A while ago, I was totally broke. I ended up with loads of credit card debt.' He looked down at the criss-cross pattern in the carpet. 'I was desperate to sort myself out. And someone offered me enough to pay it all off if I did one simple thing for him.' He glanced up briefly, saw Bradon's almost hawk-like eyes boring into him. 'Do you remember three years ago we demonstrated Dragonfly I at Farnborough?'

'How could I forget?'

'Well, what happened was all my fault. I mean, I was tricked. I've been too ashamed ever since to let anyone know, but I was persuaded to change Dragonfly's main control software.' Bradon's lips tightened. Quickly, Casey added, 'I was told it would just monitor how the craft flew, nothing else. I didn't know it would ... well, I never realised it would cause a crash. I'm really sorry.'

Casey looked up and saw anger burning in Bradon's face. *He's going to sack me right here on the spot,* thought Casey and his guts tightened further. 'I've been blackmailed for it ever since,' Casey blurted. 'By Argus – Hugo Metcalf – he threatened he'd tell you what I'd done if I didn't cooperate.'

'My cousin again?' Bradon let out a sharp sigh and shifted his scrawny frame in the office chair that engulfed him.

'I know it was a dumb thing to do. I was just naive and I never intended for anything bad to happen.'

'You were stupid more like,' Bradon snapped and pursed his lips, then drummed his fingers on the table, thinking.

Casey remained silent. Didn't dare speak. Not even breathe. He could hear his heart thumping over the hum of air conditioning.

Slowly Bradon nodded. 'The right thing for me to do would be to dismiss you instantly.'

Casey said nothing. He felt a choking sensation rise in his throat.

Bradon paused. 'But many of us make stupid mistakes when we're young and live to regret them, even I, so I'm going to give you the benefit of the doubt.' He paused again. 'But I expect total dedication from now on. As far as that incident is concerned, though, let's forget it. It seems to me you've suffered enough already. Just learn from it. Don't hide from the mistakes you make when you're young.' Bradon looked up at the ceiling as though lost in personal thought. 'We can all learn that lesson,' he said quietly as if to himself.

Casey didn't know what he meant, but ignored it and started to rise. 'Thank you. I'll never do anything as stupid again, and the company will have my total dedication.' He wanted to ask about the trials, how they'd done. Should he? It wasn't really his place. As he stood, he said, 'Do you mind me asking the outcome of the trials? I mean, did we win the contract? I wondered if what they'd witnessed Dragonfly II do in hunting down Kurt Wendell had gone in our favour.'

Bradon studied him, then shook his head. 'We didn't, I'm afraid. But then, neither did MSA.' He smiled weakly. 'Which is the main thing, of course.' Quickly he added, 'But that's not public knowledge yet, so you can't tell anyone.'

'Of course.' Casey paused, then grinned. 'And will the rivalry continue?'

'Actually no.' Bradon rose, his cheeks suddenly flushed with energy and fresh excitement. 'I'll tell you something, but this is highly confidential. It's only because of how you helped both companies last week that I'm going to mention it at all.'

Bradon stood for a moment and stared out at the gentle roll of the hills beyond the office. A pair of red kites circled effortlessly in the blue sky as if watching the cars that glinted on the bypass. Bradon turned back to face him. 'One good thing came out of this. The MOD gave us all feedback on why we hadn't won, but they specifically picked up on how well Dragonfly's vision technology performed. "The best we've ever seen," they said. Unofficially and totally off the record, they also mentioned that they considered the battery and propulsion technology in the MSA craft was top notch, much better than ours apparently. They shouldn't mention that kind of thing – it's unethical – but they reckoned that if we did a joint venture, combining the best of our technologies, we'd undoubtedly have the world's best. Apparently, they said the same to MSA, again totally off the record.'

'And will we? A joint venture, I mean.'

'We might. You can't just brush away fifty years of bitter rivalry in a night, but after Austin and I were together in that fire and afterwards the way we hunted their UAV to help them out, it kind of brought us together a tad. We're drafting a memorandum of understanding. If we can agree on that, then maybe there's hope the two halves of our family will collaborate rather than fight.'

***

The country pub was largely empty. A small group of walkers were sinking pints in the warm, two youths noisily played table football in one corner, and a single businessman chatted to the barmaid over a whiskey.

It was the following weekend, five days after Casey's visit to Bradon. He and Trish had arranged to meet up with Craig Tyler. A final catch-up before they went their separate ways.

'I'm free,' Trish said with a smile once they'd all settled

round a small table with drinks.

'Any charge?' Tyler asked.

She shook her head. 'Apparently, they found Kurt Wendell's DNA at the scene, so I guess they're going to charge him with murder along with everything else. They gave me all sorts of lectures about having done a runner, but aren't going to charge me with anything.'

Casey smiled at her when she looked up and their eyes met. He felt the beam spread further across his face into a grin.

Tyler asked, 'Did you tell them about your VAT stuff?'

She lowered her eyes. 'I explained everything from start to finish.'

'What did they say?' Tyler asked.

'They said tax avoidance wasn't their job, but they advised me to work out what I owed and to negotiate with the relevant department for some sort of repayment plan.'

'Can you manage to pay it?'

'I don't know. It feels like I've spent the whole week buried in spreadsheets. I'll find it somehow. I have to. It doesn't help that this half's profits will be shot to hell by the shop being out of order.' She looked uncomfortable again, the earlier smile gone. 'It's Beth I'll never be able to forgive myself for.' There was brief silence. 'They've released her body at last. The funeral will be the end of next week.'

'Would you like me to come?' Casey asked. 'To give you some moral support.'

'It's alright.' She shook her head. 'Cliff's offered to take me.'

Casey felt strangely jealous but he nodded sadly, wanting to change the subject. After a reverent pause he asked Tyler. 'What about you? How's the company history coming on?'

'Finished,' he said with a satisfied grin. 'All done and sent off for Mr Bradon's review.' He put down his pint. 'I need a piss. I'll be back in a sec.'

Casey shifted awkwardly in his chair. Although he'd spoken to Trish on the phone several times in the week, this was the first time they'd been together alone since the police station. He'd half expected to see the green, blue, and purple streaks back in her fringe today, but was pleased they weren't. She looked prettier without them. He contemplated the bubbles in his drink. 'Would you ...' He hesitated and started again, felt his cheeks flush. 'I wondered if you'd like to go out sometime. You know, for a meal or something. It would be a shame to lose touch.'

He felt her lay a warm hand on his. 'I'd like that,' she said. 'But on one condition.'

He looked up sharply. 'What's that?'

'That we go Dutch.'

'But that's not right. I mean —'

'Remember how all your trouble with Argus started? I think you described it as spending too much money to impress a girlfriend.'

Casey felt his face burn further. She squeezed his hand and laughed gently, a lovely soft ripple of sound. 'So, you and I will start off on the right foot, okay?'

Starting off? *Did that mean she thought they might have a*

future? He found himself grinning. 'It's a deal. Are you free tonight?'

'I'm working with Cliff trying to get the shop straight all afternoon but, yes, I'll need a break by then.'

At that moment, Tyler dropped back into his seat and Casey felt Trish's hand disappear from his. He turned to Tyler. 'If you've finished your history, what are you doing next?'

'Funnily enough, I only took that job because I'd got writer's block, but all this excitement with Argus gave me a fresh burst of inspiration. I've started to draft the outline of a new thriller.'

'Brilliant,' Trish said. 'What's it called?'

'I thought I'd call it, "Backlash",' he said and took a long slug of beer. 'If you want, I'll tell you about it.'

THE END

ABOUT THE AUTHOR

Ian Coates graduated with honours in electronics and often uses his experience of working in high-tech industries to give his thrillers an authentic backdrop. Although he followed a career in technology, his first love has always been books, particularly exciting page-turners about spies and assassins.

He won his first writing competition at the age of 14 with a crime novella. His debut thriller, *Eavesdrop*, was shortlisted in a Tibor Jones Page Tuner competition and was one of the winners in the centenary Writers' and Artists' Yearbook novel writing competition. *Eavesdrop* was published in paperback in 2014, and Audible Studios subsequently released it as an audio book. *Backlash* is his second novel.

He lives with his wife in Worcestershire, England, and is a member of the International Thriller Writers Association and the Society of Authors. A percentage of the proceeds from his thrillers supports the British Science Association.

Website: www.iancoatesthrillers.co.uk
Twitter: www.twitter.com/@ian_coates_
Facebook: www.facebook.com/ThrillersByIanCoates
Facebook author page:
www.facebook.com/IanCoatesThrillers
Blog: www.iancoatesthrillers.wordpress.com

Printed in Great Britain
by Amazon

55331358R00215